WAR GAMES

Dillon leaned against the front slope of his M1A1 in the darkness, head bowed in thought as his platoon leaders approached and stopped. Dillon closed his eyes, taking in the heavy smell of burning fuel that always accompanied tank units.

Within a few hours the Tawakalna Division of the Republican Guard would be pushing for the Kuwaiti oil fields, secure in the knowledge that overwhelming numbers and new, powerful tank munitions from Europe would allow them to slice through the single American brigade in their path.

Dillon opened his eyes and attempted to see the faces of the lieutenants he'd been training these past months. The men waited for inspirational words, needing them like a starving man needs a meal, but nothing came to him. He had never been in this position as a young lieutenant and could only imagine the thoughts running through their minds. Most of them hadn't been in the army a year, and now the security of a nation and their men's lives depended in large part on the decisions they'd make over the next hours and days.

TIN SOLDIERS

Michael Farmer

A SIGNET BOOK

SIGNET
Published by New American Library, a division of
Penguin Group (USA) Inc., 375 Hudson Street,
New York, New York 10014, U.S.A.
Penguin Books Ltd, 80 Strand,
London WC2R 0RL, England
Penguin Books Australia Ltd, 250 Camberwell Road,
Camberwell, Victoria 3124, Australia
Penguin Books Canada Ltd, 10 Alcorn Avenue,
Toronto, Ontario, Canada M4V 3B2
Penguin Books (N.Z.) Ltd, Cnr Rosedale and Airborne Roads,
Albany, Auckland 1310, New Zealand

Penguin Books Ltd, Registered Offices:
80 Strand, London, WC2R 0RL, England

Published by Signet, an imprint of New American Library,
a division of Penguin Group (USA) Inc.

First Printing, June 2003
10 9 8 7 6 5 4 3 2 1

To Melinda Britt Farmer

Words cannot convey the support, love, and critical insights you provided during the writing of this novel. Melinda, you are my best friend, my true love, and my inspiration. You keep this old tanker young and have his eternal thanks . . . and his heart.

ACKNOWLEDGMENTS

To the men of C Company, 1-68 Armor, Fort Carson, Colorado, May 1996 to August 1997—thanks for the great ride with Cold Steel. It's one I will never forget.

From a military standpoint, many have inspired. Special thanks to my mentors—Tobin Green, Steve Speakes, William S. Wallace, Dave Styles, Dave Bartlett, Ralf Zimmermann, and E. W. Chamberlain. Also to the many great NCOs who broke me into the world of tank operations and to those who later provided great support and sage counsel—Lon Hardy, Glenn Duke, Dave List, Steve Krivitsky, Jeff Gates, and all of the NCOs of Cold Steel. And thanks to Ron Bickel for making me never regret throwing a corporal into the company commander's tank as a gunner.

To Joseph Davidson, Cookie Sewell, Dave Norton, Bob Summitt, Steve Meachem, Greg Valloch, and Jackie Barnes—all of whom made valiant efforts to ensure I didn't stray too far from the mark technically. As always, any mistakes are my own and not a reflection of the hours you donated to the manuscript.

To those who helped me break into the world of writing and publishing, many thanks—Dale Brown, David Hackworth, W.E.B. Griffin, Ralph Peters, Bob Norris, Victor O'Reilly, Fred Chiaventone, Michael DiMercurio, Jake Elwell and Olga Wieser of Wieser & Wieser, Bob Kane, Sr., of Presidio Press, Paul McCarthy of McCarthy Creative Services, and last but not least, the late George Wieser.

Special thanks to a few others . . . Bill Parker and his staff at Parker Information Resources for designing my Web site, www.TheTanker.com. Bill, you're a true professional (and a great guy for a Texan). A debt of gratitude to Michael Garman, the renowned sculptor from Colorado, for allowing the image of his "Tanker" piece on the Web site. To Jody Harmon, the world's premier illustrator of armored vehicles; the use of the print "M1A2" on TheTanker.com is much appreciated.

Kudos to the Central Intelligence Agency for the use of their Middle Eastern map database. You're good people and I take back any past comments to the contrary.

To Trooper, my chocolate Labrador Retriever; thanks for keeping my feet warm under the desk during late nights of manuscript editing and for providing moments of desperately needed diversion.

Finally, I'd like to thank my wife, Melinda, and our daughters, Meagan, Dylan, Logan, and Carson. These ladies are the lights of my life. During the few times when writing became a chore, the five of them could be counted on to bring me back to earth and make clear the things in life that are truly important. My love to you all.

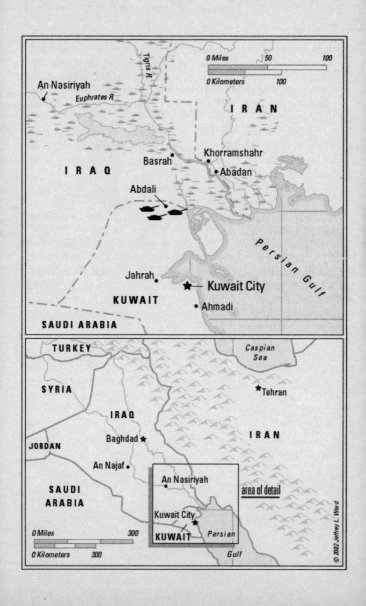

PROLOGUE

29 August: Baghdad (AP)—In a surprise announcement, Saddam Hussein today stepped down as president of the Republic of Iraq after more than twenty years in power. President Hussein cited personal reasons for the sudden resignation. A Baath Party spokesman, speaking on condition of anonymity, stated that the former president has been in failing health for more than six months. Abdul Aref, Hussein's prime minister and right hand for the past two years, was sworn in to office within minutes of the resignation. Aref, an unknown to those outside of Iraq's inner circles, is thought by many Middle Eastern analysts to be the man behind the Islamic fundamentalist movement that has slowly worked its way through Iraq's Revolutionary Command Council over the past year.

04 October: Baghdad (Reuters)—President Aref has announced that the majority Shiites will no longer go voiceless within his nation's government. While details are not clear, it is widely speculated that Aref has conducted a systematic purging of the Revolutionary Command Council, Iraq's all-powerful decision-making body formerly led by Saddam Hussein. During his first two months in office, Aref is rumored to have removed those Baath Party officials who opposed his more fundamentalist approach to governing Iraq. Additionally, Aref is said to be opening dialogue between his country and Iran. This would be the largest diplo-

matic step taken between the two nations since the end of the Iran-Iraq War in 1988.

07 October: Kuwait City (AP)—Kuwaiti prime minister Sheikh Saad al-Abdullah al-Salem al-Sabah denounced the latest in a series of troop movements by Iraq along his nation's northern border in a morning address to the National Assembly. Al-Sabah, who is also the crown prince of the small Gulf nation, says that such actions by Iraq can do nothing but erode an already strained peace.

08 October: Baghdad (*London Times*)—In an address to the Revolutionary Command Council earlier today, Abdul Aref declared that Kuwait and the other peace-loving nations of the Middle East need not concern themselves with the military maneuvers currently being conducted by Iraq. He reminds everyone that Iraq fulfilled all obligations placed on it by the United Nations as of last year and that his nation is merely conducting the training necessary to sustain a viable defense force.

08 October: Tehran (*Christian Science Monitor*)—The Iranian parliament has proclaimed a new era of brotherhood with western neighbor Iraq. Tensions have been up and down between these two Middle Eastern powers for decades, but Iraq's new tolerance toward Islamic fundamentalists has made for the most diplomatic relationship between the two nations in recent history. Exactly what this "new era of brotherhood" means in practical terms is yet to be seen.

10 October: CNN News Desk—President Drake has just announced that the United States will deploy U.S. ground forces to Kuwait in response to a request by the Kuwaiti government. The unit has not yet been identified, but is expected to be on the ground in less than two weeks. The president is quoted as saying that his intention is to stabilize tensions in the area, not escalate them. The president added that such deployments to Kuwait have be-

come commonplace for American military forces since Iraq's invasion of Kuwait in 1990, with the U.S. having a brigade on the ground almost year-round. The exact length of the deployment is yet to be determined.

Chapter 1

_____

_____

_____

Muster

Two hours earlier a hunter's moon had hung over the mountains. Now, an hour before dawn, there was nothing but darkness. A night bird lifted his head, cocking it as he heard a foreign sound. It was an eerie whine, and the source was drawing nearer. The tree he'd chosen for shelter began to gently vibrate beneath him. With a rush of wings, the bird retreated deeper into the forest, abandoning his home to this new predator.

A few feet away, an M1A1 Abrams tank slowed to a halt in a stand of pines. The tank commander, his upper body extending from his vehicle's cupola, scanned the darkness from the vantage of his perch ten feet above the ground. Speaking into his helmet's boom mike, the lieutenant called to his driver over the tank's intercom. "Shut down the engine."

The fifteen-hundred-horsepower turbine engine faded into silence. No lights of any kind were visible on the giant war machine. The tank crew was in a deadly game of cat and mouse with an unseen force, their task made all the more difficult by the necessity for stealth. It was tough playing a phantom in the night when your steed was sixty-eight tons of steel.

The lieutenant lifted the right earcup of his helmet to listen for those sounds he might not have heard

earlier due to the tank's engine noise and his combat
vehicle crewman's helmet. The helmet, commonly
called a CVC, served three purposes: to broadcast
radio messages through the boom mike running across
its front, to receive radio traffic through the speakers
embedded in its earcups, and to protect tank crewmen's hearing from the blast of the tank's main gun.
The young officer knew that if there were any heavy
vehicles moving in the area, he should now be able to
hear them. Instead he heard nothing but the sound of
his wingman in another M1A1 idling 150 meters to
his right. Three hours into tonight's mission and the
silence was almost deafening. Radio chatter through
his CVC from the company commander and the other
three tank commanders of his platoon provided distraction, along with the sounds of hydraulics as his
gunner traversed their turret in search of targets for
their 120mm main gun. He turned slowly in the cupola, a set of PVS-7 night-vision goggles to his eyes,
searching. . . .

He keyed the transmitter switch on his CVC. *"White
Four, White One. Radio Check, Over."* The anxiety in
the lieutenant's voice was clear as he attempted to
reach his platoon sergeant. This was the third call he'd
made to the White Four tank in the past five minutes.
This one, like the others, would go unanswered.

"Sir," said the NCO in the gunner's seat of the tank,
"I'm telling you, they're gone. Zipped."

The lieutenant nodded wearily. Would this night
ever end? "Roger. Take up a scan and see if you can
find whoever's out there before we stumble into
them." He shook his head. "I've gotta call the Old
Man."

"Jesus. Good luck with that, sir," said the gunner,
slipping his face back to the tank's thermal imaging
system in an attempt to locate their elusive prey.

After switching channels, the lieutenant keyed the
radio again. *"Steel Six, White One, over."*

"Steel Six," a distant voice responded.

The lieutenant took a deep breath. *"Steel Six, this is White One. My slant is two. I say again two, over."*

A barely perceptible pause from the other station. *"White One, what happened to your other tanks? I've received no contact reports, over."*

"Steel Six . . . I don't know, over."

A groan issued from the gunner's compartment. "Ohh, well done, sir. Well done *indeed*."

The lieutenant slid down through the cupola's hatch and sat in his tank commander's seat, a puzzled expression on his face. He nudged his gunner with the dirty toe of a combat boot. "What's that, Sergeant Izzo?"

The gunner, busy looking through his sights, turned and looked up at the lieutenant, then returned to his scan. "You'll see. It should be comin' any—"

A booming voice issued from the speaker in the lieutenant's helmet. *"What the hell do you mean you don't know what happened to them? Give me a sitrep, over!"*

Jumping up, the lieutenant slammed his head into the roof of the tank hard enough to see stars. He again activated the helmet's transmit switch. *"Sir . . . I mean . . . Steel Six . . . they just dropped off the net a few minutes ago and—"*

"So you're telling me that I've got two fewer tanks in my company than I thought. When were you going to share this intel jewel, over?"

"This is White One, uhh . . ."

"White One, this is Steel Six. Your mission has not changed. I need you at support by fire position Charlie Two, time now. We've got to be in position to support the rest of the battalion as they move forward, over."

The lieutenant looked at the map in his lap. In the M1A1's blue dome light he could make out little detail. He scrutinized the dot indicating his tank's GPS position taken just before calling the CO and compared it to Charlie Two's location. Only one kilometer west if he went straight over the hill to their front. By taking the low ground and bypassing the hill, he would cover more like four kilometers—screw that. *"This is White One. Roger, I'll have my two remaining tanks set in zero five minutes, over."*

"Roger, keep me informed. Steel Six, out."

The lieutenant exhaled with relief. "Driver, start the engine."

To the lieutenant's left, his loader flipped off the switch controlling the tank's communications system to ensure a surge from the start-up didn't fry the radios. As the big turbine engine spooled up and leveled off, the loader flipped the switch back on.

"Driver, get ready to move up that hill to our front. I'm going to have you stop just short of the crest so I can conduct a sweep of the far side with PVS-7s. Once we move out again, you kick this old girl in the ass . . . get us over the top before anyone I might have missed on the far side has a chance to shoot." A tanker's worst nightmare was moving over the top of a hill and having a large-caliber round or missile pumped into his underbelly.

The sound of a throat clearing issued from the gunner's hole. "Sir, I wouldn't do that. Let's go around the hill."

Once again the lieutenant reviewed his options. Option one, go straight and save three kilometers, but at the risk of being caught cresting the hill and popped by an enemy gunner—but if he was careful, he'd get to Charlie Two quickly. Option two was safer, but it would take a while, especially navigating the big main battle tank over goat trails in the dark.

"I understand what you're saying, Sergeant Izzo, but we need to get to that support by fire position now. We don't have time to go around." His decision made, White One folded his map and stuffed it into one of the leg pockets of his Nomex coveralls. "Driver, move out."

Switching to his platoon radio frequency, the lieutenant called his wingman as their tank moved forward. *"White Two, White One. Follow my move to Charlie Two, over."*

"This is White Two, wilco," the NCO commanding the White Two tank called back hesitantly, clearly not excited at the prospect of rushing over a hill.

The turbine whine of the M1A1's engine increased as the driver accelerated and moved up the hill.

Once again in the cupola, the lieutenant had the PVS-7s to his eyes. He scanned the near side of the hill and the woods surrounding the tank. While not as good as the tank's thermal imaging system, which registered heat emanating from objects such as vehicle engines, the PVS-7s weren't bad. They picked up the ambient light available, such as starlight, and used it to turn the darkness into a faint green glow. No sign of anything sinister. *So what had happened to his Bravo section? The platoon sergeant and his wingman seemed to have disappeared off the face of the earth without a word.*

As they were almost at the crest, the lieutenant called for his driver to slow to a stop. Stretching his body to its full height in the cupola, he scanned over the hill with the night-vision goggles.

"Looks good to me, Iz," the lieutenant said to his gunner over the intercom. "Clear as a bell over there."

The NCO sighed. "I hear you, sir." His face was plastered against the thermal sight. He wanted a good look on the far side of the hill as soon as they cleared the top. Until the tank moved forward his sight picture was restricted to the darkness represented by the side of the hill.

"Driver, you ready to move?" said the lieutenant.

"Roger," came the driver's tinny reply through the tank's intercom system. The sixty-eight-ton tank almost shuddered in anticipation of the jump-off.

"All right, move out."

The M1A1 shrieked as it accelerated over the crest. White One congratulated himself as they safely made it over the top and continued to accelerate downhill. He'd made the right decision after all.

The gunner stiffened at his controls as his optics displayed the area to his front. "Shit! Driver, stop the tank. Stop the damned tank and back up!"

When the tank jerked to a stop, the lieutenant's face unfortunately maintained its forward momentum. His eye smashed into the .50 caliber machine gun mounted just forward of his cupola. Applying pressure to the rapidly swelling eye with one hand, White One held the PVS-7s to his good eye. The tank was now rapidly reversing up the hill and he was having a difficult time finding what had caused his gunner's reaction as he bounced back and forth in the cupola like a pinball.

What the hell had Izzo seen . . . Oh mother of God.

A barrier of mines and concertina wire stretched in both directions at the hill's midway point. No way around it. Their only hope of survival was to get on the back side of the hill they'd just crossed, because whoever had emplaced that obstacle would surely be watching it with—

Overhead, white parachute flares burst into life, illuminating the two M1A1s on the hillside. The sounds of artillery accompanied by explosions emanated from the left and right of their tanks. At the same time several dark shapes separated themselves from the valley floor. The sounds of pyrotechnics filled the air as the enemy combat vehicles opened up on the American tanks.

A yellow light, the Combat Vehicle Kill Indicator, began flashing next to White One. He turned his head to the side and squeezed his eyes closed, temporarily blinded by the harsh light after hours of operating under blackout conditions.

A smoky female voice filled the crew's CVCs. *"Artillery hit, mobility kill. Please bring your vehicle to an immediate stop."* Before the crew had the opportunity to comply, the voice cut in again. *"Multiple direct fire hits, catastrophic kill. Please stop your vehicle and wait for further instructions. Maintain radio silence until the conclusion of the exercise. Thank you."*

From the gunner's seat, Sergeant Izzo sighed and pulled off his CVC helmet. "You know, it's almost worth dying just to hear that sexy bitch's voice."

The radio came to life. *"White One, Steel Six. That's the end of your platoon exercise. Gather the rest of your tanks from wherever they are and meet me at the After Action Review site in one hour, out."*

White One hung his head in dejection. This wasn't going to be pretty.

An hour later White One sat with the other members of his platoon in a circle of camp stools as the sun rose, waiting for a review of their mission with the Old Man. The rising sun painted the Rocky Mountains a few miles to the west a deep purple. Pike's Peak, with the season's first snow visible on its crest, was clearly visible to the group. At other times in his life the lieutenant would have been overwhelmed by the sheer majesty of the scene. Today he didn't even notice.

A crowd of senior personnel was gathered fifty feet away near a group of Hummers discussing how White One's platoon had done on the final mission of their training exercise. As the lieutenant watched, a medium-height, broad-shouldered captain separated himself from the crowd and headed toward them. The figure turned back to the group he'd just left and called a noncommissioned officer out. The captain and the NCO moved together toward the lieutenant's platoon.

Someone tapped the lieutenant's shoulder as he watched the pair approach. Turning, he saw First Sergeant John Rider grinning at him. The company's senior NCO stared at his company's newest platoon leader. "What the hell happened to your eye, Lieutenant? Fifty cal?"

White One rubbed the eye, which had continued becoming darker and more swollen by the minute. "Yeah."

The first sergeant, a tanker for years, simply nodded knowingly. A cup of steaming coffee appeared in his hand. "Here, sir. You look like you could use this. Damned cold mornings in Colorado this time of year."

White One gratefully accepted the cup. "Thanks, Top. Looks like it's about to get colder," he said, nodding toward the approaching figures.

The first sergeant looked toward the approaching men. The pair had paused en route and were in the middle of a discussion. Rider turned back to the junior officer. "Hey, sir, take it with a grain of salt. Remember, the whole point of being out here is to *learn*."

The lieutenant nodded his head ruefully. "Yeah. But, Top, I knew better than to go rolling over that hill. The CO is going to have my ass . . . and I don't blame him."

"Of course you knew better, sir . . . here," Rider said, pointing at his head. "But now you've *seen* why we go around hills and not over them. You've lived it, or 'died it,' so to speak. You won't forget the lesson anytime soon. Besides, you see that NCO with the commander?"

The lieutenant nodded.

"He's from First Brigade. When we want quality bad guys for an exercise, we make sure to ask for his platoon." Rider slapped the young officer on the back again. "Sir, you were smoked by the best. Hard to believe four Bradleys killed your tanks, ain't it?"

The lieutenant shrank. Impossible. "Bradleys?"

Any self-respecting armor officer cringed at the thought of dying to an inferior vehicle, especially one that wasn't even a tank, but rather an Infantry Fighting Vehicle that boasted only a 25mm cannon as its main gun—of course its TOW missiles evened things out somewhat.

Rider laughed and dumped the dregs of his coffee on the ground. "Yep. And don't worry about Captain Dillon. His bark is worse than his bite."

After two weeks of tutelage under Dillon, White

One had his doubts about that. "His teeth seem pretty sharp to me."

Rider turned serious. "Sir, you gotta understand where Captain Dillon is comin' from. He came up through the ranks. He was an NCO before he was an officer, so his way of training may be different than what you're used to . . . not exactly the 'kinder, gentler army.' Sure, you might have an easier time of it with some captain who only has maybe four or five more years in uniform than you do . . . but do you think you'd learn as much?"

The captain and NCO had begun moving toward them again.

"I've gotta go check on my troops, sir," said Rider. "Just remember what that old Chinaman general said: *'That which doesn't kill you will make you stronger,'* or some such shit."

Great, now I'm being quoted Sun Tzu before breakfast, thought the lieutenant. "Thanks, Top. I'll try to remember that."

As the first sergeant walked away, the captain and NCO were approaching the tank platoon.

"Take it easy on him, sir," said Rider quietly without breaking stride. "I think this one is a keeper."

Patrick Dillon turned around and threw a quizzical look at the back of his first sergeant, who had continued moving without another word. Dillon shook his head and continued walking. He stopped in front of the lieutenant.

"Doc," said the captain, "I want you to meet Sergeant Matt O'Keefe. He's the one who took out your platoon. In the real world you wouldn't be able to shake the hand of the man who killed you, so take advantage."

Lieutenant Doc Hancock rose and shook the NCO's hand. He somehow couldn't manage a "nice to meet you." "Morning, Sergeant."

"How you doin', sir?" said the young NCO. "Not a bad job last night . . . till that last charge over the hill."

"Come on, Doc," said the captain. "I want to talk to you. Sergeant O'Keefe, could you sit down with the lieutenant's platoon for a minute and compare notes with the platoon sergeant while Lieutenant Hancock and myself have a quick talk?"

"You bet, sir," said O'Keefe, turning toward the group still seated.

The captain and lieutenant walked toward the edge of the clearing and sat down among a field of large rocks.

"Take your kevlar off, Doc. Relax."

What the hell? wondered Doc Hancock. This had been the last night of his first exercise with C Company, 2-77 Armor. He hadn't been assigned to the company known as Cold Steel for two days when they'd rolled out through the gates of Fort Carson, Colorado, he as a brand-new tank platoon leader in charge of fifteen men and four M1A1s. Throughout the training, Captain Dillon had threatened death or worse if he or the soldiers of his tank platoon weren't wearing headgear of some type—either a CVC helmet on the tank or a kevlar helmet while dismounted.

Dillon removed his own kevlar, displaying a brown flattop rapidly silvering on the sides. He stared at Hancock with cold blue eyes. Reaching into a can of snuff, he pulled a pinch out and inserted it between his cheek and gum. He bent close to Doc's face and examined the lieutenant's black eye. "Fifty cal?"

Am I the only one who doesn't know to guard his face against his own machine gun? wondered Hancock. "Yes, sir."

"Doc, I'm going to be honest—my intent this morning was to rip your ass for that stunt last night," Dillon said.

Hancock's only reply was a gulp.

"Unfortunately—for me—I don't have time. Something's come up and I've got to get back to the battalion headquarters early."

Thank you, God, thought the lieutenant.

Patrick Dillon continued. "Since I can't be at your

platoon's After Action Review to hear you guys work through the mission's details, I wanted a minute alone. Here's my question, Doc. *What did you learn?* What got you and your men killed?"

"Jesus, sir. Do you want it alphabetically or numerically?"

Dillon's face remained serious. "This is why we're here. What did you learn, Doc?"

Doc Hancock thought about the question again. He'd been rolling it around in his mind since "dying" an hour earlier. "Don't roll over a hill if there's any way around it, listen to my more experienced gunner when he tries to prevent me from making a fool of myself, and . . . keep you informed."

Dillon slapped him on the back, stood, replaced his kevlar helmet, and began walking toward his Hummer. "Good. See you back at the ranch in a few hours."

Hancock watched his commander stride away. *That's it?* He almost felt let down.

C Company, 2-77 Armor, Fort Carson, Colorado
11 October, 0915 Hours Mountain

"Damn it, Sergeant Almo, turn that shit down!" yelled Dillon as he walked past his company training room. Almo, who doubled as Dillon's training NCO and Hummer driver, tended to blare Garth Brooks non-stop during duty hours. The current duo of Garth and Almo belting out "American Honky Tonk Bar Association" went down just perceptibly as Dillon continued down the hallway.

Dillon looked at his watch as he stepped into the washroom. Seeing that he didn't have time for a shower before his meeting at headquarters, the Steel commander instead settled for a quick scrub at the sink to knock off the majority of his field grime and followed up with a shave. Dillon looked in the mirror at his Nomex combat crewman's coveralls, the olive drab one-piece jumpsuit that the manufacturer guaranteed would not "melt, burn, drip or support combustion in air." *Too dirty to mingle with the staff pukes at headquarters?* The captain slapped a hand against his chest and a dust cloud enshrouded him. *Fuck 'em,* thought Dillon as he proceeded out of the washroom and down the hall.

Walking into the first sergeant's office, Dillon grabbed one of Rider's spare cups, none of which looked as though they'd been washed in recent memory. "Top, I'm heading over to the battalion to see the commander and hopefully find out what's going on."

Rider sensed something was on his commander's mind. Rising from behind his desk, he walked over and poured a cup for himself. After taking a swallow, he sighed. "*My God* but that is tasty. So, sir, any idea what this is all about?"

Dillon shook his head, wincing, as he tasted from his own cup. "Nope."

Rider nodded thoughtfully and took another sip of coffee. "You think it has something to do with this Kuwait business?"

Good question. I've been wondering the same thing myself. He shrugged. "I don't know, Top. We'll find out."

Rider smiled and tapped the side of his nose with a finger. "I got it, sir. Squash the rumors before they start. I like it."

As Dillon stepped out of Rider's office, he was almost run down by two dirty lieutenants.

"Shit, sir," said Bluto Wyatt, Dillon's senior platoon leader. "Sorry about that."

Fred Wyatt had earned the nickname "Bluto" on account of the uncanny resemblance he shared with the Popeye cartoon character—six foot three, two hundred fifty pounds, and a perpetual five-o'clock shadow on his large face. While not a fat man, Wyatt was certainly a *big* man.

His partner was Dillon's third platoon leader, Ben Takahashi, who was the physical opposite of Wyatt. The two made an odd pair. Takahashi had been in the company for a couple of months. Under Dillon and Wyatt's tutelage, he was just starting to get a good feel for his job as a tank platoon leader.

"Why back so soon, gentlemen? You guys opening the Arms Room to collect weapons or something?" With fourteen tanks in Cold Steel, each mounting three large machine guns, plus the assorted weaponry associated with the company's support vehicles, the individual soldiers' rifles and 9mm pistols, night-vision goggles, and other ordnance, collecting sensitive items and ensuring they were cleaned to standard after a field exercise was no small task. Usually a lieutenant or senior NCO would leave the field a little early to make sure the Arms Room was open and waiting when the crews began returning with their equipment. This process ensured that the soldiers "got home to Momma"—or were ready to hit the streets and meet potential mommas—as soon as possible after an extended period away from civilization and its amenities.

Wyatt stammered. "Well . . . no, sir, not exactly. Doc is taking care of that."

Dillon nodded. "Right. And the sensitive-items report due at battalion in two hours?"

Takahashi coughed. "Uh . . . Doc, sir."

Dillon crossed his arms over his chest. "And you two?"

Wyatt smiled conspiratorially and wiggled his eyebrows. "To be honest, sir, Ben here's set us up with a couple of snow bunnies for the weekend in Vail. If we leave now we can beat the traffic and be up there before dark."

"So you suckered Doc and your platoon sergeants into doing your work?"

No command was given, but both lieutenants found themselves gradually drawn to the position of parade rest, arms crossed behind their backs, feet spread.

"Rethink it, gentlemen," said Dillon, stepping into his office to retrieve his jacket and headgear.

"But, sir," implored Wyatt from the hallway, "these babes are hotties."

Ignoring the moans, Dillon retrieved his gear. As he passed his desk, the cover of the morning edition of the *Colorado Springs Gazette Telegraph* drew his attention:

U.S. DEPLOYING MILITARY FORCES TO THE MIDDLE EAST AT REQUEST OF KUWAITI GOVERNMENT

He looked from the paper to the framed photo of his wife, Melissa, and their four daughters sitting on the edge of his desk. *Patrick Dillon, my fine Irish lad, why are you starting to get a very bad feeling about this meeting?*

2-77 Armor Headquarters, Fort Carson, Colorado
11 October, 0930 Hours Mountain

"Gentlemen," Lieutenant Colonel Estes said to his company commanders, "I'm sure you're wondering what the hell's going on, so I'll get straight to the point. Third Brigade, Fourth Infantry Division is deploying to Kuwait within the next seven days. The full brigade—that means us, the other armor battalion, the mechanized infantry battalion, the artillery battalion . . . everything."

"Say again, sir?" said Captain Dan Malloy, the Iron Tigers' newest company commander.

Malloy had been in charge of A Company for one month. Command had been a whole new experience for Malloy. All of his previous assignments, with the exception of his mandatory time as a platoon leader, had been logistical billets. Because he knew his own strengths and weaknesses, the career path had been a logical choice.

Dillon's assessment of his brother-in-arms' field skills was that Malloy might be able to buy the hot dogs, but he'd have an extremely difficult time maneuvering his way to the grill.

"I got the call late last night from Colonel Jones," said Estes. "In response to Iraq's troop movements and at the request of the Kuwaiti government, Third Brigade is deploying as a show of force to emphasize that the United States' resolve has not weakened where our friends' sovereignty is concerned."

"This sounds familiar," remarked Captain Mike Stuart, the B Company commander.

Stuart had taken command fourteen months earlier, at the same time as Dillon. They were the senior company commanders and the only men present who had deployed with 2-77 Armor to Kuwait two years earlier for a similar operation. Stuart was also Dillon's best friend and only real confidant.

Estes continued. "The Pentagon believes this will be nothing more than an opportunity for us to exercise our deployment systems and get in some maneuver training. Remember, this isn't the first time that this has happened. There's a new president in Iraq, but Saddam used to pull the same tricks. The Iraqis love riding up to the border and rattling their sabers—especially when the holidays are approaching. Personally, I think they just like yanking our chain."

"Any details yet, sir?" asked Dillon. "Like an estimated deployment length? That'll be the first question we're hit with from the wives."

All present knew that similar deployments had lasted anywhere from a month to six months. A great deal would depend on the activity of the Iraqis and whether or not the no-fly zone heated up while they were in country.

Estes shook his head. "The exact layout for the operation will follow sometime later today when Third Brigade issues their operations order. They've been working on the OPORD all night. We did receive some good news this morning. Division headquarters wants to plus us up. A mech infantry company from Fort Hood will link up with us in Kuwait. Once that happens we'll task organize. Right now we'll plan on leaving A Company and C Company pure armor with fourteen tanks each. Mike, I'll probably take one of your tank platoons and give them to our new mech team. You'll get one of his infantry platoons, so you and Team Black Knight will field ten tanks and four

Bradleys. Same is happening with the Third Brigade's other two battalions—they're each being plussed up with a company from Hood. It'll be just like the good old days."

Though all of the men present knew that the United States had pretty much kept a brigade of heavy troops on call in Kuwait for well over a decade, and that this deployment was likely just another exercise, they all breathed a little easier at the news of three extra companies joining the brigade's ranks for the mission. Only a few years earlier, every tank and mechanized infantry battalion rolled to the field with four companies each. All of that changed with the army's digitization of the battlefield. Because the newer combat systems being fielded were able to communicate with each other and share the same tactical picture, the forty-pound brains that made such decisions reasoned that battalions could now get the same results with twenty-five percent less firepower. Most of the men of 3rd Brigade agreed that digitization—once they actually had it—would allow them to operate more efficiently, but in their bellies none believed the reason for cutting the battalions was for battlefield efficiency. In their minds, they were giving up combat power for budget savings. At least for this deployment they would have some insurance in the form of extra firepower.

"For now, start getting a jump on this thing," Estes continued. "Scrub your deployment packets and family support group plans. I don't want any breakdowns because of administrative SNAFUs, got it?"

Stuart raised a hand.

"Yeah, Mike?"

"Can we tell the men, sir? It won't be long before they start hearing about it."

Estes nodded. "Yeah. Get your companies together and issue warning orders. I'll talk to the entire battalion this afternoon. Besides, you know the wives will be calling soon to find out what the hell's going on. They somehow always manage to find out before we do. But tell the men to keep quiet until Third Brigade releases the official word. Otherwise we'll have every television station in town around here. And I'll have the appropriate scrotums on a chain around my neck if that happens. Clear?''

Once again there were nods from around the table. This time they were accompanied by a general crossing of legs and shifting in seats as the company commanders mentally pictured that particular form of military justice.

CHAPTER 2

That Old-Time Religion

14 October: Colorado Springs, Colorado (AP)—The 3rd Brigade of the 4th Infantry Division (Mechanized) deployed today from Fort Carson, Colorado, along with other 4th ID units from Fort Hood, Texas. The deployment, announced by President Drake just days ago, is in response to a Kuwaiti request for American troops in the aftermath of increased Iraqi activity along the Kuwait-Iraq border. Colonel Bill Jones, the "Striker Brigade" commander, says their mission in Kuwait is to deter any threat posed by Iraqi forces conducting maneuvers across the Kuwaiti border. The latest estimates have total Iraqi strength in the area at one division, roughly three times the size of the deploying American force.

17 October: *NBC Evening News* Report—"Tonight we can report to you that the contingent of American troops mobilized to Kuwait have drawn equipment and are moving as we speak toward that tiny nation's northern border. Reports say the draw of vehicles and equipment went well and the brigade will be in place within twelve hours."

18 October: Baghdad (*USA Today*)—Iraqi president Abdul Aref today voiced his outrage at the United States' latest deployment of troops to Kuwait. He said that the large number of American troops on Arab soil is an "abomination to Allah" and that this action

is an attempt by America to extend their control within the region. Aref stated that President Drake is "manipulating the royal family and the Kuwaiti government into believing they are protecting them from their enemies, when in reality the *Americans* are the enemy." The Iraqi leader called on the Islamic world to rally behind his cause.

18 October: Tehran (*New York Times*)—The Ayatollah Mohammed Khalani, leader of the Islamic Revolution, today congratulated President Abdul Aref for becoming not only a great leader of men, but a true leader of nations and Islam. Khalani proclaimed that "Aref speaks for Allah, and that the Great Satan [the United States] must once and for all remove itself from Arab soil and Arab affairs." The ayatollah has also spoken to the leaders of neighboring Arab nations during the past two days and is thought to be rallying support for Aref and his fundamentalist movement.

The White House
19 October, 0700 Hours Eastern

President Jonathan Drake, his chin resting on steepled fingers, gazed at his advisors arrayed around the conference table. In his initial term, Drake was fifty-six years old. As a professor of political science at Florida State University in the 1980s, he had grown tired of lecturing his students about what was wrong with their country's political system. Putting his money where his mouth was, he had run for and won a seat in the Senate representing the Sunshine State.

Known as a plain speaker, Senator Drake had enjoyed the confidence of his constituents for over a decade. But after three successful terms, the senator began to feel like a professional politician. Not enjoying the feeling—Drake had always fancied himself more of a Mr. Smith than a Kennedy—he had called it quits. His last act as a United States senator was to initiate legislation that limited the number of terms that both senators and representatives to the House could hold. In his mind, this was the only solution to the personal power quests running rampant throughout Congress. Maybe, just maybe, it would solve the problem of politicians worrying more about how to stay in office than in carrying out the duties they had been elected to accomplish.

The Clinton scandals of the 1990s, however, had put a sour taste in Drake's mouth—a sour taste regarding the climate in the White House, a sour taste regarding how Congress had handled the whole affair, and a sour taste for the American political system in general. Drake had begun to feel the need to make a difference again. Giving up the early retirement he'd just begun learning to enjoy, he ran for the presidency. In a close vote, he became the first Independent elected to the Oval Office.

Washington insiders didn't know what to make of their new president. His vice president was a woman more conservative than Reagan, his secretary of state a flaming Democrat, and his secretary of defense a former air force officer. The only similarities among them were that they were hands down the best-qualified candidates for their respective posts.

The current minicrisis in Kuwait was President Drake's first foreign policy test. Thus far there'd been myriad economic and domestic issues to deal with. The U.S. economy hadn't seen lofty returns, as were present in the late 1990s, in a few years; pro-life and pro-choice advocates once again were at each other's throats; the price of oil, having only recently stabilized, was once again on the rise. The list went on.

Kuwait's request for assistance came on the heels of Iraq's new president initiating a series of large-scale military maneuvers in the extreme southern portion of Iraq. So far, President Aref's forces had not strayed across the border, but Kuwait was nervous. Other than

Kuwait, most nations didn't consider the exercises a threat.

Except for the odd bombing campaign to punish Iraqi air defense units for lighting up U.S. fighters in the no-fly zone with their radars, things had been fairly quiet for the past few years. As time passed, Iraq appeared to be willing to go along with the mandates imposed upon it by the United Nations in 1991. A year earlier the U.N. had lifted all sanctions on Iraq because the majority of their demands had been met and they were tired of public outcry over the unnecessary hardship the sanctions imposed on Iraq's citizens. Most of the world regarded this as a positive sign and felt the Middle East was moving in the right direction, although a few intelligence agencies still insisted that disturbing questions remained unanswered regarding Hussein's stocks of chemical and biological weapons.

The president looked over his advisors, his gaze finally resting on the secretary of state, Adam Ridley. "What do you have for me, Adam?"

Ridley cleared his throat and adjusted his bow tie. Worldwide, the bow tie was his trademark. In Ridley's office, his walls were adorned with photos of himself wearing a bow tie in front of the capitol buildings of more than a hundred nations. The Sunday political commentators joked that Ridley had lobbied for his current posting not because of his qualifications—which were extensive—but to broaden his collection.

"Mr. President," the secretary of state began, "the situation along the border appears to have stabilized over the past few hours. I recommend at this juncture that we attempt to arrange some sort of summit between Iraq and Kuwait. I'd suggest Jordan as an intermediary."

The president nodded. "I like it, Adam. Have you attempted to start the ball rolling?"

Ridley adjusted his tie and nodded. "Yes, sir."

Sitting back in his chair, President Drake crossed his arms over his chest. "I'm curious as to the responses you've received. I've placed a few calls myself, and I've only heard back from Kuwait, Bahrain, and Qatar." Drake cocked his head and stared at Ridley. "Don't you find that a little strange, Adam? While I try to keep things in perspective and don't want to get too caught up in the title, I am the president of the United States."

The sarcasm in that last remark caught the senior diplomat off guard. "Mr. President," the Secretary of state said after taking a few moments to compose himself, "the only representatives I've managed to speak with thus far, in governments other than those you mentioned, are staff underlings. I admit it *is* a bit unusual, but—"

"Keep working on it and let me know if you make any progress. At this point I feel it prudent to look at alternatives—just in case there's a reason behind the cold shoulders."

"Mr. President," Ridley quickly broke in, "if you are talking about military alternatives, well, I must say I feel we are being a bit premature."

The president looked thoughtful. "Gentlemen, what if, and I do mean what if . . . what if, between Iraq and Iran, enough pressure is brought on the friendly and neutral Arab states that they feel forced to stay out of any Iraqi power play? Assuming, of course, that they don't outright support one."

"Could you elaborate, Mr. President?" asked Ronald Newman, Drake's secretary of defense. Newman was a retired air force general. In military circles he was well known as the most decorated fighter pilot of the Vietnam era.

Drake rose and began pacing, hands clasped behind his back, head slightly raised. His former students at Florida State would have recognized it as his standard teaching posture. "Iraq *still* retains the largest and best-trained army in the Middle East. Iran by far has the largest population. The governments neighboring them are already feeling the potential force of this alliance."

The senior military men nodded understanding.

The president continued. "All we're hearing from Iraq and Iran are promises of peace, but we have no idea what they're saying behind the scenes to their other Islamic brothers. Are they using threats to keep their neighbors out of a potential fight? Or promises of a powerful and united Arab people? Perhaps they're suggesting a new period of Islamic enlightenment is in order, with Iraq and Iran in the forefront. I hazard to guess that they would probably use a combination of these threats and promises to achieve their purposes."

Drake stopped pacing and gazed through the window into the Rose Garden. He took in the beauty of the flowers for a moment, then turned to look at the assembled group of men whose task it was to aid him in making the decisions the American people counted on him to make.

Drake's next words were spoken slowly and deliberately. "Gentlemen, should the Iraqis decide this is the time to prove themselves in the eyes of the world, we'll likely see no support from our western allies, with the possible exception of the United Kingdom."

Newman spoke up. "Alone, sir? You don't think the rest of the West would support us?" With Newman at the table were the chairman of the Joint Chiefs of Staff, General Tom Werner, and the director of the Central Intelligence Agency, Christopher Dodd.

Drake shook his head. "I've spoken quietly with most of my counterparts this morning, and most of them can't afford to. Every nation that supported us during the Gulf War has undergone massive military cuts. Not to mention that a large portion of their forces remains tied up in peacekeeping operations in Europe and elsewhere." He shrugged. "Welcome to the twenty-first century, gentlemen. It's not about fighting—it's about 'keeping the peace' around the world.

"A couple of the European heads of state outright recommended that we stay out of this one." The frustration was clear on Drake's face. "If it turns into an armed conflict, the only way that our 'allies' would become involved is if the flow of oil were threatened."

"And it wouldn't be, Mr. President?" asked Werner.

Drake turned to Dodd and nodded. "Chris just briefed me a few minutes ago on some disturbing information that several of his field offices have turned up. You'll understand why I brought you all in here an hour earlier than our scheduled meeting. Chris?"

Drake sat down and motioned for Dodd to take the floor.

The CIA director stood. "Some unofficial calls have gone out from Baghdad to various heads of state—heads of state to nations we have always considered friends. The callers have assured these heads of state that not only will the oil flow go unchecked if a change takes place in the region, but that the cost per barrel will actually be cut—significantly. Quite an incentive not to get involved in a confrontation they can't really afford anyway. Add to this the fact that they're all concerned about oil prices creeping up in recent months. The incentive to stay out of the affair becomes very lucrative. While none of our friends outright said yes, it was quite clear that the offer was well received by the majority of the major players."

Everyone in the room soaked in this information.

Dodd returned to his seat. "And they can do it with a clear conscience by continuing their support of U.S. forces involved in 'justifiable' military actions, such as Operation Enduring Freedom."

Newman's eyes bored into Dodd. "Director, is it your opinion, based on information at hand, that Iraq will attack Kuwait?"

Dodd shook his head slowly. "I can't say that with any degree of certainty, but when you put it all together, that's my assessment. Add it up." Dodd held up a hand and began counting off the indicators. "The military movements. The behind-the-scenes calls to

our allies. The lack of support from 'friendly' Arab
states. Now throw in the wild card—religious fervor.
Yes, gentlemen, on top of everything else, the Middle
East is starting to get another taste of that old-time
religion—Islamic fundamentalist style."

Silence descended on the assemblage as the advisors
considered the ramifications of Dodd's statements.

The president stood. "Thank you, Chris." Turning
to his military advisors, Drake addressed the secretary
of defense. "Ron, let's start taking a look at worst-
case scenarios. What's the composition of the Iraqi
force north of the Kuwaiti border?"

"Mr. President," answered Newman, "the force is a
Republican Guard armored division, the Tawakalna.
This division is part of their Southern Corps, headquartered out of Al Fatthul Mubean Command Center. It was part of this same Tawakalna Division that
the Second Armored Cav duked it out with at
Seventy-three Easting during the Gulf War's most serious ground fighting."

Dodd interrupted. "They're at full strength?"

Newman nodded. "The Iraqis lost a lot of their
ground forces during Desert Storm, including half of
their tanks. Since the embargoes lifted last year, however, they've pulled out all the stops where rebuilding
and modernization are concerned. The Republican
Guard units, unlike their Regular Army counterparts,
are all at full strength. It was three of their divisions
that accomplished the seizure of Kuwait in four and
a half hours in August of 1990. Additionally, the
Guard gets the best and latest equipment."

Drake chewed on that information for a minute,
then turned to Dodd. "What information do we have
on their other troop movements?"

Dodd looked uncomfortable. "Mr. President, key-
hole satellite imagery indicates two other Republican
Guard divisions, the Madinah and the Hamourabi, are
currently conducting higher than normal maintenance
operations at their command centers. These are the

other two divisions of the Southern Corps. Their activity indicates that they're moving somewhere—and soon."

The president began to pace once again, but this time his head was tucked down. His former students would tell you that this indicated Drake was looking for answers. "How does this compare to our forces currently on the ground in Kuwait?" asked the president.

The secretary of defense answered without referring to his notes. "Sir, we look good for now. It's about three to one in favor of the bad guys, but we have better equipment—and better soldiers. Those numbers don't include the Kuwaiti forces. The Kuwaitis are armed with M1A2 tanks, which is a definite plus for our side."

The president ceased pacing and looked up. "They've got a newer version of our tank than *our* own troops in the theater?" he asked incredulously.

"Sir, if I may . . . ?" said General Werner.

The president nodded. "Go ahead, General."

"Sir, the Kuwaiti M1A2s—the export version of our newest tank—have some fire-control features that are superior to those of the M1A1s our troops are manning. They also have a few other upgrades that are improvements on the design of the M1A1. The Kuwaiti M1A2s, however, don't have the same armor protection as the A1s—i.e., they die easier."

Drake nodded and looked at Newman, satisfied for the moment. "Aircraft and ships in the area?"

"About twenty-seven warships and two hundred aircraft in the Gulf, sir. The aircraft numbers could change if our allies continue the cold shoulder treatment and pull the welcome mat out from under our airbases in the region. We can count on the navy carrier group currently in the Gulf for about fifty fighters and bombers. If push comes to shove, we've got another group that's currently on patrol. It can be on station within five days." Newman took off his reading glasses and looked directly into the president's eyes.

"I would suggest, sir, that we start moving that carrier group toward the Gulf—any time now."

Drake nodded. "Do it. This is probably a good time to discuss my conversation with the British prime minister. They don't like the smell of this business any more than we do and are sending in a carrier group of their own. He assures me it will arrive on station to support our operations in a week."

Newman was clearly pleased as he jotted a note regarding the British warships. Every little bit helped.

Christopher Dodd cleared his throat. The director of Central Intelligence had worked his way through the system the hard way—from field agent all the way to the top. With a good reputation, for a spook, Dodd was known as one of the hardest working men in Washington. Clearly, something was bothering him at the moment.

Drake looked at him and raised an eyebrow. "Chris? Something to add?"

"Yes, Mr. President. The Iranians. We have no idea how they will play into this scenario, if at all. We do know that they have two heavy divisions currently positioned in southwestern Iran, vicinity Abadan." Dodd gestured with a laser pointer to the digital map of the Middle East that took up an entire wall of the room. He zeroed in on the city of Abadan, just a few miles east of Kuwait. Two red boxes sat next to the city. It seemed to the assembled advisors as if these boxes, each representing a force three times larger than the American unit in Kuwait, were leaning towards the border, ready to jump across. "That's close, Mr. President. Very close."

"Great," muttered Drake, loosening his tie. "All right, we have to look at reinforcing the unit we have on the ground in Kuwait. Who are they, Ron?"

"The Third Brigade, Fourth Mechanized Infantry Division, sir," answered the secretary of defense. "Currently they're located near Abdali in northern Kuwait." Lifting his own pointer, Newman illuminated the blue box drawn close to the Iraqi border.

President Drake, looking at the graphic symbol representing his forces, the forces of the American people, once again marveled that so much of the world's attention seemed to be drawn time and again to such a small nation. The 3rd Brigade icon was almost as large as the country of Kuwait itself. His next question was addressed to both Newman and General Werner. "Are they good enough to hold until we can get more forces on the ground, should it come to that?"

Newman picked up a document that had obviously seen a lot of handling of late and put his reading glasses back on. "Sir, they completed a rotation at our National Training Center at Fort Irwin, California, three months ago. We make the training cycle there as close to actual wartime conditions as possible. The opposing force stationed at Irwin, the Eleventh Cav, do not look at themselves as training tools. They fight in that godforsaken piece of the Mojave Desert month in and month out all year—and they're accustomed to winning. Hell, it's a point of honor for those guys. Most brigades that go against them win one battle out of five—two at the most. Third Brigade defeated the Eleventh four of five times. That's . . . unusually high."

The SECDEF took off his glasses and placed the document back on the conference table. Slowly he looked up and into Drake's eyes. "It must be noted, however, that they've undergone a seventy-five percent turnover in leadership since returning from that rotation."

The president's jaw dropped. "Ron, I *have* to ask. Why didn't we send them to the *training center* with the new leadership in place, instead of training up people that were about to leave the unit?"

Newman shook his head slowly. "Sir, that's the way it's worked for the past several years. The system is broken. The attitude is that if you screw up an NTC rotation, your career is over. No one wants to go into one with rookies. They take an experienced force, then rotate their leaders upon returning to home station."

"Who's in command of Third Brigade?" asked a dejected Drake.

"Colonel Bill Jones. He was with the Twenty-fourth Mech during Desert Storm. Commonsense guy, sir—just your type."

The president smiled slightly at this piece of information. "Well, some good news for a change." The pacing began anew. "Now who can we send to lend Colonel Jones a hand?"

Newman sobered. "Sir, I assume you're talking heavy mechanized forces?"

Drake looked appraisingly at the SECDEF and nodded. "Ron, God knows I'm not very conversant in these matters. That's why I have men such as yourself and the chairman to turn to—but yes, I would think heavy forces are what's needed here."

General Werner, looking like a thoroughbred in the gate before the big race, fielded the question. "Sir, with all due respect, you let me send *one fucking heavy division* over there, and there won't be enough Iraqi equipment left to attack a ladies' church social."

Werner wasn't known for his etiquette. Competence had gotten him where he was, which was the highest military office in the country. Known as a field general, he had served as commander of the 3rd Armored Cavalry Regiment, the 1st Cavalry Division, and III Armored Corps. "The problem, sir, is that the only forces we can get in there quickly are the airborne infantry troops out of the Eighty-second at Bragg." The big head shook sadly. "Great soldiers, but pretty speed bumps in the open desert against enemy armor."

"What about the new interim brigades I keep hearing about? Aren't they designed to deploy quickly?" asked Drake, referring to the new forces composed of medium-weight armored vehicles being formed at Fort Lewis, Washington, and a few other posts.

Werner shook his head. "Sir, we can send them, but we're not doing them any favors. Those guys are busting their asses learning that new equipment, but they're also pretty much writing the doctrine for the new organization as they go. We can get them and their stuff there quick, but . . ."

The president nodded. "Very well, noted. So who can we send, and how long before they can be there?"

"The Third Infantry out of Fort Stewart and the First Cavalry out of Fort Hood are our heavy rapid deployment forces. Currently Third Infantry is on the string. We can start movement of their advance parties from Savannah within twenty-four hours, main bodies within seventy-two hours. Problem is, they'll have to draw equipment in theater just like Third Brigade did. The C-5 Galaxies, as big as they are, can only carry one M1-series tank at a time—and let me tell you, sir, the loadmasters aren't thrilled about transporting even one. A tank weighing over sixty tons makes for high adventure if it starts slipping around at thirty thousand feet."

"Do we have enough vehicles in theater for them to draw from?" asked Drake.

Werner shook his head. "Sir, we've got a brigade set in Kuwait—the one that Third Brigade just fell in on—and another set in Qatar. We can move one of the brigades from Stuart in to draw the Qatar set once they land. The remaining troops will have to wait for the prepositioned floating stocks—large ships we keep at sea loaded down with combat equipment for contingencies in areas where we don't have equipment. We pull the prepo ships into port every few months to do maintenance on the equipment they're carrying and to pick up any parts the equipment might need. We'll get some of the boats moving toward the region now, with your permission, sir."

Drake stopped pacing and turned to his senior uniformed officer. "Do it. So, we've got one brigade on the ground now, more troops en route within the next few days, which means . . ."

Werner finished the sentence for him: "Another brigade pointing gun tubes north within seven or eight days—we still have to move that Qatar brigade over three hundred miles north to get them in position— plus two more brigades ready to draw off of the pre- positioned floating stocks when the ships arrive in port. Also, sir, I suggest we fly in the Eighty-second now. They can secure the international airport at Ku- wait City and be prepared to support future operations."

"I concur. Now for the big question. Will the Third Infantry reinforcements get there in time, General?"

The old soldier shook his head. "Sir, I wish I could tell you. All I can say for certain is that this is Third Brigade's fight for the next week."

"Okay, consider the orders given. Get the Third Infantry and Eighty-second moving. Now what about the Iranian threat? Recommendations?"

The chairman was thoughtful. "We can begin down- loading the marine ground forces that are with the carrier group to secure the port site. Once the port's secure we can position them against the Iranians in the northeast. That's a thin shield against two divi- sions, Mr. President. It would be nice not to have to worry about that flank, but we'll work it and come up with something. They are marines, after all."

"Okay, notify Central Command. Let's get the ball rolling and issue the appropriate orders. Keep me posted on the troop movements and status of the sec- ond carrier group. I hate to leave, but I've got to prepare for a press conference. Unless of course any- one wants to trade jobs for a little while?"

A few smiles showed from around the table, but no takers.

"If there are no further questions?" Drake said, picking up his jacket and sliding an arm in the sleeve.

Secretary of State Ridley, ready to burst from his seat, could no longer contain himself. "Mr. President," Ridley almost squealed as he stood, "I *must* say that sending more troops into the area is only going to *inflame* the situation. I implore you, sir . . ."

Drake raised a hand and turned the SECSTATE
off. "Right now, Secretary Ridley, I just don't give a
damn. General, get those troops from Stewart and
Bragg moving. Maybe somebody will start talking to
us now."

Werner smiled at Drake, for the first time truly
seeing the president as his commander-in-chief.
"Wilco, sir."

Tehran, Iran
19 October, 1400 Hours Local

The two men sat on cushions facing each other across
a small table. Both were aware of the irony. Former
enemies, now partners in planning retribution on a
mutual enemy. The formalities had been observed and
it was time to discuss the issues consuming them both.

Since the 1979 overthrow of the American-backed
Shah of Iran, the real power in Iran had belonged to
the religious leaders. The Ayatollah Khalani, seated
now with Iraq's new president, ran the church—and
for all intents and purposes, Iran. Reports of a new
and more democratic government aside, Khalani still
held the real power in his country. He sipped his tea,
looking at his guest. Aref, he noted, had not only been
Hussein's right hand, but had managed to steal his
looks—heavy-jowled, dark hair, and mustache. And
he insisted on wearing a military uniform, as his fa-
mous predecessor had, although Khalani knew he'd
never served a day of service in Iraq's armed forces.

"So," asked Khalani, "how go your . . . maneuvers?"

The younger leader smiled and bowed his head.
"They proceed well. The Tawakalna Division is my
very best. Their commander assures me that all is
ready for the next phase of our operation."

Khalani gazed at Aref shrewdly over his tea. "You
seem confident, which is good. I have asked you this
question before, but I will ask one final time. Do you
really think it wise to provoke the Americans?"

Aref looked at the old holy man defiantly. "I know what I am doing. Something that should have been done long ago, something that must be done if my people and I are to regain the honor we lost to those infidels. We must again be able to look our people, and our neighboring states, in the eye. We cannot allow a pitifully small kingdom such as Kuwait, which historically by all rights should be ours, to sit on its riches while the Iraqi people continue to suffer from the years of sanctions we had to endure because of both them and the Americans. And to add to the insult, they again now call in the Americans as their mercenaries."

"I understand," said Khalani quietly, but with an edge to his voice. He carefully set his cup on the table before looking again into Aref's eyes. "Just do not forget our bargain."

"How can I forget?" asked Aref, a note of sarcasm in his voice. "Do not think me impertinent, Wise One, but one-third of all proceeds from the Kuwaiti oil fields is a very high price."

Khalani smiled. "Yes, a high price. But too high to pay for a secure eastern border while you carry out your 'holy mission?' Too high when my troops await only your call to support you in battle against the infidels? Too high to pay for the influence I alone can gain for you in certain Islamic circles? Too high a price for the alliance that will eventually make us the most powerful nations in the Middle East? Even the Saudis are bowing to our combined weight, sitting by and doing nothing. Their relationship with the United States had already begun to erode since the bombing of the American facility in Dhahran, which you might also thank me for."

The old man stared at the tea leaves in the bottom of his cup. Swirling them slowly, he continued. "A high price? Yes. Too high?" Putting down his cup, he looked Abdul Aref in the eyes and smiled. "I think not."

Abdul Aref nodded, resigned to the fact that he

must, for now, continue his pretense of subservience. After he made an example of the Americans in Kuwait and had occupied that cursed little country, he would deal with "The Holy One."

"You are right, of course. I do not mean to be impertinent, but I have many things on my mind. The stage is almost set, and with Allah's will, all of the wrongs suffered against my people will soon be rectified."

Khalani nodded shrewdly and looked at his guest with a hypnotic stare. "I understand, and you will enjoy a place in the Kingdom of Heaven for your endeavors. I merely warn you not to underestimate the Americans. As much as I detest them for their part in the Westernization of my country during the Shah's regime, they are still a formidable power. In Afghanistan the Taliban experienced the resolve of a provoked America, to their bitter sorrow. Do not let your pride be your downfall."

Aref responded with confidence. "We will be successful. Of that, I have no doubt. The only allies they have remaining in the region are insignificant—either looking to support their decadent lifestyle with American gold or to protect them from our great nations. Kuwait, Bahrain, Qatar—*they will all feel my wrath*."

The Iraqi leader realized immediately that he'd misspoken and looked to the ayatollah, smiling. "I mean, of course, the wrath of *Allah*."

The old man inclined his head and smiled knowingly. "Of course. But have you given thought to what Israel's reaction to our enterprise will be?"

The younger leader waved a hand dismissively. "The Israelis are so caught up with the Palestinians that they have no time to worry about what is happening outside their borders. I plan to go to great lengths to ensure they see no threat against them by my forces." He smiled. "Besides, they are likely as tired as we are of the United States dictating policy to them. They may even see it as a fortuitous time to root out our Palestinian brothers while the world is caught up in larger events."

The ayatollah nodded gravely. "Yes. Sacrifices, unfortunately, may have to be made for the greater good. We will have time in the years to come to deal with Israel."

Aref returned to the subject at hand, glancing at his watch. "Even now the Americans are receiving notification to remove their forces from Saudi soil." He nodded at the ayatollah in acknowledgment of his counterpart's assistance in this coup. "That was not difficult once both of our governments assured the Saudis that their neutrality would ensure their kingdom's sovereignty remained intact." He waved a hand dismissively. "At any rate, as you say, they'd already tired of the Americans' presence in their country . . . we merely gave them the excuse they had spent years looking for."

The ayatollah looked thoughtful. "But even if you're successful in seizing Kuwait and destroying the Americans already there, the infidels still have the ability to bring more troops and equipment into the fight."

Abdul Aref smiled slyly. "I have long been planning this war and have thought through this contingency carefully. My council and I do not think it likely the Americans will bring in more forces. We will attack with only three divisions of my Republican Guard—the Southern Corps. That will be enough to quickly annihilate the one brigade of American troops across the border."

Khalani interrupted at this point. "I mean no offense by what I'm about to say . . . but what makes you believe you can defeat the American brigade, even with superior numbers? During the Gulf War, you didn't destroy even *one* of their tanks with your T-72s."

Aref had the look of the fabled cat that had eaten the canary. "A little surprise is in store for the American forces. All of our T-72 tanks are uploaded with new ammunition of Swiss manufacture. We've tested it against armor with capabilities similar to that of the M1. To say the testing went well would be an extreme understatement. Believe me when I tell you that the American tanks are no longer unstoppable." He laughed heartily. "No, far from it."

"Allah be praised. But . . . again, what makes you think they will not send more troops?"

"If we are successful in defeating the Americans in open battle and have possession of the territory, and the other kingdoms in the region acknowledge our new borders, the Americans will not continue to fight. At that point the American people would cry out against their government. It would be clear to them that the only reason their sons and daughters are dying is for oil, not friendship or stability." A sly smile appeared on his face. "We can also make it known quietly that we will extend to them the same oil prices we offered the Europeans. In the end, their greed will guide them. They will see the wisdom of our offer and accept."

Khalani smiled at his younger counterpart. He knew there was nothing to be gained by asking further questions. Aref's plan would work, and Iran's position would be furthered—or it wouldn't work, and Iran could still move from the shadows and occupy a portion of the vacuum created by Iraq's defeat. In either case, he won. "Yes, Allah has indeed smiled upon your people to send them such an enlightened leader."

Colorado Springs, Colorado
19 October, 1300 Hours Mountain

Melissa stared at the small television she kept on the kitchen bar. Lately, as now, it stayed tuned to CNN. The current experts being interviewed were an ex-director of the Central Intelligence Agency and a professor of Middle Eastern studies at the University of Chicago.

"But, Professor, can't you see that Iraq has nothing to gain from this? Even Hussein never attempted to retake Kuwait after the beating Iraq received during the Gulf War!" The ex-director had been getting more and more agitated by his fellow analyst.

The professor calmly straightened himself, as if his opponent's outburst had been physical, and then resumed his own attack.

Shaking his head, he began. "Sir, how *you* can say that Iraq has nothing to gain is beyond me. You must consider the current situation in its entirety, to include Saudi Arabia directing us to withdraw our military from within its borders. The Middle East is changing rapidly. In 1991, Iraq was alone. No one in the region supported Saddam Hussein's attempted takeover of Kuwait. The nations of the region *requested* us to force the Iraqi withdrawal. Such is not the case now. I believe Iraq would have little or no opposition from its neighbors if President Aref chooses to attack, so long as he has limited objectives in mind."

The ex-director was turning blue. "Excuse me, Professor, but those *limited objectives* would include seizing a sovereign nation and killing American troops!"

"That is correct," said the professor with quiet authority as he took a sip of his water.

The other man shook his head as if he were dealing with a child. "The combined weight of the Arab armies couldn't defeat Israel in '48, '67, or '73. We and our coalition partners sent Saddam packing in under one hundred hours in '91. Yet you sit there and tell me that Aref thinks he can get away with . . . with . . . with what is tantamount to the *murder* of our one small unit in Kuwait?"

The professor placed the cup carefully on the table next to his chair and spoke to the other analyst as he would to a child. "I'm not saying that Iraq can or can't 'get away' with their actions," he responded. "What I am saying is that I know the Arab mind-set. And *that* mind-set, especially where Arab unity is involved, tends to blend fantasy and reality. It is *that* mind-set which for centuries has caused them to attempt feats that are beyond their ability to achieve. Combine with this the fact that we are talking about a country that we disgraced. If in attacking they can regain their honor, seize a piece of territory worth hundreds of billions of dollars, *and* be the unifying force in the Arab community, I would say it is *quite likely* that they will attack before we have a chance to reinforce our troops in the theater."

Melissa Dillon, arms crossed tightly across her breasts, was watching the debate with such intensity that she didn't hear the small footsteps approach and stop behind her. Her stomach tightened when her youngest daughter's voice asked, "Mommy, what does that man mean? Is Daddy in trouble?"

CHAPTER 3

———————

———————

Assemble

"Guideons, guideons, Steel Six, over."

Dillon stood in the cupola of his tank and patiently waited for his platoon leaders to answer. If they did it right, finally, they would respond in order by platoon.

"Red One, roger, over," called Wyatt.

"White One, roger, over." *So far so good,* thought Dillon as Doc called in.

"Blue One, roger, over."

Hallelujah and praise Jesus. *"Congratulations, gentlemen, on your first successful net call. . . . Meet me on the ground at my fix in zero five minutes. . . . Out."*

Translated into English the message meant: Great, you didn't screw it up for once. Get your butts over to my tank . . . now.

First Lieutenant Thad Mason, Dillon's executive officer, was standing on the ground in front of Dillon's tank. Dillon had watched the former West Point nose tackle grow from a green second lieutenant who knew nothing about tanking to a trusted second in command. Mason's primary role within the company was to ensure that the tanks stayed running and to monitor the task force command frequency. This freed Dillon to do other things—like run the company. Mason, his voice reminiscent of James Earl Jones, was perfectly suited for the job of Cold Steel's mouthpiece. He could gush pure horseshit, but the voice—it gave everything he said instant credibility.

Dillon removed his CVC and laid it over the .50 caliber machine gun in front of his cupola before clambering down the tank. He landed in a cloud of dust next to Mason. Looking up—Mason stood over six feet four inches—the Cold Steel commander smiled. "Well?"

Mason, refusing to have his lunch interrupted, continued to spoon Meal Ready to Eat, better known as MRE, pork and beans into his mouth. Around a mouthful of beans, he finally said, "Well what, sir?"

"The bet, you big freak," continued Dillon.

"Ohhh, the bet. Didn't you say they'd get it right by *yesterday,* sir? I think *you* owe *me,*" said Mason.

Dillon looked at the massive lieutenant impassively and nodded. "You're gonna welsh, aren't you? You're a fuckin' mooch."

Mason frowned and the spoon of cold beans stopped halfway to his mouth. "I'm no mooch."

"You lost another six-pack. No big deal. Definitely no reason to pout like a three-hundred-pound baby."

Mason became indignant, folding the slabs of muscle he passed off as arms across his chest. "Sir, when we started this whole betting business, you said we were betting beer. *Beer.* Being a hail-fellow-well-met kind of guy, I agreed. You didn't say shit about what kind of beer. Now every time you win, you expect me to pay you off with that eight-dollar-a-six-pack British shit—"

Dillon interrupted his large subordinate with a warning finger. "Steady, Thad. Not shit . . . Newcastle." A faraway look came into his eyes for a moment. "Nectar of the Gods, my boy. Nectar of the Gods."

Mason shrugged. "Whatever. I ain't payin' eight dollars for a six-pack of beer." He shook his head resolutely, satisfied he'd come up with a course of action he could live with. "Nope, ain't gonna happen, sir."

Dillon looked at him seriously. "So you *are* gonna welsh?"

"I ain't welshing, sir. I just ain't payin'. . . ."

"Yeah, yeah, I got it." Dillon stroked his chin. "I could lower my standards, temporarily, you understand." He turned to Mason again. "Heineken?"

A grunt was Mason's only response.

Dillon changed the subject, sure that he was making no headway. "I wish to God we'd had time to do some company-level training before we left Carson."

Mason nodded. "Yeah, they're doin' all right on the platoon stuff, but they're not used to operating together."

The men leaned casually against Dillon's tank, C-66, as they waited for the platoon leaders. They had been in the tactical assembly area for a little more than twenty-four hours. Engineers had worked throughout the night on their company position, as well as those of the other company/teams. Currently Steel's tanks were arrayed in a large circle that provided them 360-degree security. A six-foot wall of sand made up the circle, with the unit's tanks scattered inside of the perimeter, gun tubes facing outward. In the middle of the defensive position were the company command post, the medics, and other support assets.

"Thad, run through our current status before the platoon leaders get here. I've got to be at the task force operations center in a half hour."

"Roger," said Mason, wiping his hands on his nomex coveralls. He pulled a battered green army notebook from his pocket. "We've got twelve of fourteen tanks fully mission capable. C-12 has a hydraulic leak, but the part is on hand and it should be up within the hour. C-34 has a computer malfunction and the mechanics are still troubleshooting it. Every tank has a full basic load of ammunition on board. We're up on fuel, MREs and water."

Mason stuffed the notebook back in his pocket and looked at Dillon. "Now, sir, can I ask you a question?"

Dillon had been scribbling in his own notebook as Mason dictated. He stopped writing and closed the notebook. "Shoot."

"Sir, what the hell's going on? We deployed here for what I understood to be a show of force. Then they rush us out of Doha as fast as we can draw our equipment. The next thing you know we're being issued war stock *service* ammunition instead of the expected *training* ammunition. I took care of the platoon leaders by telling them we always draw service ammunition when we deploy to foreign theaters of operation. But between you and me, I'd like to know what's *really* going on."

Dillon wondered how to tell Mason that he'd been wondering the same thing himself when the ammunition trucks had delivered the depleted-uranium-tipped main gun rounds.

"Thad, I have no idea," said the captain, looking off into the distance at his approaching platoon leaders. "Whatever's going on, I should find out at the task force briefing. The key for now is to be as close to one hundred percent as we can, because I don't like the looks of this. I need you and First Sergeant Rider to make sure you check out the platoons while I'm gone. Don't make the boys nervous. Just keep them occupied and make sure they're doing the right things."

Mason nodded. "Wilco, sir." He wasn't satisfied with the answer, but he'd been with Dillon long enough to know that his commander wouldn't bullshit him. He might tell him he couldn't talk about the operation, but he wouldn't lie.

They watched the platoon leaders approaching on foot across the desert. Dillon pulled a can of Copenhagen from the recesses of one of his coverall pockets. After popping the lid, he put a pinch of snuff in his mouth. Without looking at Mason, he offered the open can.

The big XO turned to his boss. "Sir, why do you

always offer me that crap? I've never once accepted, nor do I intend to."

Dillon turned to him. "Always a first time."

"Not for *that*."

They continued watching the approach of Cold Steel's junior officers.

"Damn but those guys carry a lot of crap," said Dillon as his platoon leaders moved closer.

Mason nodded once. "Yep."

Two of the lieutenants were loaded down with large wooden map boards and leaders' bags that carried the majority of manuals the army published. The two platoon leaders, Hancock and Takahashi, were working up quite a sweat when they finally reached Steel's ranking leaders. Only Bluto Wyatt was traveling light. Dillon looked up at the sky, silently asking for guidance.

"Dr. Green," said Dillon slowly and patiently. "Have we had the block of instruction on the proper method of transporting a map on the mechanized battlefield?"

Wyatt had nicknamed Charlie Hancock "Dr. Green" the day he reported to Cold Steel. His thinning hair, tall and lanky build, and wire-rimmed glasses made him a ringer for the television doctor. Most people went with the more informal version of the nickname, simply calling Hancock "Doc." Dillon made an exception when he was about to drop the hammer on Hancock, preferring at those times to go with the longer, more formal version.

Hancock had had this type of question posed to him by Dillon several times over the past few days. The wrong answer would not be good.

He looked to his fellow platoon leaders for support. Although Doc couldn't see any low earth orbit satellites overhead, Takahashi and Wyatt appeared to be busily counting them. Obviously, there was no aid forthcoming from that quarter.

He glanced at the XO. Mason just looked him in

the eye and rolled a plastic spoon around in his mouth as if it were a fine Cuban. Definitely no help there.

Finally he turned back to Dillon, who was smiling at him. *Oh God,* thought Doc, *now I know how Little Red Riding Hood felt at Grandma's house.*

Dillon's approach to their training since arriving in Kuwait was 180 degrees different from that morning back in Colorado when he'd sat down with Hancock for their little chat. The junior platoon leader couldn't begin to count the number of foreign-soil ass-chewings he now had under his belt.

Hancock cleared his throat. "Sir . . . uh . . . I believe we did discuss it, but I can't remember your exact guidance." Doc held his breath, then exhaled a sigh of relief as Dillon's gaze swung to Ben Takahashi. The fires had shifted and he was out of immediate danger.

"Ben, can you help Doc out? Or does it escape you as well?" asked Dillon as he turned to his Third Platoon leader.

Takahashi had a look of utter desperation on his face. He opened his mouth to speak, but nothing came out. Everyone stared at the gaping orifice, mesmerized. They waited patiently to hear what would eventually issue from the depths. After a few seconds, the mouth slowly closed.

"Well?" asked Dillon, shaking his head in confusion.

Takahashi opened his mouth again with the same result.

Wyatt leaned on the front slope of the tank behind Dillon, grinning at his fellow platoon leaders' discomfort.

"Listen up," said Dillon calmly. "If you haven't noticed, you're a long way from home in one of those far-off and exotic places you signed up to see. My concern is that if you can't get the little things right, what's going to happen if the proverbial shit ever hits the proverbial fan?" Dillon looked each of his platoon leaders in the eye before continuing. "If you're cruising at speed across the desert with a plywood map board larger than a Little Caesar's pizza box, it is going to: number one, get caught in the wind; number two, proceed to beat you about the face; and number three, blow off of the tank. Finally, number four, you will have to turn around, go back, and retrieve said oversize map. This will cause you unwanted embarrassment in front of your platoon. Furthermore, if you begin receiving artillery, how are you going to get the damn thing into your turret?" He looked back and forth at his two young charges. "Does that discussion ring any bells?"

The two platoon leaders nodded.

"All right, get yourselves some map cases and get rid of those boards. You're not at the Armor School anymore, so don't worry about pretty—worry about functional." Dillon spun around. *"Lieutenant Wyatt, why the hell are you smiling?"*

Wyatt's considerable bulk went two feet vertical.

Dillon jabbed a finger into the big man's chest. *"You should have helped them out before they got to me!"*

Bluto Wyatt went to the position of attention without thinking about it and looked straight ahead. "Sorry, sir."

Dillon took a deep breath and sighed. "At ease, Bluto. Relax."

Wyatt, not sure if Dillon was being literal or not, moved his arms behind his back and went to the position of parade rest. Better safe than sorry.

Dillon looked seriously at Wyatt. "Damn it, Bluto, you're a good platoon leader, but I need you to start sharing your knowledge with these guys. This isn't a contest. I'm counting on you. Understand?"

"Yes, sir," said Wyatt, finding sudden interest in the sand around his boots.

Dillon backed up and put his hands on his hips. Slowly he surveyed his young leaders. "All right, listen up. I've got to get to a briefing at the task force tactical operations center. While I'm at the TOC, I expect you to conduct precombat inspections. I also expect you to get your tanks boresighted. Ensure you enter the computer data for *service* ammunition, not training ammunition. And get your perimeters squared away— I *will* be looking at them when I return. Questions?"

Dillon looked at each of his lieutenants in turn. Each responded with a negative shake of the head.

"All right, get to it." Dillon put on his kevlar helmet and other equipment, grabbed his map and notebook, and walked toward his Hummer where it sat in the center of the assembly area. As he and his driver departed in a cloud of dust, the lieutenants could just make out strains of "Friends in Low Places" from the stereo Sergeant Almo had smuggled into Dillon's Hummer.

"Is it me, or is that about as close to a father-son talk as the CO's had with us?" asked Takahashi, watching the vehicle recede into the desert haze.

Doc nodded. "Yeah, Ben, something weird's definitely going on."

"All right, you heard the man, you chuckleheads," said Bluto. "We've got work to do. I'd make sure it gets done right before Captain Dillon gets back."

The big man began walking toward First Platoon's perimeter. Abruptly he stopped and turned. "I'll be by in an hour to check you out, so have your shit wired tight."

As the other two lieutenants stared after their counterpart, Mason returned to his pork and beans, a smile on his face. Yes, the worm was definitely turning.

Central Command Headquarters, Baghdad, Iraq
20 October, 1455 Hours Local

"Are you sure, General?" said Abdul Aref into the secure phone. "You know the price of failure. . . . Very well, proceed with phase two as scheduled. Rest assured the other divisions will reinforce you within six hours of your attack."

Ending the call, Abdul Aref dialed another number

from memory. He patiently waited until a noncommittal voice answered.

"Tell your master that his nephew wishes to extend his greetings." While the Iraqi leader had confidence in his own intelligence section's ability to hinder American eavesdropping efforts, he was not so sure regarding his new ally's equipment.

The wait was not long.

"Yes, nephew?" said the papery voice on the other end of the line.

"Hello, Uncle. I thought you would want to know. My staff has completed preparations for our banquet and the festivities will begin shortly."

Khalani listened to the news with a smile. "I've received information indicating that our guest list is growing—have you heard of this?"

Aref had been briefed on the American reinforcements earlier. His voice was dismissive. "Yes, yes, I've heard. We will take care of the visitors already here for now. Be sure that we are also considering appropriate entertainment for our new guests."

Abdul Aref's staff felt, and he agreed, that America would hesitate to send more of her sons to their deaths after seeing how quickly the U.S. brigade currently in Kuwait was annihilated. Particularly when regional and world support was not with them. If they did choose to send more troops into the fight, he would make them pay dearly. One thing the United States had never been wrong about—his nation's supply of biological and chemical agents was extensive, and he was prepared to use this arsenal if necessary. No, he did not believe the Drake administration had the stomach for that type of war, despite their apparent commitment to Kuwait. By the prophet, had the man not selected a woman as his vice president? That alone told him much about his opponent.

Khalani's voice was doubtful. "You remain certain of success then?"

Aref smiled thinly at the question. What did a holy man know of war? One American brigade was all that stood in the path of his plans. This brigade was nothing compared to the force preparing to sweep down on it from the north. They would be overwhelmed, as effective against his Republican Guard divisions as the tin soldiers he'd played with as a child. And once these tin soldiers fell, Kuwait's riches, and the power in the Middle East, would be his. "Yes. It is inevitable, Uncle. *En shallah*."

Iron Tigers TOC, Northern Kuwait
20 October, 1500 Hours Local

Dillon sat patiently as the task force S2 went through the intelligence piece of the operations order. As the enemy situation was briefed, the Steel commander annotated unit sizes, dispositions, and locations on his personal map. Dillon kicked back on his field chair and mentally compared the current enemy information with what had been briefed at the morning update. There were no real changes, which was reassuring. While Dillon wasn't afraid of seeing how his men would match up against Iraq's most elite forces, there was an awful lot of them. Prudence was definitely called for.

Lieutenant Colonel Estes stood and moved to the front as the Two stepped away from the briefing charts and mapboards.

"Gentlemen," began Estes, "there are a couple of things the Two didn't tell you. I wanted him briefing you on hard intel only—here's the rest of the story. I just returned from a two-hour meeting with Colonel Jones. The gist of that meeting was that the United States' status in the Middle East has changed dramatically in the past twenty-four hours. Many of our long-time regional allies, with a few obvious exceptions, would like to see us out of here."

Estes pointed at the map, indicating the area to their south and west. "Case in point. As of this time tomorrow, all U.S. forces must vacate Saudi Arabia by order of the Saudi government." The assembled group of officers and soldiers stirred uneasily. "That's right. All of the airpower and Patriot missile batteries in Saudi are in the process of staging for redeployment, are in the process of moving, or are already gone. The Pentagon is shifting as many of the fighters and missiles as possible to Turkey and the few Arab states in the region still friendly to us, but there are only so many facilities."

Estes paused. "Next, it is believed that the Iraqi division across the border will attack within the next twenty-four to forty-eight hours."

Most of the audience stared at Estes in open-mouthed disbelief. One captain, a veteran of several Kuwait border tours, stifled a laugh. The type of operation that the Iron Tigers were currently conducting had been going on in Kuwait for well over ten years. Some of the deployments were more high-stress than others, depending on how Saddam was feeling, but since 1991 there had been no ground action between the U.S. and Iraq.

"Let me be clear, gentlemen," Estes continued, staring down the offending captain, "I am not joking."

Estes paused to read his leaders' reactions, particularly his commanders. Stuart and Dillon returned his stare, as did Nelson Bowers, the infantry company commander assigned to Task Force Tiger. As Estes feared, Dan Malloy looked as if someone had his hand wrapped around Malloy's balls and was applying pressure to the point of pain.

He focused on Malloy as he continued. "Men, we have trained for worse than this. Sure, the Iraqis on the other side of the border have a three-to-one advantage against us. Under ordinary circumstances, that makes it a fifty-fifty proposition—but we're better than that. You may not know it, but I do." Estes shifted his eyes, holding contact with each of his commanders and members of his staff. "I've watched you, your companies, and your platoons train. I've watched this staff take a stinking brigade operations order and work magic with it so that our companies have a quality plan to fight. I know what all of you can do. But that's not enough. You've got to know. And your men have got to believe. With that said, I'll turn it over to the S3." Estes sat down in a field chair near the map.

All eyes turned toward Major Dave Barnett, the task force's S3. Barnett was tall and lean. A nattier officer than most of his armor brethren, he sported a mustache thicker than normally seen in army circles. Barnett suspected that this didn't exactly endear him to the brigade commander, Colonel Bill Jones. Jones had confirmed this suspicion the last time they'd met. "Dave," Jones had said, "why would you attempt to nurture on your lip what grows naturally around your asshole?" Since the encounter, Barnett had begun applying wax to the mustache and rolling the tips into small points. With careful cultivation, it was now almost at the point that Barnett himself was satisfied with his efforts. It was, plainly speaking, a magnificent piece of facial hair.

Barnett's job as the S3 was planning the battalion's, or when their tanks were mixed with infantry, as they were now, the task force's, battles. During missions he positioned himself at the predicted pivotal point on the battlefield so he could provide Estes with the best recommendations possible. Inevitably his advice was sound and his situation reports delivered calmly—a rare thing on command radio nets.

Barnett began in an even, controlled voice. "Gentlemen, our mission is to move ten kilometers north to positions overlooking the main approach into Kuwait. We will set a deliberate defense and stop any Iraqi forces attempting to penetrate."

As Barnett briefed, he pointed to the large map depicting the graphics for the upcoming mission. "As you can see, the brigade is straddling the major approach into Kuwait City. Kuwaiti units equipped with M1A2 tanks, Yugoslavian M-84 tanks—consider those T-72s for all practical purposes since that's the vehicles they're a variant of—and BMP2 infantry fighting vehicles are on Third Brigade's flanks. It should be reiter-

ated that while the Kuwaiti M1A2s have more modern
fire-control systems than our tanks, they do not have
the same armored protection."

This was something that everyone knew, but Barnett didn't want anyone lulled into a false sense of
security regarding their flanks. Troops tended to think
the M1A1 incapable of destruction by enemy direct
fire. The U.S. Army version of the M1A2 offered even
better protection, along with an improved fire-control
system. But the systems sold to Egypt, Kuwait, and
Saudi Arabia didn't include the top secret armored
protection incorporated into the American tanks. Better safe than sorry considering that alliances in the
region had shifted faster than desert sands over the
years.

Barnett continued. "If the Iraqis hold true to form,
they'll attack along the route we straddle. The terrain
is better and they like to orient off of highways for
command and control. We are in the center as the
Third Brigade main effort. Task Force 2-35 Armor
will deploy in a battle position to our left, covering the
flank approach that runs through the wadi complex to
our west. They're heavy, with three tank companies
and one mechanized infantry company, same as us.
Task Force 2-8 Infantry will defend from the high
ground to our right. They're mech heavy with two
mech infantry companies and one tank company.
They'll take advantage of the elevation at their position for long-range TOW shots with their Bradleys.
While 2-8 has the easiest piece of terrain to cover,
they are also losing a team that will be assigned as
the brigade reserve, so they're a little shorthanded."

Barnett paused and turned to the assembled soldiers. "Any questions on how Colonel Jones plans to
deploy the brigade?"

Nelson Bowers raised a hand.

Barnett pointed at Bowers. "Nelson?"

"Sir, no questions on the brigade's disposition, but
could we break long enough to send warning orders
to our companies. We need to get them moving now."

"Good point, Nelson, but we're getting ready to send those warning orders out for you. Your XOs will start moving the companies while you're here receiving the order. You should get to your new battle positions about the same time that your troops do. That work?"

The infantryman nodded. "Hooah, sir."

Barnett continued. "After receiving our final instructions from Third Brigade, our task organization remains unchanged except for the addition of a few combat multipliers, such as two FOX chemical recon vehicles and a couple of ground surveillance radars."

The S3 Air pulled the task organization chart up and pointed out unit compositions as Barnett briefed them. "Task Force 2-77 Armor is now designated Task Force Tiger. We'll have the following company/teams under our control. A Company, 2-77 Armor. . . ." Barnett looked toward the A Company commander.

"Yes, sir?" answered Dan Malloy.

"Your call sign will be Anvil. Your composition, fourteen tanks."

Malloy scribbled the S3's words down verbatim, though it was the same task organization he'd had since taking command.

"B Company," said Barnett.

"Yes, sir," called out Stuart.

"You will detach one tank platoon to B Company, 2-8 Infantry. B Company, 2-8 will give you one of their mech infantry platoons. Call sign Team Black Knight. Final composition, ten tanks, four Bradleys."

Stuart nodded as he wrote the changes to his task organization. "Got it."

"C Company."

"Sir," answered Dillon.

"No change. Call sign Cold Steel, composition fourteen M1A1s."

"Roger," answered Dillon, returning to the map he'd been reviewing.

"B Company, 2-8 Infantry."

"Hooah, sir."

Barnett turned serious. "Nelson, unfortunately we already have a B Company in the battalion, so my staff and I worked long and hard to come up with a totally original call sign for your team—a call sign that will have all of your grunt brethren in the infantry battalion green with envy. Care to guess?"

Bowers rolled his eyes. "Sir . . . not Team Mech?"

"Give that man a cigar! Team Mech, composition, ten Bradley Fighting Vehicles plus the tank platoon discussed earlier from Team Knight. Nelson, you and Mike get the hand-offs for the exchange of those platoons worked out before you leave here, and it needs to happen soonest."

Both captains "rogered" simultaneously.

Barnett continued. "With the addition of my tank and Tiger Six's, that's a total combat strength of forty-four M1A1 tanks and fourteen M2 Bradleys. Gentlemen, we can kill a lot of shit with that kind of firepower . . . *if* we execute properly."

Barnett paused to let the company/team commanders catch their breath before moving into the defense plan. "Okay, gents, here's how we'll crack this nut. . . . Are any of you familiar with Rommel's African campaign of World War Two?"

Dan Malloy raised a hand and smiled smugly. He might not be a warrior in the minds of the other company commanders, but he'd always been number one in his military history classes.

Barnett smiled. "Well, Dan, I'm not fucking Rommel and this isn't fucking northern Africa, so forget everything you know. . . ."

As the meeting broke up, Dillon and Stuart headed for the exit, pausing only long enough to secure their gear from the makeshift hooks hanging around the inner edges of the briefing tent. Adjusting their 9mm pistol shoulder holsters and protective masks, the commanders draped their remaining gear around their shoulders, grabbed their helmets, and strode from the TOC.

As they walked toward the group of command

Hummers a few meters away, Dillon turned to his friend. "So what do you think?"

Stuart kept walking as he answered, shaking his head. "I guess with all that's been going on it shouldn't come as much of a surprise, yet somehow it does. After seeing this same mission pulled over and over again by different units, to be the one sitting here when they tell you thousands of Iraqis are going to be screaming across the border with the sole purpose of waxing your ass . . ."

Dillon nodded. "At a personal level, it's a bit of a shocker. I think that's the sentiment you're attempting to express?"

Stuart stopped at his Hummer. "Fuck you very much, Dr. Freud—but yes."

Dillon smiled at his friend. He was having the same thoughts himself. "It's no big thing, Mikey. It's what we do."

Stuart returned a tight smile and took Dillon's hand in the gathering twilight. "You got that right, buddy. See you on the high ground."

Dillon turned to his own vehicle, then hesitated and turned back. "Hey, Mike?"

"Yeah, man?" said Stuart, climbing into the large all-purpose vehicle.

Dillon opened his arms wide. "You need a hug?"

Stuart, laughing, turned to his driver and gave the classic cavalry forward signal with his arm. "Get us the hell out of here."

**Cold Steel Battle Position, Northern Kuwait
21 October, 0635 Hours Local**

Dillon looked at his platoon leaders. They had as little as twenty-four hours to prepare their defensive position. He now had to find out how much they'd really learned in their time together. Dillon had his XO, platoon leaders, fire support officer, and an engineer lieutenant with him. They stood in the middle of a large open area north of the company battle position.

"Okay, guys, we've done this before. The only difference is that this time, the target effects from your weapons will be just a *little* more obvious. That and the fact that if your tanks don't reposition to alternate firing positions after you fire a couple of rounds, they will be toast. Some Republican Guard tank commander will fire your ass up, given sufficient opportunity."

Dillon waited a couple of seconds before proceeding to make sure the last statement sank in. Training time was over. Tanks wouldn't be magically brought back to life if a stupid mistake occurred.

With the early-morning sun at his back, standing in the middle of the piece of desert where he intended to kill the majority of the forces attacking into his engagement area, Dillon gestured with his arms at the surrounding desert. "To begin with, you're standing in the middle of our engagement area. Can you see our left and right limits of fire?" He pointed to the Battlefield Reference Marking System panels on the ground that the company's gunners were to use as left- and right-side reference points. Ground forces used these panels, called "brims" for short, throughout their engagement areas to mark and divide the battlefield. Day-Glo orange on the side facing friendly forces and desert camouflaged on the side facing approaching enemy troops, they also had several distinctive patterns on the friendly side so gunners could quickly distinguish between different reference points.

Dillon continued. "All right, big picture. Our task force is in the center of the Third Brigade defense. The 2-35 Armor is deployed in that broken terrain to the task force's left. 2-8 Infantry is deployed on that high ground to the right."

Dillon stopped speaking and looked closely at his young leaders. They stared north at the endless desert, stared as phantom tanks rushed south, bent on their personal destruction. They weren't hearing a word.

"Damn it, stay with me!" yelled Dillon. All eyes snapped to him.

"We're with you, boss," said Bluto, settling back into the here and now.

Dillon shook his head and pulled his Copenhagen from a pocket. He thumped the can twice, opened it, and took a pinch before continuing. He offered the can to the lieutenants. All heads shook no simultaneously.

Dillon shrugged. "Look, fellas, do you think I'm not scared? I could shit my pants, but none of us has the time for that. What we have to do is get our acts together and carry out the jobs we're trained for."

In the silence, Dillon could hear nothing but the murmur of the mild desert wind blowing from the west. *Start slowly,* he told himself. *Get them back to the basics.*

He looked at Hancock. "Okay, Doc. From what direction do we expect the attack to originate?"

Doc immediately pointed north. "Sir, the major avenue of approach is from the north. The terrain in the west where 2-35 is defending is slow-go, what with the wadi system running through it, but they could try it. The rocky high ground to the task force's east denies the enemy our right flank." Hancock quit speaking, suddenly aware that he actually had a clue as to what was happening.

"Good," said Dillon.

He turned to Takahashi. "Ben, what's the next thing we want to identify?"

"Where to kill them, sir," answered Takahashi.

"Correct. And where is that?"

"Where we're standing."

"Very good." Dillon grabbed a stake and jabbed it into the ground at his feet, then picked up the hammer he'd brought along. He slammed the stake with the hammer. "Right"—another smashing blow—"fucking"—one final downward stroke—"here!" The leaders stared at the spot, no doubt in their minds where Dillon wanted enemy blood to saturate the desert floor.

Dillon turned to Mason. "XO, have the brim representing the company target reference point emplaced here. Also, tape thermal pads on it in the shape of a cross so the gunners can pick it up in their thermal imaging systems. But don't have the pads activated until sunset. They're only gonna be good for a few hours, so we don't want to waste them."

Mason nodded, took note of the grid coordinate on his GPS receiver, and then copied the information into his notebook. "Wilco, sir."

Dillon turned to the engineer, who was under his control for the upcoming mission. He hadn't worked with the lieutenant before, a fact that he didn't like at all. "Sapper. What can you do to persuade the bad guys to move into our engagement area and how can you keep them here long enough for us to finish them?"

The lieutenant carried a clipboard, but he didn't refer to it. "Sir, my primary mission for your company, after digging in your tanks, of course, is to put in a blocking obstacle forward of your position to pin the enemy. If I remember correctly, most of your tanks can kill past three thousand meters with the depleted-uranium sabot round, correct, sir?"

Dillon nodded.

"Sir, I'd suggest putting the obstacle—three-tiers of concertina, reinforced with antitank and antipersonnel mines—just south of your company target reference point. If that's here, I'd start it about fifty meters back toward your position and run it from east to west. That way they'll have to stop here, allowing us to hit them with the company's combined fires."

"Go on."

"Yes, sir. Additional engineer effort will be focused on emplacing turning obstacles on the flanks. If we work it right, he'll think he's working his way around the obstacle, when in actuality we're herding him right into our engagement area."

Dillon liked the way the lieutenant said "our" engagement area—it was a good sign when attachments thought of themselves as part of the team. The kid would do. "Talk to me about the obstacle effort in the rest of our sector."

"Yes, sir. We're putting out disrupting obstacles starting thirty-seven hundred meters forward of the task force. This obstacle will be primarily composed of the new WAM mines—wide-area munitions that use acoustic and seismic detectors to pick up the movement of enemy armor and then fire a top-down explosively formed penetrator to defeat the target's thin top armor. Very nasty stuff, sir. The WAMs won't stop the enemy, but that's not the intent. They'll force the Iraqis to slow down and break up their formations as they enter the engagement area. When they try to drive around them, assuming they see them, they'll flank themselves, allowing the Bradleys better shots at max missile range."

Dillon held his hand out to the engineer lieutenant. "You've got a job. Coordinate through the XO on the priority of the digging effort and for any help you might need getting those obstacles constructed."

Dillon turned to his fire support officer, First Lieutenant Jake Dumphy. "Jake, where are you and your Fire Support Team going to locate?"

The fire supporter had been with Dillon nine months. They had a good working relationship and Dillon trusted the artilleryman's judgment. That was why, despite the fact that it was Dillon's responsibility to plan the indirect fire targets, he based most of the decisions on the recommendations made by Dumphy. While his tanks could kill up to four thousand meters out, the indirect fire provided by the 155mm artillery could strike approaching enemy targets over eighteen thousand meters to their front. Even though the indirect fire wouldn't kill many enemy armored vehicles, it would definitely upset his timing and execution. It's hard to get people to do what you want when the ground is shaking as if in the throes of a seven-point earthquake and no one can see as dust and sand are thrown hundreds of meters into the air. If the panic doesn't kill you, the shrapnel will.

Dumphy pointed back toward the Cold Steel battle position. "I'll locate behind that high ground two hundred meters to the rear. My crew has already started making a hasty fire plan for the company position and are working up some recommended targets and triggers."

"Good." Dillon reached out and gave the stake designated as the company target reference point, or TRP, a shake. "I also want you to work up a target here. When enemy vehicles start stacking up behind our obstacle, I want the arty coming in heavy."

The FSO made a note and nodded. "Check, sir."

Dillon hesitated. "One last thing, Jake."

Dumphy looked up from his notebook, pen poised.

There was a fine line between preparing for the worst and giving his young leaders the feeling of impending doom. Dillon looked at his artillery officer first, then at his platoon leaders.

"Jake, I want artillery targets plotted over each platoon position."

Dumphy understood. "Roger."

Dillon looked at his lieutenants one last time. "Gentlemen, I *do not* expect to fire artillery onto our own positions, but if something happens to me and you see we're about to be overrun, I expect you to call for smoke to obscure your move, pull out of those positions and call down all of the artillery you can get. Clear?"

Solemn nods were their answer.

"Okay, I'll get with you platoon leaders one on one in a minute to finalize the selection of your positions. Bluto, I'm putting First Platoon in the center, so I'll be at your position as soon as we get finished here. You'll be our main effort and have the primary responsibility for overwatching the blocking obstacle. I'll meet you at your BP in one hour to sight it in." Dillon looked around at the men. "We miss anything?"

"What time does the Counter-Recon team go out?" asked Doc.

"Good question. Team Knight will be in position

by noon." Dillon hated the thought of Stuart and the Scout Platoon moving out during daylight hours. It was a cardinal sin, but one that couldn't be helped given 3rd Brigade's time line to defend. Lieutenant Colonel Estes needed his eyes forward.

Dillon pointed to the northern horizon. "They'll take up station along Phase Line Pickett. Check your graphics and you'll see that Pickett is six kilometers to our front, running east to west. The scouts will continue north and establish a series of observation posts along Phase Line Sheridan. Sheridan also runs east to west, and is ten kilometers to the north. Remember, Knight will pull back through us, time to be determined. We don't want any fratricides because of itchy trigger fingers, so place your tanks on TIGHT for direct fires until Knight withdraws. I reserve the final approval to engage any targets prior to that time. If you can't get me, you guys make the call, but be sure of what you're shooting at. Anything else?"

The looks on their faces told Dillon there would be no further questions and that his team was ready to get down to business.

Cold Steel Six pointed an index finger into the air and twirled it. "Good. Mount up."

Phase Line Pickett, Northern Kuwait
21 October, 1200 Hours Local

"Tiger TOC, Black Knight Six, over," called Mike Stewart over the task force command net.

"Knight Six, Tiger TOC," the radio operator at the task force tactical operation center answered.

"Tiger TOC, Knight Six. Lighthorse elements established in observation posts along Phase Line Sheridan. Knight elements established along Phase Line Pickett. Graphics will be at your location within three zero minutes, over."

"Knight Six, Tiger TOC. Roger, over."

"Knight Six, nothing further, out."

Stuart sat in the cupola of his tank and looked over

the counter-recon graphics one last time before sending them to the TOC for incorporation into the task force's plan. Had he missed any avenue that the Iraqi recon forces could exploit? He didn't think so, but it was a wide sector.

The scouts, call sign Lighthorse, were arrayed in observation posts, or OPs, forward of Team Knight. The Scout Platoon consisted of six Hummers sporting a mixture of .50 cal machine guns and Mark-19 grenade launchers. Each vehicle contained a driver, a vehicle commander, and a scout in the backseat. When establishing OPs, two of the Hummer teams would consolidate to man one observation post in order to keep fresh personnel on the lookout for enemy movement into the task force's sector. They were Estes's eyes and ears forward and therefore an invaluable asset. The scouts' primary problem was a lack of armored protection, so they only used their .50 cals and Mark-19s in self-defense mode. Their radios were their primary weapons.

Upon detecting enemy movement in their sector, the scouts would call Team Knight, the Counter-Reconnaissance Force behind them. Stuart would maneuver his team's tanks and Bradleys into position to intercept and destroy the enemy reconnaissance vehicles before they could report Task Force Tiger's disposition to the Iraqi force's headquarters.

Stuart climbed off his tank and walked to where his XO waited. He handed the lieutenant the graphics he'd been looking over. They, like all military graphics, consisted of a series of alcohol marker notations on clear plastic. These graphic control measures included the positions of Team Knight's tanks and Bradleys, scout OP locations, and the team's targets and obstacles. Once at the TOC, the staff would incorporate them with the graphics of the other company/teams and then issue a consolidated set so that everyone was operating off the same sheet of music.

"Randy, take these back to the TOC. And make sure you stay on the specified withdrawal route; we don't need you getting shot up. I'll make a net call to all of the companies letting them know you're en route." Stuart began to climb onto his tank, then turned back to his XO. "Hell, turn your headlights on to be on the safe side. Just make sure you have them off on the way back up here. And stop at Steel's command post and let Captain Dillon make a copy of the graphics to forward to his men. They're behind us, so if anyone gets tasked to come forward and support us, Steel's the likely candidate. Ask him for a copy of his company's graphics, to include the obstacles they're emplacing. I don't want to stumble into a minefield trying to get back behind friendly lines."

"Roger, sir, anything else you want me to tell him?" asked the young XO as he took the graphics and tucked them into his canvas leader's bag.

"Yeah," said Stuart. "Tell him that we intend to withdraw after we've destroyed the lead recon forces, but before their main body attacks. It could be a fine line so far as timing goes. I don't think we can count on the Iraqis using the established recon time lines we're used to seeing at the National Training Center, so we may be in a big hurry when we move back through Steel's position. Coordinate the recognition signals with him or Thad Mason."

"Roger, sir." The XO gave Stuart a final wave and moved off.

Stuart climbed back into his cupola and put his CVC on.

Holding the transmit key down, he began his message. *"Guideons, guideons, Black Knight Six. My Five element is en route to the task force TOC. He is moving on Route Dagger with white lights on. Please do not shoot him as he just got laid for the first time the night prior to deploying and he's really looking forward to trying it again. . . ."*

CHAPTER 4

Probes

Phase Line Sheridan, Northern Kuwait
21 October, 1345 Hours Local

The battered four-wheel-drive truck trudged slowly through the desert. The two bedouins inside exchanged glances. They knew they were getting close to the Yankee lines.

"Lieutenant, are you sure the Americans will not shoot us when they see our truck moving toward their position?" asked the driver.

The man in the passenger seat turned toward his younger companion with a smile. "Taha, how many times must I to tell you? The tales of American soldiers killing and eating babies are highly exaggerated. Besides," he laughed, "why would they shoot a pair of lowly bedouins? I tell you, it was a stroke of genius by the reconnaissance company commander. The Americans are looking for armored reconnaissance vehicles probing their lines, not old rusty trucks carrying shepherds in search of their missing sheep."

The scout lying prone in the observation post tracked the truck's movement as it proceeded bumpily across the desert to his front. Positioned on a slight rise, dug in, with a desert-patterned camouflage net pulled over his hole, he was invisible unless someone stumbled onto his position. Pulling his radio close, he began transmitting while keeping watch on the vehicle through his twenty-power binoculars. Even though he was much too far away to be heard, out of habit the scout whispered into the handset. Too often Scouts had to send their reports as the enemy was passing close enough to touch, so it was an SOP derived from necessity.

"Lighthorse Six, Lighthorse Two, over."

"Lighthorse Two, this is Lighthorse Six, over," answered the scout platoon leader.

"Lighthorse Six, I have a civilian four-wheel-drive truck containing two men. I say again two men, northern section of Sierra-One, moving south, over."

At his position three kilometers to the east, the Scout Platoon leader looked at his map. He annotated the details of the spot report. *"Lighthorse Two, any weapons visible? Over."*

There was a slight pause. Lighthorse Six could see the scout in his mind, straining through the binoculars to see every detail of the reported contact.

"Negative. They appear to be civilians, but I cannot see clearly into the truck, over."

"Roger Two, stand by. Going higher."

The lieutenant selected by the battalion commander to lead the Scouts is generally an experienced tank platoon leader who has shown he can think fast and make smart decisions. The current Lighthorse Six was no exception, but at the moment, he wasn't sure what to do. He didn't want to scream, "The sky is falling," because two Arabs were riding around in a truck. Then again, he didn't want to take any chances. Since he was attached to Stuart and Team Knight for this mission . . .

"Knight Six, Lighthorse Six, over."

"Knight Six," answered Stuart.

Lighthorse 6 glanced at his map as he sent the report higher. *"Roger, Knight Six, I have a civilian truck . . ."*

After signing off from the scouts, Stuart sat back and thought about his current predicament. The Rules of Engagement, or ROE, clearly forbade them from interfering with the local population. If he called the TOC, there was a better than even chance some knucklehead pulling radio detail there would tell him to let these guys go.

But what if they weren't locals? One thing he'd learned at an early stage of his military career was that it was easier to beg forgiveness later than ask permission now.

Stuart marked the reported location on his map in red to indicate a possible enemy vehicle in sector. He looked at the blue marks on his map indicating the locations of his own elements. It looked as if his closest reaction force was his attached mech infantry platoon.

"Blue One, Knight Six. Did you monitor Lighthorse's message? Over."

The mech infantry platoon leader answered quickly. *"Roger Six, monitored. We just got eyes on the contact. The truck's moving slowly and continuing south. He's coming straight at us, over."*

Stuart nodded to himself, his decision finalized. *"Blue One, I want you to stop that truck with as little force as possible. See what type of equipment they have on board, over."*

"This is Blue One, wilco."

The Iraqi recon team pulled around the corner of a wadi and stopped cold. Directly in front of them was a Bradley Fighting Vehicle. The barrel of its 25mm gun was locked onto them and it looked hungry. The sergeant in the top of the Bradley motioned with an open hand for them to halt.

"Sir, what are we to do?" screamed the driver. "I thought you said we wouldn't be stopped!"

"Do *not* go to pieces on me," the team leader said through the forced smile he was directing toward the Bradley's crew. "Now do as I say. Back up slowly. Very slowly."

The driver joined in smiling and waving as he started backing the truck up.

The Iraqi lieutenant's smile was real now. "You see, Taha? The stupid Americans sit there. Now we know where their front lines are. The idiots are going to just let us leave. . . ."

The officer was suddenly thrown forward into the windshield as the driver slammed on brakes. He reached a hand to his mouth and felt the bloody stump that used to be a front tooth. "You stupid son of a crippled goat, I told you to move slowly! You are driving like a madman! Why have you stopped?"

The driver's head was turned toward the Iraqi lieutenant, but not by choice. His left cheek had the barrel of an M16 rifle pressed to it. Despite the seriousness of the situation, the lieutenant couldn't help thinking that his driver resembled a man who had partaken of sour milk.

Behind the rifle stuck in his driver's face stood a soldier in desert fatigues whose face was painted light green and tan. The soldier looked at the Iraqi lieutenant and smiled. "How y'all doin' today? If it's not too much trouble, how 'bout just staying put till my sergeant gets over here, all right?"

The man looked like a smiling fiend from hell, and sounded like one of those country-western singers he'd heard on the Yankee Armed Forces Network radio station.

A slight pressure on his back caused the lieutenant to look slowly over his own shoulder. A similarly clad figure stood next to his door with an M16 rifle. This one wasn't smiling. Looking the Iraqi in the eye, the figure spoke. "Yeah. What he said."

The lieutenant turned back to his driver. "Be still, Taha," he said in Arabic. "I will handle this."

"Sir . . . there are more of them behind us."

The team leader turned in time to see six infantrymen fanning out around their old Toyota.

The Mech Platoon sergeant was on the ground with his platoon's dismounted element. He took a small squad radio off his belt and keyed it. *"Blue One, Blue*

Four. SITREP follows. We stopped the truck. Truck attempted to leave area. We have stopped it again. I'm preparing to search it now, over."

The Iraqi recon lieutenant thought he was beginning to get through to the Americans. He described a camel with his hands, exaggerating the hump. Following this, he put a hand to his forehead and looked in every direction. Some of the American soldiers were beginning to smile at his antics. *Fools,* thought the recon team leader.

He looked at his driver and a cold shiver ran down his spine. The frightened soldier was slowly reaching between their seats for the lightweight machine gun hidden there. If it was found, it could be easily explained. Many of the locals carried firearms. Some Bedouin trucks even had large-caliber machine guns mounted in the rear. But if the idiot pulled the weapon on these soldiers . . .

Feeling sweat bead between his eyes, the lieutenant spoke slowly and quietly. "Taha, listen to me. Release the weapon. If you pull it out, we are dead."

The driver was sweating profusely and his hands shook. "No, Lieutenant, they know. They are m-m-merely toying with us. If we surprise them, we may be able to g-g-get out of here before the rest can react." Warm fluid had begun flowing down his leg into a pool on the floorboard.

"Do not pull that weapon out! Do you hear me!"

The corporal from Tennessee had been watching the driver since they'd stopped the truck. He now called to his platoon sergeant as he tightened the grip on his rifle, the butt pulled to his shoulder and his cheek in position along the stock in order to retain a good sight picture. "Sarge! You better get over here! Somethin's goin' on and I don't like the looks of it one little bit! I think this boy just pissed hisself! And the other one's sweatin' up a storm and screamin' at him!"

*   *   *

The lieutenant felt like staining his own trousers as he saw the driver's hand close firmly on the weapon and begin to withdraw it. "Stop, fool. Do not—"

The driver pulled the machine gun out and began to swing it toward the American overwatching him. He made it halfway.

The two soldiers standing on either side of the truck didn't hesitate. The sounds of brass bouncing off the hard desert floor was drowned out by the screams of the Arabs as both of the infantrymen emptied their rifles through the truck's windows.

Stuart had heard the small arms fire less than a minute ago, but it seemed ages. He knew that the Mech Platoon had their hands full if anything had happened and that they'd report as soon as possible, so despite wanting to radio for a situation report, he restrained himself. In frustration he scanned with his binos toward the reported location, knowing he wouldn't be able to see a damned thing.

Finally, the call came in. *"Knight Six, Blue One, over."*

Stuart keyed his transmit switch. *"Knight Six."*

"Knight Six, this is Blue One. Truck attempted to open fire on our dismounts. Both Arabs are K-I-A. I say again, both are K-I-A. We sustained no casualties. Found something interesting in their vehicle. Suggest you come to our location ASAP, over."

"Roger. En route, out." Stuart prayed that whatever they'd found in the truck was good. If not, and they'd killed a couple of civilians, no . . . better not to think about it.

A mile to the west, another truck was spotted by the 2-35 Armor's Counter Recon Force. Five minutes later, having assured themselves the Bedouins were not a threat, the truck was released so that the Arabs could continue their search for their missing livestock. The soldiers that had spotted them returned to their concealed positions, on sharp lookout for enemy reconnaissance.

Iron Tigers TOC, Northern Kuwait
21 October, 1430 Hours Local

"So what does it mean, Phil?" Estes asked his intelligence officer as they looked at the situation map.

The S2 pulled out the weapon of choice of every staff officer of every army in the world—a telescopic pointer. He employed the pointer as a master fencer a foil, moving it with swift thrusts around the map. "Sir, this red pin indicates the location where Knight took out the truck. The subsequent search of the truck resulted in the discovery of a cooler with a false bottom—a very professional job that we might not have noticed if a round hadn't rattled the cooler enough to dislodge the bottom slightly. Inside the hidden compartment were a portable radio and a map. The map contains symbology indicative of Iraqi reconnaissance operations." He turned to Estes. "Interestingly enough, sir, though you might not realize it, the Iraqis utilize a combination of Soviet and British military doctrine." He returned to the map. "You can see here that—"

Estes's face barely moved. "Phil."

The S2's pointer ceased its sparring. "Yes, sir?"

"Could you bottom-line this for me? Like . . . right now?"

The captain cleared his throat. "Certainly, sir. The Iraqis seemed to have a very good idea of where our forces are located, to include elements way in the rear. Damned strange. These guys, and I'm sure there are other teams like theirs, were trying to confirm their boss's guesses. Note that they've made slight changes to the graphics, reflecting our actual locations when they differed from their estimate."

Estes turned to the S3 Air. "Have you called this up to Third Brigade yet?"

"Roger, sir," answered the junior captain. "They

were pretty pissed initially. Said we violated the Rules of Engagement. Once I told them about the radio and the map they were a little more understanding."

Estes couldn't help smiling. "I'll bet. Has anyone taken a look at the radio to see what frequency they were using?"

The captain shook his head. "Sir, the radio caught a couple of rounds, so it was hard to tell much of anything from it. They said the truck looked like something out of *Pulp Fiction* when the firing finally died down. You know, that scene where Travolta is holding the pistol on the guy in the back of the car and—"

Estes held up a hand. "Yes, yes, I'm familiar with the film." He turned to the other men in the TOC. "Anything else, gentlemen?"

"Sir, I've spoken with the brigade S2," said the intel captain. "It turns out we're not the only task force who encountered 'bedouins' this afternoon. The 2-35 Armor ran into some down in the wadis." Silence followed for a moment. Then the Two continued. "They let them go."

"Shit," said Estes as the impact of the words hit him. "What you're telling me is there's a damned good chance the enemy knows the disposition of the forces on our left flank?"

Major Barnett spoke for the first time. "Sir, I caught the conversation between the 2-35 commander and Colonel Jones on the brigade command push. It wasn't pleasant. The colonel directed him to reposition as many of his forces as possible, particularly the ones in the area the bedouins had gone through, while continuing to maintain security within his task force's sector."

Estes didn't look happy, but nodded. "Okay, we'll have to hope that does it. Who do we have adjacent to 2-35 Armor?"

Barnett didn't bother referring to the map. "Anvil, sir."

Great, thought Estes. "Okay, call Captain Malloy.

Tell him I don't have a warm and fuzzy about that flank and to orient a few positions that way. I want at least one platoon of tanks to be able to shift to that sector quickly."

Barnett nodded. He'd made the call ten minutes earlier.

3rd Brigade, 4th ID TOC, Northern Kuwait
21 October, 1500 Hours Local

Colonel Bill Jones, commander of 3rd Brigade, exhaled a couple of lungs' worth of smoke and stared at his operations map. The numerous colored symbols wouldn't mean much to the average person. To Jones, each icon represented a group of his soldiers. Some he knew, others he didn't. But he loved them all, because they were *his* men—and women. He couldn't forget the women. No longer was it enough to worry about your men dying or being captured. Now add to that the concerns that only a father with daughters, such as Jones himself, could have.

Jones shook his head in defeat and pulled out another cigarette. He thumbed his Zippo, lit up, and looked at the souvenir from another war. One of his NCOs had given him the lighter during Desert Storm after watching Jones bum lights off others for a month. Two days later the man was dead. He'd driven a Hummer over an antitank mine in a "cleared" area.

Jones closed his eyes and exhaled. Now the Zippo was like Jones himself—a little worn, but still with some usefulness left in it.

He looked around the operations center and spotted Sergeant Major Jack Kelly. Kelly, the brigade operations sergeant major, had worked with Jones off and on over the years. Jones had considered it a personal coup that he'd snagged the sergeant major when the old soldier arrived at Fort Carson a year earlier. If the REMFs, a polite acronym for "rear-echelon motherfuckers," at Division Headquarters had known Kelly was transferring in, he'd be pouring coffee from a silver pot to the brass right now. The veteran NCO was one of those soldiers every general officer in the army seemed to know from one posting or another. He would have been a very nice addition to the division staff. Jones laughed to himself. He hadn't given the fuckers a chance.

"Hey, Sergeant Major, that pot of coffee ready?" inquired Jones in a gravelly voice.

Kelly stared at Jones in awe. He hadn't seen the man eat a bite in three days. His diet seemed to consist of nothing but coffee and cigarettes. "No, sir, but it'll only be a couple more minutes. I'll bring you a cup when it's ready."

"No, you won't, Sergeant Major. Christ on a crutch. People wait on me hand and foot around here. I draw the line at being allowed to pour my own coffee."

"Yes, sir," Kelly laughed. He knew Jones had no idea how highly regarded he was by his troops. They'd follow him to hell if he asked. All he'd have to say was that Satan had fucked up and was in dire need of an ass kicking, and forty-four-hundred-odd men and women would cram themselves onto the first elevator they could find that went all the way down. In twenty years of service, the sergeant major had met no other man like Colonel William Jebediah Jones. He was as hard and gritty as one of the weathered boulders along the North Wall of the National Training Center. Like the boulders, Jones had put in his time observing men fight in that godforsaken piece of the Mojave. Unlike the boulders, Jones had learned at the NTC, as well as at dozens of other training sites, and applied the skills he'd learned to leading men in combat. Still, for all his hardness, on more than one occasion Kelly had also seen the tears well up in Jones's eyes at the loss of one of his soldiers. Never in public, usually over an old bottle of scotch.

The 3rd Brigade commander turned back to his maps. His experienced eye noted the disposition of the brigade's three task forces. They were thin. He would have preferred to put one task force in reserve behind the two others, but he just had too much ground to cover. The best he could do was to pluck a team from 2-8 as a reserve. Looking at 2-8's battle position, he knew that the loss shouldn't hurt them. They had the high ground and a lot of TOW tubes to strike from long range.

Jones looked to the left and right of his brigade's positions. He hoped the Kuwaitis would make a fight of it. The 3rd Brigade was directly in the tornado's path, but they'd need the locals to contribute. More troops were on the way from stateside, but he couldn't count on them being in the fight for a while yet. No, the Kuwaitis would have to be able to hold if a push came in one of their areas. They had fielded some of the more than two hundred M1A2s they would eventually receive, but for now only a portion of their two armored brigades had the tank of choice for the twenty-first century. The majority would be M-84s, a European variant of the Soviet T-72.

The primary question in Jones's mind wasn't the Kuwaitis' equipment, but their will to fight. After the Iraqis overran them so quickly in 1990, serious steps had been taken to beef up their defenses. Initial reconstruction planning after the Gulf War, formulated with the help of the U.S. and the British, called for two additional armored brigades, both fielding the M1A2 tank and modern Infantry Fighting Vehicles. After a few years with no aggression from the other side of their border with Iraq, the Kuwaiti government's bean counters began pressuring their politicians to divert the funds to other projects. Add to this the fact that all Kuwaiti units were short in the manpower department—most were royalty, after all, so getting their hands dirty wasn't really what most had in mind—and one saw a force that was improved over what it had been, but which still couldn't hold its own borders for any significant length of time. Especially against the largest army in the Middle East. Jones shook his head in frustration, knowing that there was a decent chance that the Kuwaitis they were backing up would just say

screw it and take off south for the Saudi border at the
first sign of hostilities, waiting there for more forces
to arrive in country to help force their belligerent
northern neighbors back into their own yard. Still,
Jones had done some training with the "new" Kuwaiti
Army over the past few years. He knew there were
some good men in its ranks, men who looked forward
to a time when they could avenge the rape of their
nation that had taken place more than a decade prior.
Arab memories were long.

How the Kuwaitis would react to an Iraqi attack
worried Jones, but at the moment it took a backseat
to his concern regarding the Iraqi recon forces that
had penetrated his sector and possibly the Kuwaitis'
sector as well. The best Jones could do was some repositioning, but you had to fight with the terrain you
had—and that didn't leave a great deal of room for
major changes in his unit's disposition.

The Iraqis would probably have at least an eighty
percent read on Task Force 2-35 Armor. On the flip
side, the other task forces were digging in and continuing to improve their positions. If 2-35 could get most
of their repositioning completed before nightfall,
Third Brigade would be ready. He hoped.

Continuing to look at the map, his gaze shifted east
from 2-35's position to 2-77 Armor's sector. The Iron
Tigers. Jones hoped they lived up to the name. He
had placed them dead center across the most likely
approach for the Republican Guard division. He knew
Rob Estes was a capable commander. He also placed
a lot of faith in Dave Barnett, although he hated the
mustache. Once more he found his mind wandering
to that piece of facial hair. It really did look waxed,
but even Barnett wouldn't try to bait him like that.
Would he?

Before he could come to closure on the mustache
issue, which he never did anyway, Jones smelled the
intoxicating aroma of a Colombian roast. He turned
to see Sergeant Major Kelly approaching with two
steaming white foam cups. Standing, Jones took one.

"Damn it, Sergeant Major, I told you I'd get my own coffee." He tempered the rebuke with a smile. "But thanks. I appreciate it."

Jones sipped from the cup. "Where did you manage to dig up the good stuff? The only coffee I've seen around here besides the brown water the chow hall dishes out was some foo-foo stuff the air force liaison officer had—amaretto or some such shit."

"Sir, you know that kind of information is a trade secret," quipped Kelly. "If we told you, you wouldn't need NCOs anymore."

"Grab a chair and sit down with me a minute, Jack," said Jones, sitting on a field chair. "God knows my old bones can use the break."

Kelly grabbed a stool, turned it backward, and threw a leg over it. A complicated field move, the casual stool break took years to perfect. Doing it with a full cup of hot coffee was not to be attempted by the novice. "Oh, shit, sir, you're not that old yet. What? Forty-five or so?"

Jones looked at Kelly over his cup, blowing nonchalantly. "Damned near, Sergeant Major, damned near. But they've been *long* years. Jumping on and off armored vehicles takes its toll on a body after a couple of decades. Now are you going to tell me what the hell you've been smiling about all day? It's just not like you to have such a pleasant demeanor in front of the troops."

Kelly's grin, if possible, grew larger. It threatened to crack open his bulldog face if it expanded beyond its current boundaries. "Oh, hell, sir. I'm not that transparent, am I? But in answer to your question, yeah, I *do* have a bit of news."

Jones stretched his legs out and sat back. "Well, spill it, man! I can see you're dying to tell somebody."

Kelly's eyes began to twinkle. "Sir, do you remember my oldest son, Little Jack?"

Jones sputtered as he inhaled sharply and coffee went down the wrong pipe. "*Little* Jack?! You mean that six-foot, six-inch freak of nature you call a son?

Last I heard he was commanding a company in the Eighty-second back at Bragg."

Kelly nodded. "Yes, sir, that would be him." He shook his head sadly. "Never figured out where I went wrong with that boy. Raise him right and then he goes off and joins the infantry—airborne to top it all off. Anyway, Little Jack and his wife, Rhonda, just sent me a message. Jack the Third was born at eleven-thirty last night. Twelve pounds!"

Jones whooped and held out a massive paw to his friend. "Well, congratulations, Kelly. Unfortunately, he'll probably get his looks, as well as his size, from your side of the family—no offense to the wife of course. I blame it all on your genes."

Kelly grinned and shook the outstretched hand. "None taken. Thank God your girls took after their mother."

Jones turned serious for a moment. "So Little Jack was in Fayetteville for the birth?"

Kelly's smile faded. "Yes, sir. His company didn't leave until a few hours later. He should be on the ground in Kuwait sometime tonight or early tomorrow morning."

Jones nodded understanding. It didn't matter how old you were, no one liked to see his children in harm's way. Especially those who knew exactly what harm's way meant.

"Okay, Jack, I hate to spoil the mood before we start hugging and kissing, but it's time to talk business," said Jones, nodding his head toward the map. "You've been playing this game as long as I have. What do you think?"

Kelly took a sip of coffee before responding. "I think we looked good until this afternoon, sir. There's no way of telling how much intel those fucking rag heads bagged before we caught on to their game. I have to say, though, it was a slick ruse. Yes, sir, slicker than owl shit on a barbed-wired fence."

Jones nodded in agreement, though he couldn't help wondering exactly how owl shit and barbed wired equated to slickness. He stubbed out his cigarette on the dirt floor of the operations center. "Yeah, that's the bitch of it. No way of knowing."

Kelly continued to gaze at the map. "My opinion, take it for what it's worth, is that the infiltrations were by and large in our sector—not in the Kuwaitis'."

Jones grunted. "Rationale?"

The sergeant major shrugged. "Well, sir, I figure the Kuwaitis know the difference between bedouins and Iraqi reconnaissance if anyone does. And I figure the Iraqis know that, so they'd naturally send most of the effort our way . . . which is likely their preferred route at any rate."

Jones nodded. "You're probably right. Terrain's definitely better for mechanized movement."

"If it makes you feel any better, I've watched the Iron Tigers in the field. I guarantee you, sir, Colonel Estes is priming a few extra gun tubes in the direction of those wadis to his west."

Jones smiled and tapped his pockets. The smile disappeared. He couldn't have smoked the whole pack. He'd just opened it at breakfast.

"Here you go, sir," offered Kelly, already having shaken one of his own out when he saw the look of disappointment on his commander's face.

"You're spoiling me, Sergeant Major," said Jones, the smile returning as he reached over to take the cigarette. "Yeah, I think Estes's guys will do all right. At least they didn't let recon vehicles into the center of their sector."

Kelly nodded understanding at his commander's frustration, then stood and reached for his kevlar helmet and equipment harness. "Need anything else, sir? I want to go out and check our local security. Lets the troops see that I care," Kelly said with a laugh. His tirades over improperly placed machine guns around the 3rd Brigade perimeter were legendary.

Jones shook his head. "No, Sergeant Major, I think I'm going to go forward and check the battle positions myself. I just seem to get in the way around here."

Kelly felt a sudden surge of affection for his commander. He knew Jones hated being stuck at his headquarters and away from his troops. If he didn't have a reason to go out and see his men, he'd make one up. Nonetheless, he worried about the man. He was a big target for enemy troops, and the fact that his vehicle had several antennas atop it was a dead giveaway to any seasoned soldier that someone important was inside.

"Sir, you be careful out there. Leave your Hummer and take that Bradley the guys in Doha scrounged for you."

Jones saluted smartly. "Acknowledged, Sergeant Major. And thanks again for the coffee and smokes."

"Sure thing, sir. Part of the job," said Kelly as he donned his helmet and walked out of the operations center.

Kelly had taken two steps when he recognized a short, thin sergeant making his way toward the TOC.

"Sergeant O'Keefe? What the hell are you doing here? Can't First Brigade find enough to keep you busy?"

The young NCO pulled up short on hearing his name called. "Hello, Sergeant Major!"

The men shook hands warmly. "Well, O'Keefe? Glad to see you here, but how the hell did you manage it?"

O'Keefe looked embarrassed. "My company had just sent me to the brigade S3 shop after that last exercise against Captain Dillon's platoons. Well, I talked to the sergeant major—he and I go way back—and I told him how I had it from a pretty reliable source that our brigade would be the next one rotating over here to Kuwait, probably sometime next spring. Further, I told him that if I went as a rep with Third Brigade, it could sure help when the time came for our own brigade to deploy for a similar exercise. He couldn't help seeing the logic in my reasoning and arranged for me to join you." The NCO held his arms in the air. "So here I am."

Kelly couldn't help smiling. Although some would deny it—particularly to their wives—there weren't many soldiers who could resist the siren call of an operational deployment. Especially a field soldier such as O'Keefe. Kelly knew, of course, that O'Keefe had lied through his teeth to the 1st Brigade Sergeant Major.

"So what do we have you doing?" asked Kelly.

O'Keefe noticeably deflated. He mumbled something unintelligible.

Kelly leaned closer. "What's that?"

The young NCO looked noticeably embarrassed. "Damn it, Sergeant Major, I'm the night radio operator at the TOC! I might add that it's a very important duty! Okay?"

Kelly howled with laughter. He knew how it galled O'Keefe not being behind the sight of a combat vehicle. Then a thought struck him. "O'Keefe, it just might be your lucky day."

O'Keefe looked at Kelly shrewdly. When senior NCOs began talking favors, it was best to listen carefully, because there was generally more to it than met the eye. "How so, Sergeant Major?"

"How'd you like to get back on a Bradley?"

O'Keefe was tempted to whoop with delight, but held himself in check. "Gunner or vehicle commander?"

"Primarily gunner, but sort of both."

The light came on. O'Keefe shook his head. "Okay, I get it. No way. I've baby-sat lieutenants half my career. No more platoon leader tracks. Too much of a headache. As soon as I get one of those guys trained, they yank him from under me and send me a new one. Uh-uh."

Kelly rolled his eyes. "Will you shut up a minute? Not a platoon leader's Bradley—the commander's."

"Colonel Jones has a Brad?"

Kelly nodded. "Yeah, an old friend of his at the draw yard in Doha insisted that he take it. I concurred. All we have to do is find a crew to man it. So far I've got a driver and a couple of radio operators. I'd take it as a personal favor if you'd act as the Old Man's gunner. It would make me feel better about his running back and forth on the front lines if I knew a good man was watching his back."

O'Keefe rolled the idea around in his mind. Generally, he didn't like getting any closer to the flagpole than necessary. But . . . it would get him back in a gunner's seat and off the graveyard shift at the brigade TOC. Plus he'd heard good things about Jones. He nodded to himself, then looked at Kelly and held out his hand.

"Deal."

Kelly smiled and grabbed O'Keefe's hand. A weight lifted from his shoulders . . . or at least lightened. "Good shit. He's pulling out in a few minutes. Grab your gear and hop on the track."

He was talking to O'Keefe's back, as the young sergeant had already started running toward the operations center to grab his gear.

"Wilco, Sergeant Major!" O'Keefe yelled over his shoulder.

Kelly couldn't help but get caught up in O'Keefe's enthusiasm. His smile grew and his pace took on a spring as he continued moving toward the perimeter of the headquarters compound.

3rd Brigade, 4th ID TOC, Northern Kuwait
21 October, 1545 Hours Local

Jones turned back to the maps for a final look. Satisfied, he turned and began donning his combat gear to head to the front lines.

"Hey, Smitty," he said to the "runner" who passed as a gofer in the operations center. "Could you go tell my crew to get the Brad warmed up. I'll be there and ready to roll in ten minutes."

"Yes, sir," said the corporal. He turned and walked out as a high-pitched whistling sounded. The next thing he was aware of was Jones grabbing him and throwing him into a sandbagged bunker just outside the TOC.

"Get your head down goddamn it or that arty's going to take it off!" screamed the colonel in his ear.

Both men lifted a few inches off the ground as the artillery hit three hundred meters away. The barrage lasted thirty seconds, then moved west.

The brigade executive officer rushed out of the relative safety of one of the lightly armored M577 command and control tracks. He searched frantically until he saw Jones.

"Sir, are you all right?" yelled the major.

Jones stood. "Yeah," he said, brushing himself off. "This is just a prelude. Harassing fires spread around the rear area. The big stuff is still to come. Get with the fire support cell and see if they're going to be able to get any counterbattery fires off."

As the XO turned back to the headquarters vehicles, Jones glanced over at Corporal Smith. The soldier was just starting to peer over the edge of the sandbags. "You all right, Smitty?" asked the colonel.

"Yes, sir," answered the young soldier. Smith was obviously *not* all right. He was still shaking.

"All right, soldier, take a deep breath," said Jones. He made sure the corporal was looking him directly in the eyes. "I still need that Brad, son. Get moving." Jones watched the boy move off and breathed a little easier. You never knew how someone was going to react to his first taste of war. A lot of soldiers went their entire careers without ever experiencing what that kid just had.

Jones turned toward the operations track and yelled to the crew inside. "I need a SITREP on damage to the headquarters before I leave." The colonel paused.

"And I want to know the number of casualties before you give me anything else."

"Already working it, sir," came a reply from inside the vehicle.

"Medic! Medic!" came a scream from a few hundred feet away.

Jones began a trot toward the disturbance. As he got closer, he slowed.

Ah, shit, thought Jones.

A group of soldiers was grouped around a prone figure. Jones gently pulled the sergeant who had been screaming for a medic away from the remains of what had once been an American soldier.

"We need a medic over here now!" screamed the young NCO.

"There's nothing we can do for him," said Jones gently. "We've got to let the medics work on the casualties they can still help."

For the first time the sergeant looked at the man pulling him back from the body. His eyes widened on recognizing the eagle of a full colonel on the right collar of the BDU blouse. "But, sir, you don't understand. He was running around out here helping me get my guys to cover. If he hadn't stopped to help us, he'd have been in the bunker. He wouldn't be *dead*."

Jones had to break his eyes away from the sergeant's stare. He choked on his first attempt at a reply. "Yeah. I know, son. That's the kind of soldier Kelly was. Now help me find something to cover him with."

CHAPTER 5

Prelude to a Kiss

Cold Steel Battle Position, Northern Kuwait
21 October, 2000 Hours Local

In the darkness Cold Steel's battle position looked abandoned. For now, the majority of the company's tanks had pulled back into hide positions. In this way, any enemy recon that made it into C Company's sector would have difficulty establishing exactly where the company was defending. Only three tanks occupied their fighting holes at the moment, one in each of the three platoon battle positions. These tanks scanned with thermals to ensure the area remained secure until Dillon brought the rest of the company forward before first light.

Dillon's lieutenants gathered around his tank. He'd wanted to bring all his tank commanders in, but knew he couldn't afford to have that much of the company's leadership pulled away from last-minute combat checks. He'd depend on the platoon leaders to relay his message.

Leaning against his tank, C-66, Dillon closed his eyes and took in the heavy smells of burning fuel and large mechanized war machines that always accompanied tank units. The muffled clink of track on sprockets as M1A1s moved in the darkness, about their preparations. God, this seemed so much like the countless field exercises they'd drilled . . . yet it was so very different.

He opened his eyes and tried to make out the faces of the nearby men. They waited for inspirational words, needing them like a starving man needs a meal, but nothing came to Dillon. He had never been in a position like this as a young lieutenant and could only imagine the thoughts running through their minds. Most of them had entered the army less than a year ago, and now the security of a nation and their men's lives depended in large part on the decisions they would make over the course of the next few days.

It was getting too dark to see them clearly, but Dillon felt their stares as he began speaking. "I'm proud of the way you and your men have gotten in here and busted ass to get this defense set. Very proud. No one could have done more in the time we've had."

He paused, praying the words they needed to hear would come. "I know you're having doubts over whether or not you can handle the shit that's coming down. That's natural. *Know this*. I have faith in you. I have faith in your NCOs. I have faith in your men. I have faith in *this company*. Just do the things that we've been trained to do. Thad, where are you?"

Mason's grumble sounded behind Dillon. "Here, sir."

Dillon turned on the voice in the darkness. "Thad, if I go down, this company is yours. No time for doubts. You grab the bull by the balls and take it where it needs to go."

"Roger, sir," replied the big executive officer quietly.

Dillon turned on his other lieutenants. "The same goes for the rest of you, and for your men. Lives are going to be lost if no one is willing to get on the radio and make decisions. Is that understood?"

A chorus of "rogers" sprang from the night.

"I've heard some of your men talking about how this is going to be easy—how the Arabs can't fight. *Do not underestimate your enemy*. Give him the benefit of the doubt and you'll be less likely to make stupid mistakes. We may be better than anyone in the world one on one, but, gentlemen . . . this is going to be far from one on one. Make every round count."

Dillon knew his lieutenants were dangling on his every word and hoping something magical would come from his lips that would guarantee their own survival along with their men, if only they listened closely. But it was too late for that. Those magic words were the ones that had been spoken during the previous months of training—the words that had been spoken during After Action Reviews, when their mistakes were exposed and solutions for fixing them were brought out. Dillon hoped the lessons had taken hold.

Bluto broke in. "Sir, any change to Team Knight's withdrawal plan? They still coming through us?"

"Yeah, Bluto. But you guys are going to have to keep an ear to the radio. Remember, they're not pulling until they've destroyed the recon from the lead Republican Guard brigade. If that brigade attacks one of the other task force sectors, the call will be made on whether Knight's staying forward a while longer or pulling back. Either way, they're coming through us. You have their withdrawal route, Dagger, on your overlays. Ensure your tank commanders do as well. Don't think that the rehearsal we conducted earlier is going to make it simple. Those guys are likely to be pulling back under fire and it will not be the stately parade of vehicles coming back that you saw then. They will be hauling ass, disorganized, and the radio will be a clusterfuck with everybody and his brother thinking that his traffic is the traffic that needs to be heard by everyone else in the task force. *Don't add to the madness.* Stay calm. Stay cool. Keep control of your platoon nets, and keep someone monitoring the company net for my call—either you or your platoon sergeant. Other questions?"

Doc called out, "Changes to the chemical situation, sir?"

Dillon involuntarily shivered. Doc had broached the subject that all soldiers hated. Chemical warfare. Fighting an enemy that not only had a chemical capability, but who'd shown a willingness to use it. "No. Right now we don't *expect* them to use chemicals. Per the plan, have everyone in their chemical overgarments by zero three hundred hours and keep your protective masks within arm's reach. The intel guys say that *if* they use anything, it will be nonpersistent and that they'll save it until just before the main attack. Probably. We're in a good position because the brigade has positioned one of its Fox chemical recon sections forward, between Team Mech and us. If any chemical hits in this area, we'll know fast."

Absolute silence.

"Look, if it makes you feel any better, Aref is no idiot. He knows that if he uses chemicals, the United States will bomb him back to the Stone Age and *fuck* what the rest of the world thinks. It is *therefore* highly unlikely that we'll see any. But we'll be prepared, just in case. Anything else?" Dillon hoped he had alleviated some of their fears regarding the chemical threat. They had enough to worry about already. Himself, he wasn't sure that the Iraqi leader was playing with a full deck of cards. That made him unpredictable.

No one had further questions. Dillon nodded to himself in the darkness. His unit was as ready as it would ever be. "All right then, mount up and—"

A baritone voice sounded behind Dillon. "Sir, if I may . . ."

"Yeah, Thad, what do you have?"

"Sir, I know it'll sound a little unusual, especially from me, but could we . . . uh . . . say a prayer? I kind of promised my momma that if it looked like, well, you know . . ."

Dillon smiled. "Sure, Thad. I'll take all the help I can get. Just keep in mind that God is on the side of the tank with the tightest boresight."

The leadership of Cold Steel formed a small semicircle in front of C-66. Without comment, Dillon's crew silently descended from the tank and fell in with the group of men. Mason stepped forward and his deep voice led the assembled warriors.

"Our Father, who art in heaven, hallowed be thy name . . ."

Anvil Battle Position, Northern Kuwait
21 October, 2330 Hours Local

Lieutenant Colonel Rob Estes's tank slowed to a crawl two hundred meters behind Anvil's position. He was having second thoughts about A Company occupying this critical piece of terrain. More to the point, he was having second thoughts about *Captain Dan Malloy being in charge* of this critical piece of terrain. To an extent, you could blame Dan himself for shying away from the jobs that would have given him the experience he'd likely need before the night was over. The truth was, if they hadn't deployed, it would have never been an issue. Dan would have done an adequate job performing his daily duties at Fort Carson, would have received an adequate command evaluation report, and would have continued his march deep into the army's logistical circles.

Estes had minimized the situation to the extent that he could—he'd placed Malloy in the least vulnerable position within the Iron Tiger's sector. At least it had appeared so when he and Barnett constructed the plan. They'd expected most of the action to come from the center. Anvil had been placed on the task force left flank to tie in with 2-35 Armor. Now that the Iraqis likely had a good idea of 2-35's disposition, Anvil's position adjacent to them was critical. If an enemy force made it through 2-35 Armor on the Iron Tigers' left, the first thing they'd run into would be Malloy and Anvil.

"Anvil Six, Tiger Six, over," Estes called as his tank ground to a stop.

"Tiger Six, this is Anvil Five. Anvil Six is on the ground, over."

Estes smiled. Anvil Five was First Lieutenant Bob Waters, the A Company executive officer. One of the wiser moves he'd made as battalion commander, thought Estes, was to team Waters with Malloy. Waters was thirty years old; he had come up through the ranks. He had been a staff sergeant commanding his own tank when someone with an eye for talent suggested he go to Officer's Candidate School. Waters was experienced and calm, traits that would be vital once bullets started flying.

"Anvil Five, Tiger Six. I just pulled behind your battle position and need to link up for a SITREP, over."

"This is Anvil Five, roger. I have you in sight. Will link up with you at your vehicle, over."

"Roger. Tiger Six, out."

Estes released his CVC's transmit switch so that he could use the tank's internal intercom to speak to his gunner, Staff Sergeant Ike McCloud. "Okay, Ike, you've got the ball. We're behind Anvil's position. Keep an ear to the radio and local security on the tank."

McCloud's voice came to him through the CVC. "You got it, sir. The lady will be prepped and ready to roll when you get back."

"We may be staying. Likely the enemy will be testing the left flank tonight since that's where they had success with their recon. I'll have Lieutenant Waters pick us a good position and send someone over to guide our tank in."

"Roger, we'll keep a light on for you," replied McCloud with his best Tom Bodett impersonation.

Bob Waters saw Estes's tank clearly through the night-vision goggles he held to his face. The figure in the loader's hatch on top of Estes's tank, currently manning the loader's 7.62mm machine gun, swung the weapon in Waters's direction. Waters stopped and flicked the switch on the side of his night-vision goggles quickly two times, emitting short blasts of infrared light that were invisible to the naked eye. After he saw the loader on Estes's tank return the signal, Waters continued forward. As he walked, the Anvil XO dropped the PVS-7s from his face and let them dangle around his neck so his eyes could adjust to the darkness. Unlike the infantry, tankers rarely mounted the night-vision goggles to the head harness that is part of the equipment's kit, but instead pulled them up and used them as needed. Normally they depended on their tank's thermal imaging system to do their night-vision work, using the PVS-7s only to help navigate the tank at night or to scan the local area when they pulled watch from the top of the turret.

Stopping at the front slope, Waters waited as Estes climbed down.

"What's the good word, sir?" asked Waters.

"I was going to ask you the same, Muddy," replied Estes as he hopped to the ground.

"You going to be setting up shop with us, sir?"

"Probably. You guys are on the seam with 2-35 Armor. I want to see how much firepower you're going to be able to swing that way if we need it. Let me take a look at your graphics."

Estes sensed reluctance from Waters. "What's the problem, Muddy? Something on your mind?"

Waters hesitated. Loyalty to his boss versus loyalty to his soldiers was the issue he faced. Drop a dime on Malloy, or take a chance on Anvil soldiers dying. "Sir, I don't know that there is a problem. I don't have as much experience in planning as a lot of—"

Estes had a sense of what was happening. "Okay, okay. Just give me the graphics. I don't have time for twenty questions."

Estes turned on his Mini-Mag flashlight. He looked over Anvil's dispositions. "I see where 2-35's right-most company is. Have you tied in your position with theirs?"

Waters nodded. "Roger, sir. That's B Company, 2-35 Armor, call sign Bushwhacker. I coordinated with their commander this morning. Good man. We exchanged graphics and frequencies and have overlapping fields of fire, but those wadis worry me."

Estes's face became confused. He looke more closely at Anvil's graphics. Assuming the repositioning directive he sent down earlier had been adhered to, there should not be a problem. He looked up sharply after a few moments. "How many tanks can you reorient toward Bushwhacker's position if we get a major push from that sector, Muddy?"

Silence greeted the Iron Tiger commander's question.

Estes repeated it slowly. "Muddy, damn it . . . how many tanks can you orient over there if you have to, son?"

It was as though the words were ripped from Waters's throat. "One, sir."

"*One!* What the hell's going on? Did the TOC not pass on my order for a platoon's worth of tanks to be able to cover that area?"

The Anvil XO felt the weight of the world was on his shoulders, and Estes could see it.

"Listen, Muddy," he said, not unkindly. "I understand what you're going through. But let me make something perfectly clear. Your ultimate loyalty isn't to Captain Malloy, or me, or Colonel Jones. Hell, it's not even to the president. *It's to your men.* If there's a problem, it's got to be addressed *now.* We don't have a lot of time. Those recon probes and that artillery hitting throughout the area today indicate the enemy's ready to move, probably before first light. I've got to have a clear picture of the situation to make the right decisions."

Waters felt himself deflate. "Sir, when I returned from coordinating with Bushwhacker, our company was ninety percent complete in sighting in our defensive position. I went to Captain Malloy and pointed out the wadis spilling into our flank. I also reminded him of your message to focus some assets there. Since he seemed to be ignoring the fact that we might have a problem in that sector, I pointed it out to him again—that and the fact that we had *no* tanks—zero—which could orient fires in that direction. He said that B Company, 2-35 Armor was responsible for that area, not us. When I 'what if'ed' him, he got pissed and said if I was so worried about it, move my tank to cover the area." Waters looked up from the map and into Estes's eyes. "I did."

Estes's silence spoke bounds. Waters knew the commander was ready to blow sky-high.

When Tiger Six spoke again, his voice was icy calm. "What about the rest of the company's positions. He did direct their emplacement, didn't he?"

Waters shook his head, looking at the ground. "No, sir. He drew each of the platoons a goose egg on the map and told them to get busy."

"Did he check the platoon fields of fire and conduct rehearsals this afternoon?"

"Negative. This afternoon he directed the platoons to conduct internal rehearsals once they completed weekly maintenance checks—but made sure they were clear that the maintenance checks held priority. Only one platoon conducted a rehearsal, sir."

Estes put a hand on Waters's shoulder. "Muddy, where's Captain Malloy?"

Waters pointed to the east. The moon had risen, offering some illumination. "About two hundred meters over that rise, sir. He's got his tank positioned behind Second Platoon on the company's right flank."

Estes's hackles rose. "Is there a particular reason he's not somewhere closer to the center so he can control the company's fires? Never mind. Forget I said that. This is my problem now." He stood silently for a moment before continuing. "Muddy, this is what I want you to do. Lead my tank into a position close to yours to help you overwatch the left flank. It's too late and too dark to try moving one of your other platoons. Tell Ike I'll link back up with the tank as soon as I've had a talk with Captain Malloy."

Waters saluted in the darkness, managed a "Yes, sir," and began climbing up Estes's tank to brief Staff Sergeant McCloud.

Estes trudged through the sand toward Malloy's position.

Tawakalna Division Headquarters, Southern Iraq
21 October, 2345 Hours Local

General Hamza, commander of the Tawakalna Division, sat back on his camp stool and looked at the American positions arrayed on the map. His commanders waited anxiously to be dismissed so they could return to their brigades.

"Gentlemen," he began as he turned to them, "all is ready. I spoke with our president this afternoon. I gave him my personal assurance that the conditions were set and that we were ready to begin our attack. He asked me to pass on the confidence he holds in each of you, and to assure you of the special place you will hold in his heart, and Allah's, when our country takes its rightful place in the forefront of Muslim nations."

Many of the assembled commanders smiled at this news. Others simply nodded understanding. Not all were enchanted by the religious fervor that permeated Iraq. Most of these commanders had been members of the Republican Guard when America and her Coalition partners had humiliated their nation during the Gulf War. They were professional soldiers and knew the Republican Guard had not truly been put to the test. They savored the chance for vengeance and to prove they could fight on equal terms with anyone.

Hamza continued. "All that faces us is the Kuwaitis and *one* American brigade. Our initial attack will be through the Americans—after they are finished, the Kuwaitis will fall or run." In the weak lighting, the general's eyes took on a fanatical gleam. "One American brigade stands between us and *glory*!"

The Tawakalna commander let this sink in, then continued. "Our southern corp's other divisions—the Madinah and the Hamourabi—will be moving south to reinforce us before first light." Hamza pointed dramatically at the left side of the American defensive positions. "Our attack begins before dawn and is intended to make a penetration *here* for the follow-on divisions to exploit. I tell you that making a penetration is not enough. I want these dogs myself. The success of our reconnaissance today all but guarantees success in making the penetration. *Our division* is in a position to bring the Americans to their knees. We

will not waste the opportunity. With or without the
other divisions, the Americans will fall."

General Hamza's thoughts turned to the charred
and unrecognizable corpse he had been forced to identify upon returning home in humiliation from Kuwait
in 1991. His son had been a tank platoon leader during
the war. He was to have followed in his father's footsteps. The Americans had taken his son, now he would
take many sons from America.

Anvil Battle Position, Northern Kuwait
22 October, 0005 Hours Local

Captain Dan Malloy sat shivering in his Hummer fifty
meters behind his tank's position. He hadn't realized
the desert could get this cold.

Malloy turned to the soldier in the seat to his left.
"Driver, turn the heater fan to high."

The PFC looked at Malloy through the darkness.
"Sir, when the heater is turned on high, we have a
hard time hearing the radios. I thought I heard Tiger
Six trying to call you earlier, so I turned the heater
down."

Malloy shook his head. "Look, soldier, when I give
you an order, just execute. Your job is to keep this
vehicle up to the standards I dictate and to monitor
the radios. Period. If you can't do the job, I'll find
someone else to put in here and you can go back to
a tank crew."

The soldier considered the offer. He was tempted
to take his commander up on it, as Malloy was a royal
pain in the ass. Anvil 6 couldn't see the PFC shake
his head slowly, making up his mind that it was worth
putting up with an asshole to keep his cushy job. He
was Malloy's fourth driver. Unlike his predecessors,
the soldier meant to hold on to the position for a
while—life on a tank could be hard. Reaching forward
and turning the heater toggle switch to high, the driver
then traced the handset cables for the radios set to

the task force and company command nets. Once he had the cables straightened out, he stuffed the handsets underneath his helmet, one in each ear. By this means he could hear radio transmissions over the handsets themselves even though he couldn't hear the speakers from the noisy heater.

As the vehicle warmed up, so did Malloy's disposition. "There you go, soldier. See what a little initiative will do for you? Keep this up and you'll be promoted to specialist in no time."

The driver shook his head. *What a dick.*

Malloy sat back and mentally reviewed the past couple of days. Were they really going to war? He had a hard time believing it. There was just no way that Iraq would attack Kuwait again.

He and his company had been moved twice before settling into this battle position. Malloy was sure that once 3rd Brigade was set, the Iraqis would cease their saber rattling and head north. The artillery that had been received earlier, in Malloy's opinion, had been their final snubbing of the nose to the American force across the border. Hell, as bad as the Iraqi army was, it was probably just coincidence that they had hit *anything*.

With that thought in mind, Malloy turned his mind to other necessities, such as sleep. Even though this whole affair would in all likelihood result in no further shooting, he was sure the powers that be would leave them in this hellhole of a country for at least a month or two, so he wasn't about to start letting his body get run down. He owed it to himself and his men to be one hundred percent.

As he closed his eyes and the clicking sound of the heater fan lulled him to sleep, Malloy reflected on the problem of his executive officer. Waters knew his tactics, Malloy gave him that much. The problem was his attitude. At times it was as though Waters . . . looked down on him. Take the issue of their left flank. Given the simple mission of going to the tank company on their left and making coordination, Waters comes back and begins repeatedly pointing out that the company plan was off. Malloy knew he had done all that he could for Waters. Maybe the guy just felt he had to overcompensate for his enlisted background. But when he started questioning his commander's plan, that had been the last straw. Malloy's last coherent thought before dozing off was to talk to Colonel Estes about getting a replacement for Waters. Didn't Team Knight have a senior platoon leader who had gone to West Point? A likely candidate, that young man. Malloy could mold him into a real leader. Just as he began snoring, Malloy found himself hurtling towards the ground as someone jerked his Hummer's door open.

Anvil's first sergeant reached down to help Malloy to his feet. "Sorry about that, sir, but you've got to get this vehicle back. It's *way* too far forward. If we receive any contact at all, it's going to get blown to hell!"

Malloy was using the time spent brushing himself off to wake up. After a few moments he stopped, seemingly satisfied with his efforts. "First Sergeant Wiley, if I thought this vehicle was in any danger, do you really think I'd have it here?"

The senior NCO of Anvil shook his head in disbelief. "Sir?"

Malloy's voice took on a high-pitched, squeaking quality as he became angrier. "I said, if I thought this vehicle was in any danger, do you think I'd have it here? Simple question, First Sergeant."

Wiley considered his response carefully. He found there really was no correct answer, but finally settled on one. "I like to think not, sir."

Malloy threw a finger in Wiley's face. "And you would be *correct*, First Sergeant! Despite what our higher headquarters is saying, I really don't see this developing into a shooting war."

Wiley looked at Malloy incredulously. Why, after all his years in the army, did he have to get this knucklehead as a commander *now*?

"Sir, I—"

"Now, First Sergeant, I suggest that you get back to your job of worrying about our combat trains and let me worry about things up here. Have all of the crews performed full maintenance checks today? If they have, was the paperwork turned in to the Maintenance Team in a timely manner? What time are chow and fuel being picked up in the morning? We are having hot chow, aren't we, not MREs again? You see, First Sergeant, those are the kind of issues you should be worrying about, not what's going on forward. That's my department."

Wiley shook his head disgustedly. *Fuck this shit.* "Sir, with all due respect, you need to get this vehicle back a couple of kilometers with the rest of the ash and trash."

The squeak returned, higher now. "First Sergeant, perhaps I'm not being clear with you. . . ."

Wiley had had enough. "Oh, you're being clear all right, sir. Crystal. That's what scares me. Someone has got to point out the realities of this situation to you and—"

"You couldn't be more right, First Sergeant," came a quiet voice from behind the two men.

Malloy and Wiley wheeled. Lieutenant Colonel Estes stood ten feet away, arms folded across his chest. He had obviously been watching the men and listening to their conversation for some time.

Malloy felt his stomach sinking as his commander dropped his arms to his sides and began walking toward them. He began to salute, then remembered that Estes hated being saluted in the field. "Good evening, sir. How good to see you. I was just telling my first sergeant—"

"I heard what you were telling your first sergeant, Captain Malloy." Estes turned to Wiley. "That will be all, First Sergeant. You know what needs to be done."

Wiley nodded and headed back toward his M113 Armored Personnel Carrier, hidden in a depression one hundred meters behind them. He turned back toward the two officers. "Colonel, may I—"

"Yeah, Top. Take your commander's Hummer with you. Get it back and behind some cover."

Wiley nodded in the darkness and began walking around the vehicle to speak to Malloy's driver.

Seeing First Sergeant Wiley beginning to lead the Hummer to the rear, Estes turned his attention back to Malloy.

Malloy smiled. "Sir, if I might explain—"

Estes shook his head. "Shut up, Dan. I don't have the time or the inclination to listen to excuses. You are relieved of command as soon as I can get someone up here to take your place."

"But, sir, I—"

"Am I being clear, Captain? Is there something you don't understand?"

Malloy straightened. "Sir, with all due respect, do you have the authority to relieve me? I would like to take this up with the brigade commander."

Rob Estes laughed. "Indeed that is your right. When your replacement arrives you can go to the rear and do just that. I'm sure Colonel Jones will enjoy the distraction. Until then, you'll get on your tank and *command* this company. Again, are you clear on this, Captain Malloy?"

Malloy came to attention. "Yes, sir."

Estes turned and began walking away. "Then you're dismissed. I'm heading back to my tank. It's going to be colocated with Lieutenant Waters's tank on the left flank. I will call you when I get there. You will use the time between now and then to get this company to full-alert status. Clear?"

"Clear, sir," Malloy said to the retreating figure.

Malloy watched his commander disappear into the shadows with dawning disbelief on his face. This would ruin his career. Four years at West Point and six years in the army down the drain. And for what? Having a clearer appreciation of the tactical situation than his commander? Well, he'd discuss it with Colonel Jones. Surely he'd understand. For now, he had no choice but to do as Estes said.

*   *   *

As Estes approached his tank he heard a high piercing noise in the night sky to the west. The artillery impacted in the 2-35 Armor positions to the Iron Tigers' left. More barrages quickly followed, all in the 2-35 sector.

No great surprise there, thought Estes. When you intend to attack a position, you prep it first. Of course, the Iron Tigers would receive their share of the shelling tonight as well. The enemy was generally pretty good about not letting you feel neglected. A little artillery, maybe a SCUD or two, hopefully nothing with a chemical payload. Life was interesting enough already without that twist.

An earsplitting boom directly overhead caused Estes to drop to the ground, thinking some of the artillery was finally coming their way. He felt foolish when he realized it was friendly fighters, heading north into Iraq to take the war to the enemy. Estes stood, silently wishing them good hunting, hoping that the American military had a few goodies to even up the odds for the Iron Tigers and the rest of 3rd Brigade.

CHAPTER 6

Night Fliers

21 October: London (*London Times*)—Former Prime Minister Margaret Thatcher today publicly blasted Western Europe for leaving the United States to deal with the building crises in the Middle East on its own. Thatcher was quoted as saying, "It is a dark day when Western governments can be bought," alluding to rumors that Iraq has promised oil concessions and other incentives to countries that stay out of the pending confrontation.

21 October: CNN News Desk—". . . We've just received word from Pentagon sources that at least one American reconnaissance aircraft has been shot down while overflying Iraq. The apparent mission of the flight was to confirm the latest troop movements by Republican Guard forces north of the Kuwaiti border. . . ."

21 October: Baghdad (AP)—Abdul Aref has announced that his country is officially declaring war on the United States. The Iraqi leader stated that the United States has been warring on his nation for more than ten years and he will see justice done. This announcement was made just minutes before American positions were shelled by Iraqi artillery, killing two U.S. servicemen.

21 October: Tehran (*USA Today*)—The Ayatollah Mohammed Khalani, addressing the Iranian people in a national broadcast timed to coincide with Iraq's declaration

of war, called on all Islamic nations to rally behind the cause of the Iraqi people. Khalani ended the address by saying, "The Great Satan shall be driven from the land of Mohammed once and for all. I implore all true Muslims to support Abdul Aref in his holy quest and not to be tempted by the pleas of Kuwait, whose people have been so long under the Western boot that they have lost their way . . . lost their way past the point of being able to return to the true path on their own. Iran will support Iraq's mission of cleansing that nation and returning it to the fold to which it once belonged." So far it appears that the other nations in the region will not join directly in the looming confrontation, instead taking a wait-and-see stance.

21 October: Presidential News Conference—"The United States *will not tolerate* the acts of war perpetrated by Iraq. Our ground troops and our aircraft have been fired on and I stand here today to tell the American people *enough!* I have authorized our forces in theater to take whatever defensive measures they deem necessary and to prepare for offensive operations. Furthermore, in addition to the Eighty-second Airborne Division's deployment yesterday, I have now issued orders for the deployment of the remainder of the Eighteenth Airborne Corps, to include the Third Infantry Division at Fort Stewart, Georgia. Mobilization is occurring as I make these statements. Mechanized units at Fort Hood, Texas, and Fort Carson, Colorado, are on alert for deployment within the next seven days. I conclude this address by once again impressing upon the American people that I have the utmost faith in our troops currently on the ground in Kuwait. I wish Godspeed to these brave men and women. I'm sure that your prayers, like mine, are with them."

U.S. Central Command Headquarters (Forward), Bahrain
22 October, 0115 Hours Local

General Gus Pavlovski, commander-in-chief of CENT-COM, was happy for the first time in days. Aref had been firing at American troops long enough. Since Pavlovski and his staff had touched down in Bahrain twenty-four hours earlier, they'd been scurrying to keep up. Now the good guys were about to go on the offensive.

Still, Pavlovski was pissed. Pissed at having his troops shot at, pissed at the lack of friendly forces in theater, and especially pissed at being this far from the front lines. Like all the other grand plans for the defense of Kuwait that were written after Desert Storm, the CENTCOM Forward Headquarters in Kuwait never came to fruition. The other four divisions of the Kuwaiti military that had been planned and since cut would also have been nice. Fuck it. They'd make do, as always.

The secretary of defense had called Pavlovski when he heard the CENTCOM staff was mobilizing to move into theater. Per Pavlovski's guidance, they'd planned on moving the shop to Kuwait—and were in the middle of doing so when the SECDEF had weighed in on the issue. The secretary told Pavlovski in no uncertain terms that he didn't feel comfortable about the move. In other words: "With the current ratio of good guys to bad guys, it doesn't seem prudent to give the Iraqis the opportunity to capture a U.S. four star general, so don't go there."

That was fine. But the secretary didn't say shit about Bahrain, just a stone's throw away, so Pavlovski continued the movement and merely shifted destinations.

It was time to give these bastards a taste of what his troops had received. One of the toughest missions for a leader is to have assets available that you know can reach out and touch some asshole, some asshole you want really bad, yet not be able to use those assets on said asshole. It was all about timing. They had to synchronize their assets to do the most damage.

His staff had dusted off the contingency plans for striking Baghdad, and then updated the plans with

the latest assets figures and intelligence. All they had
needed was a little more reconnaissance than the satellites had been able to provide. No problem. At least
that's what they'd believed.

Pavlovski turned to the director of his Joint Search
and Rescue Center. The JSRC, comprised of cells
from each of the military services in theater, was the
responsible authority for coordinating the rescue of
any downed pilots or aviators. "Any word on your
pilots, Dick?"

It was obvious the air force officer hadn't slept
lately. He shook his head. "No, sir. We've got our
ears open to the emergency frequency. They have
specified times to signal us, but we haven't heard a
word. I've got to assume they're dead or captured."

It was the general's turn to shake his head. What
a fucking waste. When would the bureaucrats learn?
You can't fight modern wars with outdated equipment. They'd lost two U-2 reconnaissance aircraft in
the past forty-eight hours. Sent up to fill the holes
that satellite imagery couldn't provide, they'd gotten
a couple of pictures each before being shot down by
Iraqi SA-2 surface-to-air missiles.

The United States had long thought that the Iraqi
SA-2s were the early versions from the 1960s and
would be a minor risk to the high-flying U-2s. Wrong.
They'd been upgraded and the U-2 pilots had paid
the price for flying a piece of equipment whose defensive suite was just plain outdated. Future recon
flights would now include F-16 fighter escorts armed
with High Speed Anti-Radiation Missiles, better
known as HARMs. The thirteen-and-a-half-foot,
eight-hundred-pound missile would remind enemy air
defense crews that it wasn't wise to broadcast radar
beams at American aircraft. The F-16-fired HARMs
would guide in on any radar tracking the U-2s. Their
high-explosive warheads would take out the missile
sites for the duration of this or any other war—not
that this news would be of much solace to the families of the downed crews.

The general turned to his operations officer. "Transmit *Night Fliers*." A grim look of determination set into Pavlovski's face. "It's time for those sons of bitches to get a little payback."

Pavlovski's operations officer just had time to give his commander a "Wilco, sir" and transmit the attack order when they heard the SCUD sirens sound.

USS *Nimitz* Carrier Group, Persian Gulf
22 October, 0120 Hours Local

The admiral smiled a smile wicked to behold as he watched the black night turn into day for miles around. Moments like this were why fighting men stayed in the service—for that one day when they felt they truly made a difference.

Within ten seconds of receiving the order to commence his attack, the admiral had relayed firing instructions to his four DDG-51 class destroyers. The *Arleigh Burke*s had been prepared to fire and were awaiting orders. When those orders came, the Tomahawk cruise missiles fired within seconds of each other, each programmed with targets deep in enemy territory. Most had a rendezvous scheduled with Iraqi military command and control centers in Baghdad. The Tomahawks' terrain-hugging guidance system made them hard targets to stop. The crews of the destroyers and every other ship in the carrier group jumped up and down on the decks, fists shaking in the air. They were finally getting some. The *Night Fliers* were running.

North of Kuwait City, Kuwait
22 October, 0120 Hours Local

The two field artillery soldiers observed the bright lights in the north, followed seconds later by the sound of thunder as their tank and infantry brothers forward received the first concentrated fires of the war. It was obvious to these men that the fires weren't harassing, but planned.

"Guess the rumors at chow tonight were true," said the young PFC, turning to his section chief. "They figured out where some of our guys were digging in."

The NCO lit a cigarette in the darkness and cupped the glow in his hand. No need in taking chances, even if they were well behind friendly lines. He nodded in the darkness. "Yeah, looks that way. They wouldn't be pumping that many rounds into one area if they didn't have a good idea of exactly what they were shooting at."

The soldier hesitated before speaking again. "Sarge . . . you think they're gonna start firing those things back here?"

The NCO smiled. Sometimes you forgot just how young a lot of these soldiers were. The kid had just that afternoon shown the sergeant a six-month-old picture from his high school Junior-Senior Prom, powder-blue tux and all.

He reached a hand out and lightly punched the soldier on the shoulder. "Don't worry, Kenny. If they knew where these MLRS launchers were, they'd already be firing on us. That means they don't know and we're okay."

The MLRS, or Multiple-Launch Rocket System, was indeed a high-priority target if the enemy could locate them. Their capability to fire deep into the enemy rear was well remembered by the Iraqis. Once the MLRS crews fired their munitions, they had to move quickly before their counterparts on the other side of the border could pinpoint their location with radar and fire missiles or artillery back at them.

The young soldier turned again toward the distant lights flashing in the darkness to the north. "But why don't they let us fire? We can take out some of that artillery and get it off of those guys' backs."

Another pull from the cigarette, another shake of the head. "They've got different plans for us, Kenny.

We're not counterbattery firing. Remember that. We've got a mission, and according to the lieutenant, we'll be receiving firing instructions soon."

"Any idea what the mission is?"

The NCO nodded as he took another pull from the cigarette. "Yeah. I hear the air force found some SCUD sites today. Camouflaged out the ass. Fuckers think they're going to be able to sit out there, hide, rain scunnion on us, then pick up and run." The sergeant smiled knowingly, rubbed the cigarette out on the bottom of his boot, and then thumped it into the darkness. "Not tonight."

The battery command net suddenly came to life. *"All firing units, all firing units . . . Night Fliers, Night Fliers . . . acknowledge, over."*

"Night Fliers? What the hell does that mean?" asked Kenny.

His boss smiled as he reached for the radio handset to acknowledge the firing order. "It means, Kenny, that those SCUD site rag heads are about to become permanent citizens of the land of FUBAR."

Again, confusion. "FUBAR, Sarge?"

The NCO nodded. "Yeah, Kenny, FUBAR. Fucked Up Beyond All Recognition."

South of Baghdad
22 October, 0120 Hours Local

The flight of four F-117 Nighthawk stealth fighters, call sign Wolfpack, were almost at their target. Their flight had originated in Turkey and coincided with other flights going into Iraq, all with the mission to take out the enemy's ability to wage war. Of immediate concern to American forces were the two Republican Guard divisions preparing even now to move south. The flight's mission was to delay them.

The clear night sky made their job easier. The single-seat, high subsonic aircraft that resembled a black bat's wing was designed for just such missions. Although the 117's extremely low radar cross-section made it nearly invisible to the radar below, the men of Wolfpack all remembered that a Serbian missile crew had shot down one of their brethren over Europe in the not too distant past. Each man was determined that their craft wouldn't be the second stealth fighter shot down in U.S. history.

As they approached the target area, crews checked their systems one final time. The Nighthawk's capability to provide its own laser designation made delivering its load of two-thousand-pound laser-guided bombs relatively simple.

The flight leader listened carefully to the radio transmission he had been waiting for as they closed on their target, a Republican Guard logistics depot supporting one of the two divisions below. All members of his flight reported acquisition of their targets as the flight leader received the *Night Fliers* call. As the transmission terminated he radioed his elements.

"Wolfpack flight, this is lead, commence attack. . . ."

Like bats from hell, Wolfpack descended on their unsuspecting prey.

Iraq Military Headquarters, Baghdad
22 October, 0130 Hours Local

The general held the phone, listening to his caller. Sweat ran freely from his forehead. He dabbed at it with a handkerchief.

"Yes, Mr. President, we are experiencing some losses. . . .

"That is correct, Mr. President. Most of the damage occurred to our two divisions preparing to move south, the Madinah and the Hamourabi. . . .

"*No,* Mr. President. They're not out of the fight, it will just take some time to reorganize them. . . ."

As he listened to his leader rant and rave, the general slowly shook his head and lifted his eyes to the heavens.

"Yes, sir, but if you will recall the briefing you

received this morning from General of the Army Abunimah, you were told that the American response would likely be to . . ."

An aide slowly made his way to the general's side and waited patiently with a message. The general took the document and scanned it. "Yes, some of our missile sites in the south were hit by the cursed American rockets. . . ."

Continuing to scan the message he'd just received, the general smiled for the first time. "Yes, sir, but we did have some successful launches. I'm looking at an update on the strikes against the American Central Command Headquarters in Bahrain. The message confirms we scored at least two hits there, and even more on the military equipment stocks in Qatar. . . .

"Yes, Allah is good." The general spoke these last words almost by rote and rolled his eyes. He was of the old military order and didn't like this new mix of religion and fighting. Then he rethought his position. One could argue that Allah had deigned to save his neck for the moment with some positive news.

"Yes, sir. The Tawakalna Division is ready to launch their attack in the south. Our artillery is already firing on the point General Hamza intends to exploit. That is why I called. Sir . . . we might consider delaying the attack. . . ."

The Iraqi officer instinctively moved the phone from his ear at the verbal outburst that followed his suggestion. "Why, sir? Well, they would be opening a hole for divisions who are not yet in place to exploit it. If we delay their attack for a day or two, the Madinah and Hamourabi would be able to—

"Yes, sir, I know the eyes of the world are upon us. . . .

"Yes, Allah is *indeed* on the side of the just, but . . .

"It *is* possible the Tawakalna Division could succeed on its own. General Hamza says that he can defeat the American brigade and whatever forces the Kuwaitis have in place . . . but, sir . . . it would be wiser to wait. . . ."

"Very well, Mr. President, the attack will continue as planned. If I might make one request. We need to be prepared to send more units into this fight than just the three planned Republican Guard divisions from the Southern Corps. General Abunimah and his staff have been meeting all day. He said to relay to you that in order to ensure the success of this campaign—

"Of course I do not think I'm privy to all of your information, sir. I'm merely explaining General Abunimah's concern that the forces currently planned in the fight may not be enough if—

"Yes, sir, of course these are our very best men and equipment. . . ."

"I understand," he ended with a tired note.

The general hung up the phone and reflected that not only did religion not mix with war—neither did politics. They had before them an opportunity to crush the American military forces in Kuwait and teach the arrogant Western bastards a lesson. Why use just three divisions? If it were up to him, he would send the entire army. What did soldiers care of world opinion? You fought to win as quickly and decisively as possible in order to keep your men alive.

Standing, the general shouted to the officer sitting at the duty desk outside his door. "Captain, come in here, and bring the latest information on losses to the Madinah and Hamourabi. Also have the operations cell send those divisions warning orders that their movements south have been delayed until we can bring their strength up. Tell them to begin their marches in thirty-six hours."

As he sat once again at his desk to attend to the details of reorganizing the second-echelon forces, the general felt the walls vibrate. Staring at the smiling portrait of Abdul Aref that hung directly opposite his desk, the Iraqi officer saw the framed photograph rock back and forth on its nail twice, then crash to the floor. A series of concussions could just be heard from the city above. No surprise the Americans would strike Baghdad—and this headquarters would be a primary target. Knowing that this command center, like the other new command and control facilities spread throughout Iraq, was buried beneath twice the dirt and concrete as was customary in the past gave the general a warm feeling inside. Outside his office, figures scurried for cover. "Back to work! We are secure at this level!" He bent his head to the new fuel figures he'd been working on, then looked up again. "And get someone in here to clean this glass from the floor!"

A louder crash than previously heard caused him to look up. A fireball erupted across the outer office and spread rapidly in his direction.

The last moments of his life did not provide enough time for the general to realize that American munitions had improved significantly since Desert Storm. Deep-cover agents in Iraq's military had provided blueprints of the command and control facilities to the Americans—some at the cost of their lives. With the knowledge from these blueprints stored in their circuitry, the new generation of smart bombs was programmed to plunge into their targets—but not detonate their primary payloads until the designated depth had been reached.

U.S. Central Command Headquarters (Forward), Bahrain 22 October, 0145 Hours Local

"Sorry, godforsaken sons of bitches."

General Pavlovski's aide silently agreed as they stepped out of the bomb shelter and into a scene lit by the flames of burning buildings and equipment. "Could have been worse, sir. Reports so far indicate that we suffered only minor casualties. The Patriots throughout the theater knocked out most of the SCUDs before they impacted."

"How about Qatar? Did they try to hit the prepositioned stocks there?" asked the general. Those tanks, Bradleys, and howitzers would be critical for the reinforcements even now moving toward the Middle East from the U.S.

"They were hit, sir, but the damage is minimal. Most of the critical equipment was under concrete cover. The units in the field were hit as well, even in the rear."

Pavlovski stood motionless, the fires of burning buildings playing shadows across his face. Something kept nagging at the back of his mind. Finally, he turned to his aide. "Think about this for a second. Assume the Patriots hadn't knocked out most of those SCUDs. How much damage would have been inflicted on our field units?"

The officer didn't hesitate. "Considerable, sir."

"SCUD Bs, right?"

"Yes, sir."

Pavlovski turned it over in his mind. Pinpointing the location of tactical forces deep behind their own lines was difficult. To accurately strike at them with a missile system whose circular error probability was over a half-mile would be damned near impossible, like finding a needle in a haystack—unless someone was supplying the missile crews with the locations. Carrying it further, if that someone was providing eyes for Iraq, might they not also be passing on advanced guidance systems to lower the SCUDs' circular error? Some of the Russian variants were accurate to within fifty meters, so how hard would they be to modify? As the pieces of the puzzle began to come together in his mind, Pavlovski nodded. "Okay. Find a radio that's working and get me SITREPs on our deep attacks."

"Yes, sir."

"One more thing," Pavlovski added, "whatever equipment was damaged in Qatar, and any other nonessential stuff there, blow it . . . and make sure it's in the open. The more there is, and the worse it looks, the better."

"Sir?"

"Do it."

"Yes, sir."

Alone once again, Pavlovski laughed as he contemplated the Iraqi leadership's reaction to his night fliers. *Paybacks are indeed a motherfucker.*

CHAPTER 7

Contact, North!

Lead Republican Guard Brigade, Northern Kuwait
22 October, 0210 Hours Local

The brigade commander acknowledged receipt of the broadcast and signed off. They'd been waiting for word to commence the ground attack since the artillery preparations on the American positions had started an hour earlier. Hopefully his brothers manning the cannons had saved some of their ammunition to support his attack.

"Get the battalion commanders on the radio. Now!"

The radio operator nodded.

The colonel turned to his staff. "Very well. We are set to attack. Ali, do you have any updates on the Americans?"

"No, sir. It appears that their repositioning has been minimal." The intelligence officer shook his head forlornly, the pity of a warrior who knows his opponent is in an untenable position. "Really, they had nowhere to reposition. I recommend we attack the western flank as planned, sir."

The colonel nodded. "I concur."

Phase Line Sheridan, 2-35 Armor Counter-Recon Screen, Northern Kuwait
22 October, 0225 Hours Local

The M1A1 tank gunner scanned back and forth slowly with his thermal imaging system set to its wide-view

setting of three-power. When he saw anything remotely resembling an enemy target, he would switch
the sight to ten-power magnification to investigate.
Thus far, they'd not been able to spot a single Iraqi
vehicle or troop.

The American tank was part of the Counter-Recon
Force forward of 2-35 Armor. They'd had a busy time
of it over the past two hours. Like Team Knight forward of the Iron Tigers, his company's mission was to
engage the lead enemy elements in their sector, then
withdraw on order.

When the artillery began striking their positions earlier, they'd been forced to move to alternate positions.
The Iraqi howitzer gunners soon found them again,
however, making it clear that somewhere in the night
was an enemy artillery observer watching their every
move. The past hours had been spent in a series of
movements dedicated to survival, what maneuver
fighters had named the artillery dance. While most
tankers weren't known for their rhythm, they per-
fected this step or died. The objective of the artillery
dance was to stay one step ahead of your partner—
the enemy artillerymen. If you didn't—well, it was
worse than getting your feet stepped on.

As the gunner scanned, his tank commander threw
him the same question he'd been asking all night, but
in a voice that revealed the fatigue shared by the entire crew. "Any movement?"

The gunner paused his scanning, pulled his face
away from the sight, and shook his head. "Negative,
boss."

The deliberateness with which the tank commander
returned his face to the sight gave further evidence of
his weariness. The entire crew was ready to drop from
the stress of the past two hours. A few minutes of
adrenaline-pumping action, followed by a short period
of inaction as the crew thought, *Maybe, just maybe
that's it,* followed by a resumption of the enemy shelling. It had taken its toll on every man in 2-35 Armor's
position. Fortunately it looked as though only a couple

of the battalion's tanks had received minor damage, although one of the Bradleys had been destroyed when an artillery round impacted five feet from it.

Staff Sergeant Brady was an experienced tank commander. From his seat behind and above the gunner, he had his eye to his sight extension. This allowed him to view whatever his gunner was observing. To the right of the sight extension he'd Scotch-taped a picture of his children, a three-year-old boy and a five-year-old girl. Their smiling faces watched over their father's every move within the turret. They were his guardian angels.

The desert forward of their tank stood out clearly in the tank's thermals. Nothing moved. The only hot spots, displayed in the sight as brighter shades of green, almost white, were the areas where artillery shells had struck and which had not yet cooled. The hotter the area, the whiter it looked.

He pulled his head back and shook it. "I don't see anything either. I'll take up the scan from my position for a few minutes. Take a break."

The gunner acknowledged the message with a grunt and released his power control handles. Looking back, he rubbed his wrists. "Thanks, Sergeant Brady. Give me five minutes and I'll be as good as new."

"Not a problem." Brady took the commander's power control handle in his right hand. With it, he could traverse the turret, lase targets for range with the built-in laser range finder, and fire the tank's main gun or coaxial machine gun. Brady traversed the gun slowly left to right, then back again, scanning the sector assigned to his crew. Occasionally he'd ask the gunner to switch the sight to high magnification when he saw something that looked suspicious.

The gunner looked up and back at his tank commander as he continued rubbing his wrists. "So you think they're coming tonight, Sergeant?"

When Brady looked down and into his gunner's face, the plea was clear—*just lie to me, Sarge, and tell me this will all come to nothing*. The blue interior lighting lent the gunner's upturned face an eerie cast, corpselike. Brady shrugged. "Who knows, kid? Maybe not—shit!"

Their tank shook with the violence that only another tank could enforce on it.

"Driver! Back up, back up, back up! Gunner, take up a scan and tell me what's engaging us! Loader, make sure that the main gun is armed!"

The loader, with a sabot round already in the gun tube, reached forward and grabbed the arming handle. He slammed it into the firing position. "Up!"

The crew was thrown forward as the driver kicked their vehicle into reverse and gave it full throttles.

The driver's voice screamed out over the intercom. "I've got a shit load of flashes to our direct front!"

"Oh, fuck! Contact, north! Multiple enemy tanks and PCs!" said the gunner.

Brady threw his face to the sight extension. As his eyes focused, he barely had time to register the twenty-odd enemy tanks on line and rolling straight at them before a round exploded immediately to their front right, blinding him for a moment. The driver's wild maneuvering had thrown the enemy tank gunner's aim off just enough to cause him to miss.

"Good work, driver! Keep moving us back until we can hide behind something and take up a firing position!" He quickly keyed the CVC helmet's radio switch to give his platoon leader a report on their contact.

"White One, White One, White Two. Contact north, twenty-plus tanks, out."

Brady turned his attention back to keeping him and his crew alive. "Gunner, fire and adjust! Engage the lead tanks!" As the tank commander, Brady was responsible for designating which target his gunner was to engage, but right now that would just take up more precious time.

Immediately the gunner acknowledged. He had a T-72 in his sight and a reading of 1460 meters in his range display. "On the way!"

Their tank rocked back as the 120mm smooth-bore cannon fired. The inside of the turret filled with the smell of cordite.

"Target!" yelled the gunner. "Continue loading sabot!"

The loader had already engaged the ammunition door switch with his right knee and was pulling another sabot round from the ammo storage compartment at the rear of the turret.

The gunner screamed at the loader as he waited for another round to be slammed into the breech, his eye glued to his thermal sight and another enemy tank. "Give me another fucking sabot!"

The loader was trying to get the round into the breech as the tank raced backward in a zigzag pattern. "I'm trying, damn it!"

Finally the round was loaded and the gun armed. "Up!"

"On the way!"

The main gun boomed again and the turret of an enemy T-72 tank fifteen hundred meters forward blew into the night sky.

Brady observed the explosion. "Target! Get on the one to the right! He's got his gun tube on us!"

The sound of metal on metal overrode all else as the enemy tank fired and hit.

"Crew report!" yelled Brady, wanting to know the status of his men.

"Gunner up, sabot indexed! I'm on the fucker!"

"Loader up! Sabot loaded!"

"Driver up! I see flashes all over the goddamn place! We need to—"

The driver's scream was overridden by the sound of the M1A1 exploding.

"Shit, they've been hit!" said Mike Stuart as he watched the 2-35 Armor tank burn in the distance. That was the second 2-35 tank the Knight commander had seen destroyed in as many minutes. While Stuart had never doubted the Guard's ability to fight, an M1A1 still shouldn't have blown that easily. In past combat the American main battle tanks had sustained dozens of direct hits without being destroyed. There was something new in the Iraqi arsenal. He'd have to pass that piece of intelligence up to Estes at the first opportunity.

Stuart's team was tied into the 2-35 Armor team's counter-recon line. Thus far his team had received none of the Iraqis' attention.

"All Knight elements, Knight Six. Is anyone in contact? Over."

"Red One, negative."

"White One, negative."

Stuart waited patiently for his Third Platoon leader, Blue One. He'd give him a few more seconds. Time was a valuable commodity right now, and he had to get a report higher before Estes started prompting him. The task force commander would have to be deaf and blind not to know that something was going on, and he'd want answers.

"Knight Six, Blue One, over."

"Knight Six, over."

"Knight Six, my three-one element is reporting sporadic movement forward of his position. Just west of TRP Bravo-One, moving south-southwest, over."

Bravo-One was the target reference point at which Team Knight and the 2-35 team were crossing fires. The Iraqis were trying to split the seam and Third Platoon was there to watch. *"Roger. Understand vicinity Bravo-One. Stand by."*

Stuart turned on his blue-lensed flashlight and looked at his graphics. He'd penciled in the enemy's likely attack routes with a red marker. Those routes led straight into the 2-35 Armor position to his left. What Third Platoon was seeing made sense.

Stuart reached up and thumbed his CVC. *"Blue One, Knight Six."*

"Blue One."

Stuart continued looking at his map, feeling the rhythm of the battle begin to flow within him. *"How many tanks can you re-orient toward the contact?"*

"Knight Six, Blue One. All four tanks, over."

Out-fucking-standing. *"Roger, do not reorient fires yet. Be prepared to shift from current orientation to the west. New orientation, TRPs Mike-Four to Mike-Five, over.*

"This is Blue One, roger, understand Mike-Four to Mike-Five."

"Make sure your crews have their hatches in open-protected or closed position. Expect artillery in your area anytime."

If the Republican Guard unit facing them was attempting a penetration into 2-35 Armor's sector, they would want to separate the 2-35 combatants from other units who could support them. Artillery was a good way to do that. When an M1A1 tank commander closed his hatch to the open-protected position, only a two-inch crack remained. This small gap allowed him to squat and still be able to look outside to command and control his tank and at the same time offered some measure of protection against artillery and sniper fires.

"This is Blue One, roger, open-protected or closed, over."

"Roger. Red One, White One, Knight Six. Be prepared to shift your fires west. Red, look at orienting Bravo-One to Bravo-Three. White, Bravo-Two to Bravo-Four. Acknowledge, over."

The First Platoon sergeant answered the call. *"This is Red Four. Red One is on platoon net sending SIT-REP. He monitors. Understand be prepared to shift fires west, Bravo-One to Bravo-Three."*

"This is White One. Understand west, Bravo-Two to Bravo-Four."

"This is Knight Six, roger. Going higher."

Anvil Battle Position, Northern Kuwait
22 October, 0235 Hours Local

Estes sat in the cupola of his tank, waiting for word from Stuart. He'd heard the firing forward and knew an enemy push had begun.

"Tiger Six, Knight Six, over."

Estes pulled his map out and turned his flashlight on. *"Send it, Knight."*

"Roger, we have twenty-plus enemy vehicles attacking on Avenue of Approach One, I say again twenty vehicles, Avenue of Approach One. T-72s and BMPs. They're cutting the corner of our sector and attacking southwest into adjacent sector. My Blue element is prepared to engage. My other elements are maintaining coverage of our original sector, prepared to shift fires to the west, over."

Estes looked at the map and considered the options. Stuart was requesting permission to engage the Iraqi flank as the enemy force attacked 2-35 Armor. He made his decision quickly, but he'd have to clear it with Jones before issuing orders. . . .

"Knight Six, Tiger Six. Be prepared to have your Blue element support the rest of your team's withdrawal on Route Dagger, over."

"Roger."

"Tiger Six, going higher."

3rd Brigade, 4th ID TAC, Northern Kuwait
22 October, 0237 Hours Local

Jones's finger jammed into the map repeatedly. "You don't seem to understand me, Major. I want those fires, right *here,* right *now!*"

The brigade FSO nodded. "Sir, the guns are shifting to those targets as we speak."

Jones willed himself to calm. "Look, Buck, I know they're shifting. I need them to shift faster. Task Force 2-35's getting hit hard. I need that artillery to slow the Iraqis down so we can pull 2-35's counter-recon team out. They're forward and their shit's in the wind."

As if to emphasize this final point, a long series of Iraqi artillery impacted less than three kilometers away. Jones had moved his Tactical Command Post, commonly referred to as a "TAC", as close to the front as he dared. Unlike the brigade's TOC, which stayed well behind friendly lines and consisted of dozens of armored and wheeled vehicles and countless officers and troops responsible for tracking the battle and planning future operations, the TAC consisted of only Jones and few members of his staff in a handful of vehicles. Located well forward, the TAC's job was to fight the fight at hand, and that often meant getting dirty.

The artillery officer nodded. "Yes, sir."

The brigade command net came to life. *"Striker Six, Tiger Six, over."*

Jones grabbed the handset in the back of his Bradley. O'Keefe had worked miracles in reconfiguring the interior of the M2 to function as Jones's command and control track. Thoughts of O'Keefe reminded him of Kelly and he smiled. The sergeant major had taken care of him one last time. The kid was good.

As he keyed the radio, Jones pushed the thoughts of his friend to the back of his mind. There'd be time to mourn later. *"Striker Six, over."*

"Striker Six, Tiger Six. My Knight element reports twenty-plus vehicles, mixed T-72s and BMPs, on Avenue of Approach One. I've got one platoon in position who can engage, but I need to get my boys out of there as soon as possible. If I don't get them back behind the main defense in the next few minutes, I might not get them back at all, over."

Jones looked at the numerous red and blue symbols littering his map. He understood the reasons behind Estes's request. The situation was that the Republican Guard had acted in unpredictable fashion. Instead of leading their attack with a smaller-sized element, say a platoon or company, they'd led with a larger force—what appeared to be a battalion of tanks and BMPs . . . more than thirty combat vehicles. If the counter-recon teams forward of the friendly battalions got caught up in a run-and-gun battle with this larger force, it could get ugly fast. The numbers would be against them and they'd be trying to fight their way backward to friendly lines. Not good.

While artillery was hitting all across 3rd Brigade's

front, the attack itself centered on 2-35 Armor in the west. Jones was working on getting that battalion's counter-recon team back first. If the reports he was catching were accurate, they were catching pure hell.

"Tiger Six, Striker Six. Pull back everyone but the platoon that's in position to engage. I need them to support the withdrawl of 2-35's counter-recon force."

"This is Tiger Six, roger."

"Rob, you decide when to pull that last platoon, but give us as much time as you can."

"This is Tiger Six, wilco."

Phase Line Sheridan, Northern Kuwait
22 October, 0245 Hours Local

Stuart had been pleased with the news that at least part of his team was still in the fight. He understood why Estes wanted them back behind friendly lines, that he didn't want twenty-five percent of his firepower caught forward with no support. He also knew if Estes had been watching 2-35 Armor getting chewed up the way he had been for the past few minutes, it would take an act of God to keep Tiger 6 out of this fight. Stuart planned to stay forward with Third Platoon while his XO moved the rest of Knight back behind the task force defense.

Stuart looked into his sight extension. *Shit, still no smoke.* What good did it do to attach the Mortar Platoon to the counter-recon team if he couldn't get the fucking fires when he needed them? As if in answer to his silent question, the radio squawked.

"Knight Six, Thunder Six. Shot, over."

Finally. The shot call told him that the requested mission had been fired. Stuart continued looking north and replied, *"Shot, out."* This let the mortars know that he'd heard their call and was observing the targeted area.

A few seconds later, at the end of the precalculated flight time of the mortar rounds, Thunder 6 radioed again. *"Splash, over."*

Stuart continued to look north. Small impacts began dotting the green landscape. They quickly blazed white in the tank's thermals. Stuart keyed the radio. *"Splash, out."* From six locations smoke began rising. Soon there would be a nice, thick haze hanging between the withdrawal route and the Iraqis.

"Knight Five, Knight Six. You've got the ball. Start moving the rest of the team back. Red first, then White. Contact Steel on task force command and let them know you're moving, over."

Sergeant First Class Jeff Coats was the platoon sergeant of Team Knight's Third Platoon, call sign Blue Four. He'd been watching the attacking Iraqi formation for quite a while. His trigger finger was starting to get itchy.

Coats called to his crew over the tank's intercom. "Okay, guys, give me a crew report."

"Gunner up, sabot indexed."

"Loader up, sabot loaded."

"Driver up."

"Roger, TC's up. We're set. Now, gunner, you tell me as soon as that tank you've got in your sights closes to two thousand meters. You shoot it *when I tell you,* not before. Clear?"

"Got it, Sarge." His gunner was a corporal with little experience but a lot of potential. Under Coats's tutelage he'd grown into a fine shot—on the range anyway. The gunner continued watching the T-72 he'd been tracking. Jesus, the thing was getting bigger and bigger. Range twenty-five hundred meters and closing.

"Good. Driver, we've got cover behind this berm. Same as firing that first round, you pull up *when I tell you.* Once we move forward and begin engaging, count the number of rounds we fire. After the main gun has fired twice, you get our ass back and start moving to the alternate firing position before some Republican Guard hero has time to get a bead on us. Clear?"

"Clear, Sergeant."

Coats shifted his eyes across the turret to his loader, a man whose face was empty of all expression. That didn't tell Coats a lot, since the kid always looked like that—the boys in the platoon didn't call him Rock for nothing. "Rock?"

The large face smiled serenely across the turret. "Yes, Sergeant Coats?"

"You ready, man?"

Rock's smile broadened and the big head shook up and down vigorously. "Oh, yeah. I'm ready."

Despite the situation, Coats couldn't help grinning. "So what are you gonna do, Rock?"

"Sarge, I'm going to keep slamming sabot rounds into that breech until I run out or somebody tells me to load HEAT."

Coats nodded at Rock and gave him a wink. "Exactly right, my man. Exactly right."

As part of their platoon Standard Operating Procedure, Coats talked to the company commander. This freed his platoon leader to fight the platoon on their internal platoon frequency. Coats keyed the company net now.

"Knight Six, Blue Four. All Blue elements set. Ready to engage. Enemy now within twenty-four hundred meters. Request permission to engage once they've closed to two thousand, over."

Stuart's reply was quick. *"Hold fires until my call, Blue Four. I want one volley fire from all five of our tanks to initiate the action. Call me when the enemy reaches two thousand, over."*

"This is Blue Four, wilco."

As he made this last transmission, Coats heard Blue One relaying the information to the other Blue tanks on the platoon net. Coats understood what Stuart was up to. They were firing into the attacking Iraqis from the flank, trying to break the enemy attack long enough to pull the 2-35 team out. The shock effect the enemy would experience when losing a large number of tanks in a split second could do the trick, thus Stuart's planned volley fire. Too bad they didn't have the entire company up here. *That* would blow their fucking turbans and give 'em something to think about.

"Okay, gunner, what d'ya got?"

"Twenty-one hundred meters." The voice was a little shaky.

"Steady. Just like the gunnery range, Rudy. Wait about ten seconds. Then lase again. Just have that sight on and a good lase when we pull forward."

"Roger. Lasinnnngggg . . . two thousand meters!"

Coats felt his senses sharpen, though he hadn't thought that was possible.

"Knight Six, Blue Four, they're across the trigger line. Range two thousand meters."

"Roger. All Knight elements, Knight Six. At my command, two rounds sabot. Tophat, tophat, tophat."

The fire command told the Knight tanks several things. First, "at my command" let them know not to fire until Stuart gave them the order. Once they received "fire" from Stuart, all of the Blue tanks would open up at once. "Two rounds sabot" limited their fires to two rounds of sabot ammunition. This kept the trigger-happy crews from expending half their basic load of main gun rounds. Finally, "tophat" told all of the crews to move their tanks up into a firing position, time now. Stuart would give them a couple of seconds to get set and lock on their intended targets before issuing the command of fire.

Coats spoke slowly and deliberately into his boom mike. "Driver, move out."

The crew rocked as the tank pulled up into a firing position.

"Driver, stop." The driver slammed on the brakes. The tank gave a final shudder and stopped. The turbine engine kicked into a high whine. The crew could now engage, but as long as they were pulled up into the firing position, the enemy could also engage them.

"Gunner, you still locked on that T-72?"

"Affirmative!"

Coats broke his face from the sight extension momentarily and looked to his left towards the loader. "Rock, arm the fucking gun!"

The loader jumped forward and grabbed the arming handle. "Oh, shi . . . *up!*"

Coats' crew was ready. "Stand by. Steady . . . steady . . ."

Stuart's voice roared in the CVC helmet. *"All Knight elements, Knight Six . . . Fire!"*

Coats was listening to Stuart and timing his call to his crew accordingly. "Fire!"

The tank rocked. In the night, all that Coats could see was smoke and dust from the main gun firing. "Gunner, scan left. We'll come back and check that guy, but he's either hit or running for cover. A little more. I want to be on his wingman when the smoke clears. That's the guy that will be looking for us."

"Roger . . . I'm there."

"Up!" Rock was on the ball now, another round in the chamber and the main gun armed.

Coats kept staring into the sight extension. The smoke was clearing. "All right, gunner, there he is! He's traversing this way! Fire!"

"On the way!"

Again the tank rocked as a sabot round exited the gun tube. Now the crew was thrown forward as the driver slammed the transmission into reverse and got them behind cover.

The driver piped in on the intercom. "Hey, Sergeant Coats."

"Yeah?"

"I saw both of those tanks blow. Rudy got 'em."

"All right. Good work, guys. No time for kumbayas yet, though. There's a lot more of them out there."

**Lead Republican Guard Battalion, Forward of 3rd Brigade
22 October, 0255 Hours Local**

Lieutenant Colonel Sahaf listened to the progress of his units. The attack was going well. The brigade commander would be rewarded for this night's actions.

Those who'd fought during the Gulf War remembered well their lack of success against the American tanks. The new Swiss ammunition was functioning better than they'd dreamed possible. A copy of the American depleted-uranium round, it was having great success in penetrating the beast that had ripped through the Iraqis' ranks in 1991.

They'd now almost penetrated the American company screening the left flank. His battalion would make the hole a little wider and let the rest of the brigade break it open for the division's attack. From his position behind the lead company, Sahaf could see it all. It was his battalion's moment of glory. It was also short-lived.

Red flames streaked from the darkness to his left, followed a split second later by the sound of thunder. Five tanks in Sahaf's immediate vicinity exploded. The lead company halted in its tracks. Thoughts of glory disappeared for the moment as his battalion's crews shifted their actions toward survival against this unexpected threat.

"Got another one, Sarge!" called the gunner of B-33 as their tank repositioned.

"Good work, troop, but it ain't over yet."

The gunner nodded absently as he scanned for another target. The TC could say what he wanted, but they all knew that T-72s couldn't stand up to an M1A1 in a straight fight. The gunner smiled as another target moved unknowingly into his TIS at only fifteen hundred meters. Piece o' cake. "Identify PC!"

The tank commander had pulled out his PVS-7s for a quick scan of their local area. His heart jumped. Reaching into the cupola, he grabbed the power control handle to override his gunner, slewing the gun tube in the direction of the threat he'd seen—an Iraqi tank only eight hundred meters off of their flank. "Gunner, sabot, tank!"

The gunner, disoriented by the rapid spin of the turret, finally saw the enemy vehicle. "Identified!"

*   *   *

"Fire!" cried the commander of the enemy T-72.

His gunner engaged the American tank a split second later.

The commander watched as the American tank's onboard ammunition shot a plume of fire thirty feet into the sky as the pressure of the explosion vented through the blowout panels on top of the M1A1's turret. "A hit, but he is not yet finished. Reengage."

"On the way . . ."

The Iraqi smiled. The dreaded Abrams now died, just like everyone else. This would be a different war from the last, *praise his name*. His thoughts turned to survival as he watched flames lick from the hatches of the doomed tank. "Driver, move back towards the line of departure. There is nothing more we can do here for now . . . but we will return."

Jeff Coats, separated the last few minutes of the fight from his wingman as each moved between firing positions, saw the fireball reaching into the sky. He knew that it had to be B-33. "Driver, move to the alternate position, now!"

As the tank completed its move, Coats took control of the turret from his gunner. Within seconds he found the T-72 he was searching for, rapidly moving out of the area. And the carcass of what had been B-33. "Load sabot, from my position. . . ." Coats took the time for a final lase and to center on his target. "On the way," he said through clenched teeth. He showed no satisfaction as he turned control of the gun back to his gunner and climbed into the cupola.

Lieutenant Colonel Sahaf tried reaching the lead company's commander on the radio. Nothing. As he shifted his radio frequency to contact the company on its internal frequency, the Americans sent another volley towards his battalion. Four more T-72s shuddered to a halt.

Sahaf felt as though a cold snake had wrapped

tightly around his spine as he realized his tank was now the lead vehicle. And he was alone. All of the tanks accompanying him were in flames—all the ones behind him had stopped and had begun withdrawing.

"Driver, get us back, get us ba—"

Once the battalion commander died, so did any hope for a quick Iraqi penetration.

Jeff Coats listened as the platoon, minus Blue 3, the tank commander of B-33, sent their reports to the platoon leader. Once they finished, he keyed his radio to send the consolidated list to Stuart.

"Knight Six, Blue Four, over."

"Knight Six, send it."

"Knight Six, Blue Four. Slant three, I say again, slant three. Blue engaged and destroyed ten enemy tanks and one PC between TRPs Mike-One and Mike-Three." Coats hesitated, as if sending the call would finalize his friends' lives. *"We lost Bravo Three-Three. Catastrophic kill, no survivors. Continuing mission, over."*

Stuart's voice was subdued. *"Roger, understand. Is anyone in the platoon still in contact, over?"*

"This is Blue Four. Negative. The lead enemy victors are destroyed. Looks like the rest have pulled back."

"Roger, Blue Four. Prepare to move back on Route Dagger. Going higher."

Cold Steel Battle Position, Northern Kuwait
22 October, 0315 Hours Local

Dillon could see the flash of tank cannons to his front, followed seconds later by the booms of the big main guns. Not for the first time this night, he said a silent prayer for his friend Stuart. He picked up the PVS-7s that dangled around his neck and looked forward.

Cold Steel had occupied their battle position just before Knight started moving back. In this way they could take up the fight once all of Stuart's elements were safely to the rear.

As Dillon watched through his PVS-7s, he could see

the dust trails marking the last of Knight's main body moving through the passage point. He began to breathe a little easier. There were a lot of nervous gunners and tank commanders in his company who expected the horde to rush them any time. Dillon would be glad when all of the friendlies were behind them and they could quit worrying about a potential fratricide.

Thad Mason's voice squawked in his CVC. *"Steel Six, Steel Five."*

Dillon keyed his boom mike with one hand while continuing to watch with the PVS-7s for the returning Black Knights with the other. *"Steel Six."*

"Steel Six, Steel Five. The last elements of Knight's main body have moved through the passage point. They still have five tanks and three mortar tracks forward, over."

"Steel Six, roger. All Steel elements, Steel Six. Stay on weapons tight until the final Knight elements are through the passage point or I issue the order, over."

"Red Four, wilco."

"White One, roger."

"Blue Four, roger."

"Steel Six, out."

Dillon scanned along the Steel battle position from his position in the center behind First Platoon. Doc's and Bluto's tanks were well dug in. He could just make out some of the tank commanders' heads poking above ground level. The tanks were in tiered fighting positions. Currently they were all in the lowest position—their "hide." From this position the TCs scanned with their eyes and PVS-7s or binoculars while their vehicles remained hidden below ground level. By pulling forward in the sloped hole to the next higher level, the gunner could use his sight to look downrange, even though the tank was still hidden for the most part. This was possible because the sight mechanism on the M1 is located on top of the turret. When ready to engage enemy vehicles, the tanks pulled forward in their holes. This unmasked the gun

tube but still offered protection for the lower half of
the tank. Once they fired, the tank could back down
until they located another target, then repeat the
process.

Dillon's concern was Third Platoon. The ground
that comprised their position was rocky and the engineer vehicles hadn't been able to dig in it. God knows
they'd tried. Their Armored Combat Engineer vehicles, or ACEs, were literally bleeding hydraulic fluid
for their efforts. They managed to get one tank dug
in. The other three, plus Thad Mason's tank, were
nestled in folds of the terrain. This offered some protection, but not much. They did receive a bonus in
that it left them mobile. It didn't really matter. There
was nothing any of them could do about it. You
fought the terrain you were given the best that you
could. Period.

As Dillon waited the task force net hummed to life.

"Tiger Six, Knight Six, over."

"Tiger Six."

*"Tiger Six, Knight Six. Engaged and destroyed
twelve enemy tanks, two PCs, vicinity TRPs Mike-One
to Mike-Four. No contact at this time. Looks like the
enemy's attack has stalled. My slant is four tanks. Request permission to move back on Route Dagger. Also,
be advised. The sabot rounds being used by the enemy
are resulting in significant destruction on the friendlies.
They've got something new in their arsenal, over."*

Dillon sighed. Stuart had lost one. The Iron Tigers
had been blooded. And from the sounds of it, their
job had just gotten tougher.

*"Knight Six, Tiger Six. Roger, begin your move now.
Tell your men 'excellent work.' Striker Six reports all
2-35 elements pulled back successfully and casualties
recovered. Call once you're set in task force reserve
position, out."*

The men of Cold Steel watched the final Knight
vehicles passing silently through the checkpoint. Some
of the Team Knight tanks showed signs of battle dam-

age, but to the men watching from the darkness, the damage represented a right of passage. Knight had proven itself under fire. To a man, the soldiers of Cold Steel hoped they could do as well when the enemy came to them.

CHAPTER 8

Dawn

"Do you know who I gave assurances to today? Do you?" General Hamza cried, inches from his victim's face.

The operations officer blinked furiously to clear spittle from his eyes as he stood at attention. "Yes, sir."

The general leaned into the colonel's face even more. "Do you know what will happen if we do not accomplish our assigned mission?"

The colonel hesitated, then nodded. Historically, Iraqi leadership didn't fare well on the heels of failure.

"I will be a dead man!" Hamza turned his back to his subordinate and calmed himself. Regaining control, he turned and smiled. "Colonel, do not think that I will die alone. There will be ample blame for you to receive a portion." Hamza looked pointedly at his subordinate. "Do we understand one another?"

The man's Adam's apple bobbed once. "Yes, General."

The Tawakalna commander stepped back. "Good. Then let us get back to the business of defeating our enemy. What is the current situation?"

The colonel walked to the operations map. "As of now, our lead brigade has stopped. They had begun the penetration in the area where we had reconnaissance success earlier. As expected, the terrain allowed the Americans little room for repositioning."

The operations officer continued. "We caught them by surprise with the size of our attack. We had almost completed a penetration of their forward forces." The colonel pointed to the area where their attack had centered. "There was one American company here, screening forward of the main battle position." The operations officer now moved his pointer from north to south, indicating the brigade's direction of attack. "We attacked into the company like a fist, quickly overwhelming them. The new sabot ammunition had great success against the American armor."

The general interrupted. "So what happened? Our fist seems to have turned into the slap of a woman!"

The colonel grimaced and moved the pointer to the east. "Our observers report that an American company was here, tied into the point we were attempting to penetrate. As we initiated our attack, we received reports that they fired smoke and pulled out. It made sense. The Americans were sacrificing one company rather than losing two."

It was the general's turn to grimace. "Let me guess. They didn't withdraw."

"Most of the company did, sir. It appears a platoon remained in place to support the other company's withdrawal."

"A *platoon*? One platoon stopped a brigade's attack? But of course! That makes perfect sense! They were only outnumbered *twenty to one*!"

"Sir, when the Americans opened fire from the flank, they took out our lead company with two volleys. The battalion commander died during the exchange. Command and control was lost as the remnants of the other American company joined the battle. The lead battalion was decimated. Rather than have the rest of the brigade stumble blindly into a kill sack, the brigade commander pulled them back. That's where we stand now."

The general looked at the map and nodded with a grimace. "What is their current disposition?"

The colonel pointed. "There is a battalion, or more accurately a task force, as we have identified tanks and Bradleys mixed together, here at the point we attacked. We estimate they lost ten of their combat vehicles during the fighting last night." He pointed east. "Another task force here, which appears to be primarily tanks." He pointed farther east. "Their final task force is in this rocky terrain."

"Their reserve?"

The colonel shook his head. "Our reconnaissance has not located it. We assume it is centrally located somewhere behind their brigade. One could further assume that they would now use it to fill the losses they've taken in the west."

General Hamza looked at the array of American forces and shook his head. "Not yet. They'll wait to see if we attack in the west again before they commit their reserve."

The colonel hesitated. "Sir, we have already battered them once. If we place a chemical attack on the other two task forces in the east, it will immobilize them. They will not be able to influence the fight at all. We can wipe out the remainder of the western task force and continue our march south. Let the Madinah and the Hamourabi worry about mopping up the Americans."

Hamza looked at his subordinate. "We do not have permission to use chemical munitions. Besides, we have the forces necessary to defeat the Americans without their use and without the other two divisions. They've only bought a little time for themselves."

The colonel made one last effort. "Then, sir, may I suggest we shift our attack farther west and attack the Kuwaiti brigade. We have found a piece of their lines manned by M-84 equipped tank units. We can penetrate *there* and then hit the Americans from the flanks and rear."

General Hamza looked into his operations officer's eyes. He wasn't seeing the colonel, but the fly-covered and disfigured corpse of his son. "We will continue the attack through the Americans, as ordered. Our leader's wishes encompass more than just tactical considerations."

The general looked back to the map. "Has there been any indication that the Americans have reinforced the western position?"

The colonel shook his head. "I don't believe so, sir. We've got reconnaissance teams moving into position now to observe."

"Inform me when they have an answer."

3rd Brigade, 4th ID TAC, Northern Kuwait
22 October, 0425 Hours Local

Colonel Jones and his S3 exchanged tired looks. The night was almost over but the fighting had just begun.

"You got any cigarettes left, Tom?"

Major Tom Proctor smiled faintly and shook his head. "You know I don't smoke, sir."

"I worry about you, Tom. I don't trust an officer with no vices." Jones sipped his coffee. "Okay, we're in the lull before the storm. Task Force 2-35 is at eighty-five percent strength." He looked his operations officer in the eye. "You think they can hold?"

The major looked at the map. For the first time in his life, the list of combat losses that bordered the symbology was real. He scratched his face and realized he needed a shave, then further realized he hadn't answered his commander's question. He looked up from the map. "Sir . . . I just don't know. We could always move the reserve up. Or reposition some forces from another battle position."

Jones tapped a fresh cigarette out and pulled his Zippo from a cargo pocket. His eyes melded with the operations map over the flames as he lit the cigarette. He shook his head. "I'm not committing the reserve yet. They're in position to reinforce the west within ten minutes. From their current position they can also reinforce 2-77 in the center."

As he continued to stare at the map, Jones imagined himself in his opponent's position. He had an accurate read in the west. He knew he'd whittled down the forces there. Now he'd want to know . . . Slowly a smile spread across the craggy face.

"Tom, you worthless son of a bitch, call 2-77. Tell Estes I want him to . . ."

Cold Steel Battle Position, Northern Kuwait
22 October, 0530 Hours Local

Dillon acknowledged the order and signed off the task force command net. What the hell was this? As he considered the order it suddenly struck him what was in Jones's mind. Dillon smiled. That wily old bastard. He keyed his CVC.

"Steel Five, Blue One . . . Steel Six, over."

"Steel Five, over."

"Blue One, over."

"Frago follows. Blue element with Steel Five in operational control will move in two minutes. Mission . . ."

Thad Mason copied the order onto the border of his map and acknowledged. *What the fuck was this?* He shook his head. No time, he needed to move.

"Blue One, Steel Five. Follow my move."

A slightly bewildered voice answered. Takahashi obviously had the same questions running through his mind. *"This is Blue One, roger. We're moving."*

The five tanks from C Company pulled back from the rocks they'd been using for cover as the east colored with the promise of dawn. Once behind the company battle position, they spread out on line and kicked the tanks into high gear. They headed west into the desert. As they sped across the open sand, the tanks executed a series of zigzag maneuvers, kicking up huge clouds of dust in the process. They moved behind Anvil's battle position and continued west toward Task Force 2-35.

Forward of 2-35 Armor, Northern Kuwait
22 October, 0600 Hours Local

The BRDM scout car slowly pulled into a hide position behind the berm. The crew had worked patiently over the past two hours getting in position. Their instructions were to identify any forces attempting to reinforce the western American position. The sergeant in charge of the recon team ordered the engine shut off.

"Abdul," he said to his radio operator, "follow me."

The two men exited the vehicle, carrying only their personal weapons, a pair of binoculars, and a portable radio. The driver began draping a camouflage net over the small, lightly armored scout car. It was almost daylight and it looked as if they'd be here for a while.

Carefully the recon team crawled up the berm. On reaching the crest, the sergeant slowly raised his head above the edge until he could observe to the south. Satisfied there were no enemy forces in the immediate vicinity, he motioned for the binoculars. Again, he rose up just enough to observe south without silhouetting himself against the brightening sky. As he looked toward the area his brigade had attacked last night, he scanned slowly back and forth with the binoculars. While continuing to scan, he reached a hand down and snapped his fingers. The radio operator placed the handset in his palm.

"*Base, this is Recon Team Two, over.*"

"*This is Base.*"

"*Base, this is Recon Team Two. We are set. The*

*Americans have pulled out of their forward positions.
I can observe the fallback position they occupied and
am able to observe if anything moves into or from
there. At this time, no enemy vehicles visible. . . . Stand
by, I can hear engine noises. . . ."*

The sergeant released the handset and grabbed the
binoculars with both hands. As the mike snapped back
on its cord, it hit the startled radio operator in the
face, exciting a stream of curses targeting his sergeant's lineage.

"Silence!" hissed the team leader. "Give me the
handset."

The radio operator handed it up again as he muttered another string of curses.

*"Base, this is Team Two, situation update
follows. . . . There is a large cloud of dust moving in
the direction of the western battle position, over."*

*"This is Base. Can you give us a vehicle count by
type? Over."*

The team leader shook his head as he continued
looking through the binoculars. *"No, not yet. It appears to be a large number based off of the size of the
cloud. I will be able to give you a count when they
are closer."*

The American scouts sat silently in their observation post, looking west. They'd moved to this position
just before dawn in case their old position had been
compromised during the night attack. Their mission
was to stay low and report when and where the enemy
main body attacked. The new orders they'd received
a few minutes ago sounded strange, but it wasn't the
first time *that* had happened.

"Lighthorse Two-One, Lighthorse Six, over."

The transmission was muted on their man-portable
radio so that it couldn't be heard from over a couple
of feet away.

The senior scout picked up the handset.
"Lighthorse Two-One, over."

"Lighthorse Two-One, Six. Any change to your contact? Over."

The scout looked through his binoculars at their target, an Iraqi recon team. The team had moved into the area a few minutes ago in their BRDM and gone to ground. Per SOP, the scouts had called in mortars to take out the enemy's eyes without exposing themselves. The fires had been denied and the scouts were told to continue to observe their Iraqi counterparts.

"This is Two-One, negative. They are in a hide position and attempting to observe into the 2-35 BP, over."

"Roger. Two-One, look south and tell me if you can observe a large dust cloud, over."

The scout turned around and looked toward the friendly lines. Holy shit!

"This is Two-One. Affirmative. Anyone within a ten-mile radius can observe it, over."

"This is Lighthorse Six. You are free to continue call for fire on your target at this time. Out."

The scout shook his head, wondering what the hell all of that had been about. He shrugged. Time to get back to work. *"Thunder Six, Lighthorse Two-One. I have one PC and three troops stationary at grid . . ."*

The recon team continued observing the approaching dust cloud. As the vehicles moved into view it became clear that there was *not* a large number of vehicles, but rather just a few tanks. The team leader motioned once more for the handset.

"Base, this is Recon Team Two, over."

The sergeant heard two sounds simultaneously. His higher headquarters replying to his call and the whistling sound of the mortar rounds about to impact on his position.

The senior scout watched as the rounds impacted on the enemy recon position. It disappeared in a cloud

of dust and a roar that could be heard distinctly from
their position. He winced as he reached for the radio.
Man, that had to hurt.

*"Thunder Six, Lighthorse Two-One. Good mission.
Repeat, over."*

**Tawakalna Division Headquarters, Southern Iraq
22 October, 0610 Hours Local**

General Hamza looked at the report in his hands, then
looked back at the colonel. "This is the last report?"

The operations officer nodded. "Yes, sir. They attempted a transmission a few minutes ago, but we
lost communications." During the previous hour, the
reconnaissance effort had not gone well for the Tawakalna Division. In the span of forty-five minutes, they
had lost communications with every element they'd
sent forward.

Continuing to read over the intelligence report, the
general gave a decisive nod. "Very well. It is enough
information. It is obvious the Americans were trying
to reinforce the western position before sunrise, hoping our reconnaissance forces would not be able to
observe. Unfortunately for them, they did not quite
make it in time. "Do we know where the reinforcements originated?"

The colonel pointed to the center of the American
position. "Here, sir. We tracked their movement all
the way."

The general was ecstatic. *Did they think to hide such
a large movement of vehicles in the desert?* "Call the
brigade commanders. The attack will commence in
twenty minutes. They think we will attack in the west
again? Very well, we will show them what they want
to see—to an extent."

The colonel frowned. "Sir?"

General Hamza looked at the colonel as if he were
the son of a leper. *I really must get a new operations
officer,* he thought, not for the first time. *This one has
no mind for tactics.* "Colonel, it is obvious the Ameri-

cans believe we will attack in the west. This is clear
from the fact that they have sent a large number of
vehicles to reinforce that position. They attempted to
accomplish this before dawn so we would not know,
but we caught them at it. Now we will reinforce their
belief by attacking in the west, but only with the remnants of the brigade that attacked last night. The remainder of our division will attack where they pulled
their reinforcements from, for *there* they will now be
weak!" The general jabbed his finger into the center
of the American forces—into the heart of Cold Steel's
battle position.

Cold Steel Battle Position, Northern Kuwait
22 October, 0620 Hours Local

Dillon looked again toward the rocky, furrowed ground
previously occupied by Third Platoon. As a battle position the terrain stank, but it was better than nothing.
And that was what Third Platoon would have if they
didn't make it back soon, for they'd be caught in the
open. It was too soon to know if Jones's ruse had been
successful—but if the Iraqis had bitten on the bait, the
Tawakalna would be rolling straight at them.

Dillon closed his eyes and conducted a mental review.
When the enemy division attacked, it would be with
three brigades. Each of the enemy brigades had roughly
the same number of combat vehicles as 3rd Brigade.
What it amounted to was they'd better kill a lot more
of the enemy than the enemy killed of them. In the past
they'd counted on superior weapons and ammunition to
accomplish this type of destruction, but the new Iraqi
tank rounds were a wild card. No one had known about
that capability. Now the sides were on a much more
equal footing, though the American tanks still possessed
a significant technological advantage in optics and
shooting on the move. Still, somewhere on the intelligence side there had been a major hole that was just
now being discovered—the hard way.

The fight would be sequential once it began. When

the lead Republican Guard brigade was within range of the American howitzers, the friendly artillery would begin hammering it. This enemy brigade would continue to receive indirect fire until they closed into direct fire range of the 3rd Brigade's tanks and Bradleys, roughly two and a half miles forward of Steel's position. Friendly air would interdict the trailing Iraqi brigades, along with more indirect fires. This would separate the lead brigade in time and space from his follow-on forces.

The Americans had an imaginary line in the sand running thirty-seven hundred meters forward of the friendly fighting positions. Once the enemy crossed this line, which was marked on the ground by orange aircraft recognition panels, the Bradleys would open up with their TOWs. These wire-guided tank killers served two purposes: to strip off a few of the enemy tanks early in the fight and to force the Iraqis to break up their formations. The new WAM mines would force the enemy armor to turn in order to avoid them . . . assuming they were seen. While these minefields could be easily bypassed, this exposed the enemy armor's vulnerable flanks to the mech infantry's Bradley gunners.

When the enemy closed to three thousand meters, select tank crews would begin engaging. These "sniper crews" would be the best shooting tanks from each unit. They would engage the lead enemy tanks at long range while their wingmen observed for them. At twenty-five hundred meters the M1A1s would enter the fight in a mass. The tanks would use platoon and company volley fires to whittle down the enemy in chunks. The obstacles would be thicker now. Combinations of minefields, tank ditches, and razor-sharp concertina wire would force the enemy along the routes the Americans wanted them to take. If the enemy wanted to use the blocked routes they would have to breach the obstacle belts—a costly operation in time, equipment, and men as they would be under direct and indirect fire during the entire operation.

At two thousand meters the Bradleys' 25mm cannon fires would begin stitching the enemy's infantry carriers while the M1A1s continued working over the T-72s.

Dillon, like all commanders, knew that battles rarely happened as planned. The plan was a basis for change. And of course, the enemy gets a vote. The Iraqis wouldn't idly roll into the friendly engagement area to be killed, but would engage the American positions with preparatory artillery until their own forces rolled into danger at close range. At this point the enemy armor would attempt to close the distance between themselves and their objective as rapidly as possible, knowing they had precious few minutes before the American forces got their shit together following the arty firestorm that had fallen on them. If the Iraqis could significantly close on the U.S. positions, they would take away one of the American advantages, which was superior accuracy at longer distances. A final option in the Iraqis' pocket was the use of chemical munitions, likely delivered by some type of indirect fire system. As he'd told his men, the intel folks didn't think it was likely, but the possibility still remained.

Dillon thumbed the CVC's radio switch. *"Steel Five, Steel Six. SITREP on your move."*

Mason's voice rumbled through the helmet's receiver. *"Steel Six, Steel Five, E.T.A. zero two minutes, over."*

"Roger, Steel Five. Cut back your speed. We've got a few minutes and I don't want dust clouds trailing up to your positions. Let me know when you've reoccupied and are REDCON-One, over."

"Steel Five, wilco."

Dillon reached forward, giving his .50 caliber machine gun one last check, then settled back. He wouldn't have to wait long.

Kuwait International Airport, Kuwait
22 October, 0625 Hours Local

In the early-morning light a ragged group of soldiers worked at arranging the bodies of America's first casu-

alties of the new war on the airport tarmac. Nobody
noticed as a military cargo vehicle pulled alongside.
The NCO in charge of the detail looked down the
rows of body bags and at the silver caskets awaiting
them off to one side. Fifteen dead so far.

"All right!" he yelled in an attempt to be heard
over the constant noise of arriving and departing aircraft. "You will check each body bag for an identifica-
tion tag. You will then move the body to the casket
with the matching name stenciled on its cover. Don't
close the covers until I come through and verify a
match." The sergeant paused, pointing to a C-130 two
hundred meters down the flight line. "Once complete,
we'll secure the caskets and move them one at a time
by forklift to that aircraft. That aircraft will transport
the remains stateside. Questions?"

"Yeah," called a sullen voice from behind the NCO.

The sergeant turned. He recognized the speaker. A
troublemaker. One of those soldiers who bitched
about everything and felt like the world owed him
something for nothing. He, like most of the other
members of the detail, had been sent from other units.
The NCO shook his head. What did he expect, that
the field units were going to send back their best and
brightest as the war was just heating up? Not likely.

The NCO put his hands on his hips. "What is it?"

"Why the fuck we gotta do this, Sarge? Isn't this
the fuckin' air force's job? I thought they was responsible for loading shit on planes."

The NCO turned crimson. "Listen up, fuckstick.
These soldiers died at the front while chickenshits like
you found every excuse in the book to stay as far from
the fighting as they could. . . ."

As the sergeant continued, a squad of soldiers wearing maroon berets quickly exited the cargo vehicle
alongside the group. Each of the soldiers had silver
jump wings pinned to the left breast of their desert
utility uniforms. In contrast to the detail of slovenly
soldiers, these moved with a sense of grace, power,
and pride. At their lead was a giant captain.

"Now *you will* move these bodies," said the NCOIC of the transport detail, his finger an inch from the face of the troublemaker, "and *you will* show the proper respect while doing so. And if you don't, so help me God, you piece of human shit, I'm going to rip your . . ."

It was at this point the NCO decided that it would be worth the stripe he'd lose to kick the shit out of the soldier in question. As his arm cocked back and began to flash forward, it was caught in a viselike grip, its forward motion stopped cold.

The NCO wheeled and found himself looking into the chest of the big captain. The sergeant had a pleading look on his face. "I know what I'm doing, sir. Let me handle this. It's NCO business."

Captain Jack Kelly had heard enough of the exchange between the sergeant and the ragbag to get the gist of what was occurring. He shook his head, but the expression on his face was not unkind. "That's all right, Sergeant. We've got it. Dismiss your detail. I'm sure there's something else they can do on the flight line to make themselves useful."

The NCO looked at the name tag. "Kelly . . . we've got a Sergeant Major Kelly—" He stopped midsentence, understanding dawning in his eyes. "Sir . . . is the sergeant major . . . ?"

Kelly looked at the NCO and nodded slowly. "My father. Would you want this scum responsible for your dad's remains?"

The sergeant looked at the motley detail and shook his head. "No, sir. I would not. Follow me." He moved down the row of body bags, stopping close to the end of the line.

Captain Jack Kelly looked down at the body bag the NCO had stopped next to. The tag identified the remains as KELLY, JACKSON E., SGM. Kelly reached down to the zipper.

The NCO grabbed his shoulder. "Sir, I'm afraid it's against regulations to—"

The look Jack Kelly Jr. gave the man was enough

to freeze the rest of the sentence in the NCO's throat
and make him remove his hand as though it had
been shocked.

Kelly wasn't prepared for the sight that greeted him
as he unzipped the body bag. He'd tried to steel himself against it, but it did no good now that he was
face-to-face with the evidence of how brutally his father had died.

He softly touched the cheek, as he had so often
sitting in his father's lap as a child. Kelly's squad of
Airborne troopers formed a protective perimeter
around their commander. The soldiers couldn't shield
Kelly from the emotional turmoil ripping through him,
but they'd be damned if outsiders would be allowed
to see their commander's pain. Turning their backs,
the men allowed Kelly a few moments of privacy.

Jack reached inside his father's shirt. The blood had
dried and stiffened the uniform material. Slowly he
grasped the dog tag chain and pulled it out. Somewhere in the system they'd already taken one of the
tags. Well, they could live without the other. He detached it from the chain, after pulling his own chain
out, and attached his father's tag next to his own. He
then reached into his pocket and pulled out his wallet.
With a shaking hand, Jack withdrew a photo of his
newborn son. He placed the picture into his father's
hand, a hand that he knew so well, and folded the
stiff fingers around it.

"He'll be proud of you, Dad," Kelly whispered. "I'll
make sure of that. And . . . don't worry about Mom.
I'll take care of her . . . I promise. I . . . know we
have always had a hard time talking . . . really talking.
But, I just want you to know, I couldn't have asked
for more in a father . . . and I . . . I love you. Good-
bye, Dad." Kelly slowly zipped the body bag shut, but
remained kneeling over it as he regained control of
his emotions.

When he finally stood, his first sergeant spun and
faced him. "Sir, we'd be proud if you'd let us take
care of your father for you now."

Kelly nodded once quickly. "Thanks, Top. Carry on."

Kelly's men began loading the bodies into the caskets, beginning with the sergeant major's. After they completed this task, the caskets were moved to the waiting forklift—all but Sergeant Major Kelly's. Captain Kelly's men agreed without a spoken word that his casket would be carried to the waiting aircraft by an honor guard of Airborne.

CHAPTER 9

Battle Met

Phase Line Sheridan, Northern Kuwait
22 October, 0630 Hours Local

The scout sergeant held the binos to his face again, then reached behind him with an open hand. "Give me the handset, Ramirez."

The soldier slapped it into his palm. "Sergeant Cole—they comin'?"

Cole ignored the question as he continued observing north. He put the binos down and pulled a marker from his pocket. Bending over the map spread on the ground in front of him, the NCO annotated the location and information he'd just observed. Satisfied, Cole lifted the binos to his eyes and the handset to his mouth.

"Lighthorse Six, Lighthorse Two-Six, over."

"Lighthorse Six, over."

"This is Two-Six. I'm observing a large formation of armored vehicles, vicinity TRP Delta-One. Approximately four zero T-72 tanks and two zero BMPs. They are moving slowly southwest, appear to be attacking into 2-35 sector. Tell Lightning to fire group target Alpha five one Golf. I can adjust, over."

"This is Six, roger. Stand by."

As he waited for his platoon leader to request the indirect fire mission through task force fire support channels, Cole heard a whistling directly overhead. He grabbed Ramirez by the neck and shoved him face first into the sand. The rounds impacted five hundred meters away.

Cole released the scout. "Sorry, Ramirez. Didn't know how close that was going to be."

The young corporal spit sand out of his mouth. "That's okay. I'm sure you meant well."

Cole turned toward the area of the artillery's impact.

"Lighthorse Six, this is Lighthorse Two-Six. I am observing indirect fires, vicinity battle position four-zero, over."

The artillery continued falling in the area, all of it directed at Task Force 2-35's position. Damn but those poor bastards were being pounded. Hadn't they had enough? Cole picked up the binos for another look north. The enemy force had all but stopped while waiting for their artillery to finish softening up 2-35.

"Lighthorse Six, Two-Six. Tell Lightning to fire that group now! The enemy force is stationary. I say again stationary, over."

The seconds ticked by.

"Lighthorse Two-Six, Lighthorse Six. Shot, over."

By reflex, Cole responded, *"Shot, out."*

Ramirez tugged at his NCO's sleeve as Cole observed the target area to see the outcome of the fire mission on the large mass of Iraqi vehicles.

Cole held up a hand as he continued to peer through the binos. "Stand by, Ramirez. I'm busy."

"But, Sergeant Cole—"

Cole held up a warning finger. "Stand—by—Ramirez. It can wait."

As Cole continued watching the enemy formation, he heard heavy diesel engine noises. He looked to his right. "Ramirez?"

"Yeah, Sergeant Cole?"

"Were you trying to tell me that you saw a bunch of vehicles to the east of the first group?"

Ramirez put down the spare set of binos he'd been utilizing. "Uh-huh."

"And that they were headed this way?"

"Yep."

Cole's pulse quickened. "Start getting our shit together and prepare to make a run for the Hummer."

"Roger." Ramirez began policing up the ammo, maps, radio batteries, and other equipment that were the bread and butter of a scout observation post.

Cole jumped back to the radio. As he was picking up the handset to send the new spot report, the radio came to life.

"Two-Six, this is Six. Splash, over."

Shit. He'd forgotten entirely about the fire mission. He turned to Ramirez. "Get the hell outta here. I'm right behind you."

Ramirez shook his head doggedly. "I'll wait for you."

Cole started to argue, then held up a finger for what seemed the umpteenth time in the past hour. *"This is Two-Six. Splash, out."* He held up the binos in time to see the first group of vehicles disappear in a mass of dust and smoke. Group artillery targets consisted of multiple targets, all fired at once. There was a lot of shit falling on the bad guys, which was good. But it made it damned difficult to determine if anything was actually being hit.

"Six, Two-Six. Tell Lightning to repeat, I say again, repeat the mission. Break . . . Six, currently observing a second group of vehicles, roughly same size and composition as first group, maybe a little larger. Vicinity TRP Echo-Two and moving south. We've got to move. Estimate the lead vehicles will be on top of our current position in less than one zero minutes, over."

"This is Six. Good copy. Move to alternate post now. Call me when set. Out."

Cole threw the radio onto his back and grabbed his M16. "Goddamn it, Ramirez! When I tell you to do something, I don't have time to argue. . . ."

Green tracers stitched a line between Cole and Ramirez. Both men bolted south toward the wadi in which their Hummer was hidden. Behind them they heard the roaring diesel engine of a Russian-made

BRDM scout car. Apparently the Iraqi recon forward of the enemy unit had been watching the American scouts and had worked their way close enough to engage.

Ramirez, younger and more agile, was in the lead. Cole looked over his shoulder in time to see the BRDM pop over an intervisibility line three hundred meters behind them. *Shit.* Green tracers again streaked from the vehicle's 7.62mm machine gun. In what seemed like slow motion, Cole saw Ramirez reach for his calf, then stagger and go down as if a giant hand had swatted him on the back. Cole sprinted toward his fallen scout.

As the BRDM gunner watched, the faster of the two soldiers fell. He released his trigger. Praise Allah. Now for the other one. He shifted his sight picture slightly as the second American ran to aid his fallen comrade. The gunner hesitated. He did not like shooting a man coming to the aid of a friend.

"Why do you hesitate?" demanded his vehicle commander. "Fire your weapon!"

En shallah, thought the gunner, looking once again into his sight and bringing the second American into its picture. *Allah's will be done.*

Cole dropped his M16 to the ground when he reached Ramirez. Bending over the prone figure, he threw the still body over his shoulder and shifted it into a fireman's carry. He scooped up his rifle with one hand and looked back toward the BRDM as he started to run south once more. Again tracers tore up the ground, this time in a line running directly to his right. Cole jinked left, beginning to feel his thighs burn from his exertions. As he looked toward the opening of the wadi where their Hummer was hidden two hundred meters away, he could just make out the sound of a windswept voice.

"Get down, Sarge!"

Immediately Cole dropped to the ground, using his

body to cushion the impact on Ramirez. Cole eased from under the young scout and covered Ramirez's body with his own just as he heard the sound he'd been waiting for.

Whump-whump-whump. The dull thumping of the Mark-19 automatic grenade launcher was music to his ears. The 40mm high-explosive shells arced over the prone scouts, one round every two seconds, reaching toward the pursuing Iraqis. PFC McDermott, the final member of Cole's team, had stayed in the hide position with the vehicle. Apparently he'd heard Cole's call and had been watching for the team's return.

A dull explosion sounded behind Cole and he felt a wave of pressure and heat as the thinly armored scout car blew up mere yards from them. *En shallah,* thought Cole as he watched the BRDM burn.

He slid off of Ramirez, checking for a pulse. *Thank God,* he thought, *faint but steady.* He checked the extent of his team member's injuries, expertly working his hands down the young soldier's body. Nothing in the torso. His hands continued working quickly and efficiently. *There it is.* The calf was torn up pretty good.

A slight groan issued from the soldier and his eyes fluttered open as Cole's fingers probed his wound. He looked at the sergeant in confusion. "Sergeant Cole?"

Cole looked into Ramirez's face as he pulled the field dressing from the injured soldier's first aid pouch and began wrapping it around the wound. "Well, hello, Sleeping Beauty. Nice of you to join us."

The corporal was having trouble focusing on Cole's face. "What . . . what happened?"

"Well, I'll tell you what happened. You didn't listen to me when I told you to beat boots outta there—that's what happened . . . and I'll tell you something else . . . if you *ever*—"

PFC McDermott slid the Hummer to a stop next to his team. "You guys okay, Sergeant Cole?"

Cole broke off his tongue-lashing of Ramirez and looked up. "Nice of you to drop in, shit bird. Stand by." He turned back to his injured soldier. "Now, Ramirez, in the future when I give you an order . . ."

A slow smile spread across McDermott's face. *Yeah, they were just fine.*

3rd Brigade, 4th ID TAC, Northern Kuwait
22 October, 0645 Hours

"Sir?" said Sergeant Matt O'Keefe in obvious exasperation.

Jones, standing next to O'Keefe in the Bradley's turret, turned to him and raised an inquisitive eyebrow. He and O'Keefe had just moved forward to see what 3rd Brigade's left flank looked like following the night's fighting.

"Sir, you really shouldn't be this close to the front line."

Jones flicked his Zippo, took a deep drag off the cigarette—completely ignoring ten different army regulations regarding smoking on combat vehicles—and waved a dismissive hand. "Ah, bullshit, Sergeant O'Keefe. We're not that close."

An artillery round impacted five hundred meters away, causing O'Keefe to grab the side of the turret to steady himself.

"Sir, at least get in the back with the S3 and FSO. You don't need to worry about commanding the vehicle. That's *my* job."

Jones lifted the binoculars hanging from the strap around his neck, exhaling a steady stream of smoke, then turned to O'Keefe. "The FSO is allergic to cigarette smoke. You believe that shit? How the hell can I operate in that type of environment?" He turned the binos north, conducted a quick scan of the horizon, and then turned back to his gunner. "Besides, I can't see shit in the back of the track."

O'Keefe rolled his eyes. "Stand by, sir." He flipped his CVC to intercom. "Driver."

A nervous voice answered. "Driver here."

"Driver, I want you to back up two hundred meters.

You'll see a slight depression to your left once you've completed the move. Get us in there."

The relieved response was instantaneous. "Roger. Moving now."

Jones and O'Keefe were thrown forward as the driver switched the M2's transmission into reverse and shot backward.

Jones thumped his cigarette over the side of the vehicle and turned to his gunner. "I'm going back inside. Happy?"

O'Keefe gave a quick nod. "Yes, sir. Fucking ecstatic."

As Jones stepped down and into the troop area, the brigade S3 and fire support officer both rose from years of habit. Their helmeted heads banged into the steel roof.

"Seats, gentlemen," said Jones, trying not to laugh. He turned to Proctor. "So, Tom, do you think it worked?"

Proctor stared at the map. He'd been scribbling notes on its margins from the scouts' spot reports. "I believe so, sir. From the information we've received, the Two is calling the unit attacking toward Task Force 2-35 a brigade-minus, mainly tanks. That tracks with what should be left over from the unit that attacked into this sector last night. At any rate, for now we're calling them the same unit. But a larger force has appeared on the screen."

Jones closed his eyes and rubbed them as he mentally processed and stored everything his operations officer said. "Go on."

"The 2-77 scouts reported the larger force here, to the east."

Striker 6 opened his eyes just long enough to focus on the spot Proctor was pointing to on the map, then closed them and resumed rubbing. "Got it."

"These forces have slowed down in the low ground ten kilometers north of 2-77 Armor. Based off the reports, the Two is calling it a brigade."

Jones opened his eyes and looked to his FSO. "Buck . . . 2-35 still has priority of fires?"

Major Deerfield "Buck" Sheldon nodded. "Yes, sir. We've got some fire missions going in for them on the Iraqis to their front, but as that force is now almost in direct fire range, we're preparing to shift the priority to Task Force 2-77."

"Okay," said Jones, "now for the question of the day. Where's the Tawakalna's third brigade?"

Proctor took over, pointing north on the map. "Sir, we're getting feeds from airborne platforms, primarily Joint STARS, indicating a large formation of mechanized vehicles here—lots of moving target indicators. It appears to be at least two mechanized battalions. Its movement thus far leads me to make the call that it's supporting the brigade to the east—the one moving toward the Iron Tigers."

Jones's eyes remained closed as he leaned back and crossed his arms across his chest. "Summarize."

Proctor had worked for his commander long enough to know that the relaxed posture was anything but indicative of how quickly his mind was assimilating the information it was receiving. "Sir, we have a brigade-minus attacking into 2-35 Armor's sector, approximately two battalions consisting of a little over thirty combat vehicles apiece. We have two additional brigades behind that one. One of these brigades is trailing the other by about five kilometers. The XO has been running through it with the rest of the staff at the TOC. He said to relay that their read is the attack in the west against Task Force 2-35 is a supporting attack. The main attack will be in the east with the other two brigades, into 2-77's sector. That's where they think we're thin. They'll try to open a hole through our lines with the lead brigade and punch through and exploit with the follow-on brigade."

Jones nodded. His eyes popped open as he sat up. He looked to Sheldon. "Roger. I concur. Buck, I want close air support targeted against the follow-on brigade in the east. I want to gain some separation between him and the brigade he's trailing. That way Task Force 2-77 is only fighting one brigade at a time. Switch priority of fires to 2-77, time now. I want to start hammering the lead brigade in the east with artillery—ASAP. When they hit the obstacle belt forward of the Iron Tigers, I want them pounded some more. After that, it's 2-77's fight."

Proctor and Sheldon made their final notes.

Jones turned back to the S3. "Tom, don't move the reserve yet, but you tell that company commander to make sure he's conducted a recon and timed a route to 2-35's BP. What's the remaining strength there?"

Proctor didn't need to check his status charts. "There are about three companies' worth of tanks and Brads, sir. Their counter-recon team lost eight of fourteen vehicles. The other three companies lost one or two vehicles each."

Jones nodded slowly, a small indication of the pain the news caused him. He hated losing men, tanks, Bradleys, or anything else to these bastards. However, he also knew they'd been fortunate. A heavy price had been paid for letting the enemy get a read on their disposition in the west—but they'd held.

"Okay, gentlemen. Game time."

Cold Steel Battle Position, Northern Kuwait
22 October, 0650 Hours Local

Dillon unconsciously ran his hands over the switches of his commander's weapons station, double-checking their positions. He looked to his right at his status lights . . . good. He bent his face to his sight extension. Picture good, set for thermal imaging. It was still cool outside, so the enemy vehicles should show up nicely in the thermals. He stood, extending his head and chest out of the tank's hatch. He raised his binos, looking north. Nothing yet. He scanned left. Dust, and lots of it, to the northwest. That tracked with the spot reports relayed by the S2 just minutes ago. That would be the supporting attack heading into 2-35's sector.

Overhead, Dillon heard the sonic boom of jet fighters at high altitude heading north. He silently took back all the bad things he'd ever said about aviators in general and air force pilots in particular. The brigade was in a combat ratio numbers crunch and needed some help in evening the odds.

The artillery had shut down to the northwest a couple of minutes earlier and the unmistakable sound of armored vehicles locked in combat could be heard now, a sound that had become all too familiar the previous night. Task Force 2-35 was in it again. Dillon hoped their fight didn't spill over into his own sector, that they could hold for just a little longer. He and his company would have enough problems dealing with the fight in their face without having to worry about additional threats from their flanks.

The friendly artillery began again. Dillon judged it to be heading north at the bad guys moving into his sector. The task force had priority of indirect fires now, so the COLT teams forward with the scouts must have eyes on the Republican Guard brigade attacking south. The COLTs, formally known as Combat Observation Lasing Teams, were artillery observers stationed far forward of the main combat troops. With the mission to locate and target advancing enemy formations with indirect fires before they entered the main battle area, these great Americans didn't have overly long life expectancies. Survival depended on stealth and training, with a bit of luck thrown in for good measure.

Again Dillon heard the whistling of artillery. *Oh shit, that's not going out. . . .*

Jumping back inside the tank, Dillon worked his hatch levers, slamming it shut and locking it down. Looking across the turret, he saw that his loader, PFC Hunter, had already done the same and was now plastering himself against the side of the turret in preparation for what they all knew was going to be a wild ride.

"Guideons, Steel Six—" The first Iraqi 152mm artillery rounds impacted within one hundred meters of C-66, cutting off Dillon's words in his throat. The concussion of the high-explosive rounds slammed Dillon backward into the turret wall hard enough to knock the breath out of him.

The tank shook violently. It sounded as if a crew of street workers with jackhammers had decided to get down to business on C-66. Dug in eight feet beneath the desert floor, thus shielded from the majority of the artillery fires' effects, the tank nonetheless was rocked repeatedly as volley after volley rolled across the company position.

Dillon's thoughts turned to Third Platoon. He'd kept them as far back as possible in preparation for this moment. Unable to dig in, they would be catching hell. He hoped they were missing the brunt of it. Takahashi knew to move forward as soon as the indirect fires lifted. They would need every gun at that point, because the Iraqi main body would be following the artillery barrage as surely as Patton pissed vinegar.

Dillon flipped his CVC to intercom. "Gunner!" he screamed to be heard over the maelstrom that continued to swirl around their vehicle. No response. Dillon yelled into the helmet's boom mike again, this time punctuating the call with a swift kick into his gunner's back.

Sergeant Bickel, Dillon's gunner for the past twelve months, turned and favored his tank commander with a look that could kill. Realizing that Dillon was trying to tell him something, Bickel grabbed the sides of his CVC and squeezed the earcups tightly against his skull in an attempt to hear the message.

"Bick!" Dillon yelled, pointing above the gunner's head. "Close the doghouse!"

Sergeant Randy Bickel, the best natural gunner Dillon had ever met, all but slapped himself in the forehead at the blinding flash of the obvious. He reached up and threw a lever, closing the steel door that protected the tank's optical system. If it sustained enough damage, the crew would be back to engaging tanks in the same manner as the combat crewmen of World War II. No laser range finder, no thermal imaging system, no crosswind sensor, no built-in lead, nothing—just an eight-power auxiliary sight and Kentucky windage. They didn't have the numbers or the ammunition to win that kind of fight. If their fire control system held up, Dillon knew he and his crew could engage and destroy several enemy vehicles inside of a minute. If it didn't, their effectiveness would be cut by better than half.

Dillon threw the CVC switch forward to the radio position.

"Tiger Six, Steel Six, over." Dillon waited. There was little doubt that Estes knew of their current situation, but SOP required a report go up.

Hearing nothing from the task force commander after thirty seconds of waiting, Dillon re-keyed. *"Tiger Six, Tiger Six . . . Steel Six, over."*

After one final try, Dillon called Thad Mason. Nothing. He tried the platoons. Again, nothing. Finally, Dillon faced the fact that they had lost communications. With no contact to his company or his battalion, and their tank continuing to be rocked by indirect fires, Dillon felt as if he and his crew were in some kind of hell on earth. Their universe consisted of constant hammering and the impact of soft human flesh on cold steel as they were bounced around inside.

After what seemed an eternity, but was actually closer to fifteen minutes, the fires slowed. Finally, they stopped. More accurately, Dillon judged, they shifted south and into the rear areas of 3rd Brigade. Dillon shook his head to clear it. Not his problem. He had enough to keep him occupied.

He looked to the loader. "Hunter. Get out there and—"

Seeing that the soldier hadn't turned, Dillon realized the loader couldn't hear him. The shelling had temporarily deafened them all. Dillon reached across the turret and grabbed the PFC's shoulder, pulling him across the turret so that he could speak directly into his ear. "Get out and check the antennas! I think the artillery took them out! Grab the spares from the sponson box and replace them!"

Hunter's head nodded once quickly, then he was opening his hatch and hopping out.

"Crew report!" Dillon yelled over the intercom as loud as he could.

"Driver's up . . . and you don't have to yell, sir. I put in earplugs when the arty started," came the voice of Specialist Thompson, Dillon's driver.

"Roger, any problems that you can tell?" His own hearing just beginning to return to normal, Dillon made a concerted effort to speak in a normal tone of voice.

Dillon felt the tank move forward ever so slightly in their hole, then ease back. "The old girl seems to be functioning normally, and all my indicators are green," said Thompson.

"Roger. The loader's up," said Dillon. "He's checking things topside." Dillon bent down and tapped his gunner on the back.

Bickel continued flipping switches back and forth, checking status lights. Finally he turned in his seat to face Dillon. "Fire control systems look green. I'm running through a diagnostic test to make sure. I'll give you a yell in a minute once I've confirmed."

"Roger," grunted Dillon as he struggled with his hatch. Unlike the loader's hatch, with its single latching handle, the tank commander's hatch was a bitch to open, especially when crouching inside a dim turret. After a few seconds, he swung the hatch up and stood in the cupola.

Dillon took in the scene around C-66 with fascination. The outside world had taken on an alien perspective. It looked primordial, as it must have eons ago in its infancy. Huge craters, open wounds in the earth's face, dotted the landscape in their immediate vicinity. The surrounding air was thick with dust from the tons of raw earth that had been thrown upwards. The bloodred rising sun tried to cut through the haze, but it would be a few minutes before the dust settled enough for Dillon to get a clear picture past a couple of hundred meters.

Not being able to see didn't affect Dillon's knowledge of what was coming at him. In his mind the dozens of T-72s and BMPs moving hell bent for leather to hit the American position before they'd fully recovered from the artillery were clear. He knew without a doubt that the attack on their position was imminent.

Dillon looked toward the back of the tank as Hunter finished tightening down their second antenna. The loader gave him a thumbs-up signal.

Crossing his fingers, Dillon keyed his CVC. *"Any Steel element, Steel Six. Radio check, over."*

"Steel Six, Steel Seven. Roger. Good to have you back." The relief at hearing Dillon back on the company net was evident in Rider's voice.

"This is Steel Six, good to be back. Guideons, Steel Six."

"Red Four."

"White One."

"Blue Four."

"Steel Five."

"Guideons, Steel Six. I expect we'll be in direct fire with the enemy momentarily. I need current statuses, over."

After receiving a wilco from each platoon, Dillon heard Estes radioing him on task force command. Switching nets, he returned the call. *"Tiger Six, Steel Six."*

"Steel Six, Tiger Six. SITREP, over."

"This is Steel Six. The artillery fires you were observing shifted one minute ago. They caused us some commo problems—mostly fixed now. My elements are currently working status reports. I'll call you when I've got them consolidated, over."

"This is Tiger Six, roger. Scouts report a brigade-size element of sixty tanks and thirty BMPs have closed within five thousand meters of your position. You now

have priority of indirect fires and are cleared to engage, over."

"Steel Six, roger."

There was a pause on the other end of the radio, as if Estes was searching for something to say. *"This is Tiger Six . . . Good hunting, out."*

As Dillon gazed north, the dust continued to settle. He threw the binos to his face. *Here they come.* Dillon saw countless dots. He knew the ant-size figures were actually combat vehicles intent on his destruction, trailing dust clouds hundreds of feet into the air as they rapidly closed on him and his men.

"Guideons, Steel Six. Multiple enemy vehicles on Avenues of Approach Two and Three, moving south. Vicinity TRPs Charlie-One and Charlie-Three. Do not engage until I give the order, break . . . Steel Five, Steel Six, do you have our consolidated status report? Over."

Mason's voice sounded detached. *"Roger, Six. Our current slant is thirteen. I say again . . . one-three, over."*

The slant count hit Dillon in the gut like a brick. They'd had fourteen tanks before the barrage. Shit . . . Third Platoon. Who had they lost? *"Roger, Steel Five, understand slant one-three. Pass it higher, along with our spot report on the enemy approach. Who . . . what vehicle . . . ?"*

Mason knew what Dillon was asking. *"We lost Blue One, Over."*

Takahashi. Dillon shook his head in denial. Not a kid he'd worked with, trained with, laughed with. Dillon inwardly lashed himself, thinking of things he could have done to change what had happened. He could have found somewhere else for the platoon to dig in . . . or kept them further back . . . or . . . or a dozen different options, any one of which could have resulted in Ben Takahashi still being alive now.

The Steel commander abruptly ceased second-guessing himself. He knew that if he had it all to do over, he'd make the same decisions given the same tactical situation. But he didn't have to feel good about it.

"Roger, Steel Five, pass the report up . . . Guideons, continue to observe your sectors. Each platoon stay in your hide positions. As rehearsed, I want a company volley fire at twenty-five hundred meters when the enemy hits the obstacle belt. Until then, I don't want anyone pulling up to engage and giving away our position. Acknowledge."

Each platoon answered in turn. They were as ready as they were going to be.

The friendly artillery picked up again after having been silent for ten minutes. The guns must have been moving. After the field artillery fired their missions, survival for them meant displacing quickly to a new firing position before the enemy pinpointed their location. Utilizing radar, both sides could track the trajectory of incoming shells and trace them back to their point of origin—the firing batteries. It wasn't a good idea to hang around too long after shooting a mission.

The duet now playing out between the friendly artillery and advancing enemy force was strangely fascinating to observe. The overhead whistling opened the card. This was followed by an eruption in the face of the earth thousands of meters to the Americans' front. The enemy vehicles in the vicinity of the impact would jerk right or left, slow down or speed up, or simply keep coming. It all depended on the discipline of their crews. Except for the sound of the rounds as they passed overhead, the entire ballet was in silence until a few seconds after impact, at which time the sound finally carried back to the Steel soldiers, a dull, rumbling roar.

"Bick . . ."

"Yeah, boss."

"Your station good?"

"Roger, sir. We're ready to rock and roll. And, sir . . . sorry about Lieutenant Takahashi. He was a good man."

Dillon swallowed hard and continued focusing on the approaching swarm of armored vehicles to the north. "Roger."

As he watched the horde moving south, a T-72 attracted the attention of one of the downrange WAMs. A sublet could just be discerned as it flew in a trajectory over the Iraqi tank after the unfortunate vehicle had activated one of the mine detectors. Moments later the sublet's IR sensor, detecting the tank, fired an explosively formed penetrator that streaked into the top of the T-72's thin top armor. This process repeated itself a couple of times as Dillon watched. Finally the Iraqis, recognizing the cause of these top-down attacks, began giving the WAMs they could see a wide birth.

The easternmost Iraqi tanks passed one of Team Mech's TRPs. Set out at thirty-seven hundred meters, the markers let Nelson Bowers's men know that enemy vehicles in the vicinity of the panels were within range of his team's TOW missiles. Nothing yet. Dillon continued to observe. Suddenly blurs could be seen streaking from the Team Mech position. They all terminated in the vicinity of the approaching armor. Multiple explosions followed.

The men in the Steel battle position closely tracked the tanks and BMPs as the forefront of the Republican Guard attack headed their way. Because of dust and distance, they didn't notice as a company of BMP-2's pulled out of the main axis of attack, each armed with AT-5 antitank missiles capable of outdistancing the Team Mech TOWs by over 200 meters. Nelson Bowers's gunners, because of the rolling terrain, also did not see the threat arraying itself against them. The Mech gunners were so focused on whittling down the numbers attacking towards Steel that the small puffs of smoke signifying AT-5 launches went unnoticed until four of the Bradleys were hit.

Dillon looked east towards Bowers's position at the first explosion. As he watched, the nearest Bradley's rear door flew open. Two soldiers, both in flames, stag-

gered out of the deathtrap. The question of whether
they lived or died was settled when a TOW missile in
the vehicle detonated, causing a series of sympathetic
explosions in the rear of the vehicle that disintegrated
the Bradley and everything in its immediate vicinity.

Searching for the culprits, Dillon could barely see
the BMPs as the Iraqi commander backed his firing
line down to prepare for a second volley. *"Mech Six,
Mech Six, you've got a company of BMPs at your two
o'clock! I say again, two o'clock!"*

Some of the Team Mech crews, realizing the threat,
had already retreated into their fighting positions to
get out of the AT-5s' reach. The rest of the team
quickly followed their lead.

"Tiger Six, Mech Six," Bowers called over the task
force command net. *"My slant is now four and six.
Four Mike-Twos destroyed by AT-5 fire. . . .*

*"Break . . . my FSO is calling an immediate suppres-
sion mission on the enemy location, but until it goes
in, we're going to have to hunker down, over."*

"Roger, Mech Six. Tiger Six out." Estes agreed,
knowing he'd have to conserve as much combat power
as he could for the fighting in the days to come. Vehicles he could eventually replace, the trained crews
were much tougher to come by.

The unmistakable crack of an M1A1 cannon split
the stillness to Dillon's left. *What the fuck!* He'd have
somebody's balls for this.

"White, Steel Six. Who's engaging?"

Doc's voice was surprisingly steady under the circumstances. *"Six, White One. That's not us. The fires
are coming from Anvil, over."*

A mental picture of Malloy flashed through Dillon's
mind. *The stupid son of a bitch.*

*"Roger. Steel, continue to hold your fire. Going
higher."*

Dillon tried to remember the yoga exercises he'd
learned last year. Maybe they would calm him before
what was sure to be an ugly radio confrontation with
Malloy. After two seconds of effort he decided it just

wasn't his day to become one with the universe. Fucking Major Barnett. He should have known better than to listen to the operations officer's new age drivel. Worse, he'd paid good money for the instruction.

"Anvil Six, Steel Six, over."

Dillon could now see large numbers of 120mm projectiles flying north from Anvil's position. So far as he could tell, they'd hit nothing.

He tried again. *"Anvil Six, Steel Six, over."*

A voice shaking with excitement finally answered Dillon's call. *"Steel Six, Anvil Six. If you haven't noticed, I'm a little busy."*

Dillon rolled his eyes and tried to keep the sarcasm from his voice. *"Anvil Six, Steel Six. I noticed. You're wasting ammo and giving away your position. Hold your fire until they close."*

"Steel Six, Anvil Six. I don't intend to let them get that close. You worry about your sector, I'll worry—"

Estes, monitoring the exchange between his subordinates, cut them off. *"Anvil Six, Tiger Six. What range are you engaging at, over?"*

After a short pause, Malloy answered. *"Four thousand meters, over."*

"Anvil Six, Tiger Six. You will hold fire until the enemy closes to at least three thousand meters. Acknowledge."

"Tiger Six, our M1A1s are capable of hitting targets well past—"

"Acknowledge, over." The fury in Estes's voice dripped across the net.

"This is Anvil Six. WILCO. Hold fire until the enemy closes to three thousand meters."

Thank God, thought Dillon. *"This is Steel Six, returning to company command push, out."*

Colonel Hassan Abdulamir watched his battalions attack from an elevated position to the north. He'd seen the easternmost battalion being engaged by anti-tank missiles. While the battalion suffered a few losses, they had inflicted more on the enemy forces.

The American TOWs were out of the fight for now. Abdulamir nodded to himself. The Americans, outnumbered, could not afford to continue suffering such losses.

Unfortunately, the recon effort in this sector hadn't been as effective as it had been farther west. He scanned to the west for the Bradleys they had been engaging. Nothing. Wait . . . tank fires. Yes, definitely tank main guns, but the infidels were hitting nothing. And he now knew where the next company in the Yankee line was.

Looking between the company positions, the colonel made his decision. Reaching for his radio, Abdulamir called his battalion commanders. After he had them all on the radio, he issued their final orders. There was a large gap in the American line between their mixed team in the east and the tanks in the west. No one was perfect. Unfortunately, every commander at some point was tasked to cover more terrain than he effectively could. When it happened, the commander had to overextend his forces to carry out his mission. This left gaps. Such was the case with the Americans in their current battle position—obviously a case of too much ground and too few forces.

Colonel Abdulamir had identified the gap, a seam between American forces, and now his brigade would make the division's penetration through it. As he looked closer at the area, he could see the obstacle belt his recon elements had reported. Wire and mines. That would slow their momentum temporarily, but not for too long. He began arranging for the smoke that would be necessary to mask their breaching effort, and called his engineers to prepare them to come forward once the smokescreen was built sufficiently. Between his artillery, tanks, and BMPs, his forces would keep the American units occupied long enough to exploit the weak point in their defense and make the penetration. After all, without combat power facing them across the obstacle, it really wasn't an obstacle, was it?

* * *

Dillon saw the majority of the Republican Guard brigade shift its attack, heading straight south toward his position. The lead vehicles were thirty-five hundred meters out. He couldn't engage the vehicles yet, not with the lethal mass and shock effect that he wanted. They'd continue to wait, letting the Iraqis move nearer, and then hit them when they closed within optimum main gun range.

"Bick . . . range."

The gunner kept his sight on the lead vehicle in the closest pack of Iraqi vehicles and thumbed the laser range finder. The green LCD figure that appeared in his sight picture refreshed itself to reflect the current distance between C-66 and the tank in its sights. "Three thousand meters."

"Count it down every hundred meters from here out."

"Roger."

Hearing the pneumatic *swoosh* of the ammunition door, Dillon looked across the turret at Hunter. The loader was conducting one last check of his 120mm rounds, ensuring he had his main gun ammunition exactly where and how he wanted it. Satisfied, Hunter moved his knee away from the door's activation switch, allowing it to close. He looked at Dillon and gave a thumbs-up.

Dillon nodded. Good. He was on the ball and didn't look too stressed out. Hopefully he himself looked as calm.

"Twenty-nine hundred," called Bickel.

Colonel Hassan Abdulamir watched his supporting force approach the enemy obstacle. The artillery-delivered smoke had landed successfully between each of the identified enemy forces and the point in the obstacle belt where he intended to breach. With no enemy eyes able to see them, his forces would quickly clear a way through the wire and mines.

It was Steel's fight. Both Team Mech and Anvil were severely hampered by the smokescreen, despite the thermal systems that were supposed to cut through such obscurants. Hopefully the sun and rising heat would dissipate the smoke quickly, but as Dillon often preached to his lieutenants, "Hope in one hand, shit in the other . . . see which one fills up first." They would have to carry out the defense themselves for now.

"Twenty-seven hundred meters, sir." The timber of Bickel's voice was rising.

"Roger." Sweat ran traces down Dillon's forehead, cutting rivulets into the dust coating his face. As he watched the enemy formation continue to close on their position, he hoped that the company's tanks were dug in well enough to blend with the desert floor. It was the little things that could give away their position—a tank whose crew had forgotten to tie down their antennas; excess sand piled around a fighting position; a pair of goggles on top of a CVC helmet reflecting the morning sun into an alert Iraqi vehicle commander's eyes. Any one of these things could tip their hand. *Just a little closer* . . .

"Twenty-six hundred!"

Dillon saw roughly sixty vehicles pulling into support-by-fire positions to watch over the Iraqi engineers as they prepared to breach the obstacle belt. Four to one against them. But the enemy didn't know they were here, so surprise would be on their side. And once they closed, there was nowhere for the Iraqis to hide. There was nothing but open desert around them.

"I have over a platoon of tanks at twenty-five hundred meters, Avenue of Approach One, vicinity TRP Charlie-One. More vehicles approaching TRPs Charlie-Two and Charlie-Three. There's a buttload of the fuckers out there, sir."

Time to buy the baby some new shoes. *"All Steel elements, Steel Six. Two rounds sabot . . . at my command . . . Tophat, tophat, tophat!"*

Abdulamir could not be prouder of his brigade. They moved with precision as they set up the breach—

by far the most complex of military ground operations. The smoke was in. Two battalions were now moving into their final positions to overwatch the obstacle with direct fires. Once these support-by-fire battalions were set, events would move rapidly. The engineers would move in, breaching lanes in the obstacle belt. Once the lanes were in, his assault battalion would attack through the obstacle from their current position, two kilometers to the north, and secure the far side. Colonel Abdulamir would then lead the rest of the brigade through to hold the shoulders of the penetration open for the Tawakalna's Third Brigade. Third Brigade would then continue the attack into the Americans' rear.

The commander felt a sudden chill, thinking of his sister brigade. *Where were they?* The last time he'd spoken to their commander, he was fifteen minutes behind Abdulamir's own Second Brigade. He had tried calling again to send an update on the location the breach was going in, but had gotten only static.

He considered once again waiting until they'd reestablished contact to force the penetration. No. He couldn't let his unit's momentum be broken. They would hold the breach until Third Brigade arrived. Besides, General Hamza had made it quite clear that they were to stop their attack only on his order, not for any other reason. Abdulamir had gotten the distinct impression that the commander was under a bit of pressure from Baghdad.

Abdulamir knew that it should be short work once their forces broke into the Americans' rear area. The enemy simply did not have enough combat power to stop them. From past experience, he knew the Kuwaitis would be of little or no value to the Americans. Abdulamir was surprised they were not already on the road to Saudi with their skirts between their knees.

The sporadic American artillery was having little effect on his force, making it clear no unfriendly eyes could see them. He keyed his radio to move his engineers forward.

*   *   *

Dillon gave his tanks five seconds from the final tophat call to pull out of their holes, stop, and place a final lay on their targets. It was the longest five seconds of his life, knowing that his entire company was now visible to the Iraqis facing them.

As C-66 rocked to a stop, Dillon looked through his extension and saw the fire control system reticle come to rest on a T-72. *Time's up, asshole. "Fire!"*

The colonel watched as the sinister-looking American tanks appeared from the desert floor. Three more pulled from behind the scattered boulders to the south of the obstacle. Sabots streaked from the enemy tank cannons simultaneously, all heading on a dead line for his forces. In horrified fascination Abdulamir counted as thirteen of his combat vehicles went up in flames. He felt tricked, violated somehow, losing so many men so fast.

As the Americans prepared their second volley, the more alert T-72 crews opened fire. While the Russian-designed guns on the T-72s weren't as accurate at twenty-five hundred meters as the Abrams, the distance was within their effective range. One of the Abrams that had taken up position in the stand of rocks sustained a catastrophic hit, smoke and flame billowing into the sky. Another sagged on its tracks with a mobility hit. It would be going nowhere. In defiance the wounded tank fired again, destroying the T-72 that had damaged it. Another sabot round from his forces hit the Abrams and smoke began to escape from its hatches, along with the tank's crewmen. The fortuitous turn of events did not last, however.

The eleven M1s remaining in the fight threw another volley at his exposed forces, then another seconds later. A quick count told Colonel Abdulamir that he had lost close to thirty tanks and BMPs in less than a minute, almost half of his brigade's strength.

It was time for Dillon to stop worrying about fighting his tank and start looking at how the company was doing. "Okay, Tommy. Get us back in the hole. Bick, fire and adjust."

"Roger, moving back," called Thompson. C-66 backed up, reared skyward, and slid into its hiding position.

"I've got the gun, sir," called Sergeant Bickel.

"Roger, I'm going up to take a look around."

Dillon climbed into his cupola and threw his binos to his face. Trying to see the big picture through a tank sight was difficult. Even in wide field of view, only segments of the battlefield could be seen.

As Dillon watched from his position behind First Platoon, he saw Wyatt's tanks pull from their holes and throw a volley of rounds toward a cluster of retreating vehicles. Dillon watched as an Iraqi T-72 was hit just below the turret line on its side. The entire turret, including the gun tube, flipped a hundred feet into the air. It looked like a giant frying pan turning end over end.

Colonel Abdulamir correctly surmised that it was time to withdraw his forces. The position was too exposed and the Americans would continue to overmatch his combat power. If he could save what was left of his forces in the support by fire positions and consolidate them with the assault battalion waiting north of them, he would still have a significant combat force to draw into the fight later when the Third Brigade of the Tawakalna arrived. Lifting his radio, he called his battalion commanders: *"All units withdraw now. Regroup at the assault position."*

The Iraqis were pulling back. Dillon saw a mass of vehicles to the north, just beyond main gun range. It had to be the assault force that had been waiting for the breach to go in. He made a mental note of the location and looked at his map, placing a finger on a blue cross with an alphanumeric note next to it. Great. Dumphy already had a preplotted target on the position.

"Steel Fist, Steel 6."

"Steel Fist."

"This is Six. I've got thirty-plus tanks and BMPs, vicinity target Alpha Sierra four four zero three. What's left of their support-by-fire element is working its way back to the same location. Fire the group target. Over."

"This is Steel Fist. Already done. We should be receiving a shot call momentarily, over."

I love that guy, thought Dillon. *"Roger. Steel Six, out."*

"Identify tank," Dillon heard Bickel call over the intercom. "Driver, move out."

Dillon was thrown backward into his hatch as Sergeant Bickel guided C-66 out of its hole to engage the target. Tracing the gun tube's orientation, Dillon saw their intended victim. A T-72 had reversed course and headed north. Its main gun was still oriented south, however. More than that, it was pointing at *them*. Just as they were about to level off to engage the Iraqi tank, their own mount ground to a halt. C-66 was stuck halfway out of its hole, pointing into the air.

Dillon keyed the intercom. "Thompson! What the fuck, over."

The crew could hear the effort of their driver in the forward compartment. "Transmission . . . stuck. Stand by. I'm . . . working on it."

With the front of the tank obstructing his view, Dillon had to lean far out over the right side in order to get a look downrange. Pulling his binoculars up, he saw the Iraqi tank stop and make a slight gun tube adjustment. The stricken American tank was too tempting a target for them to ignore. *Oh . . . shit.* "Bick, can you engage from here?"

"Negative! I'm looking at the sky until we level out."

A boom to Dillon's right caused him to turn. One of his First Platoon crews had seen C-66's predicament and snapped a shot at the enemy tank zeroing in on Dillon and his men. Looking back toward the Iraqi T-72, Dillon saw the shot had been a near miss. The enemy tank was now maneuvering to get out of direct fire range.

* * *

"That should keep the bastards off the Old Man's ass long enough for them to get clear," said Staff Sergeant Rudy Vallejo, the tank commander of C-12. "Driver, back up and get us to our alternate position. That's our third shot from up here. We need to get down."

"Too late, Vee," said his gunner as he peered into his sight. "Dude's wingman just showed, and he looks hungry."

Swinging his binoculars up and in a line with the gun tube, fresh sweat popped from Vallejo's brow. The NCO knew the smart thing was to get his tank back in the hole, but a glance in Dillon's direction confirmed that C-66 was still a sitting duck. "Roger, engage him."

"On the way . . ."

C-12's cannon cracked. The velocity of the sabot exiting the gun tube erupted the sand in front of the Abrams into a cloud of dust.

"All right, get us out of here, *move!*"

Dillon saw the second Iraqi tank explode as the red streak that was a sabot round from C-12 reached it. He thanked himself for the hours he'd forced his crews to undergo gunnery training back in Colorado, to include midnights in the gunnery simulator when that was all that was available. The depleted uranium dart hit the Iraqi tank with the force of an eleven-ton truck moving seventy miles per hour, all of the force concentrated into an area less than an inch in diameter.

"Thompson, any progress down there?"

"Working it, sir!" came the driver's reply. "You bitch," Thompson continued as he labored unseen in the driver's compartment. "I treat you . . . good. I . . . baby you. And you pull . . . this shit! Why I oughta—"

The tank shook as the force of a nearby explosion rolled over it.

Dillon switched his attention between the tank that

had fired, the returning Iraqi crew that Vallejo had near-missed earlier, and the tank that was now in flames . . . C-12. "Goddamn it," he said softly to himself.

The Iraqi crew, the immediate threat gone, turned back to C-66.

Dillon saw the 125mm gun slowly swing their way. "Brace yourselves!"

The sabot scoured their turret with a sound like giant talons raking over steel.

Thompson's voice over the intercom rose in intensity. "You . . . piece . . . of . . . shit!" A horrible grinding sounded from the M1A1's transmission as the tank rocked forward and leveled out in a cloud of dust.

The crew of the T-72 didn't know what was wrong with the American tank, nor did they care. It was an outlet for the frustrations and fears that had gripped them over the past minutes.

"Target!" cried the Iraqi tank commander, seeing sparks fly as their round struck the side of the accursed Americans. "Put another round into him, gunner. I've seen no secondary explosions."

"Prepared to fire, waiting for a round!" called the gunner, keeping his sights on the stricken tank. Unlike the American crews, who used a soldier to feed the forty-pound main gun rounds into the breech, their T-72 utilized an autoloader. When a round was expended, another was automatically fed into the breech. While it had its upsides, the autoloader was slow. It seemed to be taking forever at the moment.

The tank commander's eyes grew as he saw the steel monster that was their target lunge into the air and settle in a storm of dust. "The tank is moving! *Hurry!*"

"I can see that . . . waiting for the round to be fed . . . all right, ready!"

"Fire!"

C-66 leveled out and the dust began to clear.

Thompson was in the middle of congratulating him-

self when he felt their tank rock as Sergeant Bickel
fired. Throwing the tank in reverse, he saw a puff of
smoke from the T-72. Thompson rotated his twist-grip
throttles to the stops in an attempt to gain
acceleration.

The two rounds passed within a foot of one another,
one going south, the other north. The Iraqi sabot over-
shot its target by inches. The American round struck
the T-72 below the turret ring, lifting the tank two
feet off the ground and spinning it ninety degrees.

The Iraqi tank commander screamed at his crew
over the intercom, flames beginning to lick at his feet.
"Fire! Get out! Everyone out now!"

Hearing no response from his gunner, he looked
across the turret toward his longtime friend. They'd
been together since the last days of the Iran-Iraq War,
enjoying many good times and enduring hardships together. A piece of shrapnel, ripped from their engine
as the depleted uranium projectile passed through it,
had pierced his eye. The gunner now jerked spasmodi-
cally in death.

An overpowering stench mixed with the smells of
cordite, diesel fuel, and sweat, creating a sickening
odor in the tight confines of the crew compartment.
The tank commander realized it was the stench of the
dead man's bowels releasing and retched into his own
lap. Further coherent thought fled as he grasped the
handle of his hatch to escape the deathtrap.

Dillon watched the enemy tank lurch to a stop,
smoke spilling from its hatches. He shook his head,
watching the helpless vehicle. They couldn't take any
chances. Just because the tank was immobilized didn't
mean that it couldn't still engage them or some other
friendly. He didn't intend to lose anyone else today.

"Reengage."

Bickel continued watching the doomed tank through

the sight, his reticle lying dead center over it. "Roger. Identified."

Hunter already had a sabot round in the tube. The loader threw the arming handle back and moved from the breech's recoil path. "Up!"

"Driver, move out."

C-66 lunged forward, this time all systems functioning perfectly.

"Driver, stop!" Sergeant Bickel had been looking through his auxiliary sight. Once he saw the horizon instead of the sky, he knew his optics were ready and switched back to his electronic sight.

"I've still got him, sir. . . ."

Looking through the sight extension, Dillon saw the reticle come to rest on the Iraqi tank.

Should he allow the enemy crew a few seconds to escape? Were they even now attempting to reengage C-66? Questions flooded Dillon's mind as he watched the crippled vehicle smolder.

"Fire," said Dillon quietly.

The Iraqi tank commander threw his hatch open and began scrambling from the burning vehicle. As one leg cleared the hatch, a giant hand seemed to lift him from the turret and throw him high into the air. He felt no pain, only an odd sensation of weightlessness as he heard the sound of the second sabot round impacting his tank. He hit the hard desert floor with a dull thud thirty feet from his burning vehicle.

His first sensation was an awareness that he could not move his limbs. He didn't know that this was because his spine had snapped on impact with the ground. The tank commander also noticed a peculiar odor. *Allah, have mercy on me,* he thought, finally realizing that he was on fire.

Slowly and painfully he turned his head southward, searching for his Angel of Death. He caught a final glimpse of the American tank as it slid into the earth, hidden once more. It was the last thing he saw because the flames had now worked their way up his body and above his shoulders, finally devouring his face and eyes.

Dillon and Bickel watched the death throes of the Iraqi tank silently. Only they could see the tank commander's death throes. Both had the same thought— *That was almost us.* After a few seconds, Dillon broke the spell.

"Crew report."

Each crew member checked in, calling out the status of their systems. The tank was good.

"Bick, do you see anything else?"

The gunner took his eyes from his sight and looked back, shaking his head. "Negative, not in weapons range."

He turned to the loader and gestured upward. "Hunter, go topside. Check the exterior for damage."

The loader quickly unsnapped his communication cord from his CVC, grasped the lip of his hatch, and heaved himself out of the turret. Dillon yelled after him. "And stay the hell down!"

He turned his attention to the driver. "Tommy, as soon as we get out of this mess, get a mechanic onboard and check out the transmission. I don't *ever* want another close call like that."

A sheepish voice replied. "Roger."

"Okay, Sergeant Bickel, continue to scan. I'm going up for a look around."

"I've got it, sir."

Dillon climbed into his cupola and put out a guideons call.

"This is Red One," Bluto replied lethargically. *"Slant three. Engaged and destroyed eleven tanks, four BMPs, over."*

"White Four. Slant is three. Engaged and destroyed nine tanks, five BMPs, over."

"Blue Four. Slant three. Engaged and destroyed seven tanks, three BMPs, over."

Dillon listened stoically as the reports came in.

They'd been in combat less than an hour and already he'd lost four tanks. He wouldn't know how many men that translated to until the first sergeant consolidated the medical reports. He knew Vallejo and his men were gone. Takahashi's crew as well.

"Steel Five. Engaged and destroyed two tanks, one BMP, over."

Dillon knew Mason would be jotting the figures in his ever-present notebook. *"Roger, Steel Five. Add three tanks to your total and forward the report higher. Make sure they're working an ammunition resupply. Also, find out what the plan is to get us some tanks and crews, over."*

"This is Steel Five, wilco. Going higher."

Colonel Hassan Abdulamir was a good commander. Because of this, he did not dwell on his personal fate. He was sure that his superiors would not look kindly upon today's results. He had for all intents and purposes lost two combat battalions—two elite Republican Guard battalions—to what appeared to be a single company. Six companies of tanks and mechanized infantry. All lost, most dead. As he watched vehicles struggle to reach the assault force's position and its promise of safety, a tear ran slowly down his face. So many men.

If only he could get some fire support. He was sure that another thirty-minute prep on the American company, now that their location was pinpointed, would be enough to ensure success. But his direct support guns had disappeared from the radio in midtransmission. He supposed American counterbattery fires, most probably MLRS rockets, had hit them. At any rate, he had no artillery. Nor any air support. And as usual, the Americans ruled the skies.

For now, he would not send more of his troops forward to certain death. Abdulamir wiped the tear from his face with a deliberate gesture. There was nothing he could do for those already lost, but he still had over a battalion remaining under his command.

Those men could still do battle another day. It was time to save what he could of his force.

"*Steel Fist, Steel Six, over.*"

"*Steel Fist.*"

Dillon was about to blow a gasket. They'd destroyed two-thirds of a Republican Guard brigade and now could only sit and watch as the last battalion was practically laagering just out of main gun range. The only tool available to him was indirect fires, and he couldn't seem to get them, despite the fact that he allegedly had priority.

"*Steel Fist, Steel Six. Status on fire mission, target four four zero three, over.*"

"*This is Steel Fist. Brigade shifted the guns to 2-35's sector for a few minutes, apparently they're encountering some problems over there. We just got priority back and should be receiving splash notification any . . . stand by . . .*"

Jesus, thought Dillon. *Couldn't this ever be easy? Just once?*

"*Steel Six, Steel Fist . . . shot, over.*"

"*Shot, out.*"

While he waited for the artillery rounds to complete their time of flight, Dillon opened the sponson box to his right and removed his canteen. He took a quick pull, rinsing his mouth and spitting it over the side of the tank. He then allowed himself the luxury of drinking for the first time in the past hour and a half. Reaching forward, he removed the OD green handkerchief always tied to the base of his .50 caliber mount. Pouring water on the rag, he rubbed it across his face, eyes, and neck.

Quickly stowing the canteen and handkerchief, Dillon got back to business. Through his binoculars, he could clearly see over thirty enemy vehicles sitting just outside his company's direct fire range. His eyes came to rest on a BMP infantry fighting vehicle clustered with antennas—a sure sign that it was a command track. The figure in the top of the vehicle was looking

through binoculars as well, right at him. Slowly the
figure lowered his binoculars and rendered a salute to
Dillon, one warrior acknowledging to another that the
good fight had been fought. He then turned to the
growing number of vehicles behind him and gestured
north. They were displacing. *God, we're gonna lose
them.* Overhead, Dillon heard the much-anticipated
fire mission finally going in.

Dumphy's voice rang through Dillon's CVC.
"Splash, over."

Dillon continued to gaze at the mass of enemy vehicles while pushing his CVC's selector switch forward
to transmit. *"Splash, out."*

Colonel Hassan Abdulamir dropped his salute.
Somehow he'd known the figure standing opposite
him in the M1A1 turret was the American company
commander. He should hate the man for the death
and destruction he'd been responsible for, yet somehow he could not. Like himself, the American officer
was following orders and doing what was necessary to
ensure his unit's survival. Abdulamir felt more kinship
with that commander, a fellow soldier, than he did
with the generals and politicians in Baghdad.

The eyes of his men were upon him. He threw his
arm up and gestured north. It was time to leave this
place. A few ambulances would stay to collect the
wounded. If captured, at least they'd receive decent
treatment. The Gulf War had taught them that much
about the Americans.

As his track began its turn to the north, Abdulamir
heard the incoming artillery. It looked as though the
fickle Gods of War were not yet finished with him and
his men. . . .

Dillon watched with a touch of regret as the artillery
impacted in the middle of the enemy formation. The
Republican Guard commander had struck Dillon as
noble, even in the face of catastrophic defeat. After
the first volley of 155mm shells impacted, he tried to

see if the commander's vehicle had survived the barrage. He couldn't tell. Dozens of the Republican Guard vehicles that had survived Cold Steel's fires were black and burning now, survivors of one fight only to die in another. It was impossible to tell one vehicle from the next.

The Iraqis had brought fuel and ammunition forward to support their attack. The artillery fires had ignited those, adding their effects to the destruction. Dillon estimated a little over two companies' worth of vehicles scattered to the north still capable of movement. That would have to change. Slowly he reached for the transmit switch. *"Steel Fist, Steel Six. Tell the guns they're dead on . . . give me a repeat."*

Dumphy acknowledged the order and started the process of bringing more fire to bear on the decimated Second Brigade of the Tawakalna.

CHAPTER 10

_____

_____

Flirting with Disaster

"What's the good word, S3?" asked Jones.

Major Tom Proctor had just gotten off the radio and was annotating the latest information from the task forces onto his map. He looked up at Jones. "Good and bad, sir. The Iron Tigers have for all intents and purposes destroyed the lead enemy brigade in the east, but they lost some combat power . . . four tanks and four Bradleys. We're still trying to establish where the trailing Iraqi brigade is. Our scouts haven't made contact with it yet."

Jones opened the troop door on the back of the M2 and turned around before stepping out. "I've got something on that."

He called over the intercom to O'Keefe. "Hey, O'Keefe . . . don't move this thing. I'm out back."

O'Keefe's voice came back with the tone of a parent reasoning with a child. "Roger, sir, but you should really stay inside the vehicle. Having a smoke isn't worth the brigade losing you." Since the death of Kelly, he'd taken his position as Jones's personal bodyguard very seriously.

"Damn it, O'Keefe! I'm not having a smoke. I gotta take a leak."

"Roger. Let me know when you're back inside."

Jones reached into a pocket for his cigarettes and

Zippo. Pulling them free, he looked at Proctor and shrugged.

"Okay, Tom. I just got off the phone with the Joint Task Force headquarters. They're working the deep fight. As soon as the trail brigade moved into MLRS rocket range this morning, they hammered it—hard." Reaching into the back of the Bradley, he pointed to a spot on the map thirty kilometers to the north. "Right here. We got real lucky. A satellite caught them in the open refueling. Best we can tell, they lost a company of tanks and two companies of mechanized infantry, about twenty-five percent of their combat vehicles."

Jones looked to Proctor again and smiled. "The good news doesn't stop there. Fifteen minutes ago, a flight of F-15E Strike Eagles opened up on the lead units of the brigade after it had regrouped. The initial battle damage assessment was a company of tanks destroyed, but you know how that goes. Figure they killed a platoon and slowed 'em up some. They've got another flight on station moving in for another strike."

Reaching to the map and Task Force 2-77's position, Jones summarized. "So between the rocketeers and flyboys, the trail brigade is running a little behind schedule—but they're still coming. Those guys will be pushing hard to exploit the penetration they think is going to be here."

Proctor sat a moment in silence, absorbing the information, then looked to Jones. "Okay, that takes care of what's going on with the Tawakalna, but what about the other two divisions reported moving south from Baghdad?"

Taking a deep draw on his cigarette, Jones looked to Proctor and shook his head. "I can't worry about them, Tom. Not yet. The only way we're going to win this thing is to take them down a piece at a time."

The 3rd Brigade had known this was an uphill battle from the start. According to doctrine, they could handle one enemy division when they defended. They knew with their soldiers, equipment, and air support, they could probably do a bit better. But three divisions? That was nine-to-one odds. Rumors of the fresh units from the States cheered the troops, but the fact was that the reinforcements likely wouldn't be in theater in time to make a difference. It was up to 3rd Brigade.

Again reaching to the map, Jones pointed to a red box with an oval inside it, two *Xs* on top. The box was bumped directly against a blue box that represented 3rd Brigade. "We've got a Republican Guard armor division in our face *now*. So far we've destroyed sixty to seventy percent of that division. Until the Tawakalna is finished, it receives our undivided attention."

He indicated Task Force 2-77's position in the center. "I feel good here. Scratch one bad-guy brigade. The Two says that a couple of command and control vehicles and about a platoon's worth of armor is all that made it out of the Iron Tigers' engagement area. Scouts reported them limping north." Pointing to 2-35 Armor's front, he continued. "This is my primary concern. The brigade-minus that is conducting the supporting attack to the west. I haven't heard jack shit lately on this one."

Reaching over with a black marker, Proctor struck a line through the Republican Guard unit facing 2-77 Armor, a casual gesture that meant more than five hundred men would never see their native land again. Extending his arm to the left, Proctor tapped the symbol indicating the enemy brigade attacking in the west. "We've shifted all indirect fires to Task Force 2-35 now that the lead echelon of the enemy's main effort has been destroyed." Proctor paused and shook his head. "Sir, it doesn't look good over there. I spoke to the 2-35 commander a few minutes ago. He said, 'Tell the boss that these bastards of mine have performed magnificently, and are still fighting, though I don't know how,' unquote."

Proctor held up, unsure of how far he could go with Jones. "Sir, they're done. We might consider moving some forces from 2-8's position."

Jones remained silent.

Proctor continued. "I just don't know how much more Mace can take, sir. They were shelled all night, fought off a battalion attack after that, and are fighting two more battalions now."

Jones looked as if a knife were twisting inside of him as he shook his head and replied. "I can't pull anything from 2-8's sector, Tom. They're already short from giving up a team as the brigade reserve. That puts them at seventy-five percent strength. If that northern brigade gets a wild hair and attacks east . . . you get the picture. No, they stay where they are."

He pointed at a spot directly behind 2-35 Armor. "Back to the reserve. Tell them to go here. Their mission is to ensure nothing, *nothing,* gets past them."

Jones knew that his S3 meant well. If he survived this war, Proctor would one day understand that commanders didn't always like the decisions they were forced to make. He could teach men like Proctor how to make those decisions—now if he could only teach them how to sleep peacefully afterward. He hadn't mastered that one yet himself and never really expected to.

"Tom, we've got to hold out a little longer. I saved some good news. Early indications are—and I stress early—that the other two Republican Guard divisions will be held up for at least forty-eight hours. The CINC threw everything he had at them last night, short of nukes, plus hit the command and control facilities around Baghdad."

Proctor brightened for the first time. "You think the Tawakalna commander will keep throwing forces into the fight, knowing that the other two divisions aren't going to be here to support him? Why not just pull everyone back and wait?"

Jones smiled and lifted an eyebrow. He crushed the

cigarette, which was nothing more than a smoking filter at this point, and threw it outside the track. "There's the rub. We don't think the Tawakalna commander knows how bad it is. Between the cruise missile and air strikes hitting their command and control nodes and our intel folks jamming anything remotely resembling a broadcast from the north, we're betting that the word never reached him. Odds are, without orders to the contrary, he'll continue his attack as planned."

Proctor nodded. Like Jones, he hoped the reports were accurate. They could use a couple of days to lick their wounds.

The brigade command net flared. *"Striker Six, Mace Six, over."* The sounds of close battle, of tank cannon and artillery, could be heard all too clearly in the background of the calling station.

Jones snatched up the handset. By the sound of the 2-35 Armor commander's voice, both knew that it wasn't good news.

"This is Striker."

"Sir, all hell's breaking loose here. I'm down to a slant of one-zero and four—and those ten tanks and four Bradleys are strung out from hell to high water along my front." The transmission was interrupted for a moment as metal on metal was heard. Cahill's tank was taking fire. *"The enemy is pushing what looks like three companies through our east side, mainly tanks. I'm moving what I can behind me now to cut them off."* There was a pause from the other station. *"Also, I just called for final protective fires now."*

It was indeed as bad as it sounded. Final protective fires were called only when the enemy was at your throat and your position was in imminent danger of being overrun. It was a sheet of steel rain dropped directly in front of a friendly position by every available tube of artillery, a last-ditch effort to allow the friendly force to move back. The men manning the 155mm howitzers would literally keep shoving rounds and powder bags into their big guns until told to stop firing or their tubes melted, whichever came first.

"This is Striker Six, roger. The reserve will be closing behind your position anytime now. How close are the Iraqis? Over."

As the 2-35 commander keyed his radio, the background fighting sounded as if it were intensifying. *"What color turban do you want? I have a good view of about three different styles. Sir, they're in our face. We'll try to hold long enough for the reserve—"*

The transmission cut out midsentence.

"Mace Six, say again. You cut out."

Nothing.

"Mace Six, come in!"

White noise.

Jones threw the handset in frustration. "Damn it!" Moving toward the front of the Bradley's compartment, he patted Proctor on the back. "Get ready, Three. We're moving."

"Roger. I'll try to get 2-35's XO on the horn." He yelled at Jones's back. "Sir, where are we going?"

Jones looked over his shoulder as he slid into the turret. "Forward, Tom. Forward."

Proctor nodded and went to work on the radios.

Seeing Colonel Jones entering the turret, O'Keefe ducked from the Bradley commander's hatch and moved left into the gunner's hatch. Jones climbed into his position and plugged in his CVC.

"Where to, sir?"

Jones pointed to a spot on O'Keefe's map. O'Keefe marked it and called directions to the driver. The two men stood in silence a few moments, bodies swaying as the large fighting vehicle moved rapidly across the barren desert landscape.

O'Keefe sensed his commander's unease. He pulled his boom mike close to his lips to be heard over the wind and engine noise. "How are things going, sir?"

Jones continued looking forward as he replied,

"Could be worse, Sergeant O'Keefe, could be worse. Then again, they could be much better."

Anvil Battle Position, Northern Kuwait
22 October, 0750 Hours

"Roger, Tiger Three. Tiger Six, out."

After signing off with Dave Barnett, Estes made final adjustments to his companies' statuses and locations in a matrix he maintained on the border of his map. Putting away his marker, he took a few moments to examine his unit's current situation.

Team Knight was in the task force's reserve position three kilometers to the rear. The team was on standby in case combat forces were needed anywhere in the Iron Tiger sector. Knight had completed rearming and refueling after last night's counter-recon fight. Stuart was trying to give his men some rest for the follow-on fights that were sure to come. Estes shook his head, knowing that only the most exhausted soldiers would be able to sleep right now.

Steel was in the process of resupplying ammunition. The company wasn't critically short, but the smart move was to get it on the tanks now while they were in the midst of a lull in the battle. If they waited, a resupply truck could get hit en route, rounds could run short at exactly the wrong time, or a million other problems could arise. The priority for Steel was to get some replacement tanks and crews. They could fight with ten M1A1s, cutting the platoon strengths from four tanks each to three, but Estes knew they'd need the additional firepower soon. Same problem for Team Mech. As for Anvil, Malloy's company was still intact. The bad news was that the wadi system spilling into their flank from 2-35's sector was looking more and more ominous.

It sounded like the better part of an Iraqi battalion had just overrun the eastern portion of Task Force 2-35's BP. The assumption had to be made that all

American forces in that sector were combat ineffective and that the enemy force was continuing to move. But moving where? If they continued south, the brigade reserve would be in place to hammer them. If they slid east . . . again Estes's eyes looked to the wadi system. Well, no one ever said it was going to be easy.

As soon as he'd heard Cahill's report, Estes had called Malloy and instructed him to shift two platoons west to the position currently occupied by only himself and Muddy Waters. Now that they knew nothing large was going to hit Anvil's front, they could afford it. Dillon could move something left into Anvil's sector on the off chance that an enemy force attacked that way.

Where in the hell are those tanks? *"Anvil Six, Tiger Six, over."*

"Anvil Six, over."

Well, at least he was monitoring the radio. *"Anvil Six, SITREP on the elements moving to my location, over."*

"This is Anvil Six, uuuhhhh . . . stand by."

Estes made a concerted effort to remain calm.

Dan Malloy got on the company command net again, trying to get the two platoons moving toward Estes. He didn't need any more trouble with the commander. The problem was, no one seemed to be in a rush to follow his instructions. Before this deployment, when Malloy said "Jump," he was greeted by a "Roger! How high, sir?" Now . . . well, the only thing that he could think of was that the troops had heard about the previous night's events. Estes had come up here, undermining his authority, second-guessing his tactical decisions. Somehow, word of that must have gotten out. How else to explain the lack of enthusiasm from his men?

All things considered, Malloy was fairly pleased with the way things had worked out today. The Iraqis had gone the other way once they'd spotted his company of tanks in their well-prepared positions. He may have been a little off base with his initial tactical assessment, but things were definitely looking up now. If events continued to go well, Estes might even reconsider his rash outburst of last night—and the hasty decision that followed. Malloy smiled to himself. *I bet he'll do just that.* With that reassuring thought in mind, Malloy worked even harder to get the two platoons moving.

"White One, Blue One . . . Anvil Six."

"White One, over."

"Blue Four, over."

Malloy didn't attempt to hide his irritation. *"Blue Four, Anvil Six. I called Blue One . . . I want to speak to Blue One. Standing by."*

Blue's platoon sergeant held back the reply that was on the tip of his tongue. Monitoring the exchange, the platoon leader, who had been working his platoon's move on their internal frequency, hopped up to the company net.

"This is Blue One, over."

"Blue One, Anvil Six. Have I not made it clear that I want you on the company command net, not one of your assistants? Over."

"This is Blue One. I was attempting to . . ." The young lieutenant thought it over. *Screw it. There's nothing I can say that he'll listen to.* "Roger, Anvil Six."

"Then make it so in the future, mister. SITREP on your move."

"This is Blue One. We need five minutes. The fueler didn't make it to our position until twenty minutes ago. My last tank has completed fueling and we're almost ready to move, over."

Second Platoon continued with the bad news. *"This is White One. We're waiting for the fueler that's at Blue's position. Only one of the fuel trucks showed up. The other broke down en route. Do you want us to wait for it or move now, over."*

Malloy's terse reply was cut off as artillery fires began pounding the Anvil position.

*   *   *

Waters had monitored the exchange. His other radio was set to task force command so that he could maintain communication with his wingman, Estes.

As the artillery fell to their east, his gunner called over the intercom. "Sir! I've got dust to the northeast. It's coming out of the wadis—vicinity TRP Alpha-Two. Stand by . . . contact, tanks, northeast!"

Waters dropped into the turret and looked through his sight extension.

Oh, boy. The unmistakable shape of a large formation of armored vehicles could just be seen emerging from the cloud. "Got it. Let them close to thirty-seven hundred meters before engaging."

"Wilco."

Not having sufficient combat power to achieve mass on the approaching formation, Waters wanted to slow them down and start them thinking about their own mortality and personal relationships with Allah. His gunner was good. With go-to-war ammunition, manufactured to much higher specifications than the rounds they trained with on the gunnery ranges, they could start dealing some destruction well outside of three thousand meters. It might buy them a little time.

"Tiger Six, Anvil Five."

Staff Sergeant Ike McCloud, Estes's gunner, had just picked up the approaching formation and notified his boss.

"I've got them, Anvil Five. I've passed the contact higher. The task force now has priority of indirect fires. We're working on getting some artillery . . . break . . . Anvil Six, Tiger Six." Estes's patience with Malloy was gone. *"Anvil Six, Tiger Six. Get those platoons over here. Now!"*

No response.

Malloy ignored his commander's voice. His tank shook with the nearby impact of another in a series of artillery rounds. *This wasn't how it was supposed to be. . . .*

He called over his company command frequency. *"All Anvil elements, remain in place! Monitor your original sector. Acknowledge!"*

Each of the platoons, unable to monitor the events transpiring on the task force command net, in turn acknowledged receipt of the message.

Something inside Dan Malloy, something that had been a little twisted his entire life, which had bent significantly during the past twenty-four hours, finally snapped. Another shell impacted two hundred meters away. Malloy secured his hatch and sat down in the tank commander's seat, closing his eyes and squeezing them shut as tightly as he could. Crossing his arms over his chest, Malloy hugged himself and rocked back and forth. *Just make it go away, just make it go away, just make it go—*

"Anvil Six, Anvil Five, over!"

Inside the turret of A-66, Malloy shook his head in denial. No. If he didn't listen, it wouldn't be real.

"Sir," called Malloy's gunner, "the XO is calling you. Sir? Are you all right?"

The urgency in Waters's voice could not be missed. *"Captain Malloy! Captain Malloy! Answer the radio, sir!"*

Something in Waters's tone finally reached Malloy, touched the last vestiges of what had once made Dan Malloy want to be a leader of men. *"An . . . Anvil Six, over,"* he replied in a shaky voice.

"Anvil Six, Anvil Five. I've got twenty-plus tanks and BMPs closing on our position. We need those platoons! You've got to move them now, sir!"

In the darkness of the turret, Malloy shook his head wildly, cold sweat flying from his face. *"Negative, negative. You're looking at 2-35's sector! We're under attack. I need them here. Can't . . . can't send them."*

Waters calmed himself. Something was seriously wrong with Malloy, but he didn't have time to psychoanalyze the man. *"Sir, you're not under attack. The enemy is currently to my northwest. They're about to attack our flank. You've got nothing in front of you."*

No response.

Shit, thought Waters. *Why did I ever decide to become an officer?* "Sir, the artillery hitting your position is an attempt to keep you from reinforcing this flank. The enemy is trying to isolate us. . . . you've got to move those platoons, sir—now!"

A few moments later, Waters got his final message from his commander. *"Negative. Steel Five . . . Muddy . . . you guys will be okay. I just can't risk this command by sending them to you. Out."*

Waters sat back, incredulous. The tank reverberated as his gunner fired at the approaching formation. Next to them, HQ-66 fired their opening salvo. *How did it ever get this screwed up?* wondered Waters.

Hopping up to task force command, Waters called in the situation to Estes.

Rob Estes couldn't believe what he was hearing. He'd royally fucked up last night leaving Malloy in command. He shook his head. No need beating himself to death now. It was pointless.

Standing in his turret, binos to his face, Estes watched the artillery falling behind the attacking Republican Guard forces. *"Stand by, Anvil Five . . . Lightning, this is Tiger Six. Drop one thousand and fire for effect."*

The artillery would force the attackers to button up, making it more difficult for them to maintain command and control as drivers swerved around impact areas and the crews lost sight of one another in the dust and confusion. Further, the fires would degrade their communications systems as it shredded antennas off of some of the vehicles. They might even get lucky and take out a vehicle or two. What the indirect fires weren't going to do was *stop* the armored formation bearing down on them.

To the north, Estes saw a puff of smoke as an Iraqi BMP fired a wire-guided antitank missile in their direction. "Driver, back up! Back . . . back . . . stop! Gunner, fire and adjust!"

Mentally reviewing everything that was going on in his sector, Estes made his decision. He couldn't fight the task force, his tank, and Anvil. *"Anvil Five, Tiger Six. You're now in command of your company. You know what to do."*

It took a moment for the message to sink in. *"This is Anvil Five . . . roger."*

Looking north again to the location of the BMP, Estes saw several more had joined it—they were forming a firing line. Estes quickly saw their strategy. Use artillery to separate him and Waters from outside support. Continue the attack with the tanks to keep them occupied. Put BMPs outside of their M1A1s' main gun range and then take him and Waters out with the BMPs' AT-5 missiles. With a range of four thousand meters, the AT-5 missile gunners could sit back and pick them off. *Fuck that.* He wasn't going to make it easy for the bastards.

Estes called his Mortar Platoon. The unit's six 120mm tubes could fire high explosive rounds in ranges exceeding seven thousand meters—and they could do it fast. *"Thunder, Thunder, Tiger Six. Fire mission follows. Ten PCs in the open, grid . . ."*

Waters took a deep breath. How would the men of Anvil respond to his message? It went against everything they inherently believed in and fought for . . . against the fiber of what made America's military the envy of the world. Loyalty. Professionalism. Ethics. He knew he had no choice. Muddy bent his head as if in prayer. With great deliberateness, he began the transmission that would change Anvil Company forever. There would be no turning back after this.

"Guideons, Guideons, Anvil Five. Per Tiger Six's order, I am taking command of this company. Blue, move now to—"

A voice screamed over the radio. The message had restored a spark to Malloy. *"Waters, what is this? I'll court-martial you! This is my command! We're moving back to . . . to consolidate. Our position here is untena-*

ble. You will stay off of my net and report to me when we're complete with our withdrawal! Do you read me, over!?"

Waters ignored Malloy. *"Blue . . . move now. Acknowledge, over."*

Blue One inwardly struggled as he listened to the exchange between his immediate superiors. A smart kid, he was only two months out of the Armor Officer Basic Course at Fort Knox—but this scenario wasn't one of the classroom "What would you do, Lieutenant" exercises taught in the schoolhouse. The company commander's word was supposed to be like the word of God. Then again, Lieutenant Waters was the epitome of what he'd been led to believe an officer should be. What finally made the decision for the young platoon leader was his gut. Something was going on with Captain Malloy. Something . . . just wasn't right.

"This is Blue One. We're moving, time now."

"Blue One, Anvil Six. You aren't moving anywhere or it's your ass, mister!" Malloy interjected.

Waters hung his head in dejection. What the hell else was he supposed to do?

As if in answer to his question, a voice called over the radio. *"Anvil Five, Anvil Six-Golf."*

What the hell? Malloy's gunner?

"Anvil Five, over."

"This is Anvil Six-Golf. We monitored Tiger Six's transmission and confirm that you have the ball. We're prepared to follow your lead, over."

A million questions jumped into Waters's mind. No time. *"Roger, Anvil Six-Golf. Blue, move now."*

The response was immediate. *"Blue One, moving."*

"White, forget the fuel. Move to an attack by fire position to the right of Blue, oriented northwest. Acknowledge."

"White One, wilco."

Waters knew his company was going to be stretched thin on the right side. Switching to task force command, he called Dillon. *"Steel Six, Anvil Five, over."*

"Steel Six."

"This is Anvil Five. I'm repositioning my eastern two platoons to the far west side of our company position. . . . Can you cover our right flank? Over."

"This is Steel Six. Roger, we've got you covered. . . . Good luck, Anvil Six."

It took Waters a moment to realize Dillon had addressed him as a company commander. *"Roger, thanks. Out."*

In the turret of A-66, the situation had calmed. The gunner faced his former commander, the Beretta 9mm pistol in his hand pointed directly at Malloy's chest. "Now, sir, what I want you to do is hand your weapon to the loader. There's no need for things to get any uglier. I don't think any of us wants to see lead flying around inside of this turret. If need be, we'll tie you up and put you on the back of the tank in the bustle rack."

Another artillery round impacted near the tank, shaking the crew. Every man clearly heard the razor-sharp shrapnel from the 152mm high-explosive shell pinging against the steel exterior.

The gunner looked at Malloy seriously. "I don't think you'd like it out there, sir."

**3rd Brigade, 4th ID TAC, South of Anvil Battle Position
22 October, 0810 Hours Local**

The Bradley screamed across the desert floor in the direction of the approaching dust clouds. O'Keefe was irate and pointing into the turret. "Sir, get down! Inside the crew compartment! Now!"

Jones ignored his gunner as he tried to make out details to the north. It was just too far. Another couple of minutes. Movement to his right caught Jones's attention. Armored vehicles, moving at high speed.

The turret of the M2 suddenly spun towards the approaching force. Staff Sergeant O'Keefe had dropped inside and was scanning the fast-closing formation.

"Sir, we might have a situation."

Jones reached a hand down to his commander's override handle and returned their gun's orientation to the north. "No worries, Sergeant O'Keefe. That's the brigade reserve. They're moving up to backstop."

Sheepishly, O'Keefe again stood in the turret next to Jones. "You might tell me these things in the future, sir. I'm a little young to be dropping dead of a heart attack."

Jones nodded and continued staring north, trying through sheer force of will to penetrate the cloud of dust and smoke in the distance. *Hang on, men. Hang on.*

Anvil Battle Position, Northern Kuwait
22 October, 0812 Hours Local

Hearing yet another main gun detonation to his left, Waters waited to make his call. Looking that way, he saw HQ-66 disappear momentarily in a cloud of smoke and dust. Following the glowing trail of the tank's sabot, he saw a T-72 explode as Estes's gunner found his mark. For the moment, their only concern was the Iraqi tanks. The Mortar Platoon had destroyed two BMPs with their earlier fire mission and forced the remainder of the long-range missile shooters to displace.

"Tiger Six, Anvil Six, over."

"Tiger Six, over."

"Tiger Six, Anvil Six. The reinforcing tanks are en route. Estimated time of arrival is one zero minutes, over."

Ten minutes. Waters knew that wasn't what Estes had wanted to hear. Jesus, the bastards were within twenty-five hundred meters now—nearly two companies of T-72s, with more behind them.

As he listened to the Estes's voice, it was clear he

didn't think the two reinforcing platoons would make it in time to do much good. *"Roger . . . break . . . Knight Six, Tiger Six."*

"Knight Six, over," came the immediate reply. Stuart had been glued to the radio. Despite his team's fatigue, he'd gotten them to REDCON-1 status—engines started and weapons prepped—as soon as he heard the first report of contact to the northwest. He'd just been waiting for the call to move.

"Knight, move to attack by fire position Lima Two. Be prepared to engage and destroy two companies of tanks with reinforcing mech infantry . . . acknowledge, over."

Stuart quickly scanned his graphics. Looking at the symbols overlaid on the map, he found Lima Two. A sinking feeling hit his stomach. Lima Two was four kilometers behind Estes's position. From there his team could keep the attacking Iraqis from penetrating farther . . . but he could do nothing to help Estes and Waters.

"Tiger Six, Knight Six. Request to shift Lima Two north, over."

Estes could hear the pleading note in the request. Stuart wanted to move up and save his commander's bacon. Estes couldn't allow that, as tempting as it was at the moment. By the time Knight arrived, his team would be caught in the open by the approaching Republican Guard forces. No, he'd put them where they could do some good.

"Negative, Knight Six. Occupy Lima Two. Orient north by northwest. Acknowledge."

"But . . ."

"Mike! Acknowledge, damn it!"

The voice answering Estes's call had lost all vitality. *"Knight Six . . . wilco."*

Estes's tone softened. *"Thanks, Mike. Now move out."*

The artillery fires had slowed their attackers, but now the Iraqis had gotten beneath them. The FSO was trying hard to adjust them back on—but with little luck. Hitting a moving formation with howitzers was damned difficult.

Estes and Waters had taken out six T-72s between them. Their M1A1s had proven better than the T-72s at long range, but now the Iraqis had closed within their tanks' effective range. It was turning into a knife fight. Shoot. Move. Shoot.

Sparks flew from the front of Waters's tank. Without being told, the driver slammed the transmission into reverse to get out of whatever enemy sight they currently occupied.

"Crew report!"

The driver grunted from the front compartment. "Driver up. Moving left behind that clump of rocks!"

"Loader up, sabot loaded!"

"Gunner up . . . sabot indexed! I think I see him, sir! Lasing . . . I have a good range. . . ."

As Waters began to issue the command to fire, he and the gunner saw something approaching the enemy tank as if in slow motion. It appeared to be headed over the top of the T-72, but a last-minute adjustment dropped the projectile into the side of the Iraqi tank's turret. The vehicle shuddered once as a warhead drove deep inside the vehicle and blew it sky-high.

The gunner's voice came back confused. "Sir . . . I think a TOW missile just took out that tank. We don't have any mech infantry up here, do we? What's going on?"

Looking behind them, Waters saw a lone Bradley. He was happy to have any support at all, but had hoped to see a cluster of combat vehicles in the Bradley's wake. Nothing followed.

"It looks like the cavalry's arrived—sort of," said Waters.

"Target! Good shooting, O'Keefe," Jones yelled to his gunner. They'd been at their TOW's maximum effective range—maybe a little outside it. "Fire and adjust."

"Roger."

Jones could barely hear his gunner. O'Keefe's voice was calm and quiet, difficult to make out over the noise of their fighting vehicle. Since they'd pulled within range of the Iraqis, the young NCO had been in another world. He was detached . . . mechanical.

Jones had seen enough combat in his time to recognize the symptoms. War affected different men in different ways. Some went to pieces. Most were scared shitless, but fought despite the fact. A few—a rare few—were in their natural element. They were like a major-league pitcher in the middle of a no-hitter: nothing distracted them. Pure focus. O'Keefe was in the zone.

As the driver moved to a position off the flank of Estes's tank, Jones felt as if the air had been sucked from around him. The thundering roar of a tank main gun followed in the sabot round's wake. Jones reached to the top of his CVC, expecting to feel a crease in the kevlar shell.

Directly in front of them, a T-72 had managed to close within fifteen hundred meters undetected. *This is it,* thought Jones. Their only onboard weapon that could kill the tank was a TOW missile. Unfortunately, they'd had to lower the hammerhead in order to move. By the time they stopped and elevated the launcher again, the tank crew could pump more than one round into them—one tank round would be more than enough against their Bradley. Their vehicle's 25mm chain gun could be fired quickly, but it wasn't designed to penetrate heavy armor. Their time was up. The colonel patted his pockets. *Where the hell did I put my smokes?* he thought.

O'Keefe opened with the Bradley's cannon, startling Jones and causing him to drop the pack of cigarettes he'd just located. A steady stream of depleted uranium 25mm rounds hammered at the turret ring of the enemy tank. No effect, other than a lot of sparks. Well, at least they'd given the bastard something to think about, maybe made him stain his shorts. Jones saw the T-72 make its final lay on their Bradley as if in slow motion.

The tank suddenly belched flames. O'Keefe continued pouring rounds into the enemy vehicle until it lurched to a stop. A hatch flew open on top of the tank. A shaking hand reached up, then dropped back inside as the tank's onboard ammunition blew in a fireball that reached two hundred meters into the desert sky.

Jones looked at his gunner. Sensing his commander's stare, O'Keefe looked at him and shrugged. "Twenty-five millimeter depleted uranium. Good stuff."

Jones could only nod in reply.

In the back of the command Bradley, Tom Proctor stared helplessly at the operations map. Even if the brigade reserve was called forward, they wouldn't make it in time to prevent a penetration from occurring here.

Colonel Jones had made the right call. Even now, as the two tanks from 2-77 Armor held up the advancing enemy force, the reserve was deploying into a firing line capable of killing anything battalion-size or smaller that made it through.

A valiant effort was being waged here in this small corner of hell, but the numbers would go against them soon. No, they needed a little luck. As if in answer to his silent plea, a message came through from the JTF headquarters. He listened intently to half of it before interrupting.

"Roger! You're damned right! Our current position . . ."

Lieutenant Sam Matheson jotted a note and acknowledged the change in mission. Quickly relaying information to the other three helicopters in the flight, the Kiowa Warrior platoon transitioned from reconnaissance mode to preparation for the attack.

The OH-58D helicopter wasn't the most popular piece of equipment in the army. Most old-time aviators, and just about every ground maneuver unit, would much prefer seeing the heavier and proven AH-64 Apache when the shit hit the fan. The Kiowa Warrior—a modified version of the reconnaissance helicopter—was slowly taking over the Apache's missions. It was smaller, easier to transport, and could carry virtually the same ammunition. The only thing it couldn't match was the Apache's survivability, range, and overall firepower. It didn't take a great deal of damage to bring one of the little machines crashing to the ground.

Matheson switched to the frequency she'd been given and contacted the unit requesting support. *"Striker Three, this is Cutlass Six. Understand you're in need of some assistance. My flight is one minute out, coming in from the southeast, over."*

As the unmistakably feminine voice came across the radio, Tom Proctor started. Proctor had been in the army for a while. He'd seen many changes over the past decade—some good, some bad. While a lot of soldiers publicly challenged the more radical military policy shifts, he'd always thought of himself as open-minded and willing to give change a chance.

One policy that Proctor personally hadn't approved of, however, was that of putting women in combat. It went against the code of chivalry his father had taught him at an early age. It was nothing personal. He knew that there were a lot of females in uniform as capable as he was—hell, more so. Still, something inside Proctor cringed at the thought of his daughter, or his wife, taking up arms. But here they were, and he was in no position to be choosy. But he couldn't help himself. Despite his professional military education and experience, one thought kept ringing in Proctor's head. *They're sending a girl to save us?*

The three American vehicles watched as the line of enemy tanks moved closer. Since Colonel Jones had arrived on the scene, life had become an endless cycle of shooting and moving.

Both Estes and Waters had almost exhausted the seventeen rounds of main gun ammunition in their ready racks and badly needed to transfer ammunition from their semiready racks. Both knew that the Iraqis weren't going to allow them the precious minutes necessary to effect the drill.

They'd slowed down the attacking battalion significantly and managed to take out the lead vehicles. Seeing that they weren't going to be able to quickly overrun the American position, the Republican Guard force was now in the process of maneuvering on the small group opposing them.

The Iraqis bounded forward by company. Ten tanks remained behind whatever sparse cover was available, firing at the Americans to keep them occupied, while the other ten tanks sped forward. Once the second group was set—some behind rocks, some finding gentle folds in the desert floor—they covered while the first group took up the attack. Once this group was set, they repeated the maneuver. It was now just a matter of time.

The Americans knew what was transpiring but were unable to do anything about it. Every time they moved from behind cover to engage the approaching vehicles, multiple rounds came their way. Each of them saw that there was no cover or concealment left between the attacking Iraqis and themselves. The final assault would be now.

Jones, Estes, and Waters chose their final positions—the positions from which they'd make their last stands. Each of the vehicle commanders issued instructions to his crew and dropped down behind their sights, lining them up on the closest vehicles in their sectors. Jones had the left, Estes the center, Waters the right.

When the assault came, it came in a rush. Multiple enemy tanks charging across the desert, gun tubes blazing. Jones's Bradley initiated fire with a TOW missile. Before the missile had reached its midway point, the section of tanks from the Iron Tigers engaged with their main guns. Three T-72s went up in flames. Each of the Americans quickly selected their next victim. They tried to disregard the fact that there were so many enemy vehicles behind the ones in their sights that they would never be capable of getting them all—it was numerically impossible.

As Lieutenant Samantha Matheson's platoon of 58Ds popped over the crest they were spread out on line. Quickly scanning for the reported friendlies, she picked up the two M1A1s and the Bradley just in front of them and to her platoon's ten o'clock—and what appeared to be another friendly tank rapidly approaching them from the rear. She saw a sabot round streak from the M1 closest to her. The concussion of the main gun caused her small helicopter to waver momentarily. Following the red trail of the projectile, she saw it culminate its journey in a T-72.

My God, she thought. They were everywhere. There had to be at least twenty enemy tanks to her front, staggered in two lines and attacking south. Farther north she saw a few Soviet infantry carriers—not in the fight at the moment, but her platoon would take care of that.

As soon as she'd seen the Iraqis arrayed north of her platoon, she'd automatically thought as her instructors and warrants had trained her. Number and types of threats, number and types of weapons at her disposal, the best way of combining the two. They hadn't mentioned the bowling ball that materializes in your stomach when you realize your bird is Plexiglas-to-gun-tube with men who would kill you without a second thought.

A voice that was pure Texas brought Matheson out of her reverie. *"Cutlass Six, Cutlass Four,"* called the experienced warrant officer who was her wingman. *"I think we've separated the cowboys from the injuns. We're prepared to engage on your order, over."*

Matheson shook her head to clear it. She mentally reviewed her platoon's weapons payload. For antitank engagements, each 58 carried two Hellfire missiles. Once they used those, they could go to work on the BMPs—but the tanks were the biggest threat to the friendlies at the moment. *"Roger. Okay, boys, we've got eight Hellfires between us. Let the friendlies worry about the lead tanks. We'll engage the far targets. Alpha section, you start on the right. Bravo section . . ."*

As their next rounds struck the attacking Republican Guard formation, the three command crews saw explosions in the rear of the enemy force. More explosions followed close behind. Some unknown guardian was wreaking havoc in the second echelon of their attackers. Things were looking up for the good guys . . . until Estes and Waters realized they were out of ammunition at the same time.

Strictly speaking, they weren't *out*. But they'd both expended the rounds in their ready racks. They each had seventeen more rounds in their semiready rack, but needed time to effect the transfer. When operating as platoons and companies, tankers drilled switching sectors of responsibility between subunits, one transferring ammo while the other covered their sector. With the fight currently in progress, the two Iron Tiger tanks simply hadn't had the time or the numbers to do anything other than continue to engage the attacking enemy vehicles. And now they were seriously sucking.

O'Keefe let fly with another TOW, and another T-72 went down. He yelled instructions feverishly to the crew. "Driver, back up! You guys in the back get two more TOWs ready! I'm gonna move down to that little dip off to the left. Prepare to reload the missile tubes."

The driver responded immediately, throwing the fifty-thousand-pound fighting vehicle into reverse and then accelerating into the depression. Once set, O'Keefe wasted no time slewing the Bradley's turret over the side and elevating the missile launcher. As the hammerhead on the left side of the vehicle completed its upward movement, the crew popped through the opening in the rear of the vehicle and slammed two more missiles into the empty launch tubes.

Rotating the turret once again in the direction of the enemy, O'Keefe turned to Jones. "What's the story, boss? Got us a target?"

Jones dropped his binos and turned to O'Keefe. "Oh, I don't think that'll be a problem. As Major Proctor is fond of saying, there's good news and bad news. The good news is that there are only four enemy tanks remaining. Some 58Ds, I can only assume from the Eighty-second, kindly destroyed most of the second company—what's left of them is hightailing north."

O'Keefe frowned. "And the bad news?"

Jones pointed at a group of burning vehicles less than one thousand meters to their left. "The four remaining tanks are hiding behind those toasties. They're getting ready to make their final assault—unless they're taking time out for a marshmallow roast." He looked pointedly at his gunner. "Oh yeah, and our two tankers appear to be out of ammunition."

Realizing for the first time that the Abrams had stopped firing, O'Keefe's stomach flipped. Then flopped. Four T-72s, two missiles. Of the two missiles, probably only time to fire one. *Shit-fuck-damn.* Dropping inside the turret, O'Keefe rotated it in the direction of the burning hulks. Looking to his right, he saw only Jones's legs. Forgetting for a moment that his boss was only one step removed from a general officer, O'Keefe stiff-armed his commander behind the knees, causing him to collapse into the turret.

"Sir, *please stay down!*"

Without waiting for Jones's response, the gunner turned his attention back to his optics and the remaining threat. Switching his sight's magnification level from four-power to twelve-power, O'Keefe conducted a check of his systems—good. Looking through the sight, he caught sight of the Iraqis as they made their move.

Two of the tanks pulled forward and stopped, scanning. O'Keefe knew these two would try to keep their heads down while the other two closed on their position. Movement from the left caught his eye. Yep, there were his buddies. Balls to the wall.

O'Keefe took a deep breath, not allowing himself to get caught up in the excitement. The two stationary tanks were the immediate threats. The T-72 couldn't hit worth a damn while moving. As he reacquired the stationary tanks, he saw one of them orient toward their Bradley while his wingman oriented toward the two American tanks attempting to transfer ammunition.

Conflicting thoughts ran through the young NCO's mind. *Fuck it,* thought O'Keefe. Making his final lay with the TOW crosshair, he squeezed off a missile. As he waited for the missile to complete its flight, he wondered if he'd made the right choice. The wire-guided missile looked as if it was heading anywhere but toward its intended victim as it made small adjustments in its flight path. O'Keefe had to keep the crosshairs on his selected target and ignore the other threat. The TOW wasn't a fire-and-forget munition; it had to be guided by the gunner until it impacted on target. The few seconds of flight time seemed to take an eternity, but the missile and its warhead finally collided with and destroyed the T-72 that had been getting ready to open fire on the two helpless American tanks.

Blinking cold sweat from his eyes, O'Keefe looked toward the tank that had been oriented on his own vehicle. His eyes doubled in size.

"Driver, back up! Back up! Back up!"

The enemy main gun round tore through the spot they'd just vacated.

Jones's voice piped in on the intercom. "That was all right, Keef. What are you gonna do now?"

"Get his head down," said O'Keefe. He opened with the 25mm, spraying the turret of the Iraqi tank. "That should fuck up the gunner for a few seconds, long enough to put a TOW down his throat."

Switching back to the TOW crosshair, O'Keefe fired. As he guided the missile in, he knew the gun tube staring at them was about to open fire. Just before the TOW impacted, the Iraqi gunner let loose his round.

Jones and O'Keefe were knocked to their knees as the sabot round slid across the front of their Bradley, cutting an inch-deep groove through the vehicle's spaced laminate armor. The enemy tank blew up two seconds later.

Both men knew they didn't have time to congratulate themselves. They'd been very lucky—and now had two very empty missile tubes to go along with the two remaining enemy tanks.

"Driver! You know the drill! Get us the hell out of here!"

"You don't have to tell me twice!" came a shrill voice over the intercom.

O'Keefe and Jones hung on for dear life, trying to figure out who was going to kill them first, the Iraqis or their driver. O'Keefe struggled to remain seated at his gunner's station and find the enemy tanks. "Driver, stop!"

The driver had found an old streambed that was a little lower than the surrounding desert floor and had attempted to exfiltrate their vehicle through it. O'Keefe had seen the T-72 stopped and scanning just as their Bradley was about to ram it at thirty miles per hour.

The driver, having seen the enemy tank at the same time as O'Keefe, put every ounce of leg muscle he owned into the braking effort. The Bradley came to a shuddering halt.

Removing his face from the front of the turret and spitting out a mouthful of blood and an incisor, O'Keefe got back on the intercom. "Bek uh, bek uh!"

The driver was ahead of O'Keefe and already putting distance between their vehicle and the tank.

"Wul . . . guess well twy the tain dun adin," mumbled O'Keefe around his torn-up mouth. He didn't

sound confident in their ability to take out a second
tank with 25mm fire. Looking through his sight,
O'Keefe tried to settle the gun on the Iraqi tank as the
driver maneuvered back and forth wildly in reverse
in a desperate attempt to throw off the aim of the
enemy gunner.

As O'Keefe squeezed a sensing burst of three 25mm
rounds, the enemy tank fireballed.

"O'Keefe!" yelled Jones, observing through his optical relay. "That was damn fine shooting! Three fucking rounds! Unbelievable. That DU *is* some good
shit!"

O'Keefe looked at Jones. "I din do ih!"

Jones squinted at his gunner. "What?"

Taking a deep breath, O'Keefe tried again. "I—
dint—do—it!"

"Then who the hell did?"

Both men stood in the turret as they heard a second
explosion. To their front were two dead tanks—the
second had been in a blind spot only two hundred
meters from the one they'd been engaging. The gun
tubes of both of the burning T-72s were oriented on
their Bradley.

"Who the hell . . . ?" said Jones.

O'Keefe thought about it. "Hewos?"

"Huh?" Jones looked up to the sky. "No, it
wasn't helos."

As the two looked back to the dead enemy tanks,
they were showered with a wave of sand as an M1A1
skidded to a halt not twenty feet behind them. As the
dust settled, Major Dave Barnett's figure took shape.
Leaning over his .50 caliber machine gun, Barnett was
gently tweaking the ends of his mustache. As if becoming aware of Jones's stare, Barnett straightened
ever so slightly and threw a casual salute in the brigade commander's direction before climbing out of
his turret.

"I knew it!" said Jones.

"Whu'? That i' wu' the ma-juh?" asked O'Keefe,

suddenly aware of how stupid he sounded through his swelling lips.

Jones looked at O'Keefe as if he were dealing with an idiot. "No. That he was waxing that throw rug! Look at how it's holding its shape in this heat and dust!"

Estes looked toward Waters's vehicle and waved for his newest company commander to join him on the ground. Looking up toward the tank commander's cupola, he motioned for Ike McCloud's attention. "Ike, coordinate with Lieutenant Waters's gunner. Set up security here until we get back. If and when those other two platoons show up, tell the first one arriving to spread out along this intervisibility line. Send the other back to the east side of Anvil's position."

McCloud threw a thumb in the air and hopped on the radio.

Waters threw a weary salute on reaching his commander's position.

Estes returned the gesture, smiling through his own exhaustion. "What the hell, Muddy? You know I have a no-salute policy in the field."

The lieutenant nodded. "I know, sir. But I'm not too worried about snipers at the moment . . . and you deserve it. You know . . . if you hadn't shown up here . . ."

Estes waved away further comments. "Muddy, you'd have figured out a way to kick their ass all by yourself." He looked hard into the eyes of his mustang lieutenant. "You did good work, son. Especially considering the conditions."

Both men's thoughts turned to the problem of Malloy. Waters wondered what had happened on the man's tank and, hitting on the likely answer, turned back to Estes. They'd have to take care of this problem quickly.

"Sir, about Captain Malloy . . ."

Holding up a hand, Estes pointed toward Jones's Bradley. "Let's walk."

As they moved toward the vehicle, Estes continued. "I dropped one of my radio nets down to your company command frequency and caught enough of the exchange between you and Captain Malloy to know what happened. I've already called Major Proctor and given him the *Reader's Digest* version. He's running a couple of MPs over to A-66. They're going to . . . escort . . . Malloy back to the field trains."

Estes continued in silence for a few steps, then said, "You know, Muddy, there are a lot of captains in the brigade waiting for command."

Waters waved off the message Estes was trying to deliver as delicately as possible. "Sir, I know someone will probably come up to take command. Don't worry about it. Hell, sir, you need someone in command with more rank and experience than I've got anyway. Whoever it is, when the time comes I'll make sure it's a smooth transition."

Estes nodded in silence. Despite Muddy's words, he could tell the thought of relinquishing the command he'd gained under fire bothered the lieutenant.

On reaching the Bradley, the two heard voices coming from the rear of the vehicle. Turning the corner, Estes was reminded of his last trip to Kuwait and the oil fires that had burned throughout the desert. Between Jones's cigarette and Barnett's pipe, the area resembled an international airport smoking booth.

Seeing Estes, Barnett took the pipe from his mouth and smiled. "Hello, sir. Good to see you in one piece."

"Dave, where the hell did you come from?" asked Estes. "The last time I spoke to you, you were moving up with Team Knight to oversee their emplacement at Lima Two."

Barnett waved the pipe vaguely in the air. "Well, sir . . . you're right. But when I got to Lima Two, it didn't look like a good position. I decided to move forward and see if there was something better. . . ."

Estes raised an eyebrow. "And . . ."

Sticking the pipe back between his teeth, Barnett looked at his commander and folded his arms across his chest. "One thing led to another . . . and . . . I saw what looked like a good position off to the east. Yes! I saw a good position to the east! Funny thing was, as I moved toward it . . ."

"Dave . . ."

Barnett ceased his tap dance. "Sir?"

Estes smiled. "Thanks."

Jones broke up the small talk. "Well, gentlemen, as much as I'm enjoying this lovefest, I'm afraid we've still got one more Iraqi brigade headed south, so—"

"Sir," called Proctor, sticking his head from the back of the Bradley.

"Yeah, Tom?" said Jones, turning.

The brigade S3 held up a handset. "JTF headquarters for you."

"Excuse me for a minute, gentlemen. The Joint Task Force beckons."

As he reached for the handset, Jones turned back to the group of 2-77 officers. "Waters!"

Muddy looked toward his brigade commander. He'd heard the stories about Jones—the man was a legend amongst the brigade's lieutenants—but had never actually spoken to him. He was surprised Jones even knew his name. "Sir?"

"Major Proctor told me about what happened out there. Good work."

Waters nodded. "Thanks, sir."

"What do you think of Anvil?"

At the moment, all Waters could think of was that while a higher headquarters stood by on the radio, Jones was making small talk with him. At the mention of his company, though, Waters stood straighter. "They're a good outfit, sir. Good men. The best."

"I'm glad you think so. For now, I'm gonna let you keep it. If all of this shit with Captain Malloy is confirmed, which I'm sure it will be, we'll make it permanent. What do you think of that?"

The dust on Waters's face cracked as he smiled. "Thank you, sir."

Jones turned to the radio in the back of the Brad.

He yelled back over his shoulder. "You're welcome . . . *Captain* Waters."

Two minutes later, Jones returned to the small command group. "All right, ladies, here's the scoop. Between the MLRS and the air, the third Tawakalna brigade has been held up . . . roughly ten kilometers to the north. Our instructions are to maintain our current position for now. It sounds like there's a plan for them that doesn't involve us. I also received confirmation that the follow-on Republican Guard divisions will be delayed at least forty-eight hours."

Jones gave the men a few moments to digest the information, then continued. "Rob, I know your guys have been busting their asses since we arrived, plus you've taken some losses. Your men are exhausted, you're exhausted . . . hell, I'm exhausted. But I need you to regroup the Iron Tigers ASAP. Take stock of where you stand and give me a call in a couple of hours. Let me know what you need and I'll do everything in my power to get it to you . . . even if it means paying civilian contractors in Doha triple-overtime to drive a few spare tanks and Bradleys up here. But I need to know where everyone stands as far as readiness goes."

"Sir, my men are ready to—"

Jones held up a hand. "I need solid estimates, Rob, not enthusiasm. I've seen what your men can do. They're a good bunch. Now understand where I'm coming from." He pointed to the west. "I've got the pieces of an armored task force over that rise. I've got to bring them back together somehow and replenish them. There's a force double our size due here in less than two days." He paused, thinking. "I'm going to try to get the Eighty-second to cut us some attack helos—I found out today how handy those little suckers can be. Shit! Speaking of helos . . ."

Turning back to the Bradley, Jones yelled, "Tom!"

A kevlared head detached itself from the rear doorway, handsets in each ear. "Yes, sir?"

"See if you can get that flight of Kiowas to drop by

here later, or at least the platoon leader. By God that
was a ballsy son of a bitch! After they took out those
tanks, they took off after those pesky BMPs to the
north. I want to shake that man's hand while I've still
got the chance."

Proctor pulled the handsets from his face. "*Her*
hand, sir."

A puzzled expression crossed Jones's face. "Huh?"

"*Her* hand. Cutlass Six is a woman."

Jones recovered quickly. "Fine, fine. *She's* still got
a king-size sack on her. See if Cutlass can drop by, all
right? And get O'Keefe down here."

"Roger, sir."

Jones turned back to the three men. A stranger who
didn't know better would see them as dirty, tired, and
in dire need of shaves. He saw men who represented
what the warrior spirit was all about. With leaders like
this, he couldn't ask for a great deal more. He
wouldn't forget them—the bonds tempered under the
fire of combat were strong. The others might not realize that yet, but they would. O'Keefe trudged up and
joined them a few moments later, a wet OD green
handkerchief held to his mouth.

"How you doin', Keef?"

The NCO looked at the colonel and nodded. The
colonel in turn continued to look at his gunner, waiting for elaboration. Rolling his eyes, O'Keefe finally
dropped the rag to reveal swollen lips and a missing
tooth.

"You look like *shit,*" was Jones's only comment.

O'Keefe closed his mouth, biting back his response.
He refused to be drawn into conversation until the
swelling subsided.

Jones looked at him seriously and put a hand to his
shoulder. "Good work today, son. If it weren't for
you, most of us wouldn't be standing here." Turning
to the others, Jones continued. "Gentlemen, meet Sergeant Matt O'Keefe, my gunner. I've never worked
with better."

O'Keefe, choked up at the genuine affection he heard in Jones's voice, reapplied the rag to his mouth and nodded.

"Sir!"

Jones turned back to the Bradley. "Yeah, Tom?"

"It's about Cutlass Six, sir."

"Yeah? She stopping by?"

Proctor shook his head. "Negative. Sir . . . she was shot down five minutes ago."

Jones frowned. "Where?"

"North."

Jones reached into his pocket for some Tums. "How far north?"

"About five kilometers. Her platoon had just finished expending their remaining payloads on the BMPs. As they turned south to head home, a surviving BMP caught her with its 30mm cannon."

All of Jones's attention seemed to focus on the small packet of antacid. He was having difficulty peeling the paper off and extracting two tablets. Finally, he ripped the pack down the side with a thumbnail and dumped all of the chalky tablets into a meaty palm. Popping the whole pack in his mouth, Jones chewed slowly, thinking.

Proctor continued. "The other three helos stayed on station as long as their fuel allowed even though they were out of ammunition. They saw Lieutenant Matheson pulled from the wreckage by a group of Iraqis. She appeared to be alive."

Jones looked to Proctor. "What size force?"

"They counted four BMPs."

Jones turned his attention to Estes. "Rob, that young lady pulled our collective asses from the wringer. I want you to see what you've got that's REDCON-One. Given the timing before that last Republican Guard brigade is due in here, I don't think the Search and Rescue guys would have much luck getting there in time."

Looking back at the S3, he said, "Tom, I want the grid coordinates to where she went down."

Proctor knew his boss was taking the situation too personally. He knew that he should try to talk him out of what he was planning before it went any further. He also knew that he agreed with Jones one hundred percent.

He held out a preformatted spot report slip. "Here's all of the information, sir. They were still there at last report, but it looked like they would be pulling out soon."

Taking the slip of paper, Jones handed it to Estes. "Go. Rob, I want her back—in one piece."

Estes was already moving.

CHAPTER 11

The Rescue

Dillon followed Hancock's platoon north. Ten minutes earlier the five Steel tanks had moved into no-man's-land in response to Estes's call. As the group of tanks cleared the protective obstacle belt to their front, Dillon looked back. The engineer squad responsible for the obstacle was already placing anti-tank mines across the cleared passageway they'd just negotiated. When they came back, the engineers would reopen the lane for his tanks. Still, Dillon felt a cold shiver run down his spine despite the Middle Eastern sun. They were entering Indian country and he and his men were the only cavalry for miles around.

"White One, Steel Six."

Hancock responded to the call. *"This is White One, over."*

"Spread it out some. Wedge formation, two hundred meters between vehicles. Traveling overwatch. I'll follow behind you, over."

"White One, wilco."

Dillon looked at his map, holding it steady as the wind blew around him in the cupola. *"Orient on checkpoint two one and keep to the lower ground."*

"Roger, sir." From the sound of his voice, Dillon

knew Hancock felt he was being given a little too much guidance. Well, maybe he was right.

"Good man. You've got the con. Steel Six, out."

Seconds later, Dillon watched as his newest platoon leader, if you didn't count the platoon sergeant of Third Platoon who had taken over for Takahashi, orchestrated his unit's movement. The four vehicles spread out in a formation resembling a flight of migrating geese. Hancock took up the lead at the point of the formation, while his platoon sergeant slid off his flank and slightly behind him. Their wingmen took up positions on the outside.

"Tommy," Dillon called to his driver.

"Yes, sir," came Thompson's reply from his driver's hole.

"I want you to keep us in the middle of the First Platoon wedge, about two hundred meters behind Lieutenant Hancock's tank."

"Wilco."

"Bick."

"Sir."

"Take up a nice slow scan. And no offense, but make sure you've got the main gun in safe. The last thing Hancock needs is a sabot up his ass."

Bickel couldn't help laughing at the mental picture of an impaled Lieutenant Hancock. "Roger. I confirm main gun in safe."

Dillon turned in his cupola and spoke to PFC Hunter. "You keep up a good sagger watch, Hunt. I don't want some Hero of Allah deciding we're his ticket to Paradise and plucking at us with an anti-tank missile."

Hunter's features were hidden behind the OD green "drive-on" rag protecting his face from the dust and wind. He gave his usual thumbs-up from behind his 7.62mm machine gun. "Got it, sir. One of those fuckers jumps up with an AT, I got something for his ass." The loader rubbed his machine gun lovingly.

"Good man. Just make sure that thing's on safe as

well." Loaders were the least experienced members of the crew and tank commanders generally tended to get a bit nervous when they got within six inches of a loaded machine gun, despite their training.

Dillon finally had a few minutes to relax—at least to the extent possible under the circumstances.

Cold Steel had pulled the mission of recovering the downed aviator. It had come down to them or Team Mech. Anvil was still adjusting to new leadership. Knight was too far south. Nelson Bowers's mech infantry team was better suited for the mission—with their infantry troops they could put men on the ground if necessary—but they'd been in the middle of refueling. Tiger Six had wanted someone moving, time now, so Steel pulled the mission. Dillon had left Mason, First Platoon, and Third Platoon at the B.P. to man the company's sector while he took Second Platoon with him for the rescue mission.

Dillon smiled, recalling how disappointed Wyatt had sounded when notified he was staying behind. The man's appearance belied the knight in shining armor hiding within him. Dillon would love to have his most experienced platoon out here with him, but from their position in the center of the Steel BP, First Platoon could cover the entire company sector if necessary. Besides, Doc had done all right when the shit hit the fan. He'd kept his cool and done nothing stupid to get any of his soldiers killed.

"Steel Six, Mech Six."

"Mech Six, this is Steel Six." Dillon wondered why the Team Mech commander was calling now.

"Steel Six, Mech Six. How are you looking for manpower, over."

"I've got five tanks with full crews. I can put about five men plus a leader on the ground if I need to."

"Roger, that's what I thought. Check your four o'clock."

Dillon turned in his cupola, looking back and right. He made out two vehicles—Bradleys—heading his way.

"Merry Christmas, Steel. You've now got a section

of dismounts. That's my Bravo section, First Platoon. He should be on your command push now and will answer to call sign Green Four, over."

"This is Steel Six. Thank you much. I'll bring 'em back in one piece. I just don't know if they'll want to go back to the infantry after a ride with Cold Steel."

Bowers's laugh was subdued. He was worried about his men. Mech Six didn't have to send them out, but he knew Dillon might need the dismounts. *"Roger. Just bring them home and I'll worry about how to get them back into the real army."*

Dillon felt much better about the situation now. Five M1A1s and two Bradleys against four BMPs. And he had a dismounted capability. Things were definitely looking up. Now they just had to protect against a case of the stupids. That and reach the bastards before they made it to the remnants of the Iraqi brigade heading south.

Lieutenant Sam Matheson didn't want to get out of bed. She threw an arm out. "Just a few more minutes," she mumbled.

Jesus, she didn't want to get up. The stench in her face reminded her that she was overdue giving Fang, her big German shepherd, a bath. He must have crawled into bed with her and boy did he *reek*. And why was she so sore?

Finally, Sam forced her eyes open. A round swarthy face with a lazy eye was the first thing she saw. Less than six inches from her, the man smiled darkly, revealing rotten teeth. Without thinking, she threw a stiff punch into the face hovering over her.

A hand the size of a country ham swung forward, slapping Sam Matheson viciously across the mouth. Her assailant screamed at Matheson in a language she couldn't understand.

Oh, God. It all came rushing back. The Iraqis . . . the tracers rushing up to meet her craft . . . oh, Jesus, her copilot looking at her with blank eyes, guts spilling onto his lap. . . .

Again the stinking figure struck Matheson. He repeated what she could only assume was a question.

Matheson reached a hand up, wiping the blood from her mouth. "I don't understand you!" She looked around to try to get a grip on the situation. She was lying in the back of an armored vehicle. It was a cramped space—and dark. The desert sky shone brightly through the troop door at the rear of the vehicle, four feet and an eternity away, promising false hope. And even if she reached it, then what? Outside she could see more armored vehicles and more Iraqi soldiers. And from the look of things, they were getting ready to move. The last thing she wanted was to be a prisoner. As an aviator, she'd had survival training—very realistic survival training—but all it had taught her was that getting captured would really suck.

A short, thin soldier approached the back of the vehicle and stopped, reporting to the man squatting next to Matheson. After exchanging a few words, the small soldier looked at Matheson, then turned away. The man—a boy really—appeared nervous and agitated. Matheson suspected she wasn't the reason for his discomfort as she caught the fearful glances the soldier directed toward the brute whom she couldn't help thinking of as Fang. She sent a silent apology to her loyal pet of so long ago for the comparison.

"Bisor'aa!" yelled Fang. *Hurry!*

The smaller soldier finally spoke. "Hello. My name is Private Suleiman . . . Daoud Suleiman. How . . . are you?"

His English was broken but not difficult to understand. It was obvious he either had never mastered the language or had rarely made use of it.

Matheson stared straight ahead. "Matheson, Samantha. First Lieutenant. 346-33. . . ."

Fang quickly spit a question at Suleiman. The soldier replied nervously. Fang made a short, deliberate statement, glaring at Sam while he said it.

"The sergeant wants to know what unit you're in

and what their plans are . . . and he says to warn you that what little patience he has is wearing thin."

"Matheson, Samantha. First Lieutenant. 346—"

In a flash the Iraqi sergeant cuffed Matheson once again, more viciously than before.

Private Suleiman winced. "Please. . . . He is not . . . a very good man. Your helicopters killed our officer . . . and our ranking sergeant. This man"—he indicated the sergeant with a slight movement of his head—"bullied the others into following him."

Finally, Matheson relented. "What does he want?"

Instead of answering the question, he said, "This is not the way we are taught to handle prisoners. I want you to . . . to understand that. We are not . . . barbarians."

Fang lashed out with a foot, kicking the translator in the thigh with a heavily booted foot. His look told both Matheson and Suleiman that his patience was gone.

Suleiman took the weight off his injured leg and glanced at Matheson, pleading. "Tell him something useful. It is the only thing keeping you alive."

Matheson looked at the soldier questioningly. "I'm just a platoon leader. I don't know what the plan is, or anything else that would be useful to this buffoon." She then glared at Fang, adding in a loud voice, "And if I did, I *damn sure* wouldn't tell him!"

Switching to Arabic, Suleiman spoke to his superior. "Sergeant, she knows nothing of use. I'll secure her and we can take her back for a proper interrogation."

The large man glared at Matheson. His eyes slid down along the length of her torn flight suit, fixating on the patches of flawless white skin exposed by the rips. And her hair. He'd only seen such red hair in pictures and films. Matheson's, usually shoulder-length and pinned up, now spilled around her face and shoulders in the dark corner of the combat vehicle. It looked afire. He felt something stir deep inside him. The fear that was so clear in her eyes did nothing but add to his desire. She might be an infidel, but she could still prove useful to a man. "Leave us, Private Suleiman. I will continue the questioning on my own."

Suleiman's face took on a concerned expression.

Matheson picked up on it immediately. "What did he say?"

Suleiman waved the question off. "But, Sergeant, you do not speak English. It is better to take her with—"

The Iraqi NCO reached out a large hand and grabbed the slight soldier by the throat, yanking him into his face, where his fetid breath was put to its best use. "Leave—us. Get the rest of the men on their vehicles. We depart in ten minutes."

The private fought to break the iron grip. "Our superiors will be angry! I implore you, Sergeant. . . ." Suleiman didn't realize his nose had been broken as the fist smashed into the center of his face with the force of a sledgehammer. He only knew that it was the most intense pain he'd ever felt.

"They will not be angry," said the NCO in a low voice. "They will never know she was here. She died when her helicopter went down, didn't she?"

The translator, his nose pouring blood, looked to Matheson. Silently his eyes pled forgiveness. Then he turned and stepped out of the armored vehicle.

"Where are you going?" yelled Matheson at the retreating figure.

Private Suleiman turned a final time. "I can do no more for you," he said quietly, seeing the lecherous glaze in his NCO's eyes. The soldier had no illusions regarding the lieutenant's fate. "Make peace with your God."

The last thing Sam wanted was to be alone with this . . . thing. Deep inside, she knew what was about to happen. The nightmare women feared most—at least from the time they were old enough to realize that God, for whatever reason, at times turned a blind eye to the helpless. She lunged desperately past Fang, making it halfway out of the troop door before her burly captor grabbed a fistful of her hair and pulled her back inside.

Suleiman turned at the commotion. The last thing he saw before the troop door closed was Matheson's hand reaching imploringly toward him.

"Steel Six, Lighthorse Six, over," called the scout platoon leader.

"Steel Six."

"This is Lighthorse Six. I've got two spot reports. First, we've sighted the remnants of the third Tawakalna brigade. Estimate their strength at a little over two battalions. They are ten kilometers north of the task force and moving south, grid. . . ."

Dillon wrote down the grid and marked it on his map. He compared it with his unit's current location. Shit. The gap was closing between his band of merry men and the final Iraqi unit of the Tawakalna—and one unlucky aviator was stuck in the middle. *"Got it, Lighthorse. Send your other report."*

"Roger, one of my OPs reports sighting your aviator. The Iraqis have her one point two north of checkpoint Tango Eight . . . Steel Six, she's alive, but my team on the ground believes she's in some serious shit. We saw her being dragged into the back of an infantry carrier, nothing since. . . . It's a ragtag group that's got her and it looks like they're getting ready to move out."

Dillon found Tango Eight and ran his finger twelve hundred meters north. Jesus, they were practically on top of the position!

"All Steel elements, Steel Six, stop where you are! Pick up a scan from ten o'clock to one o'clock and tell me what you see."

Jumping back to task force command, Dillon called the scouts. *"Lighthorse, we're almost there. Can your OP come up on my net to guide us in, over."*

"This is Lighthorse Six, roger. Call sign Two-Six. Stand by."

Thirty seconds later, the NCO in charge of the scout observation position contacted Dillon. *"Steel Six,*

*Lighthorse Two-Six. I've got eyes on you. I'm a kilo-
meter to your northwest, over."*

Dillon's men monitored the call. For a mission such
as this, with only a few tanks to command and control,
Dillon's SOP was to put everyone on company command. Gun tubes moved slowly back and forth, looking for the friendly scout.

"This is White One. We see him."

Dillon continued searching with his binoculars.
Movement caught his eye. An arm had separated itself
from the surrounding desert floor and waved slowly
back and forth. A rag cut from the pink backside of
a VH-17 aerial recognition panel could clearly be seen.

"I've got you, Two-Six."

As fast as the hand had appeared, it now disappeared. The desert was once again empty of all life.

"Two-Six, where's the enemy force, over."

After a moment the arm reappeared, an M16 rifle
in hand. The rifle barrel pointed due north, signaling
the direction of their quarry. *"North, roughly two
thousand meters from your current position. If you
move forward five hundred meters, you'll see them,
over."*

Dillon formulated a plan. They didn't have time for
subtleties. *"White, move up . . . slowly. Don't kick up
dust. When you spot the BMPs, stop where you are.
Green, be prepared to secure the area with your dismounts when I tell you. Two-Six, I need you to mark
the vehicle holding our aviator when I give you the
signal. Can you do that?"*

Lying in the sand, the scout looked around his position. His eyes settled on the M203 grenade launcher
attached to the underside of his M16 rifle. A forty
millimeter smoke grenade? He shook his head, answering his own question. No. Smoke could obscure
the friendlies' sight pictures. He continued looking
around, finally gesturing to his assistant. "Hand me
your SAW, Greeber." The assistant handed the
5.56mm squad assault weapon to his NCO. *"This is*

Two-Six. Follow my tracers. I may not have the range to reach the vehicle, but I'll point a finger at it."

Dillon nodded to himself in the turret of his vehicle. *"All right, gents. Here's what we're going to do. . . ."*

Private Daoud Suleiman was not happy about the current turn of events. Sergeant al-Sahaf was an animal. If only he could persuade some of the other men to aid him—but no, they were even more frightened of the brute than he was. Since their leaders had died, the others did exactly what al-Sahaf said, no questions. Besides, what was one American woman to them? Had not their own women suffered due to the embargoes sanctioned by the Americans and their pawns in the United Nations?

For Suleiman, it was different. Although he'd never tell his fellow soldiers, he had family in America. New York City. They'd brought him his prize possession— a New York Yankees cap—during their last visit. And they'd told him with pride of how everyday Americans had become heroes on September eleventh, sacrificing themselves to aid those trapped in the World Trade Center. No, they weren't all godless infidels. More than that, what al-Sahaf was doing was wrong. Wrong by regulation, wrong by the Koran, wrong by every moral code ever written. He looked around in frustration. But what could he do? He looked at the BMP in the distance. Al-Sahaf had ensured his vehicle was separated from the others, probably to keep them from hearing the screams he'd known would come.

The private shook his head. *I cannot allow this to happen,* he finally decided. Reaching into the rear compartment of his vehicle, Suleiman withdrew an AK-47 assault rifle. Take care of the beast and then the others would listen to reason. He hoped.

Suleiman walked toward the vehicle, feeling like an American cowboy in the films he'd seen during his childhood. He ignored the looks of his fellow soldiers. They were already mounted on their vehicles with engines started. They were anxious to head north, toward the promise of home. Didn't the idiots realize they'd just be thrown into another military unit? They wouldn't be seeing home for a long while yet.

Halfway to his destination, Suleiman saw puffs of dust kick up in a straight line a hundred meters in from of him. A second later he heard the report of the machine gun. Someone was sending a steady stream of fire directly at Sergeant al-Sahaf's BMP.

"This is Steel Six, all elements confirm you identify the BMP containing our package, over."
"White One, roger."
"Two, roger."
"Three, roger."
"Four, roger."
"Green Four, roger. We're standing by."
"This is Bick, sir. I've got it."
"White, Steel Six . . . Fire!"

Private Suleiman found himself knocked to the ground. As he struggled to rise, he saw the three infantry carriers containing his comrades in flames. The sound threatened to tear his eardrums apart. He got to his feet and continued to struggle toward the BMP containing the woman. He might die, but he would fulfill this one last mission. Suddenly Suleiman felt a stinging sensation in his legs. After falling to the ground again, he looked down his body. His legs were bloody and torn from multiple bullet wounds. Looking up, he saw two armored vehicles rushing at him. Stopping just outside of his company's position, the vehicles disgorged American soldiers. The soldiers quickly spread out. Systematically the Americans checked the area, paying particular attention to the burning vehicles.

Hearing a diesel engine kick over, Suleiman looked up to see Sergeant al-Sahaf's BMP move out at maximum speed. The private reached a hand toward the receding vehicle. *Noooooo . . .*

* * *

"Steel elements, Steel Six. SITREP," called Dillon, binoculars glued to the lone surviving BMP.

He could hear the wind whistling in Doc's boom mike as the platoon leader called while on the move. *"This is White One. Three BMPs destroyed. My platoon is moving north to the far side of the enemy position and establishing security."*

"This is Green Four. Enemy position secured. I only see one guy alive. He was moving in the direction of the target BMP and my wingman shot his legs from under him. Moving to target now with my dismounted element. Shit! *Target vehicle is moving, Steel Six!"*

Dillon had stayed on the backside of the enemy position for rear security with his vehicle. He was in the wrong position to intercept and knew it. Looking north, he could just make out Second Platoon. *"Doc!"*

A voice Dillon wouldn't have recognized a month earlier responded confidently. *"I've got him."*

"Move, move, move, you son of a swine!" screamed Sergeant al-Sahaf. Standing in one of the two rear troop hatches of the BMP, he rubbed the scratches lining his eyes. It was but by the grace of Allah that he was not blind. He'd have killed the she-devil—despite the tasty promise of the white flesh—if events hadn't turned. Instead, he'd had to settle for knocking her unconscious. The woman was the last thing on his mind at the moment, however.

He looked back, seeing nothing but the cloud of dust in his vehicle's wake. He was trying to put as much distance as possible between himself and the Americans. Looking forward he saw something. His goggles were coated with so much dust that he was having a difficult time determining what the object was. Ripping them from his face, he looked again. "Driver! Turn left! Keep moving! Faster, faster!"

An M1A1 tank, the devil-beast he'd seen during the Gulf War only at a distance, was bearing straight at them. Was the crazy American tank going to ram

them? He could see the commander standing in the
turret now. He was gesturing. What was he trying to
say? He seemed to be telling them to pull over, much
as a traffic officer would in downtown Baghdad. Al-
Sahaf threw a gesture of his own.

Without warning, a stabbing pain shot through the
Iraqi NCO's groin. Reaching a hand below the level
of the hatch, he touched the area from which the pain
emanated. As he pulled the hand back into the light
of day, it looked like a bloody claw was attached to
his arm. Another pain ripped through his midsection.
Before the big Iraqi could climb into the troop compartment to stop his attacker, his legs collapsed beneath him.

Sam Matheson was waiting. Her father had given
her the razor-sharp Tanto knife just before she'd deployed for the Gulf, along with the sheath that kept
the small, thin blade neatly hidden between her shoulder blades. Once she'd regained consciousness following her attack, Matheson had pulled the hideaway
weapon. Seeing her tormentor's legs and crotch in
front of her had been too good to ignore. After delivering two cuts that ensured he'd never again try to
take advantage of a woman, Sam had sliced both of
his hamstrings. In the split second it took the Iraqi to
fall through the hatch, she had glimpsed the fear in
his eyes. Good. The bastard. She swiftly delivered one
final cut—straight across his throat.

Sergeant al-Sahaf's driver wasn't aware of his vehicle commander's plight. When he called for directions,
all he could hear was gurgling over the intercom. The
Soviet equipment could never be counted on—especially their communications systems.

Seeing the American tank heading straight for him
and easily countering every evasive move he made,
the driver quit. He didn't want to die for lack of a
swifter vehicle. Stopping the BMP, the driver jumped

from his hatch. Throwing his hands in the air, he walked toward the enemy vehicle rapidly closing on him.

The American tank stopped fifty meters from his BMP. The tank commander deftly positioned it out of the Iraqi vehicle's 30mm gun's line of fire on the off chance that their stop was a ruse, while at the same time laying the M1A1's main gun on their own vehicle. The loader on top of the vehicle pointed a machine gun directly at his chest. He looked like a bandit, face covered by a rag, not moving.

The tank commander hopped down from his vehicle, landing in a cloud of dust. To the driver, he presented a threatening picture. Tall, and ironically more sinister-looking because of the wire-rimmed glasses he wore, the American moved slowly toward the nervous soldier. The tank commander never moved between the Iraqi driver and his loader's machine gun. Pulling a pistol from his shoulder holster, he walked behind the driver and stopped.

Stopping behind the Iraqi, Hancock patted down his prisoner—clean. He grabbed the Iraqi's shoulder and spun him around.

The driver looked up and saw the American loader's machine gun now orienting on the back of the BMP.

"Haal . . . haal taataakaalaam . . . Englizi?" Hancock asked the Iraqi. He was glad he'd read through the country handbook during what little down time they'd had since arriving, but he feared he was butchering the Arab language so badly that the kid wouldn't understand him.

The driver shook his head. *"Laa."* No.

So much for that. Hancock put a hand once more on the driver's shoulder, applying just enough pressure for the boy to understand he was to kneel. Doc gestured for him to lock his fingers behind his head. Once he saw the driver comply, he moved to the back of the vehicle. Grasping the rear door handle of the infantry vehicle, he yanked it open, thrusting the 9mm Beretta in front of his face in a two-hand weaver stance.

As his eyes adjusted to the gloom, he saw a woman's figure, covered in blood, eyes open and staring at him. On top of her was the largest Arab Hancock had ever seen. *Oh, Jesus,* he thought, *we're too late.*

The corpse spoke. "Hi there, Lone Ranger. If you're not too busy, could you get John Wayne Bobbit here off me? He weighs a ton."

Despite the circumstances, Doc couldn't help but appraise Lieutenant Matheson as she climbed on board his tank. Her hair was a mass of tangles, she was filthy, and her flight suit was unrecognizable. She was . . . simply the most desirable creature he'd ever seen. Sensing his stare, Sam turned. She said nothing, merely arched a lovely eyebrow. Doc turned his head, embarrassed.

It was Matheson's turn to look Doc over. "Anyone ever tell you that you look like that doctor on television . . . ?"

Trying to recover some dignity, Doc shook his head and snapped a reply. "No. Never heard that one. Keep moving, please, Lieutenant. There's a brigade out there heading this way as we speak."

Sam held her ground, continuing to look over the tank platoon leader. You know, he was actually kind of cute, in a boy-next-door sort of way.

Doc, having followed her up the front slope of the tank, gestured toward his loader. The soldier offered a hand to their passenger.

"Glad to see you're all right, ma'am," said the loader.

Taking the proffered hand, Sam climbed onto the turret. "Thank you. It's good to know *some* tankers have manners."

"Lieutenant," said Doc, "climb in the turret. We really do have to get out of the area."

Again Sam lifted an eyebrow at him, smiling.

"You're a regular knight in shining armor, aren't you?"

"Just get in the tank. And take this," Doc said, handing her a canteen of water. "We've got some rags in the turret to go along with the water. You really need to clean all of that blood from your face. You look like Sissy Spacek in that movie. . . ."

"I'm not much of a country music fan, but thanks." She smiled, took the canteen, and lowered herself inside the tank.

"I meant *Carrie,*" Doc mumbled to himself as he climbed into the commander's cupola and put on his CVC helmet. Man, he was blowing this one big time. What was it about the woman that flustered him so much? Flicking his CVC's transmit switch forward, Hancock shook his head and called Dillon. *"Steel Six, White One. We've got her. She's a little banged up, but otherwise in good shape."*

The reply was immediate. *"Roger, let's move out."*

"This is White One, moving."

"Steel Six, roger, out."

Turning to Matheson, Doc passed her his kevlar helmet as she climbed through the loader's hatch. "You might want to wear this. There's a lot of metal to bust your head open down there."

Sam favored him with a flash of white teeth. "Thanks."

Doc winced. The smile turned him on. The bloody face kind of scared him. "You're welcome."

Hancock watched her disappear into the turret. *Shit!* The Iraqi driver. Doc swiveled his head to where the young soldier still kneeled. A look of hopelessness crossed the boy's face at seeing the Americans had not forgotten him after all. He knew he was dead. Doc pointed at him, then pointed north. The soldier didn't move, not quite trusting his good fortune. Doc pointed north again and the soldier finally stood and began walking. He walked slowly, looked back a few times, and then broke into a trot.

"Hey!" called Doc.

The driver stopped, turning. Hancock threw a collapsible canteen of water as hard as he could in the soldier's direction.

The boy stared in disbelief.

Doc turned his attention to the vacated enemy vehicle. He wasn't going to leave it for some asshole to jump in and use against them later. "Gunner, take out the BMP."

The turret of the M1A1 swiveled toward the Iraqi vehicle. The gunner's voice came through the intercom. "I'm on . . . and our passenger is clear of the main gun."

Doc knew that much. He could feel her breasts on his shins, which meant she was in the tank commander's station. *Jesus.* "Fire."

"On the way."

The tank rocked backward. Doc didn't take the time to watch the vehicle blow. "Okay, let's move."

As his driver accelerated, Doc looked to his rear. Their wing tank was falling in. After a few minutes they reached Dillon's position. The rest of the tanks and the Bradleys were waiting for them. Dillon waved Doc to the front without a word.

Continuing to move, Doc called to the Steel elements. *"White, White One. Wedge, two-hundred-meter separation, gear three. Green, take up positions on the flanks. Let's get the hell out of here, gentlemen."*

From his position behind Hancock, Dillon smiled. His boy was growing up.

Doc's body rolled easily with the motion of his tank. Lost in thought, he didn't at first notice that his loader had grown a fabulous set of breasts. Feeling eyes on him, Hancock turned. Sam Matheson stood in the loader's hatch wearing a CVC, looking at him with a strange expression. She'd cleaned the remnants of her battle with Fang from her face and clothes as best she could. *God,* thought Doc, *she looks even better.* He hadn't thought that possible. He made up his mind. He was going to marry this woman.

"What?" asked Doc defensively, beginning to wilt under Sam's direct gaze.

Sam just looked at him for a few moments before speaking, then leaned over to be heard. "Thank you."

"For what?"

"For what? What do you think?"

God, but I'm stupid, thought Hancock. "Oh . . . well, you didn't really need much help. We didn't do more than provide you with a taxi service. And remind me never to piss you off."

A dark expression crossed Matheson's face as she thought of the Iraqi NCO. The man had deserved to die—there was no doubt about that. But still, she couldn't help feeling that everything had changed. In the back of her mind, she knew she'd taken other lives while attacking the Iraqi company earlier in the day. While that was true, it was different . . . more detached. This time she had seen her victim's face, felt his blood. She had been beneath his body as it released his death rattle.

Seeing the faraway look in Matheson's eyes, Doc guessed what was going through her mind. "It's not your fault. You did what you had to do."

Sam looked ahead, squinting from the wind in her face. "I know. But . . . it doesn't change the fact that I . . . it . . ." She shook her head, lost for words.

Doc wanted to reach out, to comfort her, to tell her that everything would be all right. Instead he just settled into the silence, to the sound of the tank beneath them and the desert wind.

Sam broke their reverie after a few minutes. "That was a nice thing you did."

Doc looked at her quizzically.

"The Iraqi soldier . . . the water."

"How'd you know about that?" Matheson had been inside the tank. Then it hit him. His gabby loader. "Besides, anyone else would have done the same."

Her gaze went beyond merely seeing him. It looked through him, seemed to burn into his soul. "No, they wouldn't," she said softly.

Doc looked away for a moment. "Well . . . I . . . hey, could you keep an eye out on that side of the tank? We're still not home yet."

Sam took him in with her eyes and smiled. "Okay, Doc. I've got port side security."

It was Doc's turn to raise an eyebrow. She'd already gotten tight enough with the crew to get his nickname? Man, she moved fast.

They were lost in their own thoughts as the steel beast plowed on, heading back to friendly lines. The CVC helmets and the drone of the turbine engine prevented them from hearing the sounds of battle four kilometers north of them.

15th KU Brigade, Five Kilometers South of the Iraq-Kuwait Border
22 October, 1200 Hours Local

Colonel Hashem al-Behbahani, commander of Kuwait's 15th Armored Brigade, savored this moment. The remaining elements of Iraq's once-mighty Tawakalna Division continued south, unaware of the fate that awaited them.

This was the moment for which he had waited over a decade. Al-Behbahani's 15th Brigade was composed primarily of the American M1A2 tanks. His men would make good use of the cutting-edge fighting machines.

Al-Behbahani smiled as he listened to the reports filtering in. The enemy was not occupying a wide frontage as he attacked south. Excellent. He compared the approaching Iraqis' projected path against the locations of the two companies of M-84s he'd set forward. They could not help but make contact in the next few minutes. The colonel made a few more calls, ensuring the preparations for their guests were complete. They were.

An aide approached the colonel, a message in hand. "Sir. We have initiated fire against the enemy. As expected, they are attacking enthusiastically."

The colonel nodded. He'd surmised that once the Republican Guard recognized the M-84s, they'd know they were fighting Kuwaitis. Conscious of the disdain the Iraqis held for his country's military, al-Behbahani knew the invaders wouldn't be able to help themselves. The Iraqis would attack with a vengeance, certain of an easy victory with very little effort. He shook his head. They did not realize that the forces they moved to reinforce were dead, wounded, or captured.

He turned to the aide. "Nasir, pass the word to First Battalion to launch their attack. Tell Second Battalion to stand ready."

The subordinate saluted and withdrew.

Al-Behbahani felt guilty for a moment. He knew what he did, he did out of necessity. Yet . . . how would his God judge him for the sense of joy he felt? Then again, where was his God when his wife needed help? Recovering from simple surgery at the Sulaibekhat Social Care Institution in Kuwait City when the Iraqi pigs invaded there in August 1990, she'd died from a combination of lack of medical care and starvation. The colonel's sense of guilt departed. He'd face his judgment later—his enemies would face theirs now.

The Kuwaiti M-84s lured the approaching Iraqi brigade in. As the enemy force assaulted, most missed the cloud on the horizon to the west. This cloud rapidly materialized into a battalion of M1A2s. The 15th Brigade's 1st Battalion attacked on line, initiating fires into their invaders at over three thousand meters. By the time the remnants of the Iraqi brigade managed to break contact, little was left of what had at one time been a proud force of over one hundred combat vehicles led by some of the most promising leaders in Iraq's army.

The ranking officer to survive the Kuwaiti counterattack was a major. He rallied the forces he could and turned north. Facing a court-martial and possible execution was better than certain death. Looking

back, he saw no pursuit. The Kuwaitis seemed satisfied
with exacting their vengeance on the men who had
not made it out of their kill sack. The major led the
ragged assembly of thirty vehicles toward the border.

As they approached a rise to their north, a line of
dots appeared on the horizon. What was this . . . ? The
major pulled up his binoculars. Focusing the lenses, he
saw an endless line of M1A2s, each with the red,
white, green, and black Kuwaiti flag fluttering from its
antenna. Another battalion of the M1A2s.

Allah have mercy . . .

Two minutes later, the Tawakalna Division ceased
to exist.

3rd Brigade, 4th ID TOC, Northern Kuwait
22 October, 1615 Hours Local

Doc Hancock felt uncomfortable. He'd never been to
the rear far enough to see the task force operations
center, much less the brigade's.

Man, this place is a fucking palace, he thought.

Interconnected M577 command and control vehicles
were everywhere, all under the largest camouflage net
Hancock had ever seen. Clusters of vans pulled side
by side and backed up to one another, extensions
thrown between them. Scores of staff NCOs and officers raced between structures, bundles of overlays and
maps in hand, intent on completing their missions. Between the structures, what seemed like miles of cable
linked generators to the various structures. The generators' constant hum and the smell of diesel fuel permeated the area. It reminded Hancock of the sound
and smell behind the booths at the county fair that
used to visit his hometown every autumn when he was
a kid.

This was an unplanned trip for Doc. On reaching
friendly lines, Captain Dillon had passed on to Hancock that Striker 6 wanted Lieutenant Matheson in
the rear, ASAP. Something had fallen through with
the Hummer that was supposed to be waiting for them

on the other side of the obstacle, so Dillon had told him to continue moving and drop his passenger off at the 3rd Brigade headquarters.

They'd reached the 3rd Brigade TOC in the middle of chow. Seeing Colonel Jones's Bradley near the center of the compound, Hancock guided his tank in that direction. As he pulled to a stop, a tall figure emerged from the vehicle's shadow. Not waiting for the tank to cool down and shut off, the figure jumped on board and climbed onto the turret.

Jones reached a hand out to Doc. "Son, Colonel Estes told me about the job you and your men did today. Tell Dillon and the rest of his miscreants that I appreciate it. God knows it's a sorry excuse for a company you've been assigned to, but you boys do get the job done."

Doc felt his hackles rise at the words, then realized from the look on Jones's face that he didn't mean a word of it—in fact, just the opposite. "Yes, sir. I'll pass the message on to Captain Dillon."

A figure emerged from the loader's hatch. Sam had climbed inside on reaching the brigade's perimeter, not wanting to become the center of attention.

Jones held out a hand. "Cutlass Six, I presume?"

Sam blushed and took the hand. "Yes, sir."

"Lieutenant, I . . . ah, fuck it." Jones leaned over and gave the aviator a huge bear hug. He released her and stepped back, leaving the young woman breathless. "By God! If I'd known it was that nice warming up to junior officers, I'd have tried it a long time ago!" He looked at her, seriously now, but with a twinkle in his eye. "Thank you, Lieutenant. Your platoon saved some fine men today. You ever need anything—anything—you call me. Understood?"

Sam blushed. "Yes, sir. Thank you, sir."

"All right then. You young folks climb down and grab a plate of chow. I know you've worked up an appetite. We've got spaghetti, garden peas, and chocolate milk. Yummy."

Doc shifted uncomfortably. He and Sam exchanged

looks. "Sir, I should really be getting back to the company."

Jones, having been around the block a few times, couldn't help but see that something was going on between the two young officers. He looked at Matheson, then back to Hancock. *Fuck it,* he thought. *They've been through hell and were likely to go through more of the same before this were over.* He could give them an hour or so to work out whatever it was. "Hell, son, you've got time to throw down some grub." Jones looked at Doc with his most dour scowl. "That's an order."

"But, sir, what about the brigade that was closing . . . ?"

Jones shook his head. "Don't worry about them, son. They're a nonissue. The Kuwaitis had a visit with those boys while you were on the way in."

"The Kuwaitis?" Hancock had never worked with the Arab soldiers, but he'd heard enough that he found the news surprising.

Jones nodded once. "Yep, the Kuwaitis. And they did fine work from what I've heard." He turned back to Sam. "Thanks again, Cutlass. I'll see you two over at the chow truck." With that said, he climbed down from the tank and disappeared into the gathering twilight.

The two lieutenants found themselves once more in conversation with Jones over dinner. Someone at the TOC had found a set of fatigues that were a bit on the large size to replace Matheson's ripped-up flight suit. She'd also had an opportunity to scrub what remained of Fang off her under an Australian shower— a canvas bag of water with a pull-spout attached to the bottom. As the water, still warm from the day's sun, had run down her body, Sam had tried to scrub the memory of her attacker from her mind. While she hadn't been entirely successful with that part of it, at least she felt human again.

The "hot" chow was served out of mermite cans on

paper plates. True to the colonel's word, it was spaghetti, peas, and chocolate milk. Hancock marveled that an army that was so technically advanced could come up with such combinations of cuisine. It was a wonder America wasn't a Cuban colony. The plates sat at an awkward angle on the hood of Jones's Hummer. The desert sky was dark now and they used blue chem-lites to dine by. The effect of the colored light sticks—blue-tinted spaghetti and purple peas—added to the ambiance of the meal.

"Well, Lieutenant Matheson, guess you're about ready to go," Jones said.

Her unit was sending a helicopter for her in two hours. Sam felt sad at the thought. She missed her platoon, but the men of Third Brigade had made her feel at home, like part of a family. "Yes, sir. I've enjoyed my stay, but I really need to get back to my guys."

Hancock said nothing. He seemed to be preoccupied arranging his purple peas with a plastic knife.

A group of men walked over, wanting to meet Matheson before she took off. Her actions in the air had earned her the respect of the men of the brigade. All of them knew that it was thanks to her efforts that their beloved Jones was still around. A few had found out that she could take care of herself one-on-one. As the story of her encounter with the Iraqi NCO continued to circulate, it was beginning to take on epic proportions. She'd wanted to spend a few moments alone with Doc before he returned to his unit, but she couldn't ignore the friendly group of soldiers. Sam talked to them, shook hands, and listened to stories of home and family. Even today, she thought, with women all over the battlefield, something about talking to a strange female while in harm's way caused men to reminisce about loved ones and the hearth. After a few minutes, she looked up and noticed that Doc was no longer present.

"Looking for our young firebrand?" asked Jones. Sitting on his camp stool and sipping a cup of coffee, he'd noticed the look of alarm in the young woman's eyes.

Sam was flustered. "Oh . . . no, sir. I was just, uh . . ."

Jones blew gently on the coffee. Looking into the cup rather than at Sam, he nodded and smiled. "Doc went that way a couple of minutes ago," he said, pointing to the perimeter.

Matheson blushed. "Oh, well . . . thank you, sir."

"You're welcome, my dear," Jones said quietly. Sam didn't hear him. She was already twenty feet away and moving quickly.

She found Doc sitting on a rock a few minutes later, just past the perimeter. It was so dark she almost stumbled over him. "So there you are!"

Doc looked up, startled. "Sam . . . what are you doing out here?"

Sam Matheson smiled, saying nothing.

"What?"

"You called me Sam."

"That is your name, isn't it?"

Matheson ignored the question. "Do you mind if I sit?" she finally asked.

She could hear him sliding over on the stone. "Wait . . . sit on this," she said, handing him a soft nylon blanket.

"Where'd you get the poncho liner?" he asked, standing up to make room.

She nodded in the direction of the headquarters as she helped spread out the liner. "A sergeant back at the TOC gave it to me, said it would be getting chilly. I guess he felt sorry for me, no clothes and all."

Now that's not the line of thinking I need to hear right now, thought Doc.

They settled down, looking at the sliver of moon on the horizon.

"Beautiful, isn't it?" Sam asked.

Hancock looked closely at Samantha Matheson.

"Yes, you . . . yes, it is." Doc hung his head, dying. *You idiot.*

"Doc," Sam said quietly.

He continued to look at the ground. "Yeah?"

"Doc."

Doc slowly lifted his head and looked into her eyes.

They came together slowly. Everything else that day had happened so quickly, they were drawing out this moment as if by mutual assent. Their lips touched, gently at first. Doc felt Sam's warm tongue slip into his mouth, questing. As their breathing became heavier, Doc slipped his hand from behind her back and moved it slowly up the front of her blouse, then stopped.

"I'm sorry, Sam. I shouldn't . . ."

"Shh." Sitting up, Sam slowly unbuttoned her shirt. Doc could only stare in disbelief.

Sam continued with the buttons and looked deep into his eyes. "I know this is going to sound silly, Doc . . . only having known each other a few hours . . . but . . . did you feel it? When you opened that door and I saw you for the first time . . . I just knew . . ."

Doc was having trouble breathing. He looked into Sam's eyes. "You're right. It doesn't make sense, none whatsoever. But God help me, I did. I feel like we've been together a dozen lifetimes."

Taking his hand, Sam moved it inside her shirt and settled it onto her breast, gently holding it there. She lay back on the poncho liner, pulling Hancock down with her. "I wanted to make sure it wasn't just me," she whispered.

Cold Steel Battle Position, Northern Kuwait
22 October, 1930 Hours Local

The leadership of Cold Steel—Dillon, Mason, and Rider—huddled around a Hummer. Each held a luke-warm cup of coffee. They'd finished chow and were taking a few moments to unwind from the events of the past twenty-four hours.

"Top, how are the troops doing?" asked Dillon. He knew Rider had to be exhausted. Once the battle was over, hell—before it was over, he was the man ensuring that men and tanks that fell on the battlefield were cared for. It was a rough job, and the hours sucked worse than even the combat crewmen's did. As the senior enlisted member of Cold Steel, Dillon depended on John Rider to keep the pulse of his men. How were they holding up? Were they getting enough rest? What was their morale? They spoke more freely to Rider. And the NCOs could always be counted on to give the first sergeant the straight shit.

Rider tossed the remains of his coffee into the sand. The look on his face told them why. "Jesus, I know we're in a combat zone, but that tastes like *shit*. A cup of brown water is all it is—and not very tasty water at that." Looking to Dillon, he said seriously, "They're all right, sir. Exhausted, but still too wired to get much rest. The NCOs are forcing them down for some shut-eye, nonetheless."

Rider was silent a moment, too tired to string together coherent thoughts. "I did speak to the S1 and the S4 about some replacements. We should have a few men and tanks coming forward tomorrow, but I don't know what kind of shape either of them will be in." Both men knew brigade was likely pulling clerks, cooks, and fuel handlers to replace the losses sustained throughout the task forces. And any tank that came forward could be a hangar queen with more maintenance problems than it was worth.

Dillon nodded absently. "It's something anyway."

The first sergeant stood silently a moment, then spit. "Say, sir, about Third Platoon . . . did Tiger Six mention sending a new lieutenant forward?"

The Steel commander shook his head. "He didn't say, and I didn't ask. I think a new face in the platoon, or what's left of it, wouldn't help things right now . . . especially if it's a fresh and untrained lieutenant." Dillon shook his head. "Nope, I think we're better off letting the platoon sergeant take it for a while."

Rider nodded. "Good call, sir. I agree. Changing the subject, any word from headquarters on what's next?"

Dillon looked into the night sky. He shook his head slowly. "No. Thanks to the Kuwaitis, we've gotten a chance to rest for a few hours, maybe a day. The other two Republican Guard divisions . . . I'd guess for now that that fight is thirty-six hours out. *I'd guess.* We should find out something at tomorrow morning's update at the TOC. For now, keep security out and let everybody get some sleep." He turned to Mason. "The tanks pulling security reported set to you yet, Thad?"

Holding a small blue-lensed flashlight between his teeth, Mason flipped through his notebook, stopping once he found the page. He scanned for a moment, then shut the notebook and turned off the light. "Roger. C-13, C-22, and C-32 are forward and set as of twenty minutes ago. The rest of the company's tanks have pulled back. C-65 and C-66 are alternating covering the backside and are monitoring the task force command net. The whole company's fed, fueled, and full up on ammo. No maintenance problems to speak of on the tanks we still have." Mason looked at Dillon. "If it makes you feel better, the mechanics think they found the problem with the transmission."

"What was it?"

Mason grinned. "It looks like a big cobra climbed up into the engine compartment to get warm. He toasted up real quick and died in there. Some of his pieces worked around in there and . . . well, you know. It's all fixed up now."

Dillon chuckled. "A snake. Ain't that the luck of the fuckin' Irish." Throwing the remains of his coffee out, he looked to the two men he depended on for so much. "Okay. Good work today, both of you. I suggest we all try to get some rest." He turned to walk back to his tank, then thought of something. "Thad, has Doc made it back yet?"

"He called. They're en route. Probably be another half hour or so."

Dillon shook his head as he walked away. "Poor bastard. I hate using him as a taxi service. Give me a call when he makes it in."

CHAPTER 12

_____

_____

_____

Outside the Fire

The White House
23 October, 0300 Hours Eastern

Still in his bathrobe, Jonathan Drake looked up from his desk as the door of the Oval Office opened. Holding out an arm, he invited Newman and Werner to have a seat. He'd insisted on six-hour updates throughout the current crisis, regardless of the time.

"Gentlemen"—he smiled tiredly—"thanks for coming in so early. Sorry about the jammies."

Newman returned his boss's smile through a yawn. "Sir, they don't bother us."

Drake saw for the first time that his insistence on staying updated, regardless of the hour, was beginning to impact his subordinates. "Ron, why don't you and the general send in someone else for the overnights? That would be fine with me."

General Werner rubbed a tired hand across his face. "Time to rest later, sir. We've got a war on."

Drake looked thoughtful. "Yeah. So . . . any changes? Things are still going well?"

Both men nodded noncommittally. Neither looked particularly pleased.

"What?" asked the president. "Something's bothering you. Spill it."

The chairman bit his lip. How do you tell the president of the United States that you couldn't be prouder of him for having the balls to do what needed to be done, but that since he hadn't served a day in the military, it was difficult to explain why things weren't exactly coming up roses. Instead, the general looked to the secretary of defense.

Taking the cue, Ronald Newman looked to the president. "Sir, things aren't looking bad. Our ground force, Third Brigade, did well against the Tawakalna Division."

Drake nodded and looked at General Tom Werner for confirmation that he was on the same sheet of music.

Werner, noticing the look, nodded. "Sir, those boys kicked ass. There is no longer a Tawakalna Division in Iraq's Republican Guard. The Kuwaitis finished off the last of them a few hours ago, which was a pleasant surprise. We weren't really sure what to expect from the home team, but they came through with flying colors."

Drake's confusion was apparent. "So why the long faces?"

Newman continued. "Sir, there's still a lot of enemy forces across the border in Iraq. Two divisions of those forces are expected to head south again anytime—and we don't know if more will join them or not. For some reason, Aref has so far minimized the number of units he's throwing at us. Our best analysis is that he thought he'd roll over Third Brigade and the Kuwaitis, and that we wouldn't press the issue by sending more troops into the fight."

"But even assuming that Aref does send those other divisions south, won't our airpower be able to take them down? Or at least cut back on their numbers before they reach Third Brigade?"

Werner took the burden from Newman's shoulders. He was the president's military advisor, so he would advise. "Sir, airpower is great, and we've got the best flyers in the world. But there are two things you need to remember about it. One, we don't have as much of it in theater as we normally do. Two, it can *attrit,* not *destroy,* two heavy divisions . . . contrary to what some folks would have you believe. A lot of shit is still going to make it into Kuwait, Mr. President."

Drake rubbed his eyes. God, it seemed like he'd been awake forever. And in retrospect, the midnight roast beef sandwich with horseradish sauce from the White House kitchen hadn't been a great idea. Holding his hand up for his guests to give him a moment, he opened his desk drawer and shuffled items around . . . a beeper for the Secret Service detail, the Palm organizer he had never figured out how to use. He controlled the largest nuclear arsenal remaining in the free world, but he didn't warrant antacid tablets? He shut the drawer in frustration.

Looking at the two men, he folded his hands across his desk. "Okay, I hear the problems. Recommendations?"

Newman gestured for the chief to summarize the course of action they'd agreed on.

Werner looked steadily at his commander-in-chief. "Attack, sir."

Drake sat up straighter, looking from one man to the other. "Attack? Third Brigade attack? Aren't they outnumbered something like five to one by those two divisions we were discussing?"

Well, at least the man had been listening during Tactics 101, thought Werner. "Yes, sir . . . actually more like six to one, considering the losses they've sustained. But we've been discussing something with the special operations folks. . . ."

Drake listened thoughtfully to the plan. It was bold, but a lot could go wrong. If it worked, though . . . "All right, gentlemen. I approve in concept. Show me something on paper in an hour."

Werner nodded. "Next note, sir. Regarding General Pavlovski's theory that someone is supplying real-time satellite imagery to Iraq . . ."

Newman grunted. "How could I forget? Did we confirm the CIA's information regarding the culprit?"

Werner's face twisted as if he'd tasted something rotten. "Yes, sir. It was them all right."

Drake closed his eyes and nodded his head wearily. If he held this office long enough, maybe it wouldn't surprise him what some of the U.S.'s "allies" would do for money. "Is space command ready to prosecute the contingency plan we discussed?"

"Affirmative, sir."

"Do it."

Newman nodded. "The final touches are being put on it now. We'll be ready. Sir . . . there's a final aspect of this mess that we haven't talked about. Iran. Right now they're just sitting across the border, but they are a threat that cannot be ignored. The marines we have facing them are good men, but there's not a hell of a lot of them. The Iranians *could* throw a wrench into this plan if they decide to become players and back up Aref."

Drake stood. "Chris Dodd called a few minutes ago. He's got something cooking that he believes will take care of the Iranians. Continue your planning. I'll have him here to fill you in when you come back."

Werner smiled at the SECDEF as he moved toward the door. "When the CIA has something cooking, somebody had better be nervous."

**Presidential Command Complex, West of An Najaf, Iraq
23 October, 1010 Hours Local**

President Aref loosened the collar of his shirt. "Explain this to me again, General. I'm not sure I understood you correctly the first time. Just over twenty-four hours ago, you said that your force was well capable of handling the Americans—with or without reinforcements. Now the first message I receive from you since that time *tells me that you have managed to lose your entire command*?"

General Hamza, commander of the elite Tawakalna Division, sighed on the other end of the line. Striking the Americans had been his chance to exorcise the demons that had haunted him in the years following his son's death. In a detached way, he was sorry for the loss of his men, but it was not what weighed on his soul. He'd had his chance, had bided his time over the years, waiting for the opportunity . . . and he'd wasted it. The last thing he needed at the moment was to listen to a Saddam Hussein clone berate him. "You understand perfectly, Mr. President. I have failed—failed you, my nation, my men, myself . . . my son. The fault is mine."

The Iraqi leader's face reddened as he screamed into the receiver. "I know where the fault lies! I want you here within the next twenty-four hours. I will deal with you then. Do you understand me?"

Yes, thought Hamza, *I understand all too well.* He knew the fate that awaited him once he reported to Aref. A quick trial before a military tribunal, an even quicker conviction, followed by a firing squad. "With all due respect, Mr. President, I do not think that will be possible."

"General Hamza, you will—" A shot rang out on the other end of the line. "General Hamza! General . . . answer me!"

A few moments later an unsteady voice replied. "Hello?"

"Who is this? Tell General Hamza to get back on the phone this instant!"

Hamza's aide looked at the figure lying over the desk, pistol in hand, a pool of blood slowly spreading from the head wound and saturating the reports scattered about desk. "I'm . . . I'm afraid the general is dead. Who is this?"

Tehran, Iran
23 October, 1110 Hours Local

The servant approached a figure reclining on the plush cushions of a balcony overlooking the city. Although he had been in the man's service for two years, he still got chills when in close proximity to the Holy One. When the leader was in thought, it was generally not advisable to bother him. Still, the visitor in the adjoining room had assured him that the ayatollah would want this message.

"What is it, Ahamad?" Khalani had not opened his eyes or turned to the servant.

"Father, you have a visitor. . . ."

"Did you tell him that I was indisposed?" asked Khalani, still not turning.

"Yes, Father. It is the director of security. . . ."

The ayatollah stood. "Very well. Send him in."

Bowing, the servant left the balcony.

Moments later, the director of internal security for the Islamic Revolutionary Council entered. He bowed his head. "Holy One."

"What matter is of such importance that my meditation must be interrupted?"

The man said nothing, but proffered a manila envelope.

Khalani looked at the parcel disdainfully. "Open it."

The director did so, then removed the contents and extended them, eyes averted.

A yellow sticky note was affixed to the top of a thick stack of photos. It read simply, "Stay out of it", with a telephone number written below the message.

Khalani removed the note and looked at the first photo. It was of very high quality. He quickly turned and walked to the edge of the balcony. Shuffling through the remaining photographs, he saw that he was prominently displayed in all. He recognized the other person in the photos as well, his guest following a social gathering earlier in the week. "Where did you get these?" he asked slowly.

The director of security did not look at the ayatollah. As was his duty, he had checked the contents of the package before bringing it to Khalani, and thus had seen the photos—a fact his leader would be well aware of. He walked a fine line. "They were delivered to the Algerian embassy in Washington. I assure you that no one has—"

Khalani raised a hand in resignation. "Enough. I have a phone call to make. Leave me."

The visitor nodded, bowed, and turned to depart. Khalani's voice stopped him. "Tell me, Abbas, who was in charge of security the night these photographs were taken?"

The tone of Khalani's voice sent a chill down the director's spine. He turned. "One of my best men . . ."

The ayatollah gazed from the balcony over the nation of people who turned to him for all of their answers. Better to betray a new friend than his followers. "Obviously not. He will be sent before the Council—today."

The director bowed again. "As you say, Father." Another shiver rippled down his back. Stoning was not uncommon for those who failed the Revolution.

The White House
23 October, 0320 Hours Eastern

President Drake sat at the desk in his personal office. Set within the Oval Office itself, the small space wasn't much larger than a walk-in closet. Still, it was the only location within these hallowed halls he truly felt was his own.

Before becoming president, Drake had not realized just how heavy the burden could become . . . occupying the office previously held by such men as Lincoln, Truman, the Roosevelts, and all the others. Had they felt as he did when nations and lives were at stake, dependent on the wisdom of their decisions? As if the spirits of their predecessors watched their every move, silently passing judgment as to whether or not they were worthy to guide this great nation?

Pushing himself back from the desk, Drake looked at his feet and the fuzzy bunny slippers wrapped around them. What would the Founding Fathers think of them? The slippers had been a gift from the first lady. He couldn't wear them around the White House proper, but this was his personal space and—the president wiggled his feet, making the ears flop—they were damned comfortable.

Drake had been in dire need of a reprieve from all that was going on after Newman and Werner departed. He had come here to his inner sanctum. Turning to his PC, he inserted a CD into one of the drives.

Turning to his ministereo, Drake selected his favorite music for these therapy sessions—*AC/DC Live.* Slipping on his headphones, the president turned the volume up and hummed along as "Dirty Deeds Done Dirt Cheap" reached its crescendo.

In time with the music, Drake blasted alien invaders from outer space on the computer monitor. The rabbit ears flopped madly back and forth as the presidential foot kept the beat.

Next to the screen, a red light flashed incessantly. *No rest for the weary,* thought Drake. Blasting a final alien, a particularly unsavory one with two heads and a drooling problem, he switched off the game. CNN's Web site popped up on the screen, replacing the galactic invaders. Turning to the stereo, he selected a nice compilation of classical music his sister had given him for Christmas the previous year. Now he was ready. "Come in."

The door opened and Christopher Dodd stuck his head around the corner. "Has the Secret Service caught on that you're a metal head yet, sir?" asked the director of Central Intelligence with a smile.

Drake rolled his eyes. "Their code name for me is 'Ozzie.' Does that answer your question? Come on in, Chris."

Glancing down, Drake saw one rabbit ear sticking out from beneath the edge of the desk. He quickly moved the flagrant slipper out of sight. It was bad enough Dodd knew about the music.

Chris Dodd shook his head, chuckling. "Sir, I'm the director of the CIA."

Drake looked puzzled. "What?"

"We know all about the bunnies. Your secret is

safe. Did you know Richard Nixon had a Howdy Doody doll he couldn't sleep without?"

Drake smiled. "Really?" He quickly threw up a hand. "Never mind. I don't want to know. Besides, that's not why you're here. What's the latest on our Iranian problem?"

Dodd turned the high beams on, grinning from ear to ear. "What Iranian problem, Mr. President?"

Presidential Command Complex, West of An Najaf, Iraq
23 October, 1200 Hours Local

Sitting in his private bunker deep beneath the sands of his homeland, Abdul Aref had never felt as isolated as he did at the moment—or as invigorated. The room was small, at least by his normal, opulent standards. And the furnishings were spartan—a desk, a chair, maps detailing his planned military actions, and a table loaded down with communications equipment and telephones.

Beneath the lip of the desk, a single button was inlaid so that its face was flush with the wood. Someone would have to know what they were looking for to find it. Twenty bodyguards, with no allegiance other than to Aref himself, would come charging into the bunker if it were ever depressed. Aref had drilled them four times over the past week to ensure they performed this duty to his expectations. The first time they were a bit slow. Since he'd made an example of the captain of the guard, their improvement had been nothing short of remarkable.

Was this how Saddam felt during the closing days of the Gulf War? he mused. *And Hitler as he watched the Allies close in on him?* He knew the United States possessed satellite technology that allowed them to— what was the popular example?—read a newspaper byline from outer space? They could easily find him if he operated in the open—and no doubt would spare little expense removing him. So he would stay here until his holy war—his *jihad*—was successfully concluded.

Aref laughed to himself. Even his closest staff members were convinced of his newfound religious conviction. Idiots. The only person who suspected the truth was the ayatollah himself, but he had been promised such profits that the old fox could hardly say no to their alliance.

Another nearby explosion caused the overhead light fixture to sway. The bombing had been almost nonstop for the past twenty-four hours. The Americans didn't know where all of Iraq's command and control bunkers were, but when they suspected a location, it was heavily targeted. Somehow they must have gotten information on this facility. Should he move? No, better to stay and wait it out. If they had not hit him yet, perhaps Allah truly *was* on his side. The thought made him smile. Would that not be ironic?

He had so many decisions to make. As the latest explosions ended, he wondered if he had been wrong. Might he lose this battle of wills against the United States? He admitted to himself that he'd miscalculated the response of the American president—but who would have expected such actions from a *teacher*?

Aref shook his head, awakening himself from his reverie. There was no time for second-guessing. It would not matter. Let them bomb. They would not stop him. It was time to make America pay for what it had done to Iraq during the Gulf War, and for the years of humiliation and sanctions that followed. Past time. "General!"

The door opened. General of the Army Ali Abunimah, the commanding general of Iraq's military, entered.

An impressive figure, General Abunimah came to attention, staring over Aref's head. The general was not happy. A survivor of the purges that had savaged Iraq's military command structure following their defeat at the hands of the Coalition Forces, the only reason he had remained in service was a true desire to make a difference . . . to somehow help his country regain its former strength and self-respect. It had been so long since the world had looked at them with anything other than contempt. Abunimah had over the years turned a blind eye to the actions of his leaders, actions that tore at his moral fabric. He justified this by telling himself it was for the greater good. *Stay silent, Ali, you can accomplish more by working from within the system.* This military action by his nation's newest leader, though, was almost too much for the general.

From the beginning, he had thought that this war was unwise. He did not want to see his men die for nothing—again. It had taken years following the Gulf War to rebuild his country's forces. To watch this . . . mad man . . . squander them . . .

But the reason Abunimah had been selected for his position was what held him from doing more. He was a soldier in every sense, and his loyalty would allow him to go only so far. He'd given his opinion in the early planning stages of Aref's war and been shot down. So he'd executed the plan as directed. Now, as he tried to win a war he had been against from the beginning, he was called here only to be told to sit in the hallway like a chamber servant for two hours until the president could see him. No, the general was not happy at all.

Abdul Aref motioned to a seat. "Please, General . . . sit down."

As Abunimah settled in a seat, the Iraqi leader began slowly. "I have been . . . analyzing . . . the results of our campaign against the infidels. We have not seen a great deal of success."

Abunimah tried not to laugh aloud. A phrase he had heard the Americans use came into his mind unbidden. *No shit.* "No, sir. Things have not gone well thus far." The general looked at Aref, judging how far he might go, then proceeded. "You might recall, Mr. President, that I tried to discourage you from sending the Tawakalna into the Americans without the rest of the Southern Corps ready to support them. I also encouraged you to prepare the Republican Guard Northern Corps to enter the fight if you truly wanted to defeat the Americans—sir."

Aref flared. "General Hamza said they would not present a problem, that he had the forces necessary. . . ."

Abunimah pushed his point. "Sir, I warned you— Hamza wanted vengeance, and he didn't want to share it. That blinded him. It had for years."

"Be that as it may, we still have a war to fight." Abdul Aref continued in a quiet voice. "I called you in here for counsel, not to listen to excuses— General."

Abunimah saw a flash of the man who had positioned himself so adroitly to step in for Saddam Hussein—who, if there were truth to the rumors, engineered the ex-president's "heart condition." No need to push his fortunes further. "Of course, Mr. President. Forgive me if I overstep my bounds."

"General," Aref continued, as if the exchange had never taken place, "will the Madinah and the Hamourabi be able to accomplish what the Tawakalna could not?"

General Abunimah thought about the question for a moment. "For now, they have the necessary forces for the combat ratio to be favorable to us. But the other American divisions are beginning to arrive in theater. Once they draw equipment—"

"We must act before then, General," snapped Aref. "How long until the American reinforcements can move against us?"

"As soon as they can draw combat vehicles and upload ammunition, sir. Their stocks of equipment in Qatar were damaged during our initial attacks, but we're not sure of the extent. If sufficient materiel remained intact there, they could even now be—"

Aref dismissed the comment with a wave of his hand. "My intelligence sources, which I cannot share with you just yet, General, tell me the Qatar stocks were destroyed. I have seen the evidence with my own eyes. Their reinforcements will draw from floating stocks of equipment—floating stocks that are not yet in port."

Abunimah did not look convinced. "Yes, that would mean a few more days, but if your intelligence is wrong—"

Aref slammed a fist into his desktop. "Forget Qatar, General Abunimah!" He stood and walked across the room, stopping next to the wall containing the operations and planning maps. "I want to push this while the Americans are still recovering from our first attack. Our Iranian brothers will support us in the effort."

Abunimah looked at him dubiously. He had fought the Iranians too many years to place faith in anything they said—much less to use "Iranian" and "brother" in the same sentence. "Do you truly believe so, sir?"

"I have the assurance of the ayatollah himself." Walking to the map, Abdul Aref pointed to Iran. "The two Iranian divisions outside of Abadan have only a token force of American marines opposing them. Even with close air support, the marines will not last long."

Moving his hand west and into Iraq, the president pointed to the city of An Nasiriyah, one hundred kilometers northwest of the Kuwait border. "I want the remainder of the Southern Corps, the Madinah and Hamourabi divisions, in staging areas south of An Nasiriyah by tomorrow afternoon. They will refuel and make final preparations for an attack on the battered American forces in northern Kuwait."

Aref pointed to the west of the Kuwaiti border city of Abdali. "They will move at night and begin their attack on the American positions before dawn of the following day. The Iranians will synchronize their attack on the U.S. Marines in such a time frame as to aid us in our attack. Together, we cannot fail. Four divisions of Allah's chosen against a brigade of devils and a few marines."

Moving his hand south, Aref pointed west and north of Kuwait's capital city. "By noon of the day after tomorrow, I want the infidels dead and our forces through the Al Jahra pass northwest of Kuwait City. The Kuwaiti forces, if they are still willing to fight, will go down quickly trying to keep us from entering their capital. The American reinforcements"—Aref favored his general with a smile—"will not present a problem without any tanks or mechanized infantry to field against us. Then," he said, raising his arms, "the city is ours."

General Abunimah had listened in silence. The president . . . had he learned nothing from his predecessor's example? It was never as simple as it seemed . . . and Aref was no tactician, though he apparently thought differently. "And once we successfully destroy the American mechanized forces, what of the airborne division they have in the city?"

"We'll offer the American government an opportunity to evacuate their remaining military forces—less their equipment of course. The Ayatollah Khalani and I agree they will take the offer. If not, we will send in fresh forces that can take their time cleaning the Americans from the city. Many of our men will die— urban combat is such a tedious and bloody affair— but we will ultimately win. By the prophet, *Kuwait will finally be ours!*"

The general had had enough. "Sir, why did you call me here? You have already made your plan of attack." The frustration in his voice was evident. Aref had allied himself with the devil, and together they had planned the war that he, if anyone, should be planning. A sense of foreboding fell upon the old soldier, a feeling that this time his nation might not survive the rash acts of a mad leader. Sooner or later, the Americans would tire of putting the wild dog back into his cage and opt instead to put the animal down.

"Not my plan, General," Aref replied. "Your plan. You will execute it accordingly, working out the necessary details. I want you to keep me informed on the movements of the Southern Corps. And remember, they are to be in An Nasiriyah before tomorrow night, prepared to attack."

So that was it. Aref wanted a scapegoat in case his plan did not work. General Abunimah stood, bowing. "It will be done, sir. If I may be excused, there are details which need tending immediately if your—*my* plan is to have a chance."

Aref stood. "That is the spirit, General! Very good. You are excused."

CHAPTER 13

Attack

"Son of a bitch," said Lieutenant Colonel Rob Estes, looking at the 3rd Brigade's plans map. He and the other task force commanders of the 3rd Brigade Combat Team had just received the order for the upcoming mission.

Standing next to his commander, Major Dave Barnett stroked his mustache and nodded. Looking to Estes, he uttered a single word: "Ballsy."

The other task force commanders, S3s, and fire support officers grouped around the map nodded in agreement with Barnett's insightful observation.

Jones stood behind the commanders, wreathed in smoke, prepared to answer questions. Once he'd completed the briefing, he had given his commanders thirty minutes to look over the graphics and order and discuss it with their primary staffs. They were now twenty minutes into that period. At the end of the half hour, each commander would brief Jones on his role in the upcoming mission. Called the brief back, it was a good method of ensuring everyone was on the same page before the commanders proceeded back to their units to plan their pieces of the fight.

In a few hours, Jones would drop by the task force headquarters to hear how each commander intended to accomplish his assigned portion of the brigade mission. He hoped to God that time allowed for at least a quick rehearsal, but it didn't look good.

Turning to Jones, Estes spoke what was on all of their minds. "Kind of all or nothing, isn't it, sir?"

Removing himself from the cloud surrounding him, Jones stepped up to the map and looked at the blue lines flowing north. "Yep," he finally answered.

The gathered leadership waited expectantly for him to expound on the reply. Instead he looked to each of them. "Okay, who's briefing first?"

The officers continued to stare at Jones. Reaching into his pocket, Striker 6 pulled another cigarette out and flicked his Zippo. "All right, gentlemen, let me tell you how it is. Right now we're sitting pretty well thanks to the replacements sent forward to backfill our losses. The brigade is at ninety-five percent strength—over one hundred of the most lethal tanks in the world, about half that many Bradleys, some shit-hot artillery, and all of these assets manned and supported by the finest military men and women in the history of the civilized world. If we sit here and defend"—Jones pointed north to the Republican Guard divisions identified as the Madinah and the Hamourabi—"these guys will be down to see us soon. And there's nothing to say that more Iraqi divisions won't start moving south in the meantime."

Barnett pointed at the closest Guard division. "And the Madinah is ours, sir?"

Jones nodded. "Yeah. And if all goes according to plan, they'll be hammered by bombs, fixed-wing air, and rocket and artillery fire before you ever get a shot off."

Major Jon Porter, Task Force 2-35's old XO and acting commander since the death of Mace 6, pointed south on the map at a blue icon. The unit symbol had popped up only four hours ago. "And these guys are going to be ready, sir?"

Jones shrugged. "I spoke with Spartan Six at the

JTF briefing. I know the man well. If he says they can do it, then come hell or high water he'll get the mission accomplished."

Jones looked around at his leaders, the men who would have to push this plan to the soldiers of the 3rd Brigade, who would have to make their men believers. First he would have to make *them* believe. "Gentlemen, here's the bottom line. We can sit here in our prepared positions waiting for these guys. We're dug in, have plenty of ammo, and can probably hold out for a while. Long enough for the Third Infantry Division to move up and support us? Those ships are still two days out, so not likely. Or . . . we can take the fight to him and maybe end this thing. The CINC has given us a mission. By God we *will* accomplish it. Besides," he added, "I'm tired of letting these assholes make all the moves. It's time to take it to them."

From around the headquarters, approving shouts went up. Others picked up on the whooping until the noise level was almost deafening. Jones inwardly sighed. Well, they'd bought it. Now if he himself could only be as big a believer.

Sensing someone next to him, Jones turned to see Dave Barnett. Barnett lit his pipe and let a few smoke rings rise before speaking. "Sir, that was"—he waved the pipe in the air, searching for the right words—"fucking inspirational."

Jones looked at the mustache, felt its now-familiar hypnotic tug. He looked away from Barnett, shaking his head to clear it. "Thanks, Dave."

Presidential Command Complex, West of An Najaf, Iraq
24 October, 1645 Hours Local

General Abunimah knocked on the door to Aref's inner sanctum. Hearing a voice calling for him to enter, he opened the door and proceeded inside.

"Sir," he said on entering the room, "you wanted an update on the Madinah and Hamourabi. The Southern Corps commander, Staff Major General al-Tikriti, reports that both units are in their staging positions, roughly forty kilometers south of An Nasiriyah."

Abdul Aref walked to his map and moved two pins, each representing one of his prized Republican Guard divisions. He looked east, to the Iranian divisions also marked by pins on his map. "Have you spoken with your Iranian counterpart?"

Abunimah nodded. "Yes, sir. He says we are to proceed as planned. That his forces will accomplish their assigned role. Sir . . ." The general hesitated before continuing. What he was about to say was based on pure instinct, with no proof to back it up. "This may be nothing, but the Iranian's choice of the word 'role' instead of 'mission' bothers me. . . ."

Aref raised a well-manicured hand to halt further comment. "As you say, it is nothing. A poor choice of words. They will be ready." The president turned from the map. "Of greater concern to me is that we get into position for our attack as soon as possible. I realize it will be difficult to conceal our movement from the Americans, but I do not want them to have more advanced warning than can be helped."

The general nodded. He might not think this war was in his nation's best interests, but if he was to fight it, he knew a few tricks. "Sir, the Americans will rely on two systems to find us—aircraft and satellites. The front that moved into the area of operations overnight has kept most of the American air grounded. We expect it will lift soon, but for now, it continues to aid in concealing our move south from enemy aircraft. Our second concern, the numerous satellites the Americans have in orbit, we have been addressing."

Aref was intrigued. "Go on, General. What are you doing about this problem?"

"Sir, here is the Southern Corps' axis of attack," said Abunimah, running a finger down a wide arrow leading south into Kuwait. "I have sent special forces into this area, and areas the same size to the east and west." The general turned to his president, looking him directly in the eye. "Over the past twenty-four hours, these troops have set fire to every oil well in the region I have just indicated."

"You *what*?"

The general had expected the outburst. It was why he had not briefed Abdul Aref on his plan ahead of time. "Mr. President, the fires create heat and smoke across that entire portion of the desert. The smoke obscures normal satellite imaging. The heat degrades the thermal satellite imaging. The area of burn is wide enough that the Americans will not be able to pinpoint our divisions or our axis of attack."

"Yes, but the oil we are losing . . ."

"These are controlled fires. We have engineer teams standing by to bring the wells back on-line at the earliest opportunity. Yes, we will lose a great deal of oil, but only a drop in the bucket if we are successful and control the Kuwaiti oil fields. And if we lose . . . will it really matter?"

"What of the Americans?"

The general considered the question. "If your question relates to their force in Kuwait, I can tell you that the Americans continue to occupy the same sector with roughly the same number of forces. They have replaced some of their losses, but no reinforcements. My estimate is that they will stay in their current positions and try to hold until reinforcements can arrive." He now looked pointedly at his leader. "If, sir, on the other hand you are asking about the status of their reinforcements . . . I assumed you still had access to your own channels and that those forces were not an issue."

"We will continue as planned, General," said Aref, a shadow momentarily passing over his face. He was not about to tell Abunimah that the satellite imagery being passed to him by his European friends had suddenly stopped. The plan was too far along at this juncture. "When will you give the order to initiate the next attack?"

"The Madinah will lead out at twenty-one-hundred hours tonight, sir. They will penetrate the west side of the American sector. The Hamourabi will follow and exploit the penetration. We will outnumber them six to one, more if the Iranians actually support our attack."

Abdul Aref raised a warning finger to the general.

Abunimah's face displayed no emotion as he corrected himself. "Sorry, sir. *When* the Iranians support our attack."

3rd Brigade, 4th ID TOC, Northern Kuwait
24 October, 1745 Hours Local

Jones looked at his watch, then at the sun settling below the western horizon. The rain obscured the orange-red globe, lending it a shimmering and otherworldly appearance. What was that old sailor's axiom? Red in the morning, sailors take warning? He guessed it didn't apply to dusk in the desert. Besides, the combination of the rain and the black clouds caused by the oil field fires that had moved in from the north was a problem likely unfamiliar in nautical circles.

Jones turned a trained eye to the 3rd Brigade TOC. The area was a hive of activity. He'd seen the routine numerous times through the years, these last-minute preparations for combat. The type of activity differed with the size of the unit. Here at the brigade headquarters, the Taj Mahal was breaking down—the numerous tents, tables, and maps pulled out and set up for planning were now being stored in whatever space was available in preparation for offensive operations. At the task force operations centers, Jones knew the scene would be much the same. At company level, the commanders would be calling for last-minute updates and statuses from their platoons. Within the platoons, crews would be feverishly finishing combat checks, tightening down ammo cans and petroleum products, and making copies of graphics. In a dark and twisted way, it was like watching a football team conducting warm-ups before the big game. Coaches making final adjustments to planned schemes, the receivers practicing the timing

of their patterns, the defense popping a few pads to
get loose, special teams rehearsing their small yet critical roles—all the seemingly disjointed operations leading up to one unified effort. The difference between
the two events, Jones knew, was that if his team's timing was off, if he made a bad call, if the other team
made a big play—a lot of his men were going to die.

Jones looked down at his coffee cup—empty. Glancing across his rapidly disintegrating headquarters to
the spot where the TOC's industrial-size coffeepot
stood, his heart jump-started. "Hey, hold on a second!" Jones yelled to the NCO about to unplug the
critical piece of combat equipment. The breakdown
was moving right along—the pot was always the last
piece of equipment disconnected from the generators.

Nodding his thanks to the NCO after filling his battle mug—a large travel cup wrapped tightly with OD
green military tape—Jones moved to the intel cell.
Major Tom Proctor was walking out of the back of
the S2's M577.

"What's the word, Tom?" asked Jones, sipping ap-
preciatively from the field cup. "The S2 get any imagery on the Southern Corps position?"

Proctor shook his head. "Sir, those fires are making
a mess of satellite reception. We had good locations on
both divisions yesterday as they moved south between
An Najaf and Al Kut. Based off their direction of
movement and estimated rate of march—the Iraqis are
pretty predictable—we know they're likely somewhere
south of An Nasiriyah." The Three shook his head in
frustration. "We just can't confirm their exact position."

"Any chance of getting some blue-suiters over the
area to take a look?"

The operations officer shrugged. "The air liaison officer thinks they might be able to get some aircraft up
soon if the weather moves out as predicted. Otherwise
we'll not only be sucking for reconnaissance, but our
close air support for the operation will be nil."

Jones nodded his understanding. "Well, like I always tell you, Tom—don't hinge your ground plan on

the air force. They mean well, but there's just too many variables involved in their line of work."

Proctor was silent a moment before continuing. "Sir, if we don't get a pinpoint location for those two divisions, we're not going to be able to prep them with the artillery and MLRS rockets before our attack. And we're not going to be able to suppress the enemy air defenses—which means it will be a hard sell getting the air support guys to fly in, assuming the weather clears. It could be a really ugly baby, sir."

Jones chuckled. "Well put, Thomas. Okay then, what are our options? It's almost eighteen hundred hours now. That gives us six hours to come up with something."

Proctor shrugged again. "Sir, we're working on it. My recommendation is to send warning orders to each task force to get their scouts ready to move forward of the brigade, tie their effort in with the brigade recon team and get as many eyes forward as possible. They can take artillery observers with them."

Jones nodded "That's *an* option—if it comes to it. But I really don't like the idea of sending lightly armored Hummers with nothing more for night-vision capability than PVS-7s and some TOW night sights forward to find T-72s and BMPs. For now, send out the warning order, but the plan remains to use the scouts on the flanks and lead with the armor."

The major nodded. In the desert at night, he also preferred having tanks as the forward element. They could see and shoot farther than any of the other combat vehicles, not to mention survive better if they stumbled into contact.

The men's thoughts were interrupted by raised voices from the back of the S2's M577. "I'm telling you . . . we can get them up. We've flown 'em in worse conditions."

Looking into the vehicle, they saw the brigade intel officer and a warrant they didn't recognize in heated debate. "Hey, Two," called Jones into the back of the track, "what the hell's the ruckus about?"

The major turned to Jones. "Sir, we were discussing trying to get some UAVs up to locate the Madinah and Hamourabi." The Two threw a thumb toward the warrant officer they'd heard a moment before. "Chief Gailin here thinks he can get his birds up—three of them. If he can, it could be the answer to our problems."

Jones chastised himself. He'd forgotten about the small, remote-controlled, unmanned aerial vehicles. Usually an asset located at echelons above brigade-level, the UAVs were a last-minute addition to 3rd Brigade's list of combat multipliers. Measuring just under thirty feet from wingtip to wingtip, they could be remotely piloted deep to send back video feeds of the intel they needed.

"Your birds can make it up, Chief? What about the winds?"

"They're Hunters, sir, we're good. Crosswind on takeoff right now is ten knots—that leaves us five to play with. The forward-looking infrared package will allow us to get some decent shots for you out past a hundred kilometers."

"How long can you stay up?" asked Jones. They had a ballpark idea of where the Iraqis were. They'd have to find them and then keep the birds on station long enough to relay back the information the brigade needed.

The chief considered. "At least eight hours, ten at the outside."

Jones nodded. "Two, give the chief your estimated location for those divisions. Focus on the Madinah first—that's our fight. Once we've got what we need, we can work on the Hamourabi for the Spartans."

The major gave a thumbs-up. "Got it, sir."

Turning his head toward the fire support track a few feet away, Jones bellowed for his FSO. "Buck!"

A kevlared head stuck from the rear of the track and looked their way. "Sir?"

"Buck, we're getting some UAV support up in the next few minutes. Have your guns ready to respond. The Two estimates the enemy is one hundred kilometers out—well outside our artillery and MLRS rocket range." Jones paused, looking thoughtful. "Does the reinforcing MLRS battalion have ATACMS?"

The Army Tactical Missile System, or ATACMS, was the army's only truly deep attack missile system. Fired from MLRS missile launchers, the ATACMS were designed as a tool for the ground commander to shape the fight deep and early.

Major Sheldon nodded. "Yes, sir. And they have the Block Two models. Range out to one hundred forty kilometers—antiarmor, top attack submunitions. Acoustic and infrared seekers working in tandem. Good shit, sir. FUBAR City for the bad guys. You'll need to call the JTF headquarters for permission to use 'em, but it won't be a problem. They'll work out the airspace issues."

"Roger, I'll make the call in a minute. You start working it with the guns."

Sheldon nodded and disappeared into his track.

"Chief, how long for you to get your birds prepped and airborne?"

The warrant officer smiled. "Sir, I've got a ground control station REDCON-One at our runway now with the birds preflighted. We can start sending them up inside of five minutes."

"*By God!* I like you, Chief," roared Jones. His slap to the warrant's back nearly knocked the smaller man off of his feet.

Recovering his balance, Gailin looked uncertainly at Jones. "Thanks, sir. I, uh . . . like you too."

The old warrior turned serious. "Chief, if this works, I'll owe you big." Jones turned his attention back to his S2. "I want to keep at least one of the birds on the Madinah all the way till showtime. As that division moves into artillery and MLRS range, I want to know, and I want those boys on the guns to start earning their money. Got it?"

"Roger, sir."

Jones put his hands on his hips and visibly swelled. "I do love it when a plan comes together. Let's get to work, gents. We've got a war to win!"

*   *   *

Ten minutes later, from a small dirt airstrip two thousand feet long and a hundred feet wide, the first of the three Hunter UAVs sped to takeoff speed. Its two 750cc Moto Guzzi engines whined as it climbed to an altitude of fifteen thousand feet. Any higher and it wouldn't be able to see through the clouds, any lower and it would be a ripe target for any enemy vehicle that spotted it. As its two brothers joined its orbit, the small formation flew off to the north at a cruising speed of seventy knots. The Hunters could dash at one hundred ten knots for short periods, if necessary.

The ground control station crews felt elated as the falling darkness enfolded their small craft. The soldiers knew over four thousand men and women depended on their ability to find the Republican Guard forces located somewhere to the north. They also knew they were equal to the task.

The Two looked at his map. Unlike the operations map, which showed primarily friendly units and only the broad strokes of the enemy situation, the intel map showed known and suspected enemy locations. Unfortunately, right now the vast majority of the graphics were suspected—or unknown. Looking at his watch, he saw that it was a little after twenty hundred hours—four hours before the brigade was due to move out. *Damn it, where are they?*

"Sir! Sir! We've got 'em!"

The major turned to the UAV imagery analysts huddled over their workstation. The duo was excitedly pointing at the near real time video playing across their monitor. Looking over their shoulders, the major felt a thrill of triumph. *The Madinah.*

"I'd kiss you, Sergeant," he said to the team leader, "but my wife's funny about that kind of thing." Turning to one of his one men, the S2 pointed at the display. "Get the relevant grid coordinates and call Major Sheldon. Tell him we've got his ATACMS targets."

Taking a deep breath, the major turned the handle

to open the back of his M577. As the latch disengaged, the vehicle's interior white lights cut out and were replaced by blue lighting. As he stepped outside, he paused a moment to allow his eyes to adjust to the darkness. An orange glow two feet to his left gave away the brigade commander's location. As the Two had suspected, Jones had waited outside for the critical intel piece he needed to fight his battle.

"We've got 'em, sir."

The sound of a fist slapping into the palm of a hand was heard distinctly. "Fucking A!" The orange glow had disappeared with the slapping sound. "Ooooww! Shit, that's hot! Did you notify Sheldon?"

"Roger, he's on the way over to get the coordinates. We'll pass them off to the ALO so the air force has got them as well."

"For all the good it'll do them," said Jones, looking up into the wet night.

After they had stood in silence for a couple of minutes, the rain slowed, then stopped. Looking up, the two officers saw a patch of stars appear overhead. Jones was the first to speak. "You know the good thing about things going wrong, Two?"

"No, sir. What's that?"

The major could almost hear Jones smiling. "When they start to go right, they really go right."

Republican Guard Southern Corps Headquarters, Vicinity An Nasiriyah, Iraq
24 October, 2015 Hours Local

Staff Major General al-Tikriti, commander of Southern Corps, paced impatiently within his headquarters van. With the weather clearing, he knew that his forces would soon be vulnerable to American aircraft. Walking across the room, the general stopped next to his air defense headquarters commander. "What is the status of your systems?"

The colonel stood and came to attention. "Sir, both the Corps and division air defense sections are ready."

The general arched an eyebrow at the colonel. "Indeed? We shall—"

Within the shelter of the van, all activity stopped. Ears tuned outside to a strange shrieking sound that seemed to be moving toward them. In the distance to the south—the direction of the Corps' two divisions— a series of explosions sounded.

Al-Tikriti wheeled on his communications officer. "Get the commanders of the Madinah and the Hamourabi on the radio. Find out their status and tell them not to wait until twenty-one hundred hours— they must move out at once. I repeat, tell them to get out of their staging areas now!"

Overhead, silent to the Iraqi soldiers running in the darkness to defend against an unseen foe, a Hunter UAV filmed the Southern Corps headquarters and relayed the imagery south, across an invisible datalink capable of handling ten megabits per second, to the UAV's ground control station at 3rd Brigade headquarters.

3rd Brigade, 4th ID TOC, Northern Kuwait
24 October, 2015 Hours Local

Chief Gailin watched the imagery coming in from bird number two. *Well, hello there. . . .* He quickly jotted the figures on a message pad, then double-checked the coordinates. Satisfied the information was accurate, Gailin ripped the note from the pad and stuck it in his NCO's hand. "Get this to the targeting cell. I think they'll want this one moved to the top of the hit parade."

Republican Guard Southern Corps Headquarters, Vicinity An Nasiriyah, Iraq
24 October, 2020 Hours Local

"Sir, both the Madinah and the Hamourabi report incoming missiles strikes," the communications officer reported. "They cannot confirm the extent of their losses, but they appear to be significant. The primary targets have been the tank and mechanized infantry battalions."

General al-Tikriti nodded. "Very well. Are they moving?"

"Yes, sir. As we speak."

"It is time we did the same. . . ."

The now-familiar sound of another incoming American missile interrupted the general. This one somehow sounded different . . . higher pitched.

The missile that detonated over the Corps headquarters wasn't one of the new Block II ATACMS containing brilliant antitank submunitions. The Block II missiles were being utilized against the mechanized divisions to the south. This missile was the first of a series of the trusty old Block I variety to be fired at the Republican Guard's command and control center. Each contained nine hundred fifty baseball-size bomblets. Designated the M74, the antipersonnel/antimateriel bomblets struck the command center with devastating effect.

The Southern Corps headquarters area looked like a scene from Dante's *Inferno*. Within the primary command center, General al-Tikriti crawled toward the radio linking him to his division commanders. Because he was badly burned, every inch of progress he made was torture. Al-Tikriti remembered reading somewhere that burn victims did not feel much pain after their initial moments of agony, that the nerves were deadened and that the onset of shock shut out the impulses of whatever nerve centers remained—lies.

His vision clouded and it seemed as if the radio set on the table sat at the end of a long, dark tunnel. As if Allah watched his efforts with sympathy, the table collapsed on flaming legs. The radio fell just short of the figure struggling on the floor. The general reached out a shaking charred hand and grasped the handset connected to the transmitter. He pulled it to his mouth. Trying to speak, al-Tikriti choked. Summoning all of his remaining strength, the general managed one word before succumbing to the smoke and flames. "Attack!"

Presidential Command Complex, West of An Najaf, Iraq
24 October, 2300 Hours Local

General of the Army Abunimah burst through the door leading to Abdul Aref's private sanctum. Aref looked up in alarm, then annoyance at recognizing his chief military advisor.

"Mr. President, I have been trying to reach you for over two hours," said the general.

"I have been busy. What do you require?"

Abunimah looked at his leader in shock. "Have you not received any of the reports from the south, sir?"

"Yes, yes . . . I know the Americans somehow struck our forces, despite your assurances that they would not be able to locate them."

Abunimah ignored the gibe. "Sir, you must reconsider this offensive. The Republican Guard Southern Corps headquarters is gone. . . . I must assume General al-Tikriti is dead. The Madinah and Hamourabi divisions are continuing their attack south, even though each has suffered severe losses."

The president watched Abunimah with dead eyes. "I am aware of this."

The general refused to participate longer in court intrigue. "I *know* you are aware of it, sir. . . . When I radioed the commanders to halt their attack and await further instructions, they informed me that you had ordered them to continue their mission—and to disregard orders to the contrary from myself or my staff!"

"General, you are very close to overstepping your bounds. . . ."

Face aflame with rage, General Abunimah continued. "Damn your bounds! Those are my men you so casually throw into combat! And what of the Iranians? *They have not moved an inch across their border!*"

For a moment the president wavered, uncertain. Then he recovered. Aref had tried to contact Khalani for hours and had gotten nowhere. The old man had betrayed him. He threw a hand in the air and paced like a caged animal. "I do not need the Iranians. I have alerted the commanders of the First and Second Corps that they have twenty-four hours to be in position to support the two divisions in the south. I have instructed all units to prepare their artillery to fire nerve-agent munitions in support of a breakthrough— they will do so only on my release, of course."

"*You are mad!* Sending more forces south alone will give the Americans reason enough to do something drastic. If you use chemical weapons on them"—Abunimah looked at Aref, attempting to find some way of getting through to the man—"it will be the death of us all, sir. Mark my words."

Without taking his eyes from Abunimah, Aref reached beneath the lip of his desk and pressed the concealed button. "You are relieved, General."

General Abunimah knew he had failed. Reaching to each shoulder, he tore the epaulets off. First one, then the other. He threw the symbols of his rank— the rank he had worked so many years to attain—at the feet of his president. General of the Army Ali Abunimah stood at attention for the final time. "No, sir. I resign."

Behind them, Aref's personal guards rushed into the room. Seeing the two men squared off against another, they paused, uncertain.

Aref turned to his new captain of the guards. "Major, take General Abunimah to his quarters. Allow him two minutes to gather a few possessions. Then escort him to his new lodgings . . . a cell."

The major in charge of the guard detail was clearly reluctant to carry out his assigned duty. Like the other soldiers who knew Abunimah, he held the general in high regard.

Stopping outside the general's quarters, he turned

to his onetime leader. "Sir . . . take all the time you need."

Reaching a hand to the young officer's shoulder, Abunimah grasped it. "Thank you, Major. I will be but a few minutes." He turned the handle and entered the small room he called home when at Aref's complex. As he had hoped, the major reached into the room and pulled the door closed to offer him more privacy.

Alone, Abunimah walked across the room and past the kit bag containing his personal items. Stopping at his desk, the general looked at the phone as if it were an adder. He knew what he must do, for the ultimate survival of his men and his nation—and he hated himself for it.

3rd Brigade, 4th ID TAC, Northern Kuwait
24 October, 2350 Hours

In the darkness, the two men watched with PVS-7s from the turret of the Bradley. The green landscape showed scores of armored vehicles moving rapidly across the desert.

"You ready, O'Keefe? One last ride?" asked Jones.

Sergeant Matt O'Keefe let the night-vision goggles fall around his neck and looked at Jones. It seemed as if he'd known the man forever. "Yes, sir. I'm ready."

"Okay. It's almost midnight, time for me to check on the boys." Patting the young NCO's arm, Jones dropped down and moved through the Bradley's turret and into the rear compartment. "Tom, status on the unit moves."

Proctor was busily annotating unit locations and statuses into his map matrix as the task force headquarters checked in one by one. He stopped and turned to Jones. "The scouts of each task force have moved out to the flanks, sir. They're in position. The task forces report they're twenty-five percent complete on their moves. Estimated time REDCON-One, zero three hundred hours."

Jones's experienced eye looked over the map. "What about Spartan?"

Proctor shrugged. "I spoke to Spartan Three a few minutes ago, sir. They're 'moving north with all due haste.' Even with our night vision equipment, limited visibility moves take a while."

Jones nodded. "Yeah. SITREP on the Madinah?"

"Still moving south. Chief Gailin is as good as his word. We've had eyes on them the whole way. The division contained over two hundred T-72s and one hundred BMP-2s when the UAVs picked them up four hours ago, plus their organic air defense systems and supporting artillery. As of twenty-three hundred hours, they'd sustained about twenty-five percent losses. Figure they've got a hundred fifty tanks and seventy-five or eighty BMPs remaining. The ATACMS strikes were followed immediately by fixed-wing air force attack runs." The major paused. "Sir, the bottom line is that they're hurting, but they're still coming."

"Yeah, that they are. Okay, Tom. Keep me posted. I want everything set by zero three hundred. I'm going up top to move us behind 2-77 Armor. I'm starting to feel an attachment to those boys . . . especially when bullets are flying."

U.S. Central Command Headquarters (Forward), Bahrain
25 October, 0100 Hours Local

The lieutenant colonel hung up the phone and walked to General Gus Pavlovski with a quizzical expression on his face. "Sir, I just got the strangest call from the headquarters in Tampa."

Pavlovski, in the middle of sifting through damage assessment photos taken following the air attacks on the Republican Guard, took off his glasses and rubbed his eyes. He needed a break anyway. "Okay, Charlie. What kind of call?"

Instead of answering, the colonel picked up a red pin and walked over to the map of the area of operations. After looking at the map a few moments, he stuck the pin in it and turned to face the CENT-COM commander.

Pavlovski leaned his chair against the wall, two legs in the air. Folding his arms across his chest, he gave the colonel another moment before asking, "Well?"

"Aref."

"What about him?"

The aide reached backward, still facing the general, and pointed a finger at the red pin he'd just plunged into the map. "He's there. We just received the coordinates for the underground complex where he's holing up, along with all of the specs for the location—composition, depth, everything."

The front legs of the chair crashed to the floor. Pavlovski got up and walked over to the map, looking at the pin. "An Najaf? You're sure?"

"About ten kilometers west of An Najaf, actually. Am I sure? The information is very detailed, sir, and the source of the information . . ."

"Yes?"

"The caller claimed to be Iraq's general of the army, Ali Abunimah."

Pavlovski looked puzzled. "Why would Abunimah phone Tampa, instead of here—assuming it is Abunimah."

"He didn't know the number to the forward headquarters. So he called a stateside operator and had them patch him through to MacDill Air Force Base. Things have gotten kind of crazy in that bunker, sir. Aref has put Abunimah under house arrest." The aide detailed the events that had unfolded at Aref's secret complex.

"Aref intends to use chemical munitions on our troops? General Abunimah is certain?"

The aide nodded. "Sir, the deputy CINC took the call. He's having a written report prepared for you now. It should be complete within fifteen minutes. He just wanted to give you a heads-up. The D-CINC said to pass that on for what it's worth. He thinks this is legit."

Pavlovski racked his brain, trying to remember all he could about Abunimah. Attended university in England—Oxford? One of the rising stars in Iraq's military for years. Long line of military service within his family. Loved his men. Not a politician. Now Pavlovski put himself in Abunimah's shoes. Crazy son of a bitch in charge of his country. Said crazy SOB threatens to use chemical munitions on the U.S. U.S. would likely respond with . . . what? Given the right circumstances, he'd probably do the same thing Abunimah had. Cut off an arm to save the body.

"I think it's legitimate as well," said Pavlovski. "Get the staff together."

After writing a few lines on a scrap sheet of paper, he handed them to the aide. "Here's my guidance. I want to see a plan in one hour."

"An hour, sir?" asked the aide. That was barely long enough to get the staff together and sharpen their pencils.

Pavlovski stood in front of the colonel and put a hand on each shoulder. He bent over to get on eye level with the shorter man. "Charlie, we don't have much time. The battle up north is about to kick off. If Aref feels things are going wrong and authorizes those forces to use chemicals on our troops . . . well, we might not be able to talk any shit to India and Pakistan for years—understand?"

The junior officer looked incredulous. "You think Washington would do that, sir?"

Pavlovski shook his head and shrugged. "I don't know, Charlie. Maybe. I'd think about it. Bombing Iraq into the Stone Age hasn't worked in the past— we've tried it. And we don't have the ground forces in theater yet for a proper invasion. Hell, we don't have enough forces to pull Third Brigade's shit out of the fire. How many options does that leave us, Charlie? You tell me."

The colonel nodded. He understood.

"Get the staff together. I've got a call to make."

Attack Position NIRVANA, Northern Kuwait
25 October, 0245 Hours Local

Looking at his graphics in the soft blue light of the tank's interior, Dillon frowned. *Nirvana?* And where was Task Force 2-35? Attack Position *Doors?* The helos . . . *Queen?* Couldn't the plans guys come up with a naming scheme that didn't involve bands with dead lead singers? Jesus. He liked Morrison as much as the next guy, but let's face it . . . those were some morbid fucks in plans. What about the Dave Matthews Band? Dave was the man. And Culture Club—well, maybe not. American soldiers tended to lean toward the homophobic side.

Rolling his Nomex glove down, Dillon hit the illumination button on his watch. Zero two forty-five hours. Last reports put the lead echelons of the Madinah twenty minutes out. The company was running ahead of schedule.

He keyed his CVC to check in with the platoons. *"Guideons, Steel Six."*

"Red One."

The Goo Goo Dolls. Those guys rocked—*and were alive.* Then again, Attack Position Goo? Uh-uh.

"White Four."

"Blue One."

"Guideons, Steel Six. No change to enemy E.T.A. Currently the Madinah is five kilometers out. You should start seeing hot spots to the north anytime. Weapons control status hold . . . I say again . . . hold. . . ."

Overhead, the men of Steel heard the first artillery volleys of the night coming in. Looking south, they saw the night turn to day all along their old defensive positions as the Iraqi guns and rockets pounded the location in preparation for their attack. *I hope 2-8 Infantry is still in their hide positions,* thought Dillon.

The plan called for them to stay back until the enemy preparatory fires lifted, then to rush forward and occupy before the Republican Guard began their assault. As always, a tough time line to call. If they had jumped the gun, they'd be caught in the open or—at best—sitting in their holes and getting punch drunk from the pounding at the BP.

"*. . . Also, tell your tank commanders to confirm that every instrument light in their turrets and drivers' compartments are either off or taped. They can turn them on again once the shooting starts. Call me and confirm Redcon-One once you're there, out.*"

While he waited for confirmation that his company was ready, Dillon turned his attention to his own tank. Reaching for the knob on the right side of the turret that controlled the interior lighting, Dillon turned it down until the blue light faded, then went completely out. "Crew report."

"Driver's up, driver's instrument panel dark," Thompson reported from the front of the tank.

"Loader up, sabot loaded. No lights."

"Gunner up, sabot indexed, blackout confirmed."

Dillon looked around the turret, satisfied. He knew that one enemy vehicle commander or recon team with night-vision goggles could pick up the light of a single small bulb inside a tank from thousands of meters away. He'd seen units die because of such mistakes in training. He refused to let it happen for real.

"Roger, I'm going topside. Bick, pick up a slow scan to the north."

"On it," called Bickel, moving his face to his thermal imaging system.

As Dillon stood, the turret—already oriented over the right front and to the north—slowly began moving right to left. Lifting the PVS-7s from around his neck, Dillon looked up and down the attack position. Dark. Good—wait! *What the fuck was that?*

"*Red One, Steel Six.*" Through the PVS-7s, the driver's compartment of one of the First Platoon tanks looked as if a spotlight was aimed straight into the sky. Removing the PVS-7s, Dillon could see nothing. *Driver's master power light, sure as shit,* thought Dillon.

An embarrassed voice replied to Dillon's call. "This is Red Four. I've got it, Six."

Two seconds later, the light popped out and Attack Position Nirvana plunged into darkness. To anyone approaching the position, there was nothing in the night but the desert sands and the occasional ghostly howling of the wind.

Doc Hancock stood in the turret of C-21 and breathed in the cool night air. So much had happened to him over the past weeks. He'd gone from inexperienced lieutenant to battle-proven platoon leader. Captain Dillon even showed real faith in his abilities—that was something approaching a miracle with the Old Man. And he was in love. Good God, he still couldn't believe that one.

Reaching behind his hatch, Doc felt the small pad taped in place. It was only eighteen inches by eighteen inches. Sam had pulled it from a bag they'd sent on the helo picking her up. Making him promise to tape it to his tank, she'd rushed off without saying more. Sand-colored and slightly luminescent, it appeared to be some type of new recognition panel. Hancock knew the battle labs were experimenting with some new materials on the combat ID side to try to cut down the number of fratricides. Maybe she'd gotten hold of a new piece of gear? The lieutenant shrugged in the darkness. Well, if it made her feel better, he'd leave it in place.

"Sir, I've got vehicles moving in from the north, vicinity Phase Line Buford, avenue of approach One!" called Bickel.

Dropping into the turret, Dillon put his face to the sight extension. One . . . two . . . three . . . screw the counting. That was a butt load. Too far out to tell what type. Calling Estes, Dillon relayed the spot report.

"What do you think, O'Keefe?" asked Jones.

The NCO never took his eye from his gunner's sight. "Too far out to hit 'em, even with TOWs. Besides," the gunner said, turning to Jones, "you want to let them move between 2-77 and 2-35, right?"

Jones nodded. Damn but he could use a cigarette. "Yeah, that's the idea."

"Air?"

"None available for the next twenty minutes."

"Artillery?"

Jones punched the gunner's arm across the turret. "There you go, son. Artillery!"

Dillon heard the distant whistle of the 155mm rounds overhead, heading north. As he watched, the initial volley landed behind the first echelon of the approaching Madinah.

Dave Barnett's voice was on the air quickly. Knowing the battalion's fire support officer would be riding with the commander tonight, the S3 called Estes. *"Tiger Six, Tiger Three. Tell Redleg the guns need to drop two zero zero and fire for effect."*

"Tiger Six, roger."

After a minute, the artillery ceased as adjustments were made based off of Barnett's call. Two minutes later, the American artillery hammered the first echelon of the approaching Madinah Division. From the number of rounds, it looked like the cannon cockers were pulling out all the stops, thought Dillon.

The Republican Guard unit continued moving south, slowly but steadily.

"What's the range, Bick?"

Sergeant Bickel tracked the nearest T-72 tank as it moved across the desert. Dillon could clearly see the unit markings on the side of the vehicle through the M1's thermal sight. In the reticle, the green number indicating the enemy vehicle's range changed as Bickel hit the laser range finder button on his gunner's power control handle. "Twenty-two hundred meters, sir."

The enemy force had passed Phase Line Buford and the lead vehicles were between 2-77's attack position and 2-35's attack position. The Madinah was set on a course to hit 2-8 Infantry dead-on. Behind them, the men of 3rd Brigade knew that the Hamourabi Division followed close behind, prepared to continue their sister unit's attack.

Once the enemy's first echelon closed inside of four thousand meters, 2-8 would open with their TOWs. Spread across three times their normal frontage, the mech-heavy task force would attempt to mislead the attacking Iraqis into believing that the 3rd Brigade still occupied their holes.

Five kilometers to the north were the brigade's two tank-heavy task forces. Ten kilometers separated the two American units. On order they would each attack, one from the west flank, one from the east. Task Force 2-77 currently occupied Attack Position Nirvana in the east. Once the lead echelon of the Madinah came abreast of the Iron Tigers left-most unit, they would hit the front of the enemy division on its left flank. Task Force 2-35, occupying Attack Position Doors in the west, would hit the rear of the enemy division on its right flank simultaneously. Each of the task forces would put over forty M1A1 tanks and fourteen Bradley Fighting Vehicles into the fight for their assault across the dark desert floor. Surprise was critical. The force they were striking outnumbered them two to one.

Cold Steel occupied the center of Nirvana. To their left was Anvil, to their right Team Knight. Team Mech would be two kilometers behind the task force in reserve, prepared to flex either way.

Estes occupied a position behind Steel from which he could command and control the task force. With him was Jones. Major Barnett moved off of Knight's flank. Once the attack began, it would be critical that someone keep an eye on Knight and 2-35 as they began to meet at the center of the Madinah—that would be Barnett. In situations where two friendly forces were coming together in the darkness, fratricide was a major concern. The depleted-uranium sabot rounds didn't discriminate; they'd destroy whatever they were fired at, enemy or friendly.

Estes's voice cut over the friendly artillery. *"Guideons, Tiger Six. I'm going to let the enemy formation move another thousand meters, then we attack. Task force on line as you're currently set. Mech, maintain a cushion of two kilometers, be prepared to support as ordered."*

The company/team commanders acknowledged the order and waited. This was the hard part. It was all the U.S. soldiers could do not to open up on the Iraqi division parading in front of them. The men of the Striker Brigade had quit trying to count the number of tanks, infantry carriers, and various other armored vehicles passing. It was an endless formation that kept coming on, and on, and on. Then the formation stopped.

Dillon watched the stationary Iraqi division. At forty-five hundred meters, they were still outside 2-8 Infantry's TOW missile range. The mech-heavy task force couldn't touch them. "What the fuck . . . ?"

Then the Hinds appeared on the scene.

The MI-24 attack helicopters swooped in from the north, stopped, and hovered off either flank of the Madinah. Normally used in the offense to destroy counterattacking forces, the Iraqis had decided to change things up. Like giant insects, the Hinds hovered two hundred feet above the desert floor, their weapons oriented south at the American vehicles that had just moved into their prepared positions.

The first volley of AT-6 Spiral guided missiles flew from the Hinds' weapons pylons and toward 2-8's position. Accurate to five kilometers, the missiles allowed the Iraqis to soften up the American position while staying out of the U.S. soldiers' direct fire range.

Looking south with his PVS-7s, Dillon saw flames

spouting from five different positions along 2-8 Infantry's lines—positions that used to be holes hiding American tanks and Bradleys.

Dillon dropped inside the turret and looked through the sight extension. As he knew would be the case, Bickel had the reticle laid on one of the Russian-made helos, hovering stationary as it expended its air-to-surface missiles.

"Guideons, Steel Six. Tell each of your tank commanders to select a hind and then to keep him in his sights. Don't engage until I tell you . . . going higher." Dillon switched his radio to the task force command frequency. *"Tiger Six, Steel Six."*

"Tiger Six," answered Estes.

"Tiger Six, Steel Six. We can take out those Hinds and attack as planned. The lead echelon of the Madinah is far enough . . . Tiger Six, if we don't do something fast, 2-8 is going to get eaten up, over."

As Dillon waited for Estes to reply, he looked south toward their old position. Most of the 2-8 Infantry vehicles were popping their onboard smoke generators and attempting to exfiltrate. To stay in their holes was to die. As they moved out, they presented even more tempting targets. Three more Bradleys fireballed.

"This is Tiger Six. Concur. Going higher to pass on to Striker Six. Take them out."

Dillon wasted no time in dropping to company command. *"Guideons, Steel Six . . . one round each at those Hinds. Platoon leaders, ensure you're not double-pumping. Listen up, people. As soon as you fire, we attack. Surprise will be lost and we'll need to move. . . . All Steel elements, one round sabot, helos, at my command. . . . Fire!"*

Madinah Division Forward Headquarters, Northern Kuwait
25 October, 0302 Hours Local

"Tell the helicopters to continue their attack!" screamed Staff Brigadier General Sufian, commander of the Madinah. "I want half of the Americans dead and the other half in shock when we roll into them!"

Standing in the turret of a BMP command and control vehicle just behind the helicopters and in the lead of his division, Sufian intended to win at all costs. He did not know what was going on in the north, but he had received enough conflicting orders tonight to understand that a shake-up was occurring—and that Abdul Aref was still in power. He had not heard from General Abunimah for hours, so the old man had fallen out of favor. That left but one course of action—to carry out Aref's orders to the letter.

So far his division had performed flawlessly. The Hinds had surprised the Americans. As he watched, two more fires appeared in the south. More Americans dead. Excellent.

To his front, red tracers streaked from left to right. The sound of thunder overrode his vehicle's engine noise. Then the unthinkable happened. His ten helicopters—his precious Hinds—fell from the sky in flames.

Attack Position Nirvana, Northern Kuwait
25 October, 0305 Hours Local

"Red! Move out in the lead of the wedge! Blue, take left. White, right! Move, move, move!" yelled Dillon into his boom mike. He switched to intercom. "Tommy, follow a hundred meters behind C-11."

"You got it, sir." The crew rocked backward as the big tank moved out.

Surprise was gone. The 3rd Brigade now had to live up to their name, the Strikers, and hit the Madinah fast and furious, whittling down the enemy's numbers in short order. Dillon checked his company's alignment as they moved forward in the attack. First Platoon led in a wedge formation. Second Platoon was moving into their assigned position on the right flank. Third Platoon moved to the left flank. Cold Steel was now a spear, a sharp and deadly spear aiming for the heart of the Madinah.

The remaining company teams of 2-77 Armor oriented off of Dillon's unit. To the left, Anvil moved into a wedge. Stuart and Team Knight moved up on the right. All of the elements of the task force were in position as the attack on the Madinah commenced.

In front of Dillon, the tanks of Wyatt's platoon opened fire. The other platoons followed suit. The battle damage assessment reports began flowing in.

"Guideons, Steel Six. Save the reports. Kill 'em now, we'll sort 'em later. Out."

Jones turned to Sheldon. "Buck, shift the artillery south onto the Hamourabi! I don't want those fuckers getting a chance to sneak in the back door!"

He switched his attention to Proctor. "Tom, what's Spartan's status?"

The Striker S3 bounced in the back of the Bradley. Not able to hear the joint task force over his CVC, he'd stuck a handset beneath the helmet's earcup. He turned to Jones. "Sir, they're moving into position as we speak."

Jones swayed in the rear compartment of the Bradley as it raced across the desert. "Marvelous! Keep me posted. I'm going up top."

Madinah Division Forward Headquarters, Northern Kuwait
25 October, 0315 Hours Local

"General Falahi, you must bring your division forward! We have moved into a trap and are surrounded! We have American units on each of our flanks! I need you here to support our attack! Acknowledge!"

Falahi, commander of the Hamourabi, acknowledged the distress call. He had been monitoring the events to his south. Since his division had continued moving as his sister division paused for the helicopter attack, they would soon be in position to come to their aid. "We are moving toward you now. We will be in position in five minutes."

Phase Line Buford, Northern Kuwait
25 October, 0317 Hours Local

Two kilometers northwest of 3rd Brigade, the 2nd Brigade of the 3rd Infantry Division pulled on line. M1A1 and Bradley commanders made final adjustments to thermal sights, fine-tuning their pictures on the approaching enemy formation. The Hamourabi Division—Iraq's prized mechanized infantry—slowly approached an invisible line in the sand that marked 2nd Brigade's trigger point. Fingers twitched and vehicle commanders issued preparatory fire commands as the first enemy vehicles crossed the line of death, blissfully unaware of their circumstances.

Colonel John Seacourt, Spartan Six, lowered his PVS-7s. The enemy had moved far enough into the kill zone that few, if any, would escape. *"Task force commanders, it's your fight. Engage and destroy. Out."* Two seconds later, hundreds of 120mm sabot rounds, TOW missiles, and high explosive mortars were on a collision course for the advancing Hamourabi.

3rd Brigade Axis of Attack, Northern Kuwait
25 October, 0330 Hours Local

Doc Hancock stood in the turret of C-21 as Steel and the rest of 2-77 Armor attacked west. Things had gone well thus far. His platoon hadn't lost anyone and they'd destroyed at least ten enemy vehicles. From what he could see, the Madinah Division was attempting to break contact and head north.

Small pockets of resistance kept flaring up as the more disciplined of the Iraqi units held their ground while others displaced under their covering fire. Hancock had to acknowledge that the Republican Guard were better fighters than he'd been led to believe.

Doc slammed into the side of the cupola as his gunner fired another main gun round. Momentarily blinded by the white flash from the muzzle as he stood in the cupola, the lieutenant rubbed his eyes. "Thanks for the heads up, Izzo," he said over the intercom.

The gunner sounded contrite. "Sorry, sir. That bastard popped up and was lookin' right at us."

Lifting the PVS-7s that hung from his neck, Doc scanned left. His platoon was maintaining their position off of First Platoon. Looking right, he saw the beginnings of a problem.

"Steel Six, White One, over."

"Steel Six."

Doc could hear the adrenaline pumping in Dillon's voice. The company had been in the attack for twenty minutes. Twenty minutes of rapid movement across the desert, at night, firing at and being engaged by an enemy force, and the whole time trying to keep their alignment with each other and the rest of the task force so one friendly didn't shoot another. The inherent anxiety of the mission was beginning to tell on every man in the company.

"This is White One. We're developing a seam between our right flank and Team Knight. Knight needs to pick up the pace, over."

The pause over the radio told Doc that Dillon was checking out the gap himself. *"Roger, I see it. Going higher to coordinate with Knight. Red, slow it down a little until Knight closes up. White and Blue, maintain your positions off of Red. Out."*

Doc was just dropping to relay instructions to his platoon when his tank shuddered and ground to a halt. Momentarily blinded by the sparks of what had to have been a direct hit by a sabot round, he dropped inside the turret. The first thing he noticed was the smell of smoke. As his vision cleared, he saw flames licking up from beneath the turret floor. The turret's sensors kicked on the automatic fire suppression systems. A white cloud of halon enveloped the interior of the tank as the fire suppressant suffocated the flames. Two seconds later the fire sprang back to life.

"Son of a bitch!" screamed Doc. "Crew! Evacuate the tank!"

Another detonation from nearby jarred the crew. Sticking his head through the turret, Doc saw his wingman tank, C-22, stationary and burning, its gun tube hanging at an odd angle from the catastrophic hit that the Abrams had suffered.

Dropping back into the turret, Doc saw his loader moving. As the soldier jumped through his hatch, he was knocked flat. "Shit . . . sir, I'm hit!"

"Just stay flat on the turret!" Hancock yelled. "We'll get you when we clear out."

"Sir, Cramer's not responding in the driver's hole!" called Sergeant Izzo, C-21's gunner. "His hatch is locked down, so we're going to have to get him out from the inside! Rotate the gun over the rear while I move to grab him!"

The smoke inside the turret was getting thick. They didn't have much time. Reaching down and grabbing the control handle, Doc rotated the tank's turret. The only way to access the driver's compartment from inside the tank was for the gun to be over the rear deck. Once there, Sergeant Izzo could reach through a small opening and pull the injured driver free.

Feeling the tank shudder from another enemy hit, Doc popped his head through the hatch again. He immediately saw the problem. A platoon of T-72s had found the gap between Knight and Steel. *Someone had apparently forgotten to tell these guys they were supposed to be retreating,* thought Doc. Behind the platoon, he saw more enemy tanks moving to follow the group shooting at them. "Shit! Izzo, get in the loader's station!"

"Sir, we don't have time to be fuckin' around!"

Doc looked down at his gunner. *That's okay. He's bitching—which is understandable since we're on fire— but he's moving.* "Load sabot!"

"Up!"

Laying his reticle on the nearest Iraqi tank, Doc lased. "On the way!" The tank rocked backward. The

T-72 in his sight stopped as if it had hit a brick wall and flames rolled from it.

"Target! Give me another one!" Looking down, Doc saw Sergeant Izzo slamming another sabot round in the breech. The flames in the bottom of the tank cast an eerie light on the NCO's features. He looked like a damned soul stoking hell's furnace.

"Up! Sir, that's going to have to do it! This fire ain't goin' to wait for us!"

Looking through the sight extension, Doc saw an eager T-72 move around his burning buddy. "On the way!" Again the American tank rocked as the main gun of C-21 engaged for the final time.

Doc quickly rotated the turret over the rear deck. "That'll hold 'em for a minute, Sergeant Izzo. Get ready to grab Cramer."

The gunner moved back to the turret floor. As the driver's compartment rotated into view, Sergeant Izzo reached out a hand and grabbed the unconscious soldier. "Cramer! Come on, man, we got to get out of . . . Cramer?" The head rolled back. Glazed, staring eyes and the unnatural angle of the soldier's neck told the sergeant all he needed to know. "Sir . . . he's dead."

"Okay, get the fuck out of there!"

"But Cramer. We can't leave him—"

"We don't have time, Iz! Get the fuck out . . . now!"

Jumping out his hatch and seeing the figure struggling on the top of the turret, Doc remembered their loader. PFC Gilreath was trying to wrap a tourniquet around his leg. Blood had soaked through the Nomex legs of his pants and was rapidly puddling beneath him. Seeing his lieutenant exit the turret, the boy turned and smiled through clenched teeth. "Hey, sir. Sounds like you guys have been busy down there. Could I get a little help now?"

Izzo burst through the loader's hatch next to them. "Sir, she's getting ready to blow!"

The old girl had given all she could. With multiple hits through the hull and engine compartment, C-21 had stayed intact long enough to give her crew the time they needed. She could give no more.

Grabbing Gilreath and lifting him, Doc looked the young soldier in the eye. "Sorry about this, Gilreath."

The loader looked confused. "Sorry about what? Hey, sir, what're you—"

Doc threw the soldier off the tank. The eight-foot drop wasn't nearly as bad as the alternative of hanging around longer. He and Izzo jumped before Gilreath's protests had cleared the air.

As they hit the ground, both the lieutenant and the sergeant threw their bodies on top of the loader, who at the moment was howling. "Sir, that was fucked up! You could have broken my neck."

The pressure of C-21 exploding sucked the oxygen from around the three men. As the shock wave cleared, Doc and Izzo began dragging the loader away from the tank.

Looking down at the boy, Doc Hancock smiled. "You were saying something, Gilreath?"

The loader, grimacing in pain as his injured leg bumped across the rough desert floor, looked embarrassed. "Forget it, sir."

Doc and Izzo hit the ground again as green tracers flashed out of the night toward them.

"Goddamn it!" screamed Sergeant Izzo in pain.

Doc looked to where the tracers had originated. The remaining Iraqi tanks were returning. "You hit, Iz?"

The sergeant was already ripping open the plastic shell of his field dressing with his teeth. "Yeah . . . shoulder. I'll be all right."

Reaching over, Doc helped the NCO cover the wound and tighten the dressing. "Can you drag Gilreath out of here while I hold these guys off?"

"How the hell are you gonna do that?"

Doc flared at the sergeant. "Can you drag him?"

"Yeah . . . I can drag him."

Doc held up the loader's rifle he'd grabbed from the turret roof before jumping from the tank. "When I start firing, get out of here."

The NCO looked at his platoon leader as if he were insane. After a moment, he nodded.

Doc turned his face to the sound of the diesel engines approaching in the darkness. He could just make out the low shapes moving toward them. Pulling himself from the ground, Doc began walking toward the approaching T-72s, attempting to distance himself from his two crewmen. *Sons of bitches. Try to rape my girl. Kill my driver. Blow up my tank. Well, fuck you.* Switching the weapon's selector to three-round burst, Doc raised the rifle to his shoulder and opened fire.

Attack Position Queen, Northern Kuwait
25 October, 0340 Hours Local

The company of OH-58D Kiowa Warriors waited patiently at their attack position. They'd been assigned to the brigade as a reserve force to be used if the shit hit the fan. The gap between Steel and Knight threatened to turn 3rd Brigade's right flank into one smelly mess.

The OH-58D company commander, call sign Mad Dog, listened intently to the transmission coming from the 3rd Brigade TOC. *"Roger, Striker Three. Moving now."*

"Guideons, Mad Dog, I need a platoon to cut off a potential penetration of the brigade's northern flank, vicinity TRP Sierra-Five."

Sam Matheson listened to the coordinates. She'd talked a set of maneuver graphics off of one of the brigade's plans officers earlier. Having looked over the mission numerous times, she knew that was the area Steel would likely be operating in at the moment.

"This is Cutlass. We've got it."

Before the commander could acknowledge, the four 58-Ds of Matheson's platoon were speeding north into the night.

*   *   *

Doc cringed as he heard the rifle hit on an empty cylinder. He was out of ammo. Looking back to check on his men's progress, he saw Izzo drop to the ground as more tracers sprayed in the direction of the two injured crewmen, Doc's efforts to distract the enemy tanks failing. The Iraqis could smell an easy kill and were not going to be denied.

"Shit." Dropping the rifle, Doc pulled the 9mm pistol from his shoulder holster. Taking a two-handed grip, he again opened fire. "Over here, you bastards!"

Doc finally managed to draw the Iraqi crew's attention. The tank's machine gun ceased firing at Izzo and Gilreath and began firing at Doc instead. The rounds were landing well short, but working their way toward Doc in a straight line that ultimately would not be denied.

"Look at the fool! He fires a pistol at us!" The tank commander laughed. Yelping, he dropped inside the turret.

The gunner released his trigger and turned to his comrade. "Are you all right?"

Running a hand across his forehead, the tank commander felt fresh blood from the 9mm crease across his jawline. He was no longer laughing. "He hit me! He actually hit me. Finish him! The other two are going nowhere."

The gunner put his face to the sight and squeezed the trigger again, working his rounds toward the American standing defiantly in their path. A commotion behind his intended victim drew the gunner's attention. Lifting his gaze, he froze. An American attack helicopter hovered over the lone gunman, its wicked-looking missiles aimed directly at them.

Sam had seen the recognition panel on the back of the M1A1's commander's hatch. She knew it had to be the same one she'd given Doc. Fearing the worst, she'd almost lost control. Then she saw him. The idiot was firing a pistol at a charging tank. Like a mother hen, Matheson sped her craft in his direction. On reaching him, she brought the helicopter to hover.

Matheson lined up her sights and armed the Kiowa Warrior's weapons station. "Okay, motherfucker. He may not be smart, but that's my boy . . . and you don't fuck with him." Sam released the Hellfire missile and watched it blow into the T-72. The rest of her platoon, hovering off of her flanks, took the cue. Hellfire missiles rippled from the weapons pylons of the OH-58Ds. The penetration was sealed.

"Mad Dog Six, Cutlass Six. Engaged and destroyed five T-72s, vicinity Sierra-Five. Proceeding back to Queen, over."

"This is Mad Dog. Roger. Good work, out."

As Sam turned, she looked down at Doc. He was waving.

Looking up at the helicopter, Doc knew it had to be Sam. "Thanks, honey!" he yelled, waving skyward. The helo did a little wag, then darted south with its sister ships in tow.

Holstering his pistol, Doc walked back to his men. Sergeant Izzo was working on Gilreath's leg with his good arm. He obviously hadn't made much of an effort to leave. The two men were only five feet from where Doc had initially left them. Slapping the loader's leg, Izzo laughed. "You're going to be fine, kid."

"Damn it, Sarge! That hurt!" yelled Gilreath. Reaching out a hand, he poked Izzo's shoulder wound.

"Ow!" yelled the gunner. "Why, you little shit . . ."

"What are you guys doing here?" asked the platoon leader. "You were supposed to be heading south with all due haste."

Sergeant Izzo rubbed his shoulder. "Well, sir, every time we moved, that fucking T-72 started shooting at us. Besides," he said, winking at Gilreath, "we had to wait and see if you were going to pull a knife on that tank when you ran out of 9mm bullets."

The gunner and loader howled. Doc tried to keep a straight face, but finally joined them.

Slowly the laughter faded. Each of them thought of Cramer, but none spoke of their dead comrade. There would be time for that later. Slowly, the battle moved away from them.

After a few minutes, Gilreath turned to Hancock. "Hey, sir. Was that Lieutenant Matheson?"

Doc nodded.

"Well, I guess that's all there is to it then," said the boy seriously.

Doc looked at him and cocked his head quizzically. "What do you mean?"

The young soldier looked at Hancock, finally shaking his head in exasperation. "Well, sir, I guess you're gonna have to marry her now."

When First Sergeant Rider came on their position moments later with an ambulance track, he looked at the scene before him in confusion. Their tank burning just yards away, two of the men obviously wounded, the three remaining crew members of C-21 were sitting on the desert floor rocking with laughter.

Madinah Division Forward Headquarters, Northern Kuwait
25 October, 0400 Hours Local

"Get the presidential command bunker on the radio!" screamed General Sufian. "Tell them to relay to President Aref that I want authority to release my chemical munitions. It is the only way we can stall the American attack long enough for us to regroup and counterattack. Also tell them if I do not receive permission for release within the next five minutes, this battle is lost."

Iraqi Artillery Battalion Position, on the Iraq-Kuwait Border
25 October, 0402 Hours Local

Colonel Karim al-Hamdani turned to his executive officer. "Are the firing units in position?"

The major nodded, obviously not pleased. General Sufian's warning order had been received moments before. "Yes, Colonel. They are in position. The munitions are still being distributed to the gun platoons. We should be ready for firing missions shortly."

The colonel turned to his second in command questioningly. "What is wrong, Ahmed? Something bothers you."

The major shook his head and looked into the night, where men frantically moved about, completing precombat activities. "I believe this is wrong, sir. Once we open this . . . this Pandora's Box, it will not be so easily closed."

Al-Hamdani's face reddened. "You question our authority—more than that, our responsibility—to repel these infidels by whatever means necessary?"

The major faced his commander, eyes sad. "Sir, I do not question our right or our responsibility. It is the method that I—"

"Major!"

The executive officer stood to attention. "Yes, sir."

"Because of the faithful service you have shown in the past, I will forget this conversation. Now go to the fire direction center and ensure that all is ready. Dismissed!"

After saluting, the major left. The colonel walked out of the tent and surveyed his unit's site. While the remainder of the artillery units supporting the Madinah Division continued to support the attack against the Americans to the south, Colonel al-Hamdani's battalion of 155mm howitzers had been ordered to go to ground and hide late yesterday afternoon. If President Aref called for chemical munitions to be fired, al-Hamdani's unit would receive the honor of striking the fateful blow.

His eighteen-gun battalion would remain to the north, staying just within range of the Americans. If given the order to fire, they would shoot several volleys and displace north. The United States would know what happened, but they would not be able to locate the evidence before the battalion had displaced over the border and disposed of it.

The munitions had begun arriving four hours earlier from the corps artillery site. The soldiers handling the rounds wore rubber chemical protective suits and masks. Of Eastern European design, the garments and masks were not as effective as the Americans', so the men worked carefully.

The agent present in the rounds they prepared was sarin. Originally produced in 1938 by the Germans, the nerve agent's most recent use had been in the Iran-Iraq War—unless one counted its use against a civilian population in Japan by the Aum Shinrikyo religious sect in 1994 and 1995. Colorless and odorless, a minute quantity of Sarin would prove lethal within one minute of ingestion. The chemical could be breathed in or absorbed through the skin; either way, several things would happen to its victim in short order. The first symptoms would be a runny nose and tightening of the chest. These initial symptoms would quickly be followed by difficulty breathing, drooling, and vomiting. Because the victim loses all control of bodily functions, he would involuntarily defecate and urinate. Twitching and jerking of the entire body would soon follow. Ultimately, the victim would become comatose and suffocate as a consequence of convulsive spasms.

A sergeant approached al-Hamdani, saluting. "Sir, I have been told to report that all guns are ready and the ammunition distributed."

Returning the salute, the colonel dismissed the sergeant and stepped back inside his tent. Fixing himself a cup of tea, he sat down by the radio and waited for the order that would ensure his battalion's place in history.

**Presidential Command Complex, West of An Najaf, Iraq
25 October, 0402 Hours Local**

The colonel in charge of Abdul Aref's action center rushed into his office without knocking. "Sir! This message just arrived from the south."

The president, looking annoyed, took the note. After scanning it once, he read it again more carefully. The Iraqi leader looked to the clock on his wall—the message was two minutes old. So . . . it finally had come to this decision. He had told that woman of a soldier, Abunimah, that he was prepared to authorize the release of chemical munitions if necessary. But was he?

Aref knew that his predecessor had been prepared to use nerve agents and mustard gas on the Coalition Forces during the Gulf War. Hussein had changed his mind at the last moment when the American president, Bush, had hinted that a nuclear response would follow any chemical strike by Iraq. Would Bush have actually pushed the button? Perhaps. *Would the current American president—the teacher?* That was the question. It was not as if chemical warfare had not been used throughout history. As early as the fifth century B.C. the Spartans had used sulfur fumes to overcome their enemies on the battlefields of ancient Greece. Was one tactical chemical strike on the modern battlefield all that different?

Abdul Aref looked to the clock once more. Less than two minutes to make a decision. *No,* he finally decided, *the teacher would not retaliate with nuclear weapons.* He would not be willing to stand up to the global condemnation that would surely follow such an act. So what *would* he do? Escalate the bombing campaign currently hitting Iraq? That was impossible—they were already being hit with every platform and missile available to the Americans. His decision made, Aref turned to the colonel.

"Inform General Sufian he has permission for release of his chemical weapons."

The colonel saluted and left. As he entered the hallway, he began sprinting towards the communications room. Halfway to his destination, the officer stumbled as the lights dimmed and the floor heaved beneath him. As he attempted to negotiate what was becoming an obstacle course of falling rock and mortar, the colonel could hear the sounds of bombs overhead. The hall lights went dark, replaced by the sound of an alarm Klaxon. Dimly at the end of the hallway, the officer could see red emergency lighting spilling from the communications room. Focusing on the mission assigned him, the colonel kept moving forward. He died three feet from the communications center, as a piece of concrete the size of a Volkswagen separated from the roof and crushed every bone in his body.

Abdul Aref stumbled from his office and into the hallway, nearly falling as another concussion rocked his headquarters. "Guards! Guards!" he screamed, trying to be heard over the cries of the wounded.

The major in charge of the bodyguards arrived moments later, his detail in tow. "Sir! Are you injured?"

Aref sighed with relief at the sight of his protectors. "I am . . . fine. We must make for the emergency exit at once."

The major saluted smartly, then turned to his men and issued orders. Around them, the command and control complex's infrastructure continued to give way under the massive bombardment.

U.S. Central Command Headquarters (Forward), Bahrain 25 October, 0457 Hours Local

"So were we successful?" Pavlovski asked his assembled staff.

Rear Admiral Dave Jordan, Pavlovski's director of operations, nodded. "Yes, sir. If Aref was in there, he's dead, buried, or running."

"Very well. Is our team ready?"

The ex–naval aviator nodded. "They're airborne, sir. We had to scramble to find enough Blackhawks to lift the entire battalion on such short notice, but we managed. They're orbiting now and will move in as soon as the last ordnance hits." Pausing, Jordan checked his watch. "That should be in about two minutes."

General Gus Pavlovski turned his head and slowly

looked at each man in the room. "Make no mistake, gentlemen. I want Abdul Aref's head. Whether it's attached to a living, breathing body really doesn't matter much to me at the moment."

3rd Brigade Axis of Attack, Northern Kuwait
25 October, 0630 Hours Local

"Hold up, Tommy," said Dillon in a tired voice.

Without responding, C-66's driver slowed the tank to a halt.

"All Steel elements, Steel Six. Spread out here and hold. Platoons, set up sectors of fire oriented north from ten o'clock to two o'clock. Work up your casualty reports and cross-level ammo as necessary. I'm going higher to get a SITREP. Out."

But Dillon didn't call anyone. He was just too damned tired. The sun had just begun rising when Steel and Anvil had been ordered to assault through this position and destroy what appeared to be the last remaining pocket of Iraqi resistance. They'd defeated the enemy force, but Steel had lost two more tanks in the process. Looking west, he saw Anvil pulling on line to his company's left—they had lost three tanks in the dawn assault.

Reaching into his sponson box, Dillon removed his canteen. He rinsed his mouth out and drank. From his pocket he produced a tin of Copenhagen. The silver lid of the tin flashed in the early-morning sun. Dillon began to open the can, then stopped. He looked at it another moment, then threw the snuff over the side of the tank. "Fuck it."

As he was about to call Estes, HQ-66 pulled abreast of his tank. Pulling off his CVC, Dillon poured half of the canteen over his head and face. Something had to be going on, he thought, for the commander to meet him here. Well, give them five more minutes and the company would be ready to roll.

As Dillon hopped to the ground, he found Estes

leaning against his tank's front slope. The man looked ready to drop from exhaustion.

Hearing Dillon clambering off the tank, Estes looked up. "That's it."

Dillon looked around, his gaze surveying every piece of the war-torn desert his men had just fought and died to gain. The blackened and smoking hulks of Iraqi vehicles, most still burning, littered the landscape. "Say again, sir?"

Estes joined Dillon in surveying the scene of the task force's latest victory—if ground gained and enemies destroyed at such a cost could be considered a victory. He closed his eyes and let his head fall back. "That's it. It's over, unless they start pushing more shit south."

Dillon shook his head, clearing it. "You sure, sir?"

Estes nodded. "The wind shifted north a couple of hours ago. Cleared out the smoke enough for the satellites to get some good shots on their last pass." He motioned to the dead Iraqi vehicles. "These guys were the last. A few got out, but the JTF commander has attack aviation en route to cut them off." He paused, then shook his head. Enough fighting men had died in the last few days from both sides. "They won't make it far."

The men stood in silence for a few moments, each lost in his thoughts. Estes finally broke it. "How many did you lose?"

Voice cracking, Dillon gestured at the burning tanks that littered the battlefield around them. "Shit, sir . . . this morning? Last night? During the defense? I'm starting to lose count."

Estes was silent. He knew his subordinate didn't mean any disrespect, but rather was trying to come to grips with the guilt a combat leader feels when he fails to bring his men home.

Straightening, Dillon pointed out the tanks in the loose semicircle around them that still sported crossed sabers superimposed over a skull, the symbol of Cold Steel. "I've got ten up, sir. I lost two from Second

Platoon last night and two of the replacement crews during this last assault." He stared off into the distance for a full minute before continuing. "I'm not sure how many men actually died from those crews. I've found it's easier on my soul in the short run if I think in terms of number of tanks lost. If you need the casualty figures, I'm sure First Sergeant Rider has them by now." Turning to his boss, Dillon concluded, "To be honest, I don't have the guts to call and ask for them just yet, Colonel."

Grasping the younger man by the shoulders, Estes stared into his eyes. "Patrick, two things to keep in mind, son. First, you can't ever save them all, no matter what you do. Believe me, I feel the weight of your men as well—plus a lot more. The second thing"— Estes turned the younger commander to where a group of his soldiers were gathering, breaking out MREs for a hasty breakfast—"you brought back a lot more than you lost. That's something to be proud of."

Dillon nodded. He knew Estes was right. But it was a bitter pill to swallow.

CHAPTER 14

Operation Phoenix

**Presidential Command Complex, West of An Najaf, Iraq
25 October, 0645 Hours Local**

The emergency lighting didn't extend past the main
arteries of the command complex. Abdul Aref and his
handful of guards picked their way through the par-
tially collapsed escape tunnel, their path illuminated
only by the beams of two dying flashlights. It was slow
going. Numerous times the small party had been
forced to stop and clear debris from their escape
route. Finally, after three hours of effort and setbacks,
they approached the concealed door that led to their
freedom.

Lining the stone wall of the mountain into which
the outer door was set was a series of storage compartments. Without speaking, the major's men began
drawing out the necessary equipment. Reaching into
the nearest compartment, the major removed a stack
of clothing and handed it to his leader. "Sir, please
put these on."

Taking the garments, Aref examined them in the
faint light. He smelled the garment and grimaced.
"Am I to now pose as a lowly bedouin?"

"Excuse me for saying so, sir, but the lower the
better. We do not know what awaits us outside of this
door. Better to err to the side of caution." Without
saying more, he turned to another compartment and
pulled out a battery-powered lantern. Turning the lan-

tern on, he hung it from a hook driven into the rock
wall and began searching for the other items they
would need. Soon weapons, food, water, and a working radio were laid out.

The president's heart leaped at seeing the radio was
operational. "Call a helicopter immediately. I want to
be back in Baghdad as soon as possible. The people
will expect me to address them."

The major shouldered the portable radio on his
back and tightened the straps. "It is not possible inside
of this mountain, sir. Once we are outside, I will see
to it."

Aref nodded understanding and gestured to the
door. "All right, proceed."

Walking to the door, the major stopped. The nation's best engineers had installed this escape route
and similar ones in each complex the Iraqi leader
might occupy. The doorway was built into the moun-
tainside so that it looked like a rounded rock. On the
inside, it was high-tech steel with an electronic locking
mechanism. Only the major and a handful of the other
ranking presidential guards knew the combinations to
each. Without the combination, someone would need
a few days and a lot of blowtorch equipment to
open it.

Motioning for his men to get ready to move, the
major bent to the locking mechanism and input the
numeric combination into its keypad.

**Iraqi Artillery Battalion Position, on the Iraq-Kuwait Border
25 October, 0800 Hours Local**

After hours of waiting, Colonel Karim al-Hamdani
had begun to lose faith. It looked as though his leaders
did not have the courage to do what was necessary
after all. Very well. He was a soldier, and he would
follow orders—or the lack of them.

The radio that had sat silent for so long began receiving a transmission, startling the officer of artillery.
Al-Hamdani listened to the message and silently gave

thanks to Allah. Signing off, he walked to the opening of his tent and called for his executive officer.

The major walked in, saluting. "Sir."

Al-Hamdani handed him a slip of paper. "Ahmed, you have an opportunity to redeem yourself. General Sufian and what remains of our division are in trouble—serious trouble." The colonel nodded at the slip of paper in the major's hand. "Those are the coordinates where the American brigade has halted. General Sufian has ordered us to strike before they have an opportunity to do further damage to our forces."

"Sir, only the president himself can give permission for release of chemical munitions. You know this."

The colonel's face revealed that the thought had crossed his mind. "I am aware of our protocols, Major. However, no one has been able to contact An Najaf since the Americans struck it hours ago. We must assume that the president is dead or injured. All the more reason to carry out General Sufian's tactical decision."

Handing the paper back to his superior, the major came to attention. "Sir, with all due respect, I cannot carry out this order."

Pulling his pistol from the holster on his web belt, the colonel raised it and fired a single round into his executive officer's forehead. "Very well. Then I shall do it myself."

AH-64 Deep Attack, Northern Kuwait
25 October, 0810 Hours Local

The company of AH-64 Apaches hugged the low ground and sped north at full power. They were part of an attack helicopter battalion ordered north to complete the destruction of the Madinah Division. As the aircraft moved toward a patch of open desert surrounded by rocky hills, something caught the eye of the company commander.

"Barbarians, Barbarian Six. Can anyone get eyes on what that is to the northwest in that patch of rock? It

appears to be a camouflaged position of some sort, possible Iraqi logistical center. . . ."

At that point, unaware of the danger approaching his position, Colonel Karim al-Hamdani gave his battalion the order to fire. The complexion of the war, which momentarily appeared to have reached a climax, took a nasty change.

A 152mm round passed close enough to the Barbarian Six's AH-64 to make it rattle. *"Holy shit! Those are enemy guns! Barbarians, prepare to engage . . ."*

3rd Brigade Reserve Position, Northern Kuwait
25 October, 0815 Hours Local

Things could be worse for Cold Steel. Task Force 2-77 Armor had finally gotten a break. For the next twenty-four to thirty-six hours, they were the brigade reserve. The remaining units of 3rd Brigade had pushed north and established hasty defensive positions in the event that Iraq deployed more forces south. The Spartan Brigade of the 3rd Infantry Division had occupied positions to the east and was likewise covering potential avenues of approach. With the floating stocks of combat equipment in port and being downloaded, both brigades expected to be reinforced within the next few days. But maybe it would be over before then. According to the reports filtering down, Iraq wasn't expected to continue the war. Rumors were even circulating in the 3rd Brigade rear area that they'd gotten to Aref in last night's air attacks, but the reports hadn't been confirmed. The troop grapevine was ever the source of one rumor or another.

Once they'd received word to pull south, Dillon had moved back to check on his casualties. He had thought the charred black remains that were formerly men of his command were the worst—until he saw the living casualties. Some had been inside their tanks when the onboard ammunition had exploded. Dying would have been a blessing. With third-degree burns on ninety percent of their bodies, they were in constant agony without the help of heavy sedation. Others were missing arms or legs. Dillon had moved among these men at the casualty collection point as they waited for evacuation to the rear. It was far worse than the battles themselves. Tonight he would have to sit down and write the families of these men. What in the name of God was he supposed to say?

For now, Steel and the rest of the Iron Tigers had a few hours to lick their wounds and take stock of where they stood. After the past seventy-two hours, they could use it. Dillon, Rider, and Mason were working through the details of getting their men and their machines back to speed. Rider had started a small fire and made real coffee for the first time in two days. The small indulgence was welcome.

"Okay, Thad, good work," said Dillon. "That'll bring us up to twelve tanks if you can get those parts. Top, what are the chances of getting some more people in? Without them, we'll have to shift a lot of the tanks to three-man crews."

First Sergeant John Rider didn't look hopeful. "Sir, we might get some replacements in, but it'll be a couple of days. What brigade is telling us is that we've got what we've got for now, and to make the best of it."

The radio in the back of Rider's APC squawked. Within seconds, the sergeant monitoring the task force command net ran from the back of the track. "Sir . . . they've hit the northern task forces with a chemical strike! We've been directed to go to MOPP level four, time now!" Three cups of coffee fell to the ground simultaneously as Steel's leadership scrambled to respond to the latest crisis.

**U.S. Central Command Headquarters (Forward), Bahrain
25 October, 0820 Hours Local**

"Goddamn it! Are they certain?" demanded Pavlovski.

The aide nodded. "Yes, sir. The Third Brigade's

mech battalion took the brunt of the hit. Initial reports indicate it was a nerve agent."

The general hung his head and closed his eyes. "How many?"

"One company was hit hard—over fifty percent casualties. Seventy dead so far, maybe more. They received a direct hit on their position. The rest of the battalion received early warning from a Fox section deployed forward. They got suited up quickly and only received a few exposures here and there. The brigade is in the process of repositioning, moving the contaminated casualties back, and conducting decon activities."

The bastards finally had to go and do it, thought Pavlovski. It had only been a matter of time. For nations like Iraq, chemical and biological weapons were the poor man's nuke. Enough of the shit could be manufactured in a family bathroom in twenty-four hours to take out an entire division. "All right. See if there's anything we can do for them. Whatever they need, they get—period."

Admiral Jordan hung up the phone on the far side of the office and approached. "Sir, the Iraqis who fired the strike have been identified and taken out. A company of Apaches was moving north as the strike was fired. The 64s were on them before the enemy guns had time to fire a second volley. We've got infantry and chemical personnel airborne to the location now. They'll secure the site and collect data on the agent."

The general pounded a fist into the wall. "But who's to say that some other unit won't pop the top on another strike? Or lob a SCUD with a surprise package in the warhead? You know their policies as well as I do. Only their president can authorize the use of chemical munitions." Pavlovski stood and walked to the window. "Have we heard nothing from An Najaf?"

"Negative, sir. The Third Battalion of the 325th Airborne is on the ground scrubbing through the rubble. Not many survived inside the complex itself. Aref's body hasn't been identified and the few survivors we've interrogated aren't talking."

"So we can't confirm that he was even there? He could be elsewhere and issuing orders to his troops in the field?"

Jordan nodded. "Correct, sir. Sir . . . has anyone brought up Phoenix yet?"

CINC CENTCOM shook his big head. "No, but that could change now. I'm scheduled to call the White House in two minutes to give them an update. Go ahead and get the staff together to go over the details in the event that Washington makes the call."

Jordan saluted and withdrew, leaving Pavlovski to his thoughts. They'd known this could happen since the Gulf War. Operation Phoenix was one of the United States' contingency plans in the event that Iraq initiated a weapon of mass destruction—a nuclear, chemical, or biological weapon—against American troops.

Once it became clear that hostilities were imminent the week before, A-Teams from the 5th Special Forces Group had infiltrated into Iraq and placed tactical nuclear weapons into operation at select targets. While cruise missiles fired from the sea would have proven less risky from a manpower viewpoint, if something happened and the mission was aborted while the missiles were in flight, there was no guarantee they could recover all of the warheads. So the Green Beret A-Teams had then been sent in, left their packages in hidden locations, and then exfiltrated. Now they were on standby to go in and recover the nukes if and when hostilities ended. But now that stupid idiot Aref had gone and done it, contaminating the battlefield. At this point, Washington would make the call whether or not to detonate the packages. Pavlovski himself would send the coded signal to orbiting military satellites. The satellites would authenticate the codes and initiate signals of their own, which would then be downlinked to the packages in Iraq. Clean and simple. Pavlovski shook his head in disgust. *Simple anyway.*

The general moved to his desk. He'd done everything in his power to bring this war to a conventional ending. It was out of his hands now. The general picked up the phone linking him to the National Command Authority in Washington.

West of An Najaf, Iraq
25 October, 0935 Hours Local

The soldiers moved in single file up the mountain path. It was their third patrol of the day and it wasn't even lunch yet. Raising a clenched fist, the sergeant in the lead went to one knee. Behind him, the infantrymen stopped and took up security positions along the rocky trail.

The platoon leader moved up silently with his RTO and stopped behind the NCO, kneeling. "What have you got, Sergeant Wilcox?" he whispered in the point man's ear.

Wilcox pointed to the head of the trail. It ended in a blank wall. "Sir, a piece of that mountain just, uh . . . disappeared."

"So? Mountains shift, rocks fall. What's the big deal?"

The sergeant shook his head. "I know that, Lieutenant. But they don't just *disappear*."

"What?" Squinting, the platoon leader looked again. He now saw the area that so intrigued Sergeant Wilcox—a darker patch against the tan-colored face of the mountain. "Cave?"

Wilcox shook his head. "Sir, ten seconds ago, that was solid rock. Now there's a big hole."

As the men watched, a robed figure tentatively emerged from the opening. Close behind followed another, then another, then more. Both men felt their pulses quicken.

Wilcox looked at the platoon leader. "Sir, those guys may be dressed like bedouins, but I have a feeling they're anything but. And I don't think it's Ali

Baba running out to pick up takeout for his band of thieves, either.''

The lieutenant nodded. Using hand and arm signals, he had his men establish an ambush position along the trail. Five minutes later, the group of robed figures approached. When they were within fifty meters, the lieutenant started to rise.

"Sir," whispered Wilcox harshly, *"keep your fuckin' head down!"*

"It's okay, Sergeant." The lieutenant smiled. Rising slightly to be heard, the young officer called out, "Halt!" An automatic weapon answered his directive.

"Sir, get down!" screamed Wilcox. A number of weapons now fired down on their position. Heaving on his lieutenant's legs to pull him down, the sergeant felt a gelatinous substance splash his face. Wiping his cheek, Wilcox looked at where the lieutenant reclined against their rock. The upper three inches of his head were missing. *"Son of a bitch!"* whispered Wilcox to himself. He looked left and right, checking the other patrol members—still in position and down. Pulling two hand grenades from his web gear, the NCO placed them on the ground in front of him. He got the attention of the SAW gunner crouching four feet away.

"On three," mouthed Wilcox.

The gunner nodded and settled down, weapon to his shoulder. Looking to the other patrol members, Wilcox received nods of acknowledgment. He worked the pins from one of the grenades. Finished, he looked at the gunner once more. The sergeant held up one finger, raised a second, released the spoon of the fragmentation grenade, raised a third finger. As the gunner opened up on the Arabs down the trail, Wilcox rose just enough above the boulder to throw the first grenade, then dropped. Pulling the pin on the second grenade, he allowed three seconds of count off and threw it after the first one. The other soldiers of the patrol took their NCO's lead and contributed a constant stream of lead and grenades up the trail.

Wilcox allowed thirty seconds, then called out,

"Cease fire . . . cease fire! Anybody hit?" His men checked in. The lieutenant had been the skirmish's only casualty so far.

A voice called in broken English from up the trail. "We . . . sur-ren-der. Do not . . . shoot! We are coming out!"

Wilcox slowly rose, taking up a squatting position behind the large rock he was coming to love. The Arabs were sprawled along the trail. Most looked dead. The rest weren't going to be a problem. He couldn't see the owner of the voice that had called out. "All right, Ali! You come out slow and easy with your hands on top of your head!"

After a few seconds, the figure appeared. Hands on head, the Iraqi tentatively approached.

Sergeant Wilcox rose, covering him. "Come on! This way! Real—fuckin'—slow!"

A minute later, his men had the figure on the ground and cuffed with plastic binding straps. He looked like any other Iraqi to Wilcox.

The local man raised his face, pleading with Wilcox. "Please . . . we are but simple shepherds—"

"Then why the hell did you fire on us?" snapped the burly sergeant.

"We . . . we . . . have had troubles with the soldiers in recent weeks. Sometimes our goats get trapped in the caves and we have to retrieve them."

The sergeant stared at the man. "Well, you're mighty well armed for goat herders."

Wilcox turned to his two nearest men. "Smith, Le-French, come with me to check the status of this guy's pals." He pointed at the RTO. "Louie, call the C.O. and let him know what's goin* on. Tell him we're on the way down."

The White House
25 October, 0330 Hours Eastern

From his position next to the Situation Room's electronic map, General Tom Werner stood. "Sir, as you know, the objectives of Operation Phoenix are three-fold. First, to send a message to Iraq and other nations manufacturing weapons of mass destruction that use of such weapons on U.S. troops is unilaterally unacceptable. Second, to cut out the heart of the Iraqi military, which translates to their Republican Guard. And finally, to minimize the civilian casualties resulting from the operation to the greatest extent possible."

"General," said the president quietly, "would you please go through the list of targets a final time?"

Drake looked at the electronic map. It was set to display real-time information on the current operation. Currently, five areas of Iraq had small circles around them. Werner used a laser pointer to indicate a target in the north. "Allahu Akbar Command Center, headquarters of the Republican Guard's Northern Corps." The general continued, indicating the other four targets in turn. "Al Fatahul Mubeen Command Center, their Southern Corps headquarters. Nabukhuth Nussar Command Center, a mechanized infantry division. Al Nedaa Command Center, an armored division. Adnan Command Center, a mechanized infantry division."

Moving the pointer south, the general paused when the red light touched on northern Kuwait. "The other three major Republican Guard division centers will not be hit, because these divisions—the Tawakalna, the Madinah, and the Hamourabi—have been rendered combat ineffective during the past week's fighting by our military forces in the theater of operations."

General Werner moved the glowing red light north to the center of Iraq. "One Republican Guard mechanized infantry division will remain untouched because it is headquartered in the vicinity of Baghdad."

The chairman turned off the pointer and turned back to the president. "The Guard's only other remaining forces fall within the Special Republican Guard, a division-sized unit whose headquarters is in Baghdad and whose units are spread out and fall close to major population centers. The Special Guard contains some combat units, but their primary function is to provide protection to Aref, his family, and his advisors."

"And the scope of damage from the strikes?" asked the president.

"Sir, the ADMs—"

"General, please. Try not to use Pentagonese right now. Just keep it simple."

Werner nodded. "Yes, sir. The atomic demolition units, commonly referred to as 'satchel bombs,' are the smallest tactical nuclear weapons in our inventory. The weapons were designed for Special Forces to use behind enemy lines to destroy key infrastructure like airports, railroad centers, roads, and as today, command and control centers."

The general paused. By God, the man needed to hear the real deal. "Sir, the devices will do what we need them to do. They'll destroy the majority of the Republican Guard's remaining equipment, kill most of their highly trained troops, and hopefully scare the bejeezus out of the bastards—all without putting more of our troops' lives on the line. There will be some fallout—there's no way around that—but due to the size of the devices, it will be minimal."

President Jonathan Drake turned to the other side of the room. Displayed across twenty different large, flat-screen monitors were the faces of the ranking leaders of NATO, representatives from the United States' old allies in the Middle East region, and the leaders of Russia and China. "Gentlemen, do you have any questions?"

The president of Russia, who appeared to have swallowed some bad borscht, was the first to reply. "President Drake, I cannot agree to what you plan—"

The prim representative from France didn't give the Russian president a chance to complete his sentence. "Nor, sir, can I. France will not condone—"

Other monitors began to buzz with broken English and foreign tongues.

Drake, whose face told of the inner battles he'd struggled with over the past days, wearily raised a hand. Slowly the voices settled. Once the room was utterly silent, Drake began. "Gentlemen, I made an emergency request for all of you to join in this tele-conference for two reasons—to tell you what our current plan is and to alleviate future concerns that we might initiate strikes against targets other than those you've just seen outlined in this briefing."

Drake then turned to the French representative's monitor and looked at him knowingly. "By the way, Mr. Ambassador," he asked the French delegate, "how have your intelligence satellites been operating lately? I understand you've had some problems with them recently."

The president looked over the sea of electronic faces. Some he knew; others he did not. "I will say this, and it is our last word on the matter. When Iraq threatened the border of one of our allies, we responded in an attempt to ensure that ally's stability and to keep peace in the region. Most of our other *allies* in the region not only remained neutral while their neighbor was threatened, but stopped just short of aiding the aggressing nation of Iraq by forcing the withdrawal of U.S. troops from their soil—leaving us virtually no base of operations in the region. When Iraq attacked into Kuwait, our forces and those of the Kuwaitis met them in open battle and won. This apparently did not sit well with President Aref. He subsequently ordered chemical strikes on our troops. If that were not enough, our latest satellite imagery shows not only six more divisions of Iraqi tanks and infantry preparing to move south toward Kuwait, but along with them more SCUD launchers—doubtless many of which have chemical or biological payloads waiting to be launched in order to further soften resistance against them."

An Arabic man in a business suit accompanied the representative from the Algerian embassy. He had been pointed out to Drake before the conference as a high-ranking Iraqi official. "Sir, you have no proof."

Drake, prepared for the accusation, depressed a button on the table in front of him. The targeted areas of Iraq dissolved and were replaced by the picture of an uncovered mass grave in the desert. The bodies belonged to soldiers who'd been in the center of the artillery chemical strike. It wasn't a pretty scene. Clearly, the men had been exposed to large doses of chemical munitions. Their bodies were contorted into grotesque shapes and to a man the dead seemed to scream in silent agony. A soldier stood silent sentinel in front of the grave wearing a full chemical protective suit and mask. He held in front of him a Stars and Stripes newspaper. The current date was clearly visible on the front page.

"We'll have the full facts on the attack shortly, as we now are in control of the site from which it was launched. For now, that picture of over seventy dead American soldiers will have to do."

Drake turned back to the Algerian representative, glancing with meaning at his companion first. "Sir, we have tried without pause to reach President Aref—or any ranking government official in Iraq for that matter—but to no avail. I am asking you now to open the channels available to you and inform them of the planned strikes. The only thing that will stop them is an immediate cease-fire and the unconditional withdrawal of all Iraqi forces from Kuwait."

The Iraqi behind the diplomat whispered angrily in the man's ear. The Algerian looked at Drake from the monitor. "And what, sir, if the government of Iraq, despite the loss of its most elite troops, should decide to continue its attack?"

"Captain, are you with us?" asked Drake, interrupting the diplomat.

A previously dark screen lit up, displaying a naval officer. From the array of equipment around him, it was clear he was operating from a tactical location. "Yes, sir, Mr. President."

"Gentlemen, this is Captain Young. Captain, please tell these gentlemen who you are, what you do, and more important, your current instructions."

There was a slight delay as the satellite relaying the

voice and video signals caught up, then a nod. "Yes, sir. I'm the commanding officer of the USS *Connecticut,* a Seawolf-class fast attack submarine. The *Connie* carries a mix of Harpoon antiship missiles, Mark 48 ADCAP torpedoes, and Tomahawk cruise missiles. All that should really be important to these gentlemen is that right now we have three Tomahawks with nuclear payloads ready to fire on word from our National Command Authority, the first of which are targeted on Baghdad."

"Thank you, Captain Young."

"Aye, sir," said the figure, and the interior shot of the sub disappeared.

After a few moments of consultation with his associate, the Algerian diplomat smiled. "Mr. President, I believe we can help you work out a compromise of some sort. I believe that within two days we can negotiate the withdrawal of most—"

Drake shook his head and bent to shut down the transmission from his end. "You have two hours."

There was a commotion behind the Algerian. The Iraqi official had disappeared.

U.S. Central Command Headquarters (Forward), Bahrain 25 October, 1100 Hours Local

The assembled staff of United States Central Command sat silently in the spacious conference room. Around them, steaming cups of coffee and silver platters of delicate pastries went untouched.

At the head of the table, General Gus Pavlovski stood. "Gentlemen, I have just spoken with the President." The general paused, then with great deliberateness continued. "We have been ordered to prepare the final phase of Operation Phoenix. Call the commanders of our forces in theater to inform them of the decision. As it stands, the operation is a go at twelve hundred hours local."

The officers looked at their commander, knowing that something had to follow . . . some chain of events or alternative response that would cause the order to be rescinded.

An air force colonel cleared his throat. "General . . . can we *do* this?"

Pavlovski looked at the colonel sympathetically. "You know, Al, ten years ago the answer would have probably been no. Fortunately or unfortunately, depending on how you look at it, things have changed. In the past, we'd have had to clear this through all of our allies in order to ensure we didn't lose their support. Therein lies our problem. Our allies have abandoned us. We could beat these guys conventionally—once we managed to get enough troops on the ground. But we don't have enough troops on the ground, and this maniac has already shown that he's willing to throw chemical agents at the few we do have in theater. Which brings up the second reason. If we don't do something now before the horde starts south, you can write off every American service member still alive in Kuwait."

The air force colonel stood. "Sir, I respect you a great deal, but I cannot in good faith condone this action." The officer saluted and held the gesture. "Request permission to be dismissed, sir."

Pavlovski returned the salute. "You're dismissed."

As the colonel dropped the salute and headed for the door, Pavlovski called after him. "Al."

The officer turned, hand on the conference room doorknob. "Yes, sir?"

"You've still got a job tomorrow, son . . . and frankly I don't blame you a damned bit."

The colonel smiled sadly and left the room.

Turning to the others in the room, the CINC looked over their faces. "Anyone else?"

West of An Najaf, Iraq
25 October, 1155 Hours Local

The patrol had made it down the trail five minutes before. Now as Abdul Aref watched from a kneeling position twenty feet away, an officer approached the body of the American lieutenant who had been killed. The officer lifted the poncho and stared for a few moments, then gently replaced it. Standing slowly, the man turned and walked toward him and his guard.

"Hold his head up again, Sergeant Wilcox," said the officer, a captain.

The NCO gladly complied and twisted his prisoner's head painfully upright.

The American looked at him so long and hard that Aref tried to turn his head, but the grip in his hair wouldn't allow it. As he was forced to look at the officer, fear crept up his spine.

"I'll be damned," said the giant officer quietly. "It's him."

The Iraqi leader felt a sense of vertigo. He'd hoped to be marched away and grouped with the other prisoners of war. He knew that if that happened he'd soon be back at one of his fifty presidential palaces. It looked as though it was not to be.

The American squatted in front of him. "My name is Captain Jack Kelly. I am the commander of C Company, Third Battalion of the 325th Airborne Infantry Regiment. You are my prisoner and will be accorded rights as stated by the Geneva Convention." Kelly leaned closer, almost into his face. "But so help me God, you give me an excuse, and I'll cut your heart out myself. Clear?"

Aref squinted as he looked into the man's face. He was but a word or a gesture from death, and he knew it. "Yes."

Standing, Kelly called to his radio operator. "Get me the battalion commander on the line. ASAP."

Kelly stared at the prisoner as the RTO made the call. His fingers brushed the handle of his bayonet as he thought of his father, of the young lieutenant lying behind him beneath a dusty poncho, of all the lives this *one man* had impacted in such horrible ways.

"Sir, the battalion commander said we have to get to the pickup zone now. Choppers are on the way."

Kelly turned to the corporal. "What's going on, Midtlaen? Did you tell him who we had here?"

The young soldier shook his head. "I tried. He cut me off and said to get the fuck out of here, time now."

"Give me the radio." Kelly took the handset. "Put me on division command."

The RTO looked incredulous. *"Sir?"*

"Just do it, Middie!"

The corporal turned a switch on the radio a few positions and nodded. "Go, sir!"

Kelly wasted no time. *"All stations this net, all stations this net, this is Wolverine Six. We have secured the target. I say again, we have secured the target, over!"*

A pompous voice immediately answered Kelly. *"Wolverine Six, you and the other units have orders to clear out. I'm giving you . . ."*

There was a ten-second pause, and then a different voice came over the radio's speaker. *"Wolverine Six, we understand your transmission. Are you certain it is the target? Over."*

Captain Jack Kelly looked at the man in question. Since his father's death, he'd memorized every line, every blemish, every hair of the individual he held responsible for that death and so many more. *"Affirmative."*

"Roger, stand by."

In the division CP, the colonel speaking into the radio grabbed a different handset and screamed into it: *"We have Hannibal in hand! I say again, we have Hannibal!"*

An answering voice confirmed the call.

Turning to the dumbfounded major from whom he'd taken the radio handset, the colonel smiled coldly. "Well, Wally, how does it feel to be the man who almost single-handedly ensured the first nuclear strikes since World War II?"

CHAPTER 15

_____

_____

Homecoming

25 October: CNN News Desk—"This just in . . . American forces in Kuwait have captured Iraqi President Abdul Aref as he was attempting to escape from an underground complex. White House sources further inform us that the Iraqis have requested a cease fire while they attempt to sort their government. . . ."

05 November: Baghdad (Reuters)—In a brief ceremony this afternoon, General Ali Abunimah was sworn in as Iraq's interim president. Abunimah, the former head of Iraq's military, said that his first official act would be to take custody of former president Abdul Aref from the United States. He added that Aref will be placed on trial for crimes against the state. The rumors in Baghdad are that Abunimah severed diplomatic relations with Iran within minutes of taking office.

19 November: Kuwait City (AP)—Sheikh Jaber Al-Ahmed al-Jaber al-Sabah, the emir of Kuwait, today made a rare public appearance. In a prepared statement, Kuwait's ruler announced formal relations with Iraq. Since taking over Iraq's government two weeks ago, President Ali Abunimah has gained the confidence of the emir by turning over hundreds of Kuwaiti political prisoners previously reported by the Hussein and Aref governments as missing or dead. These prisoners, held since late 1990 in Iraq, said on being re-

leased that the changes Abunimah has already brought to Iraq are startling.

20 November: Colorado Springs, Colorado (UPI)—A 4th Infantry Division (Mechanized) spokesman confirmed this morning that the Fort Carson soldiers still in Kuwait will return home in two days. The soldiers of 3rd Brigade defied the odds and twice defeated superior forces from Iraq's elite Republican Guard in the fighting that took place in Kuwait a month ago. The first flight will contain the 3rd Brigade's casualties. Specialists have been busy over the past three weeks equipping a special treatment facility at Fort Carson's Evan's Army Hospital to deal with the soldiers injured in the Iraqi chemical attack during the last day of fighting. In a side note, the Kuwaiti government announced plans for a massive memorial to the 3rd Brigade soldiers who died in the defense of the Kuwaiti people in what is coming to be known as the Second Gulf War. The monument will feature life-size marble replicas of an M1A1 tank and an M2 Bradley Fighting Vehicle and will be placed on the site where the seventy-six chemical casualties of the Striker Brigade are buried.

Colorado Springs, Colorado
23 November, 1300 Hours Mountain

As the aircraft made its final approach into Colorado Springs, Dillon felt his stomach flutter. It had been over a month since he'd seen Melissa and his four daughters. A lot of things had changed since then, not the least of them he himself.

Turning in his seat, Dillon looked down the length of the aircraft at his men. Clad in desert camouflaged battle dress uniforms for the chartered flight home, they laughed and talked nonstop in their excitement. Dillon smiled slowly. The conquering warriors returning home. They'd seen the elephant and lived to tell about it.

The smile disappeared as the faces of the men he

had lost flashed through his mind. The first nights after the fighting, there had been no dreams, only nightmares. Slowly, very slowly, that was changing. Now Dillon dreamed of his lost men, but they were not dreams of his men's suffering or their deaths. These dreams were more the journeys of his troopers taking a respite from their final resting place at Fiddler's Green, the tankers' and cavalrymen's Valhalla, to wish their commander peace.

Turning to his window, Dillon watched as the Rocky Mountains came into view. He often had to leave Melissa and his girls. On his return, the sight of the majestic Front Range and Pike's Peak always seemed to be saying welcome home. An end to another leg of his seemingly eternal warrior's odyssey.

As he stared at the snowcapped peaks, Dillon thought of his family and what their lives would be like now. He'd only been able to call home a few times before the flight out of Kuwait City. Prior to that, he and the other men of the Iron Tigers had manned positions along the now-stable Kuwait-Iraq border, keepers of the new peace during the initial postwar period. Though he'd attempted to sound upbeat during their brief conversations, he knew that Melissa could hear the darkness that had taken root in his heart. He only prayed the worst was behind him.

Next to Dillon, First Sergeant Rider stood and began his final duties of the trip home. "All right, shitbirds! Shut your pie holes and sit down. Everybody look next to you. You should see one of two gentlemen, either Mr. M16 Rifle or Señor Beretta Pistol. If you do not, you better find them in the next five seconds! Do not let me find a weapon on this aircraft while you're on the ground hugging Momma! Speaking of Momma, on landing you *will* file out of this aircraft in an orderly fashion, not make a mad dash for those sassy ladies sure to be lined up outside!"

If possible, Rider's voice became louder as he warmed to his topic. "Once off of the aircraft, if Momma or your sweetheart runs to you, you will kiss her warmly but quickly, assure her of your undying love, tell her that you will take care of her needs later, then proceed smartly to the Customs Station! Is that clear, gentlemen?"

"Clear, First Sergeant!"

Rider couldn't help but smile. They were a good bunch of boys. The smile turned to a snarl. "And one final thing. We are a kinder, gentler army. Should you find a microphone in your face, you will *not* use profane language! Are you little bastards clear on that issue?"

Once again the plane roared with the men's response. "Clear, First Sergeant!"

Jones, looking through the window of the aircraft carrying his command group and staff, watched the rolling hills of some Midwest state slide by. Turning to a passing flight attendant, he touched her elbow. "Ma'am, seeing as how we'll be landing in a couple of hours, you can go ahead and pass out the pleasantries."

Tom Proctor, seated next to Jones, looked at his boss with a raised eyebrow. "Pleasantries, sir?"

Jones waved his unlit cigarette, privately damning the FAA. "Tom, my boy, I gladly pass on to you the knowledge of how to win the hearts and minds of soldiers, acquired over a lifetime of military service. The boys are almost home, so I'm gonna give 'em a little present—something they've been missing for too long."

"And what would that be, sir?"

"Alcohol."

"Sir, that's against regulations."

Jones looked at S3 and shrugged. "They can sue me," he said. "Now where the hell did I put my bifocals?" he asked no one in particular, feeling his pockets.

"Sir," said Proctor, trying not to smile, "they're hanging from your neck."

Reaching down, Jones secured the glasses and slid

them on the tip of his nose. Looking to his protégé, he clucked, "One day you'll start losing track of things, young smart-ass. Hope I'm there to see it." Reaching into the seat beside him, Jones retrieved some paperwork.

"What's that, sir? It's about time you relaxed a little."

Jones paused, looking at Proctor over the tops of his bifocals. "Tom, this is my last official act before taking a well-deserved vacation."

They were interrupted as the attendant paused next to their seats, handing each of them a plastic cup of ice, two cans of Coca-Cola, and two small bottles of Jack Daniel's.

Proctor looked doubtful. "Sir, I hope you set some kind of limit on this so things don't get out of hand before we land and meet the brass."

Jones nodded. "I did."

"You did?" Proctor asked, surprised.

The attendant chimed in brightly. "He did. Six bottles each, maximum. But that figure is . . ." She looked to Jones for help.

Jones smiled at her in a grandfatherly manner. "Negotiable, darlin', negotiable."

"But, sir . . ."

"Shut up, Tom." Reaching into his carryon, Jones extracted two shot glasses and winked. "Had a batch of these made up special in Kuwait City before we flew. Notice the detail in the brigade crest?" Filling each of the glasses, he handed one to Proctor.

Proctor, resigned, shook his head and lifted the glass. "So what are we drinking to, sir?"

"New beginnings." Jones smiled, lifting the glass in one hand and his paperwork in the other.

"What's that?"

"Doc Hancock's leave papers."

"There are a lot of guys taking leave, sir. What's so special about Hancock's?"

Jones drank deeply and sighed. "I've still got the magic touch," he said, waving the form. "These are for Doc's honeymoon. Seems he's marrying a certain young aviator on Christmas Eve."

Fort Bragg, North Carolina
23 November, 1515 Hours Eastern

"If you don't behave, I'm going to take you straight to bed. Yes, I will," Rhonda Kelly cooed at the crying baby. Walking through the Kelly home's front room and rocking the infant in her arms, she was rewarded with a large smile. "There's my big boy! You're such a *good* boy!"

"Do you know how much it turns me on to hear you talk like that?" came a voice from the front door.

Wheeling, Rhonda Kelly saw a large figure standing in the open doorway. Wearing a green Class A uniform with trousers tucked into shiny black jump boots, Captain Jack Kelly's freshly cut flattop threatened to burst through the top of the doorframe.

Rushing to him with the baby, his wife squealed with delight. "Jack!"

Kelly laughed as he embraced her. "Easy! Don't crush my boy."

After a few breathless moments, Rhonda pulled away. "I thought you weren't coming home for two more days!"

Kelly looked uncomfortable. "They wanted a few of us back early. They're having a ceremony or something in Washington tomorrow. I thought I'd surprise you with a little vacation."

"Ceremony?"

Kelly blushed and looked uncomfortable. "Yeah, for my guys. I get to tag along."

Rhonda looked at her husband knowingly. "Well, Mr. Tag-along, it wouldn't have anything to do with that, would it?" she asked, pointing to a new addition to the living room wall. A *USA Today* front page hung in a frame. The headline read IRAQI LEADER CAPTURED. The full-color photo showed a particularly vicious-looking army captain in desert fatigues and maroon beret leading the ex-president into a military headquarters building.

Kelly's blush darkened. "Oh, Jee-sus, I had no idea . . ."

Rhonda smiled. "That you'd return a hero? According to that article, if it weren't for you and your men, Abdul Aref would likely still be free. The president even referred to you in a speech on television last night."

Kelly continued to stare at the wall with a slack jaw.

"Doesn't anyone around here know how to shut a door?" asked a voice behind them.

In the front door stood Martha Kelly, Jack's mother. Rhonda had attempted to dissuade her mother-in-law from going back to Colorado alone to settle her and the sergeant major's affairs, but Martha Kelly had insisted. She had felt she needed to say good-bye to Big Jack in her own way, in their own home. From the smile on her face, Rhonda Kelly knew her mother-in-law was going to be all right.

"Mom!" Jack rushed across the room and snatched the small woman from her feet, grasping her in a bear hug. Finally releasing her, Jack reached inside his uniform shirt and pulled out his dog tags. Unsnapping the metallic link, he removed one of the three small silver tags, handing it to his mother. "I thought you might like to have this. I was able to spend a few moments with Dad before they brought him back."

Martha took the small piece of metal in her hand and looked at it: KELLY, JACKSON EZEKIEL. Smiling, eyes wet with unspilled tears, she held it a moment. Reaching to her son's chain, she replaced the tag and snapped the clasp closed. "I think your dad would have liked for you to have it. I've got Big Jack with me all the time, right here," she said, lightly tapping her breast.

Colorado Springs, Colorado
23 November, 1330 Hours Mountain

Over two thousand people were on hand to greet the first unit redeployment from Kuwait. Standing back

one hundred yards from the aircraft, the families were
kept at a distance. To their front, every general officer
remotely associated with the 4th Infantry Division or
III Corps waited at the base of the steps leading to
the aircraft door.

"Are they ever going to let them off the plane?"
asked Melissa Dillon impatiently. She and the girls—
Meagan, Hannah, Logan, and Carson—had waited patiently with the other families for the better part of
two hours. While the sun was shining and the sky
was cobalt blue without a single cloud, the cold winds
rushing down from the Rocky Mountains had made
life less than comfortable for the crowd of loved ones
and onlookers.

Carson, the youngest Dillon, looked concernedly at
her mother. "They *can't* keep Daddy on the plane,
can they, Mommy?"

Melissa smiled and began to answer, "No,
honey . . ."

The 4th Infantry division band began playing "The
Army Song" full blast as the first 3rd Brigade troops
departed the aircraft.

"There's Daddy!" screamed Logan. She broke loose
from Melissa's hand, ducked under the crowd tape,
and was speeding across the tarmac as fast as her five-
year-old legs could carry her.

"Logan, come back here!" called Melissa. Holding
Carson in her arms, she knew she'd never catch the
child. "Logan . . . oh, you go, kid."

The crowd roared its approval as the child pushed
past the generals and launched herself into the open
arms of a desert-fatigued captain who had just stepped
from the boarding ladder onto American soil. Flash-
bulbs popped and video cameras rolled, recording
what would become the homecoming picture seen
around the world.

Two military policemen rushed forward to inter-
cede, only to be halted by the 4th Infantry Division
commander.

"Sergeant, I don't think we have a problem here,"

said the general, smiling at the ranking military policeman.

The MP paled and saluted. "Roger, sir. No problem at all."

The father and child stood at the base of the stairs. "Hey there, angel," said Dillon, squeezing Logan tightly to his chest, tears spilling down his face.

"I missed you, Daddy," sighed the little girl, content now that she was in her father's arms again.

Dillon looked into her face and felt the warmth and love flow through him like a river, taking with it the darkness that had been with him for too long. "I missed you, too, darlin'," he whispered through his tears.

Gathering the child tightly to his chest and ignoring the assembled VIPs, Captain Patrick Dillon walked away from the aircraft and toward the rest of his life.

A MILITARY WRITER WHO "TRANSPORTS READERS INTO THE COCKPIT."
—San Diego Union–Tribune

Robert Gandt

WITH HOSTILE INTENT

"Aerial flight scenes more thrilling than a back-to-back showing of *Top Gun* and *Iron Eagle*, this red-hot piece of military fiction is certain to keep readers riveted."
—*Publishers Weekly*

0-451-20486-7

Brick Maxwell is back in

ACTS OF VENGEANCE

When a motor launch carrying the *USS Ronald Reagan's* top brass is attacked, the U.S. vows a swift reprisal. Enter skipper Brick Maxwell and his roadrunners—the jocks who fly the F/A-18 Super Hornets. Their mission: a deep air strike in northern Yemen. But their target—the commander who master-minded the attack—has laid a deadly trap for Maxwell and his fellow warriors...

0-451-20718-1

Look for Gandt's new novel, *Black Star*, coming from Signet in November 2003